POINTS of LIGHT

Books by Linda Gray Sexton

POINTS of LIGHT

A NOVEL

BY

LINDA GRAY SEXTON

LITTLE, BROWN AND COMPANY

BOSTON   TORONTO

FIRST EDITION

The author is grateful for permission to reprint excerpts from the following copyrighted material: from *Sons and Lovers* by D. H. Lawrence. Copyright 1913 by Thomas Seltzer, Inc. All rights reserved. By permission of Viking Penguin, Inc.; from "In Blackwater Woods" from *American Primitive* by Mary Oliver. Copyright © 1983 by Mary Oliver. First appeared in *Yankee*. By permission of Little, Brown and Company in association with the Atlantic Monthly Press; from *The Little Disturbances of Man* by Grace Paley, Viking Press, 1956. By permission of New American Library; from *Disturbances in the Field* by Lynne Sharon Schwartz. Copyright © 1983 by Lynne Sharon Schwartz. Reprinted by permission of Harper & Row, Publishers, Inc.; from Dylan Thomas, *Poems of Dylan Thomas*. Copyright 1945 by the Trustees for the Copyrights of Dylan Thomas. First published in *Poetry*. Reprinted by permission of New Directions Publishing Corporation; from *The Complete Letters of Vincent van Gogh*, New York Graphic Society, 1958. Reprinted by permission of Constable Publishers and Little, Brown and Company; from *To the Lighthouse* by Virginia Woolf. Copyright 1927 by Harcourt Brace Jovanovich, Inc.; Copyright renewed 1955 by Leonard Woolf. Reprinted by permission of Harcourt Brace Jovanovich.

Library of Congress Cataloging-in-Publication Data

Sexton, Linda Gray, 1953–
    Points of light.

    I. Title.
PS3569.E886P6   1988   813'.54   87-17087
ISBN 0-316-78200-9

The characters, places, and events portrayed in this book are fictitious. Any similarities to real places or persons, living or dead, are purely coincidental and not intended by the author.

RRD-VA

*Published simultaneously in Canada
by Little, Brown & Company (Canada) Limited*

PRINTED IN THE UNITED STATES OF AMERICA

To my mother,
who taught me to listen for the sound of the word

The eternal question whether we can see the whole of life or only know a hemisphere of it before death . . . The sight of stars always sets me dreaming just as naively as those black dots on a map set me dreaming of towns and villages. Why should these points of light in the firmament, I wonder, be less accessible than the dark ones on the map of France? We take a train to go to Tarascon or Rouen and we take death to go to a star.

— Vincent van Gogh
The Letters of Vincent van Gogh

Contents

POINTS of LIGHT

PROLOGUE

Summer 1986

Quickly, as if she were recalled by something over there, she turned to her canvas. There it was — her picture. Yes, with all its greens and blues, its lines running up and across, its attempt at something. It would be hung in the attics, she thought; it would be destroyed. But what did that matter? she asked herself, taking up her brush again. She looked at the steps; they were empty; she looked at her canvas; it was blurred. With a sudden intensity, as if she saw it clear for a second, she drew a line there, in the centre. It was done; it was finished. Yes, she thought, laying down her brush in extreme fatigue, I have had my vision.

— Virginia Woolf
To the Lighthouse

A Vision of Jamie

Before that day, painting had always been a simple act of control for me: look, visualize, and transfer that barn, that face, that flower. With my mind and hand I described what, or who, or how I saw. But on that summer afternoon something happened — a strange new heat ran down and over the edges of my canvas — and it was then that I knew, for the first time, that something was askew, ajar.

There was the color, for one thing: Strontian yellow, Cinnabar green, Vermilion, and Cadmium orange. Colors that abused my brush, bending and caking the bristles with their thickness, they were so bright. Color leaking out of the silver Holbein tubes with their tight caps, colors I had never before even broken the seals on. I couldn't seem to stop myself; I was squeezing the oil paint directly onto the canvas — no mixing or blending with turpentine at all, just straight pure color. I was using my brush as I once might have used my fingers.

I was painting Jamie from memory — although he wasn't far away, just playing on the other side of the garden with his trucks. I could see the tipped-up visor of his Red Sox baseball cap disappear and then appear again as he stood and then sat behind the screen of tomato plants. I was on the near edge of the flowerbed, where I often worked after lunch, under the shade of a pine, my blonde hair clasped up off my neck with a barrette, the fair skin on my long arms and legs already freckled and browned from the direct summer sun. Ordinarily I did not paint much from memory, relying instead on what I could see and touch, but I didn't need to see my son to know his profile, the outline of his face, the texture of his skin and hair. I knew him better than I knew myself.

My husband, Sam, had taken both of the girls over to the barn with him after lunch. It was the blacksmith's day at our farm, and his rusted truck rattling up the drive earlier this morning had gotten the kids wild with excitement. Jamie had darted back and forth between the anvil and the cross-tied animals, getting in Mr. Barker's way, trying to touch the red-hot curves of iron, getting yelled at and jostled aside, and shrieking with two-year-old glee each time a smoking shoe was dropped into the bucket of cold water with a hiss. I'd had to take him up for a nap right in the middle of lunch because he'd fallen asleep with his forehead in his plate.

But Anna, on the other hand, couldn't wait to run back to the main floor of the barn and had stuffed down her sandwich. Her Shetland pony, Duet, was due to have her hooves trimmed this afternoon, and Anna was determined to be there to quiet her. We were expecting a foal out of Duet later in the summer, and Anna was very protective of her pregnant pony. She'd taken Meggie with her because lately she'd liked to tote her younger sister around everywhere. Each foray to the chicken coop for eggs or to the pasture to help whistle in the new colts, all the little errands to the tack room for a grain scoop or bridle, to the garden for a basket of tomatoes — every one was an opportunity to pour out on Meggie's willing and credulous ear the amazing amount of information Anna had been told or overheard, truth and misconception mixed together in a wise and startling brew: horses wore shoes so their feet wouldn't get cold, chickens had wings so they could cuddle their babies three at a time, the rooster crowed because he was really an alarm clock, and Shetland ponies were pint-sized because they'd been made especially for kids.

And Meggie loved to listen. Where her twin brother would have run impatiently from the onslaught of big-sister information, Meggie just stood and packed in each new nugget, blue eyes wide, a squirrel hoarding her nuts for winter. At night sometimes I heard her in her crib, repeating Anna's phrases over and over, getting them just right in private in a way she never would have done in front of us; I'd stop in the hallway and smile, listening to that little voice lisping the facts of our everyday life like nursery rhymes.

After tucking Jamie in, I set up my paraphernalia in the garden, savoring the solitude. The only other sound of human activity came from my mother-in-law, Tobie, banging around in the kitchen, yelling at the three sheepdogs who crowded her feet as she sifted and measured ingredients and then floured both hands and board to knead a loaf of sourdough. She won prizes at the local fairs for the knack of her moist and even crumb; at first I'd wanted her to teach me, but I'd never been able to duplicate her magical expertise of knowing just how much flour, how much kneading — enough but not too much. Slowly it had occurred to me that maybe she wasn't all that anxious to make clear her mysteries. But there was a lot she did teach me in the first years of my marriage to her son: how to butcher a cow, tend a garden, curry a horse, diaper a baby. For a long time I thrived on those lessons — until I tired of always being the apprentice.

Tobie didn't approve of letting Jamie run around in her flowerbeds, any more than Sam had approved of letting him bother Mr. Barker earlier; and when Jamie had bombed through the door to join me an hour later, I'd had to promise, somewhat resentfully, to make sure he didn't do any damage. He liked to play in the sunflowers — there was a field of them behind the compost heap — chasing the birds in circles, and then he'd even enticed me away from my painting preparations into a game of hide-and-seek. Over and over he'd given himself away. Bubbling, high-pitched giggles spilled out from behind those broad green stalks and made me laugh along with him until I had a stitch in my side and couldn't chase him anymore. That was when I had limped back to my easel and brushes.

Jamie liked to pick the black-eyed Susans, too, tromping into his grandmother's garden bed, but she yelled at him whenever he did because most of the time he ended up with a handful of blossoms on stems just two inches long. And with pollen smeared from ear to ear, as if he'd been eating corn on the cob lathered with butter. But today he promised to be very careful, so I let him do it — in secret, defying my mother-in-law the way I'd once defied my mother — and I stopped setting up my palette to watch him.

Once again he proved just how precise he could be when he wanted. Crouched down low, squatting in the warm black earth of Tobie's chrysanthemum bed, he broke the stiff stem, snap, against the ground. I felt a thrill of relief: I couldn't have done it better myself; in fact, I would have to claim I had done it myself. It hadn't always been like this, I thought, turning back to my easel. So much had changed when Meggie and Jamie, the twins, were born. Some intricate balance shifted two years ago, everything: Sam and me, Anna and me, Tobie and me. Nothing was as simple as it had been before.

Now Jamie pushed himself up with both hands and came to lay the flower across my knees. I saw again, with pleasure, how much he resembled me, how much he was of my flesh. "Mommee's flower," he said with pride. "Color Mommee's hair. Color my hair." I looked up at him, puzzled, trying to decode his minisentence, and then, with a small mental leap, I grasped his meaning: the mum was a deep yellow, just the color of my hair, just the color of his hair. I looked at him with awe, almost with reverence. To have made such connections when he'd only just turned two seemed a miracle. He had grasped the abstract; he had grasped the infinite; he had grasped reality. I saw him a mathematician or a botanist, definitely an artist — and wanted to laugh at myself.

I smiled my joy and he smiled back. Our eyes held steady, his as clear and translucent a blue as the marbles you shoot as a child. Cobalt blue. Eyes he had inherited from me. In that instant he let me into his heart, and for that I forgave him the mudpie he'd built on top of my new canvas last week, the dumptruck loaded with cow flops I had found hidden in his closet the day before yesterday, and all the Spaghettios in his hair and mine after yesterday's tantrum-filled lunch. I even forgave the pencilled scrawls I furtively washed from the walls of his room each morning, a kind of drawing I knew he couldn't help. I didn't need to forgive the drawings as Sam or Tobie would have, had they known about them. I didn't need to forgive because I understood.

"I dood tit!" he said, pointing at the flower on my lap.

"Yes," I said, "you did it, you picked it perfectly." I hugged him and pulled him up across my knees. He snuggled in against me, warm, tender; he was my only cuddler. "It's a beautiful flower, Jamie." The smell of baby shampoo drifted up from his curls, and I rubbed my lips over the softness at the nape of his neck.

If I had believed in God, I would have said a blessing radiated over us in that moment: some kind of pure ethereal bliss; an ascension. And as he squirmed down and away from me to go back to his trucks, I suddenly wanted to paint that feeling in my heart, the moment when a mother and son exchange something immutable, something untranslatable. I had caught the girls with my skill many times before, but Jamie had always eluded me: too quick, a hummingbird flashing his many colors, and then, more quickly, gone. It would be a beautiful painting — idyllic, lyric, soaring — a mother's song, in oils.

I began without even a sketch. I would wing it, just start in free from any lines or distractions, or maybe preconceptions, and paint him as I had envisioned him in that instant. And so I began, pulling my Red Sox cap with its visor snugly over my head, laying out brushes left to right from smallest to largest, digging into the box of paints at my feet, uncorking the turp, setting out three cotton rags for cleaning. The canvas was already up on the easel, but I made several minute adjustments in its position, and then stood to do five deep knee bends and ten side stretches. My blood was buzzing. I was ready.

I centered first on Jamie, with the warm colors that I usually chose: the Jaune Brillant number 2, with its soft beige tone, for his skin; the Naples yellow, understated like a summer afternoon's late light, for his blond hair; the Violet gray, softer still, twilight, for his blue eyes. I was working quickly already, my brush flickering down into the white, afraid I would lose the impetus, the mood. The garden seemed less important; I made it soft, nearly a pastel blush against the background. In my painting it was spring.

I concentrated on Jamie. I painted each stroke as I would have touched him. The brush lapped at his forearms, soft peach now as they picked the violet iris; the brush traced a finger of sunlight down across his forehead; the brush rubbed dampness into his curls as he knelt on pale green. I worked for a while, absorbed, the warm wind lifting the collar of my spattered workshirt, tickling the nape of my neck with long wisps of hair which had escaped my cap. It was developing as I had planned: Impressionist in style, a painting that relied on subtlety and light, effective harmonies, indistinct outlines. I paused, ready to begin the figure of the mother. I tried to see how she would fit into the composition. I hesitated. Something was keeping me from putting her where I'd planned, where I had purposely left the space.

I sat back for a minute and studied what I'd done. Something was missing. Something was eluding me. Without thinking, instinctively, I put up a new canvas.

I lifted my head briefly to check that Jamie was still absorbed with his trucks, and my hand felt its way down to the paint box, back to the tubes of oils. Even as my mind said, *No, it's too strong,* my hands were squeezing color out onto my board, setting up a new palette in vibrant, violent color, color with which I had never before been comfortable. The color of the harsh autumn which would surround me in a matter of weeks, months. Bright oranges, scarlets, sharp yellows. A new image was pushing its way out. The yellow jackets, confused, were drawn to my colors as to pheromones, mistaking them for flowers. They buzzed and landed in the pools of paint on my board. Ordinarily I hated bees. Now I ignored them.

I spread the color directly on the white canvas. I pushed my brush through Cadmium orange, Viridian, and Strontian yellow. These were the colors in my head now. I could not mute them, no matter how hard I tried. The colors went on, very fast, in a thicker impasto than I had ever dared use before. The shapes grew clearer, with a lot of motion — more fluent motion — to the brushstroke. Jamie's face was no longer indistinct, no longer a happy blur, but a small triangle of sadness; the lines of his body were angular, strained by the intensity of his crouched posture.

My brush moved to the sky, painting there a desert, a huge orange sun surrounded by stars, yellow stars out in the daytime, not hidden even now by their parent sun, and shining with the same arid heat. Highest noon, the colors said. Down to the ground, the garden was relegated to a mere strip in the forefront, the sole anchor for the small boy. An imaginary field of bright yellow hay, undulating, stretched beyond, to the horizon. There was no mother in this painting.

I drew dark outlines around the big sunflower heads, zinnias, and chrysanthemums, around Jamie's body and face in a color I despised: Raw umber. A hedge of milkweed pod the same hue rimmed the periphery of the painting like a border. There was not a shadow on the canvas. The sun and the stars echoed the Strontian yellow of the hay, metallic and harsh.

My hands were shaking. I was very tired, I told myself, I had to stop now. In the right corner I put a title, "Vision of Jamie," in the Raw umber, and in the left corner I signed my name, "Allie Yates." But it was not finished, and I knew I would work on it again. It was still alive and demanding of me. How strange that a canvas could make me feel bewildered and uneasy, almost unnerved.

Jamie brushed up against my side. He stood quietly beside me, looking at what I had done. I did not mind his eyes on my work. I reached down to take his hand, and we stayed there, silent, staring at the painting.

I did not understand myself. I did not understand the isolation I had painted or where it had come from. My own vision frightened me: my son crouched alone in that stretching field of sunflower, hay, and zinnia, and I could not reach him.

PART I

THE BIRTHS

July 1984

He took his thumb out of his mouth and placed his open hand, its fingers stretching wide, across my breast. "I love you, Mama," he said.

"Love," I said. "Oh love, Anthony, I know."

I held him so and rocked him. I cradled him. I closed my eyes and leaned on his dark head. But the sun in its course emerged from among the water towers of downtown office buildings and suddenly shone white and bright on me. Then through the short fat fingers of my son, interred forever, like a black and white barred king in Alcatraz, my heart lit up in stripes.

> — Grace Paley
> "A Subject of Childhood"
> *The Little Disturbances of Man*

Sam

The twins came on a raw, drizzly Saturday, in a week that had been all rain. The sky was a grayed-down purple: it looked bruised, as if it were tired from carrying the weight of so much water. The earth had given up trying to absorb it all; there were puddles everywhere, and mud, lots of mud, ankle-deep, that sucked the boot from your heel at every step.

I got my first contraction at the breakfast table, but I didn't say anything to Sam, or to Tobie. Anna was whining about her eggs again. She hated eggs, but eggs were cheap because we still owned over a hundred smelly broody hens. Her straight blonde hair was still uncombed; her sparkly brown eyes dimmed now with petulance; her full-lipped mouth curved downward in a pout. I rubbed my eyes against the green cast the circular overhead fluorescent sent out and reached over to switch on the small metal lamp at the end of the long trestle table. The glow felt like sunshine on my face, the skillets hanging on the wall over the fireplace pinked up, the dishes on the table changed from gray to beige. We all looked healthy again, snugged in together, our early-morning babble filling the space of the big kitchen and making it cozy on this bleak day. For a minute I deliberately forgot to wonder about that pain, a pain which might, or might not, be the start of my labor. "Do you want some yogurt?" I asked, turning to Anna. Tobie looked up at me from her mug of tea, her upper lip puckered in the vertical grooves that came from years of drinking the strong astringent brew. She knew instantly that something was going on. I'd given myself away by breaking the house rule of never offering Anna an alternative meal when there was something perfectly good in front of her. Tobie liked to say that our kitchen wasn't a McDonald's with four different kinds of hamburg. Still, lately I'd been feeling sorry for Anna: she sat there like a queen in her highchair today, but her two-year term of happy terror was about to end — and she didn't even know it. I looked away from my mother-in-law's probing glance and stirred my bowl of yogurt and prunes.

"Yogut, yogut! Booburry yogut!" Anna cried, banging her spoon in rhythm and trying to pull her bib over her head.

"I'll get it, Allie, you stay put," Sam said, pushing his blond hair back off his forehead. He unfolded his long legs from under the table and clumped across the floor to the refrigerator, narrowly missing the tails of Tobie's sheepdogs with his boots. The smell of barn drifted from him as he passed behind my chair and I inhaled deeply. It was a rich smell, of manure, hay, molasses-soaked grain — the smell of the earth, a smell that wrapped up all my feelings about living here on this farm. I loved that smell so much I didn't even mind the scattered brown shavings he left across the wide oak planks of the floor. Every day before breakfast, he and Joe — the only hand at BoxTie for nearly twenty years — had to feed and water all the animals. With fifteen brood mares, the stallion, five Shetland ponies, all the chickens, and enough livestock to keep us from hitting the IGA for meat during the winter, it took quite a while.

Sam and I were always up by five; Joe and he expected a

big breakfast at seven sharp before starting to muck out the stalls and pens. At nine-thirty, after Anna's hour of *Sesame Street* in front of the old black-and-white set in the kitchen, after I got the laundry started, the beds made, the kitchen swept up, and Anna settled in with Tobie, I was free to go up to my studio in the attic and paint for a few hours before lunch. Except maybe not today, I reminded myself, feeling the beginnings of another contraction across my abdomen. If the twins came today, Sam and I wouldn't make our usual Saturday-night trip into Manchester for the movies either.

"That new gray's favoring her left hind leg," Sam said to Tobie as he slammed the Kelvinator door closed. "She picks it up real quick." He put the bowl in front of Anna. "Joint's not hot though."

"No abscess in the foot, neither," Joe added. "I checked it out 'fore coming in." He mopped his last bit of toast in the grease on his plate and pushed back his chair. Joe didn't talk much, just gave you what you needed to hear with no frills. I always thought Tobie and he would have made a great pair.

"You might have a look," Sam said to his mother as Joe went out the back door.

Tobie nodded, pulled her dentures out of the back pocket of her Levi's, and slid them into her mouth; she never drank her tea with them in. "Expect the paddock's still a mudhole." She paused to adjust the teeth. They were the only thing on her person that ever needed adjustment: her hair was iron gray, straight, close-cropped, and she never fiddled with or patted it; her body was tall and stringy, and she never hitched at pants, belt, or shirt; she was comfortable with her body and her aging. "Maybe she twisted her leg when you turned her out yesterday." She had a way of contracting her words, of making two syllables one, so that "mudhole" sounded like "muddle" and "yesterday" became "yest'dy."

Sam didn't sit down again. He looked anxious, just in the way he stood, with his tall, slender frame kind of hunched forward, and the way he kept brushing his hair back off his forehead with the flat of his palm. A lot depended on the three new mares he'd bought at auction last week: he'd been too nervous to turn them out to pasture and had just been exercising them on the lungeline in the paddock. He was smart about his animals, but everybody makes a mistake sometimes, and he wanted Tobie to go out with him right then. I got up to clear my plate and gave his hand a squeeze. He reached over to tweak my bottom as I went by. Even with my big belly, he had remained affectionate and ready anytime I was. "Why don't you go over with Sam," I suggested to my mother-in-law, clattering the dishes down into the sink. "I can finish up here."

Tobie had been halfway up out of her seat when I spoke, and at my words she sat back down again. "Go on ahead, Sam," Tobie said. "I'll be along soon." She fiddled out an unfiltered Camel from the soft pack in her breast pocket. The match threw a spark as she scratched it across the top of the table, and she inhaled, long and hard. Smoke streamed out her nose.

Sam didn't seem to hear her and his dark-brown eyes got a stubborn, faraway look to them. "Think I'll have another cup," he said, taking his mug to the stove and refilling it from the dented tin pot. Then he sat back down at the table; I realized he intended to sit there long enough to pressure her into moving. For once I wished he'd just be direct: say what he meant, ask for what he wanted. But that wasn't the way they communicated.

I began to scrub the iron skillet, irritated at myself and at him and at her — but I didn't say a thing. She was ornery sometimes; Sam had his own ways of handling her, and I'd learned it was better to stay out of it.

After a minute Tobie brought over a stack of dishes and slid them into the dishpan of soapy water, her cigarette still between her teeth. Suddenly the smell of bacon grease and smoke made me feel sick. I stood sideways at the sink and fought the nausea blooming up in my stomach by starting to sing "Old MacDonald." In the middle of every verse I paused to let Anna fill in a different animal, her eyes dancing with pleasure as she yelled horse, cow, pig, hen, dog, mouse, bird, and banged her spoon in rhythm. The sick feeling diminished and I smiled at Anna, making wild noises to illustrate her choices.

But a minute later another contraction tightened down and brought our duet to a stop. Even so, again I pushed away the idea that my labor was beginning. I wouldn't admit it, but I was afraid, more afraid than I'd been when Anna was born. This time I knew what I'd gotten myself into — and this time I was carrying twins.

"Go! Out! Side!" Anna demanded in precise toddlerese. I heard Sam snort with laughter, and I took my hands out of the greasy gray water, turning back to lift her from her highchair. Her dark-brown eyes shone, delighted at the expression on my face: she'd sculpted her blueberry yogurt into an abstract heap with her fingers and was streaking it like purple warpaint across her forehead, cheeks, and chin. I started to smile.

"Nothing served by giving the child a second meal," Tobie said, going over to move the plate beyond Anna's purple fists. "You laugh at her, Sam, and she'll think it's the thing to do." She gave him a look.

"Oh, come on, Ma," he said, trying to squash his smile. "Anna's not such a bad girl — just artistic like her mother." He reached under the table and tickled Anna's knee.

I closed my eyes and leaned against the stove, wondering how long it would be before I could get back to my work again after the babies came. The knobs dug into my spine and centered me there for a minute: "Woman Leaning on Stove"; someday I would paint it, I resolved, in tones of deep purple and gray, maybe in casein.

Tobie was sizing me up with her trained eye. She'd been born on a farm in Nova Scotia, to a mother who was also the local midwife, and she had spent a lot of her adolescence beside her mother and her mother's patients. She'd learned the trade well and even now helped out some of the women in Arrowsic who were too superstitious or poor to go to the hospital when their time came.

When I'd first come to New Hampshire, I'd been taken aback by the large families who lived in tar-paper shacks, with rusted-out pickup trucks beached in the front yard. Two or three generations of women always sat rocking on the front porch; the children grew long-legged and ragged in the dirt; the TV antenna on the roof was the only clean and shiny object in sight. I'd never seen rural poverty before; in the city, poverty was different. This was so elemental, so stark, set in contrast against the riches of mountains and woods. It was to shacks like these that Tobie often went in the middle of the night.

But Tobie didn't say anything to me now, just hefted Anna under her arm and bore her across the room. It always surprised me how much weight she could juggle around; she was over sixty now, but her arms were still young — not like my mother's, whose flesh jiggled when she applauded — and her shoulders were right angles, square and sturdy. I straightened my own shoulders and scrubbed a little more fiercely. How could I be afraid of a mere childbirth when this woman had faced her husband's cancer by refusing to send him to the hospital to die and nursed him instead on a cot in the living room for three months? This woman had learned to run a farm, from barn to books, and kept her home afloat too. It seemed she might run the whole world. I remembered then, in a brief flash, how she'd taught me to fish when I first came to Arrowsic. The picture in my mind was as sharp as if it were yesterday: she'd stood knee-deep in spring water rushing down from the mountains, her feet white against the pearly black stones of the riverbed, her khakis rolled to mid-thigh; Tobie never used boots, and I loved her for that. I needed someone who was as strong as I wanted myself to be — someone to show me how to go about it — and Tobie was that person. She'd showed me how to bait my hook, cast the line, and wait; how to dig the hook out of the lip, mouth, or stomach; how to gut it, scale it, fry it, eat it.

At the deep porcelain sink I squirted more detergent into the dishpan while Tobie baptized my daughter under a stream of cold well water. "No point in dilly-dallying around, Anna," she said in the face of the ensuing roar. "Shampoo your hair with yogurt, and we'll just be rinsing it out."

I flipped her a dishtowel and frowned against the next contraction, sneaking a look at the kitchen clock. They were fifteen minutes apart.

"She'll come out to the barn with me," Tobie said, toweling Anna with vigor. Anna never held still under my hands, but she didn't dare squirm when Tobie was washing her up — a fact which was beginning to infuriate me. "Got to call Tyson's and order more chicken feed, take a look at the mare. Might as well let her run 'round out there." She allowed her hand one lingering stroke before swatting Anna on the bottom of her overalls, while I hid my smile and soaped a glass till it squeaked. "Run get your jacket and we'll give your mother some peace."

I turned back to the sink, grateful, and afraid I'd tell her so. That was something else I'd learned in the four years I'd lived here: Tobie didn't like to be thanked.

When I heard the screen door slam I trudged upstairs and sat, winded, for a minute on our bed to catch my breath. It felt like my belly was sitting on top of my lungs instead of the other way around; there wasn't any space left inside of me for air. I straightened the blue braided scatter rug with my big toe and turned on the bedside lamp.

Right away its yellow glow drove back the chilly light that

came in from the windows and I felt warmer. I ran my hand down the spines of the stack of library books on my night table. They were an eclectic mix — John Irving and T. S. Eliot, Thomas Hardy and Agatha Christie. Books for pleasure beside books I hadn't had a chance to tackle during my college years. Every two weeks I journeyed to the public library in Manchester with our neighbor, Sarah Mack; I chose things I thought I ought to read, things I had missed in my four years at college, things I had an urge to catch up on. I was always fighting a sense of not being educated enough, of having left too much of my city self behind. The library and its dark-spined volumes were the one part of my past I didn't want to move beyond. Overdue notices connected me to urban streets.

But, mostly, the books sat. It seemed to take forever to read even one chapter, let alone a whole book or the stack of five I always chose. At the checkout desk I was like the fat lady in line at the supermarket with her hoard of sweet and starchy treasures. Each night I climbed into bed beside Sam, opened the thick, boardy pages, and promptly fell asleep. And it was even more true now that I was pregnant again. I was a lazy pregnant lady, too tired for reading, but I didn't want to admit it — and so every two weeks I took the books in and renewed them.

Another contraction tightened the lower part of my belly now. This one hurt; it made me hold my breath and sit still, my hands resting on the hardening mound of my abdomen. If it lasts less than a minute, I thought, then I'm carrying two boys. Tighter, tighter, and just like that it started to soften up under my fingers and was gone. I looked over at the windup Big Ben on the bureau. Forty-five seconds. A positive sign.

When Anna had come I'd wanted a girl. I was terrified of having a boy. What do you do with a boy? I'd asked Tobie, who had a pragmatic answer for everything I could think to ask. It had seemed impossible that my female self could spawn a male, anyway. I would know what to do with a girl: a girl I would be able to understand, know, talk and share with, but a boy would be an alien creature.

When the twins began to move inside me, I'd been possessed by a strange, unexpected itch — like the pregnant woman in "Rapunzel" who craves at any cost the magical salad leaf, rampion, and so goads her husband into climbing over the witch's wall to procure it. In just that irrational way did I want the babies I was carrying to be boys. Boys: different from what I had and what I was.

I got off the bed and stripped the four-poster down, bringing the birthing sheets from the hall closet. The rubber sheet we'd used when Anna was born in this room went over the mattress first, then a Turkish towel, and then the linen, washed clean but stained. Tobie had used these same sheets when Sam came, in this bed with its carved finials. Before Anna's birth I'd welcomed the sense of history and looked forward to sharing my debut into motherhood with her, but now I was more sensible: the sense of history was, in the end, simply a shared history of pain, women's pain, unlike anything a man could ever know or imagine.

I stacked a half-dozen clean towels on the dresser. The room was ready. A hot shower then, with a lot of soap everywhere, luxuriously long — long enough to steam up the medicine-cabinet glass. It didn't matter that in a little while I would be sweaty again. A shower was part of my preparation, an important way of getting control. Two contractions in a row made me sit on the edge of the claw-foot tub; after they were over I turned the shower handle hard left, cold, and put my face up into the water.

I stood in front of the full-length mirror by my window to comb out my long blonde hair, which was beginning to streak up gray in back and over my ears, but I couldn't see that today in the dim light from the outside. If it took less than fifteen strokes to untangle my hair the twins would be boys,

I decided; more and they would be girls. As I got close to fifteen I lost count on purpose and twined my hair up on the back of my head with a big metal barrette.

Still naked, I stopped to look at myself with a tight mixture of awe and fear, closing my eyes to picture, for an instant, my old, slender body, that reedlike body I had grown with and into. But when I opened my eyes the mirror showed something entirely different: I had swallowed the globe like some creature from a Greek myth; the world outlined itself between my ribs and pelvis. When I looked at myself like this I could see parts of me that I hadn't seen in months: my thighs (sturdier now); my pubic hair (stretching out into an even bigger triangle as my belly stretched); my feet (long, narrow, uncertain of their burden); my breasts (lying on top of my stomach, waiting to nurture and be nestled into); my nipples (dark, dark, dusky dark, like a black woman's). My body had given itself over: it was no longer mine. A contraction moved across my belly. I could actually see it harden, and I rested my hands there, fanned open wide, as if I were holding a basketball. My fingers made a net across the taut skin.

I turned away and pulled on my last clean pair of maternity dungarees and a plaid workshirt. The thought of bending to tie my sneakers was comic, so I shoved my feet into my slippers instead and turned to go finish up my morning chores.

"How far apart are they?" said Tobie from the doorway.

I didn't even look at her, but just turned mechanically to the top of my dresser to straighten the hairbrushes and the penny jar, the receipts for grain and equipment I always found jammed into Sam's pockets, as well as the miscellaneous elastics, bobby pins, and spare change. The dresser was a maple chest that Sam and I had picked up at a yard sale on our honeymoon in Vermont, and I thought back to what a perfect day it had been: we'd spent all morning in bed, then eaten a huge brunch of eggs and smoked ham in the inn's main dining room, then gone for a drive. On that drive we saw an old barn with a grayed sign propped against its doors: USED FURNURTURE.

"How far apart?" Tobie asked again.

I kept straightening. Admitting it would make it real. There could be no turning back. In my mind I began to paint us standing there, the silence long and gray, thin violet light from the window, a yellow pool from the lamp by the bed.

"Ten minutes," I answered finally.

"You could go faster this time."

"Or slower. Or it could be false labor."

I heard her snort and turned to fold the lavender quilt back from the bed and stow it in the closet.

"And I suppose that's why you're making ready?"

Outside the window the rain was just a drop now and then on the puddles in my garden. The tomato plants were still climbing the towers of their stakes, but the beans and lettuce were ready for picking. Although I'd attacked the weeds last week, finishing with mosquito bites at the backs of my knees and a rotten neckache, there were already a lot of scraggly new interlopers poking their heads through the mud and making my nice, even rows look unkempt. "I thought I might work a little in my garden this morning," I said, as if I hadn't heard her, knowing at the same time how stupid I sounded. I bit the inside of my cheek and wished I could just go and lay my head on Tobie's shoulder. Another contraction snaked up inside me.

"It's raining."

"A little rain doesn't bother me."

"And how about a little mud?" She still stood in the doorway, her solid, square form blocking my exit. She wanted me to stay here; she wanted me to begin. My fear turned into anger.

"It's not time," I said stubbornly, opening Sam's drawer and juggling his pile of jockey shorts. "There's five loads of wash today, the interfacing on Anna's dress to do, the linen closet isn't straight yet —"

"Don't be a twit," she interrupted with impatience. "All of that'll keep. You should be putting your feet up now." She watched as I had another, this one strong enough to force me to sit. She came in and stood in front of me, so that I had to look up at her. "We need to take a look at you. See what's what."

"I don't want to, I don't want to do this again," I said, panic running my voice in a circle.

She rested her hand on my shoulder, almost like an accident. "We got through it last time, we'll do it again."

Somehow her tone reassured me. And her touch, too. Maybe it was that someone else was taking charge, and suddenly I felt incapable of any decision, however small. Here was someone who would stand between me and my body, between me and the driving force of shoving babies out into the world. Tobie would be my voice when I could not speak. She and Sam would help me through the birth as they had helped me through Anna's.

I pulled my pants down and lay back on the bed, staring up at the ceiling. Tobie came back from washing her hands. "You're two fingers open," she said, pushing down on my belly as she shoved up hard with her other hand. "Take a rest now and I'll go tell Sam to get Sarah Mack." Sarah was one of the few locals who had welcomed me, an outsider, after Sam and I had married. She was a regular visitor at BoxTie and always came in for tea after our biweekly library excursions. She lived right down the hill from us, and her own son and daughter-in-law lived just a bit beyond that. Freddie Mack was one of Sam's old schoolmates, and we took in an occasional movie with him and his wife.

"I don't like bothering her yet, when we're not sure."

Tobie snorted. "*I'm* sure. And she told me again yesterday she'd watch Anna when you were ready."

"I don't want Anna up here." I rose on one elbow.

"She'll learn soon enough." Tobie headed out the door to wash up. In a minute she was back. "For sure you don't want Doctor Loring? He'll come down if we ask."

The entire family had been going to Nat Loring since he'd set up practice the year Sam and I married. He was an affable, easygoing sort and had even managed to charm Tobie. Still, I preferred to do this on my own, so I shook my head. "The three of us did fine all by ourselves last time."

"Two may be harder than one," she warned.

"I don't want anyone else."

"Fix yourself up, and I'll be back." She left, talking to herself and yelling to the sheepdogs, who'd followed her upstairs. Tobie's dogs loved her and moved with her in a pack. At night they crept into her room one by one and settled in hairy heaps across the floor like big bags of laundry. One of the massive animals inevitably managed to nestle up next to her on the bed and would open a sleepy eye when I stumbled by her room in the early morning. The vague scent of animal always clung to Tobie, a kind of perfume.

"Some tea might be good," she muttered as they all tromped down the stairs together.

I took off my shirt and bra and put on one of Sam's old flannel nightshirts. It was comforting to feel cloth worn soft by his skin against my skin. In spite of innumerable washings in strong laundry soap, the smell of his body lingered in the fabric, overpowering the smell of clean. It was as if he were putting his arms around me.

Puttering around the room, I waited for the next contraction and hoped Tobie would hurry back. Some people in town thought it was strange that I had my mother-in-law for a midwife — they told me so every time I went in for groceries — but it didn't seem strange to me or Sam. I'd been terrified of hospitals ever since my tonsillectomy when I was ten. It was comforting to know Tobie would be by my side:

beyond her reputation as a fine midwife was her performance right here on our farm; she'd saved a lot of animals who might have died under less determined hands.

In fact, when I'd first met her four years ago she had been in the barn, down on her knees with her arm up inside a mare, trying to get a foal out.

It had been one of Sam's most valuable horses who'd gotten her baby stuck, one of the very first he'd bought to start the breeding end of the farm. I was just a bystander, having met him only that hour in the far pasture down the hill. I'd driven up to Arrowsic from Manchester, where I lived in a rented room, to do some painting. I was working on my first commission from Hallmark Cards — a set of rural watercolors for their Easter series the following spring.

It was a perfect field for my illustration: pastel yellows and greens, the soft blue of tiny wildflowers that grew en masse in the long grasses, grazing cows and horses, a silvered barn topping the rise a quarter-mile away, and the mild swell of the mountains as a backdrop. The day was sunny and hot for so early in May, and the field smelled of pink clover and sun-baked earth. I set up my easel happily, unscrewed the cap of the large thermos of clean water that would enable me to have clear colors several hours from now, took out my thumbhole palette, and began to rummage in my paint box for the watercolors that would catch all the glory around me. I took out a big badger sweetener for blending and some sable flats as well, did some pencil sketching for a while, and then began to block the painting in. Not until a strange man came over the breast of the pasture did it occur to me that I was trespassing. Covertly, I watched him approach.

He had a long, easy stride, and his tanned arms swung with his body's motion, the sleeves of his workshirt rolled up; a study in fluid movement, he tilted his body back at the hip to compensate for the slope of the hill, and he moved down without slipping, scrambling, or hurrying. Then he

stood before me, broad shoulders pulling the worn cotton of
his shirt tight across his chest.

"What d'you think you're doing here?" he asked.

"And just who are you?" I countered.

"The owner of this field, for one," he said. "Sam Yates for
two." He was even taller and leaner than he'd appeared at a
distance, his blue jeans dropping from narrow hips and a flat
belly. His straight blond hair was short but it still fell over his
forehead. He came around behind me and looked at my
watercolor. I had to lock my hands behind my back to keep
from flipping it facedown on the easel. It made me nervous
when people looked at my work before it was finished; it
made me nervous when people looked at my work, period.
And so I stood very still, rigid really, wishing he'd just go
away.

"And who are *you?*" he asked, interrupting his perusal of
my painting.

"Alice Sterne," I answered stiffly.

"Well, Alice Sterne, my barn's too much to the left in this
painting of yours," he said.

I didn't respond. Who cared if the barn were dead center
or in the foreground? It was none of his business anyway.

"And you should ask permission before you go setting up
on other people's places."

I looked up at him again and met the impact of his eyes
for the first time. They were a dark coffee-colored brown.
And soft. With thick, bristly blond lashes. No man should
have lashes like that, I thought critically, dropping my eyes
in an attempt to get control of myself and think of a reply. It
wasn't that he was simply handsome, though undoubtedly
he was. The clipped edge of his hair was starting to grow
over the rims of his small, well-shaped ears; his nose was
long and pointed; his mouth was very broad. His features
were bold, I decided, risking another upward glance, and I
liked that. I liked it a lot. He started to smile, a wide, warm

smile. Even his eyes crinkled up at the corners. I blushed as I realized he'd been teasing me.

"You haven't seen a Guernsey, have you? A calving Guernsey?" he asked, putting his hand to his brow for shade and scanning the edge of the pasture. "She didn't come in for her feed this morning."

It took me a minute to focus on what he was saying, to stop staring and begin to think again. "Cows?" I asked, somewhat stupidly, astonished. I gestured with a broad sweep of my palm. A whole herd was spread before us across the hill.

"No, no, not out there in the open," he said with impatience. "She's *calving*. She'll have tucked herself off somewhere." He started toward the trees and stone wall that bounded the field. "Want to give me a hand?" He smiled back at me, shrugging his straight, broad shoulders and letting his dark eyes tease me again. "As rental for your easel space."

I laughed, already out of breath, but tagged after him uncertainly nevertheless. Some instinct would not allow me to let him just walk away, but on the other hand, what did I know about cows, calving or otherwise? I'd been raised ten miles outside of Boston, in a working-class suburb where everyone was either a bank teller or a shoe salesman. My father worked the furniture department in Sears, Roebuck. I didn't even like to *remember* my years in Massachusetts: I'd been born when I moved to New Hampshire after college.

I was an art major at Boston College, but my life-drawing classes didn't interest me. Or anatomy. Or bowls of fruit. I spent most of my time in class looking out the window and drawing the trees, the flowers, whatever was *outside* the hothouse of the studio. I wanted to paint things that moved, that blew, that danced, that grew. I was impatient; I didn't want to learn the basics. In biology class, in choir practice, in a bar with friends, talking with my roommate before bed — I always felt distracted. I wanted to be somewhere else, doing something else. Only in bed with a man did I get absorbed and involved and free from my own critical inner voice; it was easier to give and take with my body, in the dark, than it was over a cup of coffee the morning after.

I held something back from my studio classes and from the teachers that taught them, and so I held something back from what I painted there. There was a key somewhere that would unlock what was really inside of me, more than just my good eye or a fine sense of draftsmanship; I was still looking for that key the day I met Sam, and until I'd found it I was loath to show anyone anything.

On summer weekends when I was little, my parents used to take me to the big state fairs in New Hampshire. They liked the ball and rifle games you could never win, the junk jewelry and stuffed animal prizes, the hot dog and Sno-Kone stands. While my father tried to shoot down a line of yellow ducks, I'd sneak away and lose myself in the crowd. I backtracked to the barns where cows and horses stood head-to-head, lines of them munching their hay, dropping their manure. Away from the grinding machines of the midway and its rides, I discovered that the quiet of the animal noises, even their smell, excited me.

My parents would find me an hour later, leaning on a cow's stall in a state of blissful unawareness, patting the animal's nose, rubbing my cheek against the soft fur, pestering some owner with questions, or curled up on a bale of hay sketching. I had no idea of how much time might have passed. They were always angry; they were afraid for me, they said. I was their only child.

They were afraid, I'd thought resentfully, of everything: of animals, of highways and planes, of the unknown crash and bang. They had padlocked their lives up in a yellow shingle house in the suburbs, out of the city, out of the country — away from anything with a beat, a pulse, a rhythm of its own. At the ocean I wasn't allowed to swim, at the fair I wasn't allowed to ride, in the city I wasn't allowed to walk alone. In our small front yard at home even the big sycamore was off-limits.

One summer vacation we took a trip to New Hampshire for a whole week, to Lake Winnipesaukee, where we rented a small cabin on the edge of the water. There were too many tourists doing too much waterskiing and eating too many clam rolls for it to be rural or rustic. My parents wanted to see all the sights, so we spent our days at the Flume and Lost River, in the Polar Caves, or buying moccasins, balsam candles, and sachet bags stuffed with pine needles at a Totem Pole Outlet. At night I dreamt of visiting the small towns where people actually lived, and on waking I resolved to return here alone someday, to this place where thick stands of conifers lined the mountains a dark, furry green.

When I was seventeen my father died, as earthbound as he had lived: electrocuted by a bare wire in the Christmas lights he was stringing across our front hedge. It was almost embarrassing, except that he was my father. My mother and I missed him in ways we did not, could not, talk about. We sealed up our pain and kept it as mysterious and sacred as a religion. He and I hadn't ever done much together, and so I invented things we might have done. I embellished in my mind the memory of what we did: the few baseball games, the trips to the supermarket every Saturday, the one county fair where he'd relented and taken me on the salt and pepper shaker and I'd clutched his hand in delight and fear. I missed what had not been between us even more than I missed what had been.

In my sleep I kept turning corners — at school, in the department store, in the kitchen — and there he was. Some part of me refused to believe he'd just stopped. Not even my paintings just stopped. Every night before bed I checked the stars, changing my position to change the patterns I could see: I kept looking for the design of my father's face, or his initials, or even the shape of his big brass belt buckle.

The Friday night before my college graduation, I dreamt I was living in a cabin in the woods, throwing pots. Behind the cabin was a shed with eighteen shelves of vases, mugs, platters, and bowls, and each piece was a deep, extraordinary blue. I woke from that dream and lay there thinking. I hadn't known what to answer when my mother and friends asked what I was going to be doing after June came and went, and suddenly here was a new possibility. Still, I hesitated, almost afraid. I had craved change for so long, but craving and doing were two separate things.

Allowing my own sense of adventure to carry me forward, I packed my parka, my paints, my astrological charts and books, and caught the seven A.M. Greyhound to Manchester, New Hampshire, where I rented a room, got a job as a waitress, and found myself painting a portrait of a woman throwing pots. My mother was in despair and called me weekly, begging me to come home. She couldn't understand why I would leave our comfortable life to go to a strange town where I knew no one.

And I was lonely at first. There was no one for me in Manchester. A big mill town with a river rushing down its middle, it was an ugly place — not at all what I had dreamed of. I wanted to move out, into the countryside, but I had to support myself, and there were jobs in the city. So I stayed, dated a few locals who came into the Grille, made some casual friends of the other waitresses. And kept painting. Painting was about all I had then, some sort of communication with myself. And I continued to dream of, and paint about, the time when I could move on.

My dreams began to tell me what was coming, like a horoscope, a forecast of intent. When I moved to Manchester I started to keep a journal of those dreams, and each morning when I woke up I wrote the last night's episode in my spiral-bound notebook — even before brushing my teeth — in as much detail as I could remember: the colors, the smells, everything. My best paintings began to emerge from the journal, where the real details of a day lived merged with the shadows and mystery my subconscious provided.

I'd been in Manchester nearly two years when I met Sam Yates. Two years of waitressing and doing sketches for calendars and newspaper ads, and then, finally, my major job from Hallmark had come through, with just enough money so that I could quit my job at the Grille and spend all my time painting.

Sam and I had looked for a long time that day before we found the cow and her calf at last; his plaid shirt had sweat in circles under the arms and in an arrow up the back. I was so wiped out from climbing up and down the hills and valleys that I could only gasp. Sitting at an easel hadn't done much for my wind. He didn't seem like he talked a lot anyway.

I trailed behind him. Maybe it was because I was moving more slowly and he so fast that I was the one who saw them first. They were hidden behind a small ring of oak trees at the far edge of that big pasture, the cow already standing, the calf already nursing. I pointed.

He ran to them as if he weren't tired at all and sat down on the rock wall near the cow's head. He looked so relieved that I started to laugh.

"She's my ma's prize Guernsey," he explained, stroking her nose. "I'd really hate to lose her."

"But I thought cows did this all the time." The color rose up red in my cheeks: here I was with a strange man, discussing birth. I felt as shy as a teenager — like a virgin, which was absurd, considering the four years I'd spent at college. I smiled at him and sat down, leaning against the stone wall.

"Sometimes you can have trouble," he said. His eyes lightened to the color of caramel in the sun, and I felt as if I were falling somehow, falling into him. I was afraid I was going to blurt out something stupid, so I looked away.

"We've got a mare with a foal laid wrong up in the barn right now," he went on. "Yesterday I thought this calf might be coming rump-first too." He smiled and pulled a piece of grass from the clump at my feet. He picked up the Turkish towel he'd been carrying and began to wipe out the calf's eyes and nose, with great care and tenderness despite his big hands. I liked that he was doing something because it meant I could watch him openly. I liked to see the expertise with which he handled this delicate operation. "Looks like she managed, though," he added.

I put my head back and closed my eyes into the sun; it was hot and bright and red against my eyelids. I was warm and more relaxed than I'd been in a long while. I didn't mind being quiet with this man even though he was a stranger. We didn't need to make a lot of noise to cover the silence, just sat there listening to the suck-suck-suck of the calf on its mother's teat. I opened my eyes and caught him staring at me. I could tell what he was thinking, and I blushed again, looking away.

"So, you said you're an artist?" He straightened up and swung a neck rope around the heifer. I rose reluctantly and we began to lead her back up the hill. The calf tagged behind, not steady yet. I put my hand on his warm, damp flank. He didn't move away.

"I'm doing a set of Easter cards," I answered vaguely, thinking about what would happen when we got back to my easel. I didn't want to go back to work now. I wanted to walk for a while with Sam and his calf. "Your pasture's beautiful. It'll make a pretty watercolor."

He bobbed his head and turned his face down toward the cow, embarrassed. I was surprised at how much he let his pleasure show. Later I realized that my passing remark was just a piece of conversation to me, but to Sam it was justification: the farm was his — each sharp pitchfork, mound of hay, bucket of grain, the health of every animal. When his father died of cancer, Sam had left his junior year in college to come back to help his mother, and he'd done it gladly. He came home, right to where his father had said he'd belonged anyway. And with no one around to point it out, without the need to rebel, he'd stayed, stuck with it, let himself love it. There are some people who fit into their work the way an egg lies against its shell. They never struggle. Sam was one of those. I fell in love with him because he was, like the land, a combination of opposites: vulnerable and tough, rough and gentle, open and yet hidden. Even then I think I sensed that he was the conduit to what I wanted to paint.

We walked right past my easel without hesitating and kept on talking. We put the cow and her calf in a clean box stall. Sam gave the new mother a drink of water and then showed me around. I forgot all about my work. We found Tobie and Joe with the foaling mare Sam had mentioned earlier.

"The whole world must be giving birth today," I said as we stood in the door of the stall.

"Or not giving birth, as the case may be," said Tobie, who was kneeling on the floor in the middle of the wet bedding with her arm up to the elbow inside the mare's body. All my romantic fantasies of bucolic life on a farm fled before this grotesque reality. The mare lay on her side, obviously exhausted. Sam went to kneel beside her head and stroked her neck. She flickered her eye at him, but that was all.

"She's given in," Tobie said to Sam. "Not even straining anymore. I can't get the foal to turn nor the vet on the phone either."

Sam's face was grim. He didn't bother to introduce me to his mother or to Joe. Later he told me Bay Lady was the first mare he'd bought for the farm, a fine Arabian, and he loved her the way a boy loves his first pony.

"I guess you'd better get the ropes then," Tobie said to Joe.

They'd already forgotten about me, and I perched on the edge of the hay rack uncertainly, afraid to get in their way, wondering what they could do with a rope. But I wanted to stay. I was drawn to the drama, and — without even knowing it — I was painting the scene in my head: the bright vermilion of blood against the yellow straw, the harsh light from the overhead bulb, the black rubber water bucket turned on its side, the determination on their faces. Soon I was on my knees too, painting forgotten, handing them tools, towels, taking a turn on the ropes when the others got tired.

An hour later we managed to get the foal turned right side to, and with a last effort the mare pushed and we pulled, and in a gush of water the colt was born. We all cheered. The instinct to nurse her baby was strong, and the mare struggled up. The colt wavered on his pipestem legs and then, with Tobie's help, found the teat. I hugged myself, curiously moved. Tobie handed me a towel and asked me to rub him dry. I wanted to cry, but I put my arms around him and toweled instead, imitating what I had seen Sam do earlier with the calf. The foal nuzzled at his mother while Tobie checked him over, handling his fuzzy body with the same strength and gentleness I'd seen in Sam's hands. It struck me then how unusual it was to see such teamwork between a mother and son, how remarkable it was to find a son still living with his mother in a society where children did not remain at home past high school. Maybe it was a mark of loyalty. If so, it was a loyalty I envied.

Remembering the first time I'd met Tobie made me feel better for myself now as I lay there on our bed and watched the rain strike the windows, timing my labor pains with the Big Ben on the dresser. I would live through this, I decided, I would live to watch Anna grow, to love my husband, to paint innumerable pictures, to watch my tomatoes turn red and ripe in the garden.

But I wished Sam would hurry and come upstairs. I really

needed him now. He was probably still working on that lame mare, and we'd have to start the Lamaze breathing patterns pretty soon. I twisted impatiently on the sheets, and, for a minute, I resented the farm's hold on him and his devotion to it. Unbidden to my mind came a picture of my mother when I was little and sick in bed as she trudged up the stairs with a tray of chicken-rice soup, toast, and a glass of milk. Sam, too, would be willing to bring me that tray, but first he would prioritize: was there time, was it urgent, did I really need it. He was a practical, pragmatic man, a temperament he had inherited, in part, from Tobie. Now this similarity aroused in me a deep ambivalence: on the one hand, I was jealous of his love for that demanding other woman — his land; and, on the other hand, I loved him the more for the hard muscles and sweat, the undeniable expertise which enabled him to move with ease in such a mysterious world.

Now I looked back at the clock. I'd been in active labor an hour and a half. Anna had taken ten hours to get born, but this time I was sure it would be better. This time I knew what I was doing.

I shook off any feeling of self-pity. At BoxTie there was just too much to do and too little time. To push myself, to see how far I could stretch, was one of the reasons I'd come to live here in the first place; Sam was only taking care of his end of things. He would come when he could. I reminded myself sternly of the pioneer women, having their babies in covered wagons, and of Chinese farm women, dropping them in the fields like stones. I readied myself for another contraction: they were three minutes apart now and regular, so that I could prepare for them a little. I turned on my side to ease the pressure in my lower back and massaged my thighs. I thought of good things, of the long, slow nights we'd spent in this bed, of the night our pleasure had conceived Anna, here in this room, and then, further back in memory, I re-

membered the very first time we'd ever made love, only a
week after I'd met him in the pasture that day.
He'd called me in Manchester and invited me back to BoxTie
for supper. The sun was just going down behind the gray-
shingled farmhouse, staining Tobie's rose garden a deep blood
red, when I drove up the gravel drive. Sam was waiting for
me in a rocker on the front porch, his sleeves rolled back to
the elbow, exposing the smooth, hard length of his forearm.
Over the roof of the house the pine trees bowed and whispered, a deep and extraordinary green. I envied him being
able to live in such a beautiful place.

Tobie made chicken stew and BoxTie mashed potatoes, using
fresh cream from the Guernseys and celery seed from the
garden. I remember that I ate a lot — it had been good to eat
something real after all the grease from the Grille — and that
I couldn't look much at Sam. The sensation of sliding and
falling right down into his eyes was even more intense than
it had been before. My chest was so tight it was hard to
breathe.

Afterward we were supposed to go to the drive-in, but a
mare had just come into heat and Sam had wanted to take
care of her right away. The late spring light was fading, slant-
ing down into the paddock gold and green, shifting with the
dust in the air. I leaned against the fence and watched,
thunderstruck and captivated by the sheer size of the stallion,
his excitement, his prancing dance and squeals of pleasure
as he scented the mare. I tried not to stare, my own fascina-
tion embarrassing me.

Sam handled the excited Arabian with ease, walking him
in quick, tight circles, while Joe stood at the mare's head,
soothing her. At Joe's nod Sam brought Shadow Man to the
mare's hindquarters. He sniffed and curled his lip up in delight, showing his teeth, rearing to mount her. She kicked
Shadow Man three times before he managed to straddle her,

and then Sam quickly pulled her tail aside, out of the way, still maintaining a good hold on the stallion's head. In a few thrusts it was over. So fast, I thought, a little disappointed that the excitement had ended so quickly.

"Some first date," Sam said to me as he walked the mare in circles to keep her from expelling the sperm.

"I thought it was . . ." I looked at him out of the corner of my eye. "But I didn't realize how fast —" I stopped short then, color heating my cheekbones again.

"Well, it gets the job done," he said, sending me a puzzled look. "We should have a foal out of her next spring." He turned the mare loose in the pasture and we walked back into the barn to check on Shadow Man. "See you, Joe," he called, as the other man headed out the main door, lifting his hand in a goodbye.

We were alone in the big space of the barn, except for the animals, rustling and pungent. We peered in over the top half of the stallion's door. He was pacing.

"This guy's my chance," Sam said, glancing at me in the barn's half-light. It was beginning to turn dusk now. "Like your painting, I guess. I want this place to be more than just a chicken farm, more than what my father left." He sighed. "My father was too worried about losing what he already had. He wasn't interested in dreaming — only in surviving." He paused, shuffled his foot back and forth over the floor. "I can understand that better now, I guess, seeing as it's taken all we've saved for the last four years — and everything Dad put away too — to buy this guy." He gestured with his thumb and then reached up to swing the top half of the door closed.

"No, don't," I said, my hand reaching out to stop Sam's. I didn't want him to close that door. "Look how beautiful he is." I wanted to stay near the stallion. In the half-dark his white coat was luminescent: he shimmered like a ghost. I watched him, the strong legs, the heavily bunched muscle of his hindquarters, the curved half-moon of his neck. Every

sinew was lean and hard. I looked into his face. It seemed
more than human: he knew exactly what he was, and I envied
him that.

"We're out on a limb now." Sam paused and cleared his
throat. "After all, I'm still real new at this. When you think
that my mother's been working with animals for the last . . . ,"
he paused, counting, in his head, "twenty years, I'd guess.
There's nothing I do that I don't clear by her first."

"You're lucky you get along so well."

"Sometimes she gets under my skin, but mostly —" He
broke off and shrugged. "She stood by me from the start.
And it's good to have someone sharing the risk."

"Why do you put yourself down like that?" I was puzzled.
"You've got a natural sense of the business, I can see it just
from the way you handle the animals."

"Nothing's a sure thing. There's disease and accident and
stillbirth — one disaster after another just looking for a home."
At his vehemence I felt suddenly ignorant, sorry for my dis-
missal of his anxiety. "Just about anything you can think of
could ruin everything." Then he smiled, a wide, vulnerable
grin, and my feeling of insecurity vanished.

"But, well . . . ," I objected, and let myself, for the first
time, give in to my longing: I touched the back of his hand
where it lay across the top of the stall door. I ran my finger
down the length of tendon mapped beneath the sheer sheath
of his tanned skin. "Risks. When I moved to New Hampshire
I didn't know if I'd be able to paint here or not. I still don't
really know."

"You're not afraid of much, are you?"

"Yes, I am." I turned and looked into those eyes of his. I
sensed that he admired me, that he found me brave. "I just
don't let it stop me. And neither do you."

"Something in common," he said, squeezing my fingers.
His grip was strong. "And what else?" I felt strange, confused
almost, as if I were awake in one of my dreams. I kept looking

into his eyes, and he pulled me to sit beside him on a bale of hay to the right of the stallion's door. The length of his side pressed against the length of mine. He put his arm around me, and I turned slowly toward him, floated out toward him, kissed him. The inside of his mouth was very soft, but he kissed me hard, with force, his lips covering mine in a wide, wet circle. We stopped for a minute and then began again, this time for a long time. It was as if our mouths were the center of our bodies and we had fused around them.

"Could we?" I asked, not really believing I was initiating this. I didn't know him at all, and that made it even more exciting. There was no one to see us but the animals, breathing there, only a few feet away. I could see almost nothing by then. It was like being in a black box with no windows.

"Here?" he asked, sounding incredulous. Then he laughed and moved toward me. He kissed the side of my neck first, tracing his tongue upward in a long wet line, licking the edge of my ear. Behind his half-open stall door, Shadow Man was restless. He wanted more, I thought. One mare wasn't enough. Or maybe he knew we were there.

Sam's hands slid up under my shirt onto the skin of my breasts, and I crossed my legs, squeezing my thighs against each other in excitement. I was already wet. His calluses were rough as he rubbed the flat of his palm over my nipples, bringing them up into points, and then he squeezed them hard, rolling them between his fingertips. I pushed my hands up under his shirt, across the fine hairs of his chest, and then edged downward below his belt. He leaned back to make room for my hand and sighed. I was shaking with my own desire. I wanted him in a way I'd never wanted anyone before. Hand up under my blue-jean skirt, I pulled down my own panties.

He hesitated for one more minute, looking around into the dark, but then knelt and unzipped his pants as I stepped out of mine. I could just make out his face as he leaned toward me, intense, urgent, no smile. No hesitation. I had gotten to him: we could have been on the side of a mountain or in a parking lot — he could think of only one thing now.

He pushed into me, not quite rough, but not gentle either: he knew what he was doing and he did it. He wasn't worried about pleasing me, I realized, he simply seemed to assume he would. The smell of sweat and the musk of horse clung to his shirt and in the hollow of his collarbone. I thought of the stallion, of the mare with her head held, who had felt no pleasure. For me it was different. I was wet, slippery, heated with my own power, heated with his strength. I arched up against Sam with a deep noise I'd never made before, surprised to feel myself feeling so much. Wild, almost. All sense of control dissolved, all conscious thought. I just felt: everything I was in that moment centered in my body, in the pure sensation of his body inside mine.

Sam started to move faster, his rhythm matching mine, but then I circled my hips a little to the left and suddenly he slipped out by mistake.

We stopped, startled by the abrupt disconnection, but then I groaned and started to laugh, and when I did, so did he, a deep, husky laugh. It was the first time I'd ever laughed with a man during sex, and I loved him then — for his lack of pretense, for his ability to let things be exactly what they were.

He pushed back inside me and then stopped again. "Look," he whispered.

I turned my head and looked up. A last bit of daylight had filtered in through the west window of Shadow Man's stall, silhouetting his head as he hung it over the door. He glimmered against the dark of the main corridor. He was watching us. His nostrils were wide, inhaling the smell of our sex. His eyes were tiny stars of light. I stared back at him and my hips began to move, undulating around Sam, drawing him in even deeper. Something about having been interrupted made all sensation more intense now. I was losing myself to him as he was lost in me. His rhythm got quicker, harder; I wrapped my legs around his waist and he held his breath against my neck. I clasped his body tight into mine, quivering, nearly there. I kept staring at Shadow Man and I saw myself, for perhaps the first time — even as I pushed back against Sam, even as we tightened down, even as we both came closer and closer, I kept staring. Sam lifted my legs back toward my shoulders, he went down into me so deep it almost hurt, and I spread myself wide, and then widest, and then I bloomed up under him, and he into me, as I watched us through the eyes of the animal.

That night I dreamt I married Sam, there in the barn; the next month I asked him for a date at City Hall, startling even myself with my own impetuous decision. With a smile he warned me that our life would be quiet and solitary. Most of his friends had left Arrowsic for college and never returned. There wouldn't be much except the work and each other. I didn't care.

But my mother did. She was angry when I called to tell her she was a new mother-in-law. I'd robbed her of her only chance at a wedding: no napkins with our initials, no dance band, no cake in waxed paper to dream on. Flat out she said I was crazy, didn't know what I was doing, had made the mistake of my life. "On a farm, Allie?" Her voice overflowed with incredulity, indignation, betrayal. She was so hurt that she refused to come and visit us in my new home for two years. When I'd moved to Manchester after college she'd been distressed and depressed to have me so far away, but my precipitous marriage to a horse breeder gave her anger the foothold it needed to blossom into righteous fury. She felt I'd cut her off and out: totally alone in the small suburban house, she used her hurt as a shield against any overture I made. I turned instead to Tobie, who had a particular way of accepting the things that happened to her and didn't waste a lot of energy fighting the inevitable.

But the ease with which I'd married was not paralleled by an equally easy adjustment to life on BoxTie. It was not merely a game, not some simple adventure. Breeding and raising horses — running the farm — was Sam and Tobie's livelihood, and I quickly found there was a lot of gritty detail I didn't like at all. Mucking out manure-filled stalls right after breakfast made me nauseated, and so I retreated sheepishly to the easier tasks of getting meals, doing laundry, and making beds. It didn't take me long to realize that Tobie and Sam accounted for every penny spent; if I wanted paints and brushes and canvases I would have to work to buy them. And so I did not give up my commercial work, as I had anticipated. I kept on looking for jobs, dreaming up landscapes and still lifes, giving over what I earned in exchange for the free time to paint. And little by little the presence of the animals, and the earth, and the seasons around me swelled into a rhythm inside of me, a rhythm that gradually began to edge itself into my paintings, as I had hoped it would. My new life was not all I had dreamt it would be, but it was enough.

Now another hard contraction came down, and then another, and I started up my breathing exercises smoothly — the exercises Sam and I had memorized from a Lamaze book bought in the city before Anna was born. It felt good to be working at last, instead of just lying there. Again I was pioneering, again I was strong and in control. There was pleasure in doing something I was good at. There was nothing to rely on here but myself and Tobie and Sam: no medications, no surgery, no anesthesia. Just me and my body. For a minute I thought of my own mother, lying drugged and unconscious in a hospital while they dragged me out of her with forceps. I did not want that. I wanted to be awake, to be the Creator, to give life.

Another contraction started, right on the heels of the one

before, and I checked the clock. They were speeding up. I began breathing again, concentrating, but still thinking that *convulsion* would be a better word for this — less neat and tidy than *contraction*. Contraction sounded like you could control it, or ignore it, but who could ignore this wild animal of a uterus? My body was turning itself inside out, over and over, wringing itself dry. I kept breathing, light, steady, determined.

Tobie appeared with a basin of water, a scissors, and a ball of twine. Sam was right behind her. She came to the head of the bed, put a cold washcloth on my forehead, and took my pulse, while Sam started to mimic the breathing pattern to help me keep the rhythm. He held my hand, he locked his tenderness against my pain and told me again that I would be all right. "I'm here," he said. "You're brave. You're fine."

The contraction ended, but another one started right away, and then there was a slam deep inside me, a slam so hard I thought my hipbones would break — like being hit by a Mack truck, but from the inside. I lost my rhythm and my breath. One of the babies' heads had engaged in my pelvis. The bag of waters broke and gushed out between my legs in a warm river. I riveted my eyes on my husband's face and started the breathing pattern again. I sucked the air in and out of my lungs. I focused on the rhythm. It was a litany, and we were the preacher and the congregation. I stifled an absurd urge to laugh, to scream, but it was like a cough, tickling featherlike in my lungs. I started to giggle; it bubbled out the corners of my mouth and made me lose my rhythm again. I looked into Sam's eyes and we began to laugh, great big belly laughs. And as we laughed, we knit ourselves up together, tight, just the way the pain and the pleasure knit themselves up together in my body, inseparable, and in that instant of birthing and life, so were we.

Three Mothers

I had been here before; I would be here again. Time was simply a circle in space and I was locked in motion, spinning like the sun, orbiting toward the inexorable beginning or end. Had I known what would happen to us, I might have tried to lean a little to the left or the right, tried to affect the course we took. I might have given in that day the twins were born, just exhaled my way out of time, out of the pain of the moment, out of the pain to come. But I didn't. I struggled and heaved and tried to get my babies born.

It was late afternoon, nearly four-thirty. The gray light from the windows was turning purple and lavender with shadow. I could hear the rain, heavy again, against the glass. I'd been in labor nearly ten hours now, hard labor for over nine.

Sam was still by my side, holding my hand — although I'd noticed that he was massaging his fingers in between contractions. I worried I was hurting him, but he said he didn't care: it was his way of sharing some of the pain, and I could appreciate that. At the end of each contraction I was glad he was there, but at the beginning, as the pain began to mount, I mostly wanted to scream at him, kill him, have him kill me. Of course, with some logical, but remote, part of my brain I realized that this was all typical behavior for a woman entering the last stage of her labor. The desire to quit breathing and just scream, the need to give in and give up, and the urge to murder the man who'd put you in such an unforgivable position — it all spelled one thing: transition.

Tobie was listening to my belly with the same stethoscope she used in the barn. She didn't like what she heard, I could tell. But I was too busy to pay her much attention. I'd been in transition for the last hour, my legs shaking uncontrollably, the contractions storming in nonstop — no time to think or worry. Sam held my legs to help control the tremors and breathed with me, five accelerating and decelerating breaths, then four, then three, then up again. Anything to push back the dreadful pain, the pain that could make you lose your mind, pain that you had to swim through, like a strong current which threatens to pull you under forever. I wanted to desert my body and be someplace else, but the only refuge was a hidden corner of my brain. The laugh we'd shared seemed ten years ago.

"Is it all right, Ma?" Sam asked as there was, at last, a pause.

"The heartbeat of the one further back seemed a little on the slow side that last contraction," Tobie said, taking a minute to mop my face with a cold cloth. I was shivering now, on fire. I leaned over and vomited into the pan beside the bed. I had never wanted a drink of water so much in my life.

"What's wrong?" I lay back on the pillow to try and rest.

"I want to check you again." Tobie washed her hands in the basin by the bed. "Bear down against me," she instructed as she felt my insides. "Good," she said, relief on her face. "Nearly five fingers. You'll be ready to push soon."

I turned my face to the wall, away from Tobie and Sam. I wanted to go to sleep, I wanted to leave this place.

Five more contractions and then the urge to push came

over me in waves. I squatted on the bed, leaning my forehead and my ungainly weight against Sam. He put his arms around me tight. I was crying and didn't even know it. This was the worst, this was pushing down into a pain so deep I could never climb out. All thoughts of control were gone. I was sure I would split myself wide open like a gutted chicken, I would push my insides out through my own vagina. This was pushing body and mind into a black, black hole. This was pushing down into death.

I was running now, running away from the pain in my mind, looking for anywhere to hide. I held my knees in my sweaty palms and thought, in desperation, of my painting — my painting, which was more me than even my body. I centered on it in my mind; in that moment I rooted my life in it.

Pushing a baby out is like painting, like pushing an idea out, forcing it through a mass of mental blocks, forcing the obstinate brain to give up its gifts. My first real drawing came when I was six, one afternoon in our kitchen. I'd been sketching for several years without understanding what I was doing: it was like doodling, a nervous habit, a tick that kept my hands busy. My schoolbooks were filled with little drawings around the white margins, thumbnail portraits crowded the paper napkins we used every day on the table, but this was the first time I'd deliberately taken an entire blank piece of paper and a smudgy number 1 pencil — not a crayon, but a pencil, which could be controlled — and made a full-fledged drawing.

My mother was fixing vegetables at the sink, working on dinner as she did every day at four-thirty. I was doing my homework at the kitchen table, working on a page of spelling. I looked over at her for a minute and wondered how it must be to peel potatoes every day at exactly the same time. I flipped the page of my notebook and put the pencil down on the clean white sheet. At first it was a challenge, a game, to see if I could do her face in profile, if I could catch a likeness just for fun — but then it became something entirely different.

Something began to happen inside of me. As I drew I suddenly saw beyond the lines of the page to the insides of the room, beyond the straight square of the sink and the motion of my mother's hand. I groped for the right lines, like reaching over the edge of my bed into the dark. I didn't know what I was doing, but some instinct made me draw a triangle for her shoulders and back, a frail slope, and, using the side edge of the lead, the light as it came through the window across her face. I put my love, and my fear, down on blue-lined notepaper. Later, I recognized I'd drawn the trap I sensed but could not understand so young: a woman who peels potatoes day after day and grows dusty and fragile.

I'd been so proud, though, of the way I'd caught her mood, but when I showed it to her she'd smiled. "What a *nice* picture, Allie," she said.

I'd looked at it again. It wasn't nice at all. It was worried and tired and silent. It puzzled me that she couldn't see it.

In the beginning I'd showed her everything I drew, but then, after a while, I stopped. She and my father thought everything I did was "nice." Only after I had asked over and over for several months did they take me seriously and get me some charcoals and blank white paper — for my birthday present. My mother was upset that I didn't want to do coloring books. "Practice staying inside the lines, Allie," she'd say with exasperation at my leaps of creativity.

By the time I was ten I didn't want to hear the word *nice* ever again. I began to accept that they didn't understand — and didn't want to — just the way most kids accept their parents' limitations. I painted a thick, tough hide around my secret ambitions. I knew I would be painting and drawing for the rest of my life, whether or not they chose to help me. Once I had started to draw, nothing could stop me, and I even drew under the covers at night with a flashlight. The drawers of my bureau gradually filled up with the people of my world: my teachers, chalk in hand; my friends, roller skates slung over their shoulders; my parents reading, arguing, kissing; my block, with its tall sycamore trees, level concrete sidewalks, small squares of green lawn.

Later I realized my parents ignored all my industry because they were threatened — afraid to look and see what I was really doing and know what it meant for my life. So they passed over the drawings they couldn't deal with, and focused on those which were pretty and safe. They asked me to do birthday cards for family occasions, usually watercolor or pastel. In their minds I was like the accomplished girl who can manage a few pieces on the piano; it never occurred to them that one day I might want to play in a concert hall.

My mother and I found something else to share. She was a good seamstress and she loved to make things; sewing didn't ask for much talking or thinking. We started with potholders when I was four and moved up to dresses when I was ten. She never ripped out my uneven stitches, never straightened my seams or flattened my puckered hems. She never tried to show me by doing it better herself. She just let me improve on my own, a good teacher who worked by my side quietly. It taught me how to be persistent, how to work hard on something and get better at it.

When I was a freshman in high school, my art instructor suggested that by now I should be studying with someone recognized, but my parents were only puzzled by this idea. And so he was the one to help me master the basic techniques and the "craft" of painting. I learned how to choose a ground suited to the paints I would use, which brushes to use for what — red sable for watercolor, hog bristle for oil — and what effects could be created with brights, flats, filberts, and badger blenders. He taught me that a painting knife yielded a thick impasto, that a sweetener made the best wash, and finally, that intricate care was required for maintaining these precious and expensive tools.

He encouraged me to try more abstract pieces, to get away from my own traditionalism, but I didn't like Abstract Expressionism, Pop Art, Op Art, or Action Painting. I still wanted to tell a story with my brush and couldn't bring myself to discard old methods natural to me simply because they had been used before. They were integral to the way I spoke when I painted. While he revered Klee, Rothko, Mondrian, Pollock, Stella, even Vasarely, my favorites remained van Gogh, Monet, Manet, Cézanne, Degas. These artists excited me: they forced me to think of the possibilities of line, color, expression of face and body and emotion. The others made me feel I had run into a concrete wall.

Under my instructor's tutelage, I made up my mind to lead a different kind of life. I resolved that once I left home everything would change for me. I might spend my afternoons walking around the mall with a pack of girls, looking at things we couldn't buy. I might go to Dustin Hoffman movies and dance to Stevie Wonder. But underneath I was restless with the normal, uneventful peace of our teenage years: it lulled us, it made us fat and content as overfed cats. I didn't want to spend the rest of my life wearing a haircut made popular by a skater and made common by masses of middle-class high-school girls.

During my sophomore year, boys began to call for dates. After movies or dances we went to park on the side of Bearskin Road, overlooking Route 128. The cars were lined up bumper to bumper, and sometimes it was hard to find a spot; parking there wasn't exactly an original idea. The police cruisers went by, flashing their lights in on us. I loved sex in spite of the places in which I'd found it: I loved the darkness of it, the abandonment to pleasure. I didn't want to play games the way the other girls did. I wanted to touch and be touched. But I held back; there were still rules.

It was only slowly, very slowly, that I began to let myself know how different I already was from the other girls, and not just about sex. They knew exactly where they would fit, how their lives would bend and twist; it seemed to me theirs would be a long, flat road: technical school (dental hygiene was the popular one my senior year) or junior college (work hard to get your M.R.S.), then engagement, marriage, and babies, with hobbies on the side. But when I envisioned my future, it was greedy and rich and full of self-absorption, a passionate portrait of dedication: wearing my lucky Red Sox cap, I would work impossibly long hours in some garret studio with a cigarette dangling from my lips — although I didn't smoke, even then — and wrestle to produce a brilliant and complex oeuvre. Naturally the succession of lovers would be moody and dark. There were to be no diversions like husbands or pets, much less brats who tugged and whined and distracted me from my colors and shapes.

I wanted to see more, not less. I spent hours away from my friends, fabricating chores my mother had never assigned as an excuse to escape, and these hours were like cold, clear drinks of water. I haunted the Museum of Fine Arts, spent hours staring at the works of others. I came home from those secret jaunts exhausted, but excited.

Still, I could see how easy it would be to let myself slide, seduced into an ordinary, safe way of life. And so by senior year I'd learned to keep my differentness locked inside. I stored it away and let my friendships grow casual. I studied with my peers, I went to choir practice with them, I even auditioned for the school play with them — but I shared less and less of myself. And I kept my paintings in my bedroom closet and put away my own laundry so that no one would look at them.

For all those years my work remained a private part of me. I kept it hidden because I sensed instinctively that once other people were allowed in, I would have to declare myself and my intentions. Even more, I knew that to show a painting meant it was finished, and I didn't want my work to be finished, to leave or move away from me, like something being born, or dying.

When my father suggested I apply to a college where they had a major in interior decorating and get some training in a "practical" field, I only smiled. My parents were flabbergasted to hear that, at the instigation of my teacher, I had applied for a scholarship in art to Boston College. And college was, as I had hoped, a little less confining. Here at least I was able to study the fine arts with experienced lecturers and learn what had gone before me; here I could work side-by-side with some competent, and a few quite gifted, people. But mostly I continued to use my classes to absorb technique, and I never did find a mentor. Maybe my stubborn rejection of all that surrounded me was just a way of making sure that my work remained in my closet.

I was waiting, without even knowing it, for something — a particular rhythm — to force me outward. That's why I'd come to New Hampshire in the first place. The city was killing my instincts, and instinct was integral to what and how I wanted to paint. I was sure I belonged here, where the seasons revolved, where full bloom was followed by slow fading, where things were born and died on the land, in their home.

After Sam and I were married, I'd told Tobie I didn't want any kids. I had already told this to Sam, but he'd only laughed. He didn't take me seriously. His mother did.

I had enough to do with my painting, I explained to her, and with helping Sam around the farm. Tobie sized me up, her face implacable. "What're you so afraid of?"

"Nothing," I'd denied, defensive.

She'd sat back in her chair, lit up her Camel, and stared at me a little longer.

"My mother was in labor with me for over twenty hours," I said after an uncomfortable silence. I paused as it occurred to me that my mother and I had never talked about it. "My father told me she nearly died."

"Don't get it in your head that everything's happened to your mother'll happen to you. Life doesn't work like that." But I kept using my diaphragm anyway. Not even Sam could change my mind. And he began to bring it up with increasing frequency. After we'd been married nearly a year we had our first big fight about it. In Arrowsic, Sam said, brides usually got pregnant on their honeymoon; we were about to celebrate our first anniversary and people were starting to rib him a little when he went to town. It was our first major battle, and at the end neither had won or given in. We were a complement in stubbornness and strong will. He was determined to change my mind and I was determined to change his.

I didn't want to admit to him, or to Tobie — much less to myself — that I was indeed afraid. Of the pure biology, of the life-giving, of the uncontrollable. Nothing felt more out of control to me than being pregnant: to have your body inhabited, to be taken over — irrevocably. And then the continual responsibility for someone else's life, with no time or space for your own. This was something Sam couldn't seem to understand. It terrified me, and I simply couldn't bring myself to do it. In my heart I still wanted to be responsible only for Allie.

Then one day I was helping with the evening feeding. I came to the pasture gate and dumped a load of grain into the long trough for the animals who were turned out during the summer. The yearling who'd been born the day I'd first met Sam trotted up to the gate, whickering at me; I'd gentled him, I felt bonded to him somehow, having been there at his troublesome birth. Although he'd been weaned long ago, he still liked to nurse on my fingers, and he did for a minute that night before shoving his nose deep in my armpit and inhaling the smell of my body.

He was asking something of me, some touch, some connection, and it stirred me in a sensual, almost sexual, way. I stood, electrified by that velvet muzzle, mesmerized by a pull which came from deep inside of me, an urge, my own ambivalent need to succumb. The lowering sun fell across us in a long golden streak. The horizontal lines of the fence defined the space in which we stood, and held us together. I looked up at the sky and saw a pale yellow moon.

I spent the night in my attic studio, painting as I had not painted in a long time. Inspiration forced its way out, this time in tempera: that colt and me, carved upon the face of the earth in a maternal embrace. And at two A.M. I went downstairs, to Sam, this time without my diaphragm.

After so many years of careful birth control — just the right amount of jelly, the precise insertion, the timed removal — I was nervous at first about being without protection; making love was a little bit strained. Even so, it was only three months later that my period didn't arrive. And then when Anna got stuck inside me, Tobie had just reached up and eased her out. Who needed forceps? I had my mother-in-law's strong hands.

My own mother didn't understand natural childbirth, open space, or living with the land. Six months after our wedding, Sam and I faced her refusal to come and visit us and left BoxTie for the weekend to drive down and visit her. She was suspicious of Sam at first, guarded though polite, but his direct look, his gentleness with the shrill little terrier she'd bought since I left home, as well as his willingness to pitch in with the dinner dishes, began to wear down her defenses.

We went for several visits that first year and continued to invite her up to the farm, but she just made excuses. Her anger began to wane, though; she was forgiving me by inches. By the time I got pregnant, she wasn't so much mad as she was baffled by what I had chosen, and when Anna was born she consented to come to Arrowsic for her first visit — to meet her only grandchild, to see my new home, to meet my mother-in-law.

You didn't lie around in bed after childbirth at BoxTie; there was a routine which had to be followed, chores to be done, a work quota to be met. Tobie allowed me to linger in the four-poster with Anna tucked under my arm for two days, till my milk was in, then I was back up and proud to be so strong. I wanted my mother to see me in my element — it was more of my old pioneer fantasy — and so I told her to come on the Saturday after Anna arrived.

After recovering from the sight of my family's old Buick pulling up the gravel drive, smack in the middle of my world, I led my mother out to the barn to find my mother-in-law. Anna was sleeping. My mother wanted to see her right away, but I thought we should wait. I really wanted to get the hard part over with first. I knew she would love Anna; Anna was easy to love. What I didn't know about was myself — what I had at last become, my new life, my new family. Would she love these things too? Would she still love me?

I was very tense. It seemed awkward to introduce my mother to Tobie. Tobie and my mother were so different. With my choice of Tobie as mother-in-law and BoxTie as home, I would be telling my mother something about myself, something she probably wouldn't want to know. And for the first time in years I let myself know how much her approval did matter. Ignoring it hadn't made my need for her go away.

Sam was finishing the morning's load of mucking out and gave my mother a careful hug. He said Tobie was over getting a wheelbarrow of fertilizer for the rose beds. This was a polite way of telling us that she was shoveling shit.

My mother and I walked down the main corridor of the barn, stepping carefully, and went through the small back door which led to the foot of the manure heap. The pile was a mountain which towered over our heads, probably about seventeen feet high now. This year we would have to have some of it carted away. Joe was on top, bringing fresh loads from the newly cleaned stalls, and so the pile itself was steaming in the clear, cool morning air. The fragrance was rich — very rich.

We walked around the pile, and I was just wondering if Tobie had gone back into the barn when I spotted her on the far side. She was filling her wheelbarrow to the very top, tamping it down with her sneaker.

We walked over. "Tobie Yates, Lynne Sterne." I introduced them, looking at the ground the entire time. My mother was very polite. She even offered Tobie her hand, which Tobie just as politely, and incredulously, refused to shake, turning her grimy palms upward.

My mother's face had that glassy look which covers dismay. As she stood there in her peach polyester pantsuit and Fayva sandals, with her blue-rinsed coiffure and her red lipstick, I knew it was hopeless. The halves of my life — past and present — could never merge, not even in the interests of the future. I was embarrassed by my mother and by Tobie, and then mad at myself for being embarrassed at all.

I took her back to the house and showed her around, noticing for the first time the dust kitties under the tables and beds, the battered furniture, the old plumbing. Tobie and I never worried about dusting or polishing; it was enough just to maintain a basic sort of order. When I was young my mother had scoured the house with Pledge and Lysol and Vanish every week and vacuumed once a day. Again our differences overwhelmed me, and I talked a lot to cover the nervous silence between us, dumping another load of clothes into the washer as I started to fold the baby's things on top of the dryer.

We went upstairs to check on Anna, and she was awake and crying. My mother bent down and scooped her up, took her to the rocking chair, and sat with her.

She held Anna and sang to her, and for a minute I wanted

to cry. Anna stopped bawling and just looked deep into her grandmother's eyes. It was the first time anyone from *my* family had held my baby. There was something so lonely about the way my mother cradled Anna against her chest, and I wondered what she did all day now that she had no one to peel potatoes for.

"You used to love this song," she said. "Whenever you cried it calmed you right away." It came to me with a jolt then: she had held me, loved me, sung to me. She had mothered me the way I was trying to mother Anna.

"When she cries," I said tentatively, shyly almost, "I get frantic . . . I guess I don't know what to do."

"When you were first born," she said, smiling, rocking Anna back and forth on her shoulder in an easy rhythm, "you cried a lot." She laughed, remembering. "And *I* cried a lot."

We smiled together then, with pleasure at the sharing, and suddenly I wished there weren't so much distance between us now, physical or emotional — the distances I'd put there on purpose.

We went downstairs, talking about babies — what helped with teething, croup, the best way to fold a diaper. It was the first time I really listened to her: I needed her expertise. We made lunch together, trading the baby back and forth, and I remembered her favorite sandwich was a BLT and took out the precious fresh bacon from the porker we'd slaughtered a few weeks before.

Tobie, Sam, and Joe thundered in at noon, hungry and hot, and tore into those sandwiches. My mother ate around the bacon, too polite to pull it out of the sandwich and put it aside. I could see it was too fatty for her. Tobie also noticed, but didn't say anything.

"Is something wrong, Lynne?" Sam asked, concerned. "You haven't had a bite."

She smiled at him and fluttered her hands. "It's the heat, I guess. I'm not used to such a long drive and the heat."

"Thermometer's up over eighty," Tobie affirmed. "Never known it to be so warm this early in May."

Anna stirred in her basket by the fireplace and began to whimper. Our attention shifted away from my mother. I got up to go to the baby, but Tobie looked up, surprised.

"Let her be, Allie. No harm in letting a baby cry a bit. The world can't always be running to her side."

I stopped, chastened, and a little angry underneath. Anna was *my* baby, and it was humiliating to be reproved in front of my mother. Anna's whimper changed to a full-scale scream.

My mother pushed her chair back and rose, moving past me silently. She scooped Anna up, settling her into the niche between her chin and collarbone, rubbing her back with a smooth circular motion. Anna struggled, red-faced, for a minute, made a noisy wet burp that brought curdled milk up onto my mother's peach shoulder, and then snuggled down in and went back to sleep. My mother sent me a triumphant look over her granddaughter's soft bald head. Moving gently, she settled into the rocker and leaned back with a contented sigh.

"She'll have her mother stomping the floorboards all hours of the night," Tobie observed, scratching a match on the table and lighting up a Camel.

My mother turned her head to look sideways at Tobie and then waved her hand back and forth through the air over Anna's head. "Better open the window, Allie," she said, waving, rocking, and staring at that cigarette. "Babies shouldn't breathe smoke."

The window was already open. I smothered a laugh and sent Sam a look. He too was stifling a grin. After a minute of silence Joe pushed his chair back with a loud scrape.

"Back to work," he said, smiling at me. "Nice to meet you, Mrs. Sterne."

She nodded imperiously from her moving throne.

I waited for Sam to get up and follow, but he didn't. He was enjoying this scene too much. He pulled a chair up next to the rocker and hunched in close to my mother. "How about that nose," he said, drawing her into a discussion of Anna's beauty. "Your side of the family?"

Tobie was still stubbornly puffing away, and now that my mother was more relaxed I felt a little sorry for Tobie. As I began to clear the table I saw she was watching, covertly, the attention her son was paying my mother. My mother laughed then, putting her head back, and gave Sam a look of admiration. "Allie," she called to me as I stood at the sink, "I've never seen a man so out and out stuck on a new baby."

"Can't help myself," Sam said, prying Anna away from my mother and parking her up on his broad shoulder. "She's so beautiful I'm just plain in love." Anna wrinkled her old man's face and stuck her tongue out. Sam did likewise.

My mother laughed and looked back at me with a teasing expression on her face. "He pretends to be tough, but underneath he's an old softie."

"Carson was like that too," Tobie said in a low voice, the words escaping her as she slipped back, remembering.

"Probably runs in the whole family," I said, smiling at her.

Tobie stood up at that, embarrassed, and went to the refrigerator. She fixed two glasses of her special iced tea, with mint from the garden, and then crossed the room to set one in front of my mother. "When you don't see her much you need do a little extra holding, I expect," Tobie said grudgingly. Some sort of peace had been achieved among us, forged by the littlest Yates.

The heat didn't make my afternoon's work any easier. The knacker had delivered the sides of beef from the cow we'd slaughtered the week before; it was time-consuming, messy work to butcher it up for the family, and it was my job. And although I would never have admitted it, especially with my mother there, I was very tired. Sam told me not to be silly, that the heavy work and standing around on my feet for those hours would be too much for me, and I could see my mother agreeing, gratified that someone had said aloud what she was thinking. She appreciated the way he protected me; maybe she was falling a little in love with him herself. "Go up and take a nap," she urged me. "I'll watch the baby."

"Listen to your mother." Sam put his arm around me.

Tobie's left eyebrow chinked up a notch. I knew perfectly well what she was thinking, and I was determined to prove that I belonged here. I smiled at Sam and gave him a shove to show I was no suburban housewife who needed pampering. "I'm fine," I said firmly, tying the big apron around my still stretched-out waistline.

"Sam's right," my mother went on, continuing to argue. "This isn't a good time to be pushing yourself."

I didn't answer, just started opening and shutting drawers, gathering together my tools.

"So I'll help," my mother said, lifting her hands in a gesture of despair and shaking her head at Sam. Silently I gave her a big apron to cover her clothes.

I began to carve out pot roasts and oven roasts, steaks and sirloin tips, cubes for beef stew and scraps for ground round. I was good at this and I enjoyed it despite my fatigue. There was something very precise, very decisive, about separating the muscle from the bone.

My mother fluttered around the edges of the counters; she didn't know what to do and I didn't know how to help her help me. Mostly she tried to wipe up the mess before I was finished. She was used to getting her meat in neat cellophane packets from the A&P. When she'd offered to help she couldn't have realized what she was getting into.

"So much juice," she said, shaking her head as she squeezed out the big sponge. A stream of red water sluiced into the sink. She poked at the heap of fat discarded on the chopping block and didn't even try to touch it: it was beyond her. "I never knew meat had so much blood in it," she said with a grimace. "I never thought about what went into my hamburger."

I kept whacking away with my cleaver, separating sinew from fat, fat from bone, and wrapping up the white packages of carnage like a machine. I didn't say anything. I was irritated by her disgust and once again feeling our distances. There was nothing wrong with any of this: it was good, honest work.

She sat down at the trestle table and stared at the set of Ginsu knives she'd brought as a gift — ordered from a TV advertisement — which lay on the kitchen table untouched, too lightweight for this job. I looked over at her and saw the lines on her face, her unarticulated sadness at our separateness.

"I wanted to bring you something," she said, spreading her hands wide in a helpless gesture. "But this . . . this was like bringing a snowshovel to the North Pole."

Suddenly the whole thing seemed funny, and I knew she was right. I began to laugh and then she laughed and then we laughed together, laughed until the tears ran down our cheeks at the absurdity of it all.

After we stopped laughing she came and put her arm around me. "I didn't know what you needed before I came, but now I do. I'll send you one of those intercoms you can plug into your electrical outlet. Then you won't have to run over the stairs to check on Anna."

The baby started to cry from her basket near the fireplace. Pleased she was awake, my mother went to get her, and I crossed to put my arm around her shoulder as she sat holding Anna. I could smell her deodorant, see the face powder where it lay in a pink dust across the pores of her nose. I tried not to touch her with the red wet front of my apron as I hugged her. "Could you take a look at this?" I picked up the baby sweater I was knitting from the chair. "I've balled something up, but I can't figure out what."

"Here," she said, pointing to a row of stitches near the bottom, "you've got your pattern reversed way back here. You should've been purling, not knitting."

I groaned. I'd have to rip out a month's worth of work.

"You never were a knitter, Allie," she observed. "Do you want me to take it home and unsnarl it?"

I hesitated: it was the one and only thing I had knit for Anna's birth, and I wasn't sure I wanted her taking it over. Then I saw the look on her face and realized she was eager to be included. I nodded, slowly, and she smiled.

When she drove off later that night, I was sad to see her go, but we had made a date for her to return in a few months. I didn't think she'd liked what she'd seen, but she'd accepted it. In the end she'd even laughed. Maybe there was hope for us: maybe I'd finally grown up enough to see that I did need her after all.

"Push, Allie, push," Sam entreated.

"Bear down," Tobie barked.

I looked up at them, not sure of where I was anymore, lost between my body and my head. Yet I strained once again. My face reddened, my eyes grew hot from pressure. I couldn't keep it up much longer. I was in trouble: these babies were not sliding out like Anna had. They were stuck somewhere in the dark abyss of my body, and I was tearing myself apart inside every time I pushed.

Tobie made me lie down and listened again to the babies. Sam stroked the hair back from my forehead. I started to cry, and he soaked up my tears with his shoulder. Tobie looked at Sam, her face grim. "I don't like it," she said. "The heartbeat's even slower. God help us if it's the cord. Go phone Dr. Loring."

I closed my eyes as Sam ran from the room. I was going to die, my babies were going to die — and it was my own fault. We'd known all along the birth might be difficult, and

Tobie had been nervous from the start about delivering twins. I'd been stubborn about having them at home like I'd had Anna. Anna's birth had been easy, despite my fears.

As I lay there bleeding, the twins caught in the vise of my body, one of them perhaps already beyond saving, I wanted my mother. To hold my hand. To stroke my head. To tell me it would all be fine. I needed her faith that you could just close your eyes and life would work out around you. Why hadn't I asked her to come?

"Allie." Tobie's voice was stern. "I know you're hurting, but you've got to push again. I've almost got my hand under the jaw of the first. A little more and I can help it out."

"Maybe we should wait for the doctor," I said, terrified.

"We can't. We're losing the heartbeat."

I looked into her face. She was telling me to fight for my children.

Sam rushed back into the room. "He's out on a call. We're on our own."

"Allie, forget about the pain and push," Tobie said then, her eyes unrelenting. "If you don't, there'll be far worse pain to come."

I heard the threat in what she said. I stopped thinking about my mother, about my work, about Sam. I thought about my babies, trapped there inside me, dying. I had a powerful love for them even though I knew them only through the wall of my belly. I took a deep breath and I shoved with all the power I owned. I bore down, I drove myself out of sight with the push. Tobie reached up inside me and slid the head out.

I looked between my legs and saw it sticking from my vagina, bloody, wet, wrinkled. I pushed again: the shoulders came through and then the body. "It's a girl," Tobie said. She handed her to Sam and tied off the cord.

Another contraction drowned out her words, obliterating my reaction, and I started to push again, another hard, horrible push. Tobie reached up inside. "No, no, don't push now,

Allie — I'm easing the cord." She worked for a minute, her face strained and maybe even frightened. "It's around the neck." I panted and blew, fighting my urge to bear down, wanting to scream.

At last she nodded, and I gave way with relief to push myself into oblivion: I gave myself, body and soul, to this last child, and I felt him move down and out of me, first the head, as big as a bowling ball, burning as it passed from my body, then his shoulders, nearly worse, and then, with no effort at all, his body, slithering out like a fish. I knew before I saw that he was a boy, and I didn't care anymore what I had been through. I only wanted to hold him. I held out my arms.

Tobie ignored me. Working quickly, she cut the cord. He was a deep, deep blue.

"Give me my son," I said.

She didn't answer. She spanked him on the buttocks, hard, but he didn't twitch, didn't take a breath. She turned him on his stomach and struck a sharp blow between the shoulder blades, then flipped him, ran her finger around the inside of his mouth, lifted him and began to breathe into him.

I watched. I couldn't move. Sam and my new daughter waited on the other side of the room. "Please, God," I whispered.

She pinched his foot hard and he jerked. He gasped. He gulped for air. He turned from dark blue to bright pink. A furious wail filled the room.

"So you're a screamer," Tobie said, smiling down into his angry wrinkled face. "And will you look at the size of you! No wonder your poor mother had a hard time of it." She lowered him into my arms, and I watched him beat at the air with his fists. Another contraction told me the placenta was on its way out, but I just held him and pushed at the same time. I would never let him go. He had nearly killed me with the pain of his birth, and that pain bonded us now.

"James," I whispered, giving him his name as I rubbed

some vernix from his skin with my index finger and examined him to make sure he had all his fingers and toes. "You're a Jamie for sure. And Megan," I said, turning to Sam as he looked down into the eyes of our youngest daughter, "is she all right?"

He nodded and held her aloft.

"Beautiful," I said.

"But look at the difference in size. She's tiny — must get it from her grandmother." Sam looked over at Tobie and laughed at his own joke.

"Let me have her, Sam."

We traded and I stroked her soft cheek, her tiny fists. After a minute, she closed her eyes and slept. I gave her to Tobie, who swaddled her tight, and I took Jamie again, who was now howling. Here was my boy: feisty, hungry, demanding already, and even more precious because there was only one of him. I set him at my breast and stroked the dark nipple against the rosebud of his tiny mouth. How good it felt, how warm and close, as he eagerly took me up. I let him draw my body into his, and I let my heart go with it, belong to him, become one with his. I looked into his eyes, slitted into dusky blue crescents against the new light, and let love grow so strong that I would kill to keep it.

PART II

PAINTING

July 1986

From the size and scope of one human body you
can discover immense secrets of the universe.

— Lynne Sharon Schwartz
Disturbances in the Field

A Question of Luck

Because he had nearly died, Jamie was even more precious to me. Maybe I held him a little closer because of that, maybe I kept him nearer my heart than Anna and Meggie. It was harder when Jamie learned to walk than it had been when Anna did. I didn't want him to fall down, bump his head, or bruise his knees. It was harder not to run and catch him, harder to let him learn in his own small way about hardship, pain, the consequences of actions. I wanted to protect him; I wanted to wrap him in a bunting that would shelter and keep him, pink and tender and unscathed — forever.

Just after his first birthday, he took the pencil from the kitchen table and drew a big scribble on my market list. Within the month he was making "pithers" everywhere, wide, looping scrawls that did not then resemble anything, but which shortly began to display his sense of tactile control. I took one of those drawings to Nat Loring when the twins went in for their eighteen-month checkup, a drawing that exhibited more proficiency with the crayons than even four-year-old Anna had. Nat admitted he'd never seen such early development of a child's fine-motor ability and was amused by my maternal pride, but cautioned me not to get too excited yet — sometimes children seem gifted at something for a while, and then revert back to a more ordinary level.

Despite his warning, I continued to hope, and to feed: I decided he might have fun fooling around with fingerpaints, and he did, even though Meggie could barely hold her crayon upright, and Anna had just gotten into painting herself. He liked playing with the bright colors and mixing them to make different shades, and I began to buy special children's art supplies for him on my daytrips to Manchester — tools which would fit his small hands, pots of paint which could not tip, anything to encourage him as I had not been encouraged. When he was ready he would not have to beg for his first charcoals.

I even began to leave a pad of paper and crayon in Jamie's crib every night so that when he roused he could amuse himself if I wasn't awake yet. Lately he'd taken to climbing out of the crib, and his early-morning arrivals into our bed made Sam irritable. Over the last few months, Jamie's rambunctious ryhthm had begun to grate on my husband. Of course, Jamie was more active than either of the girls, more noisy, more cantankerous, more demanding of time and effort and attention. And, although I fought it, he drew more from my heart.

As coordinated as he was with his hands, he was still a clumsy toddler with the rest of his body, and while he could draw a circle, he regularly tied his feet in a knot. One day I tried to stop him from climbing onto Anna's tire swing in the back garden, but then I heard my mother's voice in my ear, forbidding me to climb the tall sycamore in the front yard when I was six. For the first time I saw the scene from her point of view instead of my own. For the first time I felt fear, saw the broken bones, heard the cries of pain in my mother's imagination. I understood her better now: she shimmered in front of me, a ghost, but I didn't let that vision stop me. My son was eager and ready for this simple challenge. I wouldn't let my fear cripple him.

Holding my breath, I watched him clamber onto the swing and then fall right off. But when he cried, I just wiped his face and showed him how to hold on more tightly.

A strength I didn't know was in me surfaced. Jamie's curiosity — his restlessness, his intensity — forced me to grow in a way Meggie's quieter nature couldn't, in a way I wasn't ready for when Anna had been the same age. By the time Jamie turned two, I believed I could live through nearly anything he could dream up. His birth changed me and changed us, changed the way we lived and the patterns we kept to.

His body clock, which led him to wake much earlier than either of the girls, altered our morning routine in particular: where Sam and I had used to go out to the barn together while Tobie watched Anna before breakfast, by the time Jamie was a toddler, Tobie and Sam went together to the barn at five-thirty. Anna had learned to sleep later, and Megan did so naturally, which left Jamie and me, partners, to start the household chores.

On this morning he helped me lug the laundry to the machine, carefully loading his yellow plastic shopping cart with one of his shirts, a pair of pants, socks, and his teddy. While I got breakfast on, he trotted around the kitchen on his sturdy legs, opening cabinets and drawers and imitating me in reverse by pulling things out as I tried to put them away. On his head he wore the large pink Tupperware bowl he called his "Morning Hat." At supper he would switch to green. Middle of the day, it was his Red Sox cap, and only his Red Sox cap.

Because the girls were still asleep above our heads, I tried not to clatter too loudly as I pulled the frying pan from beneath the heap of time-blackened pots. Jamie stirred a saucepan of Cheerios with a ladle.

"I cook Chee-toes," he announced proudly when I asked what he was making. I steered around him to the refrigerator, and ten toasty little O's went crunch, crunch, crunch under my sneakers. "Damn," I said, scraping my foot against my leg and wanting to say something much worse.

"Damm, damm, damm," sang my echo happily.

I sighed and reached for the eggs I was going to scramble, but the wire basket was empty. Sam must've made himself a fried-egg sandwich, or two, before bed last night. I swore — but this time silently. Some days I just didn't feel up to all this. Meggie had been awake at two and then again at four last night, asking for water, and I was tired, the kind of tired that started at my mouth and ended in my brain. My eyes were grainy and my head ached. Working today would be hard.

"Come on, kiddo," I said, reaching down to take Jamie's hand, "we've got to go for some eggs."

"Ekks!" He scrambled up, a glint in his eye.

I sighed again. "Ekks" was one of his favorite games: he'd need a tight rein today, I saw, or he'd be wild and unstoppable.

The screen door banged shut behind us as I stopped short on the back stoop to look around, really opening my eyes for the first time that day. Sun turned the tin weathervane on the barn roof a pinked copper, and it spun slowly in a cool wind. The heads of the sunflowers behind the garden were only pale yellow now, and a new strain of roses grew up against the weathered shingle of the house in what the Burpee catalogue called "gentle peach." The mountains behind the west pasture, on the far side of the barn, were shadowed green because the sun had not yet found them, and there was a softness about that seemed more like spring than deep summer, a softness which came with the hour in my part of New Hampshire.

Jamie had stopped to play with the stones in the gravel drive as I gawked at the scenery, but I took his hand now, urging him with that motion in the direction of the barn. Still, we took our time, and I matched his baby steps so as not to hurry him. I let him pull the petals from a primrose, put a handful of stones into the egg basket on my arm, decorate his Tupperware hat with dewy morning grass. Our sneakers soaked through at the toes. I was savoring the peace, the stillness of the landscape before us, and this unusually quiet moment with my son. I wanted it to continue, untouched. The wind rustled through the pines; the cows bellowed to be fed in the far pastures; there were the clanking of feed buckets and the thump of a bale of hay as it was thrown from the loft. These were the sounds of the day beginning here, on our land.

But as we approached the barn, reality returned. Jamie began to tug on my hand, leaning all his weight against the length of my arm to hurry me from my lingering stroll. And when we got to the main doors, he was like a parakeet free from a cage. He dropped my hand and ran down the dark main floor, hollering and whooping, and made straight for the ladder into the hayloft, which he was forbidden to climb.

The loft was one of our special places. From its windows you could see the pastures and mountains, solid green of varying hues stretching for miles around. The kids and I sat up there and read most every afternoon, curled into a nest of hay, after I had finished in the studio and they were up from their naps. Jamie loved reading with me there best of everything, and even after Meggie and Anna had grown bored and gotten up to do something else, he would beg for just one more story.

But the ladder to the loft was high, narrow, dangerous — one of the few places I felt justified in forbidding. We used the back staircase up to the loft and he knew it, which was why he always tried to climb the ladder. When I shook my head menacingly he took off again, this time for the chicken pens on the far side of the barn.

I followed more slowly and passed Joe wheeling a barrowload of molasses grain to the outer stalls. He nodded and paused. "Thought we might let Anna try walking Duet over some cavalletti today," he said, a smile creasing the deep grooves of his face. "Pretty soon that pony's not going to be comfortable with any gait 'cept walking."

My expression must have been surprised, for he went on with a broad smile. "Anna's getting a real fine seat. Start them young and they're not afraid of anything." I nodded and went after Jamie reluctantly, distracted by thoughts of my oldest's progress.

Looking for eggs this early in the morning was a detestable job, and I always got as many as I could at once so I wouldn't have to do it again the next day. I hated the smell, and the flutter of the stupid birds against my legs.

I started into the dimly lit pen, moving with care so as not to rile them. Getting in and out quickly was the trick. Jamie stood beside the door watching — for once not running around stirring them up — and as I slid my hand under one feathery bottom after another, he slipped from my mind. I was thinking again about the oil painting of Jamie in the garden, considering what still had to be done, and why it troubled me so. I was dreading going back to it this afternoon.

It was a bountiful haul of eggs: my basket was full to the top, I'd slid two into the pocket of my denim jumper, and I had another in my hand. This would keep us for at least three days, provided Sam didn't make any more midnight raids on the refrigerator. I looked up then and saw that I'd left the door to the pen unlatched. Jamie was gone.

I stopped for a minute and thought about going to look for him. I thought about the ladder. But I was nearly done, and without a single squawk. He couldn't get into any trouble that fast, I decided, so I hurried to finish up, concentrating on the last row now, balancing two more of the hard brown ovals in my left hand.

With a sudden whoop Jamie was back then, running through the door with a cowbell in his hand. He stormed the hens, ringing the bell as if the barn were on fire, crowing with delight, and they scooted from one end of the pen to the other in a mad babble, crashing against my legs.

The noise hurt my ears and I hollered at him to stop, but yelling made the chickens even more frantic. My hands were full so I couldn't catch him, and I stood there stupidly, trying to keep my balance, but it was like fighting a feathered surf. He kept right on, running and ringing and screeching, "Ekks! Ekks! I mek ekks!"

I tripped over a fat chicken then and the handful of eggs smashed against the floor. I started after him, enraged, and determined to get hold of that bell — the racket he was making would scare them so they wouldn't lay for a week and there'd be hell to pay with Tobie — but he managed to slip by me again, losing only his hat. My chasing seemed just a new variation on his game. He laughed and teased me with his eyes, ringing his bell nonstop and giggling. Then I slipped on the slimy mess of broken eggs and went down in the pen, right on my backside, with a thump. I couldn't help myself: I was so mad that I started to cry.

Jamie stopped dead in his tracks, alarmed. "Mommee, you hut?"

Nothing about this day was going right. I was angry and out of breath and tired. My crying got louder, faster, and then suddenly turned into semihysterical laughter. There was nothing to do but laugh: this kid had me outfoxed. I pulled a chicken feather from my hair.

"What's going on in here?" Sam leaned over the door and looked down at me with disapproval. My knees were covered with chicken manure and egg yolk, there were shavings in my eyebrows and no breath in my lungs. I looked back at him and waited. For the explosion.

He started to laugh — then fought it and struggled to put a stern expression on his face. "Jamie, you bring that bell right here — and right now."

Of course, Jamie didn't hesitate. He marched up to Sam and handed the bell over casually, as if he'd just been safe-keeping it for a while, as if it were something he was allowed to play with, as if I hadn't been trying to take it away from him for the last five minutes. "He y'go, Daddee."

Sam reached out and ruffled Jamie's tousled mop of curls as he took it. "No more riling the chickens like that — understood?"

Jamie nodded sheepishly and then just stood there, his head down, staring at the toes of his new red Keds, his eyes sneaking to the side to watch my reaction and see if he was going to be punished. He looked so guilty and so clever all at once that laughter pushed up the corners of my mouth again.

Sam was still choking back his own hilarity and hung the cowbell back on its hook to distract himself for a minute.

I stood up and brushed off my knees, still fighting the belly laugh tickling deep inside.

"Whatever you do, don't tell Mother why breakfast is behind," Sam said over his shoulder in a choked voice, not turning back to face us; he walked away, and on the far side of the barn I heard him let out a great big bellow of enjoyment.

I smiled to myself, relieved and pleased that this time we'd shared a moment of laughter over our son's head instead of arguing. I picked up my basket, setting Jamie's hat back over his curls. I took his hand and stuck my tongue out at him playfully. "I know you like getting Mommy in trouble with your grandma," I said, "but how about being good for the next five minutes?"

He grinned up at me, his teeth white and even as seed corn.

On our way out I stopped to latch the pen securely behind us and to throw the broken shells into the trash barrel at the side of the door. When I turned back to take Jamie's hand again he was gone. This time I didn't think twice. I just clutched my basket against my chest and ran. I knew where he was, and I was not annoyed, not mad, not out of breath, not amused. This time I was scared.

When I got to the main floor of the barn he was silhouetted against the bright daylight coming through the wide and open doors, his little legs pumping hard to outrun me. I prayed that this one time he would indeed trip and go sprawling. But he reached the ladder to the loft and his Tupperware hat fell to the floor as he started up.

"Jamie Yates! You stop right there!"

He laughed.

It was another game — a terrible game. I wanted to scream at him and run for all I was worth, but I was afraid to startle him. A quick movement might make him look down and let go of the wooden rungs.

He was halfway up now, probably fifteen feet off the ground. I made myself walk slowly, casually, to the foot of the ladder. I put my basket of eggs down carefully. No more would be broken. I would climb up, I decided, my brain working slowly against the deep-freeze of fear. If he knew I was behind him he'd just climb all the way to the top, and then we'd go down the back staircase like always, hand in hand.

I put my foot on the bottom rung, tilting my head up and back and keeping my eye on his bottom. The Oshkosh engineer overalls my mother had sent seemed close enough to grab hold of. He looked down at me then and giggled. "Mommeecum too?"

"Mommy will come too," I answered firmly in a voice that

surely belonged to someone else's body. "Wait for Mommy in our reading place. I have a book for you."

"No, no," he said, smiling and giggling again. "*I* cum *Mom-mee.*"

It took a second for my brain to decode what he'd said. By the time I did, it was too late.

I watched him in slow motion: first his fingers uncurled, then they straightened, then he balanced on the soles of his feet, then he leaned back against a pillow of air. He clapped his hands. Freefall.

He was delighted by the sensation — like diving from a tree branch into a summer river, I thought, although he'd never done that before and would certainly never do it now. His eyes were very wide as he plummeted past me, the air pushing his blond curls back from his forehead. He didn't know enough to be scared. He was only two years old. He was still smiling as he hit.

There was a loud thud. His body bounced off a bale of hay and rolled onto the barn floor. He lay facedown, his right arm underneath him, his blond head twisted to one side. I couldn't move. I just hung on that ladder, a scarecrow on a hook, no skeleton, no muscle, no brain — just hung in the air while my son lay there, smashed and bleeding. I couldn't have gone and turned him over for anything or anybody. It was beyond me.

And then his leg moved. And a minute later his left hand. Still I hung there.

He sat up. His eyes were unfocused, dazed. His nose was bleeding. He looked around, and finally I realized that he was looking for me. I made a little croak.

He looked up. "Do 'gain?" he asked, with hope.

I skidded down the rungs of the ladder to drop in a heap beside him. My hands flew, prodding, poking, hoping to heal, all the first aid I'd ever read whipping through my mind: internal bleeding, shock, broken bones, severed spinal cord.

I popped the buttons off his shirt to get to his chest and listen for his heartbeat, check for a carotid pulse.

His legs still bent at the knee and ankle, his fingers still curled around mine, his mouth still smiled even though he'd chipped one of his front teeth. He was not only alive, he was all right.

That was when I started to shake with rage, and fear moved over to make way for anger. I put him across my lap and for the first time ever I spanked him: round, hard slaps that stung my hand. He started to wail, scared at last. How many times had I threatened a spanking, but never followed through? Unlike Tobie, I didn't believe in spanking.

From behind me, Sam pinned my arms against my sides. "What're you doing?" His voice was incredulous.

I couldn't answer. My voice was gone. I started to sob, choking out the one word, *ladder*. My whole body shook. I kept clutching at Jamie, wanting to make sure of him.

"You've got to watch him, Allie," Sam said. "How many times've I told you?"

"I'm not a bodyguard!" I snapped, tears stopping. He didn't understand how hard it was to protect an active little boy. And he didn't understand how guilty I felt already. "How many times have *I* begged *you* to shorten the goddamn ladder!"

"Gaw damm lad-der! Gaw damm lad-der!" Jamie chanted, slipping away from my embrace and spinning in a drunken circle. He stopped to put his Tupperware hat on at a jaunty angle and flashed us a gap-toothed grin.

Sam and I looked at him in amazement and started to laugh. "Scare of the week," I said, leaning my head on my husband's chest. "Maybe we can sell the TV rights."

"We'd be rich — this kid's got more tricks than an encyclopedia salesman." He reached over and pulled Jamie down on his lap, tipping our son's head back with the cup of his palm. "But maybe we should finish spanking him first," Sam suggested, getting serious again.

"Don spak me!" Jamie said, indignant, squirming to get free.

"He's had enough," I said, shoveling my hair back from my forehead.

"We're much too soft on him, Allie," Sam said.

I opened my mouth to object, but then looked away.

"How far up did he get?" Sam asked, changing the subject.

I pointed. "Why didn't he break something? He wasn't even scared! He was smiling!"

"That's probably why — he didn't tense when he landed. Like getting bucked off." Sam shook his head. "We got real lucky this time."

"Lucky," I repeated. I wondered if it was just a question of luck. We got up and each of us took one of Jamie's hands. We walked back to the house for breakfast, slowly.

"Out!" Jamie demanded imperiously from under the long visor of his Red Sox cap. "Wanna gee out!"

"Get out!" Meggie added importantly, nodding her curly blonde head.

I looked at them both in exasperation as they stood up in the shopping cart and threatened to tip it over. For a minute I hated this day which had begun so badly, hated them, hated my whole life: exhaustion made me irrational, and my headache was worse. If I'd had a trash can I'd have looked a lot like Oscar the Grouch. I pulled a loaf of Wonder bread — the only kind Anna would eat — from under Meggie's feet and took the lettuce from Jamie's hands before he threw it over the side. "Wan ball," he said, his lower lip starting to thrust out. "Wan *geen* ball."

How could he be so impossible after having nearly killed himself on that ladder this morning? How could I be losing my patience again so soon after our miraculous reprieve? "It's not a ball," I snapped. "Now *sit* down!"

"Gee out," Jamie demanded inexorably.

"Get out," Meggie confirmed.

"O-kay," I gave in. I planted a kiss on each of their cheeks as I hefted them over the edge of the cart and set them down in the aisle of the IGA. Tobie had insisted on doing some farm business right in the middle of my studio time this morning, and although I'd decided resolutely that I might as well get something accomplished, I was annoyed; I wanted to get back to the painting of Jamie, even though I dreaded facing it. Our unnerving incident in the barn this morning had made me want to abandon the portrait entirely, but the compulsion to finish it and triumph over its disturbing implications was equally strong.

"Now you two stay close to Mommy," I said, giving them their instructions and shaking my finger under their noses. "Understand?"

They nodded, very solemnly, one after the other.

"Anna," I said, turning to my four-year-old, "can you get me two cans of the red coffee?" I pointed.

Anna trotted off, long skinny legs flashing below her shorts. She was going to be as tall as Sam, I thought, smiling at how grown-up she was becoming. I started to load cans of tomato soup into the cart. At least there was more room for the groceries without the twins as cargo. As we moved down the aisle, they pushed the cart and watched me, while Anna worked as runner for the easy-to-reach items. I loved having a helper, a real helper.

But after five minutes Jamie tugged at my hand impatiently. "Go too?"

"Go where?"

"Me go mik?" he asked hopefully. I hesitated. I wanted to encourage him, but there were real hazards here. I wondered how easy it was to split open a milk carton. Still, the dairy case was only one aisle over and the milk right at the front. He'd be able to reach it and probably carry it too.

"We get milk?" Meggie asked, refining her younger brother's request. She tipped the scales: her face was so earnest I couldn't resist. I nodded.

"But just one carton," I said, holding up my index finger. "And you be *careful.*"

They took off down the aisle, their sneakers smacking against the linoleum, and I told myself I must be crazy. I hurried through the rest of the soups, the relish, the ketchup, the paper towels, the sugar, the number 9 spaghetti, the dishwashing compound and managed — with Anna's help — to round the bend into the dairy aisle only a minute or two after Jamie and Meggie. I could see them at the far end, standing on a milk crate, pointing into the dairy case and talking about which container to pick. Meggie was voting for the blue carton and Jamie the red. They seemed all right, so I stepped up to the butcher's counter and let Anna choose three hens; I'd used the last of our own frozen stock night before last, and we wouldn't be slaughtering again till next week.

Anna told the butcher she had to pinch the skin — the way she'd seen Tobie do — "to see how old it is," and I smiled at her intensity and concentration, loving her at that moment just for not being two. By the time we got back to the dairy section, Meggie had a small shopping basket over her arm and Jamie was taking eggs from a carton and laying them in the basket, very carefully, one by one. "He y'go," he was saying as I rolled up, "one mommee ekk, two mommee ekk, three mommee ekk!" His face was flushed with triumph as I looked into the basket, and I clapped my delight that he'd counted correctly — Anna hadn't learned to count until this year — because, sure enough, there were three unbroken eggs rolling around in there. But then I saw that there were also four on the floor. Yolk oozed across the linoleum.

I just looked at them and sighed. Meggie turned her eyes

down and looked meek. "I sorry, Mommy," she said. "We made akdent."

"Accident or not," I said wearily, "you've made a mess — now you've got to clean it up." I unwrapped a roll of paper towels, thinking that if I had to look at any more little yellow yolks today I'd scream. Mr. Baskins, the owner of the IGA, walked by us in silence, returning a minute later with a trash basket. He didn't say a word. The Baskinses were used to my kids making mischief. If it wasn't noise and running up and down the aisles, it was breaking a jar of sticky jam on the checkout belt. I was sure Mrs. Baskins was tempted to lock up when she saw our old Ford wagon pull in to angle-park at the sidewalk out in front.

Anna helped me pick up the shells while Meggie and Jamie made a new game out of shampooing the floor with egg slime. After a while the towel absorbed it all, and I pushed cart and kids toward the checkout.

"And add on four eggs, please, Mrs. Baskins," I said as Anna and I began to unload.

She rang up the extra price without comment. Her hair was bottle-brown, and the symmetrical rows of sausage-shaped curls were rolled up tight against her head, showing lines of pink scalp in between — as if her curlers were still in. She didn't like to brush out her set right away, she'd told me once. Letting it sit awhile made it last longer.

Ina Robards had come through the front door and swung around to stand at the end of the conveyor belt as I began to unload. Nodding at me, she leaned on the edge of the counter to talk to Mrs. Baskins. Her voice had always irritated me, a grating, nasal whine, so I was never glad to see her come in, and she slowed down Mrs. Baskins's pudgy fingers on the register as well.

"I had it direct from Ted Mullins," she was saying confidentially to Mrs. Baskins, running a fingertip back and forth over the hairy mole on her left cheek. "He was up on her place last month for over two weeks, building some fancy room for all her paintings and that stuff."

The word *paintings* riveted my attention. Who could she be gossiping about? But I didn't want to ask. As an outsider I'd had to smile hard to win over the locals when I first moved to Arrowsic. Although they seemed to accept me now, it was a grudging sort of acceptance, and dependent on my discretion.

Jamie had taken a Golden Book off the rack and was pointing out the pictures to Meggie, while Anna continued to help me. "You want the book, too?" Mrs. Baskins asked me, interrupting Ina.

I flushed, embarrassed, and then nodded, scanning the rack of newspapers and magazines to the left of the register as Mrs. Baskins wrapped up the meltables in heatproof bags.

"She must be a weird one," Ina continued, making sure she talked loud enough for everyone to hear. "Living up there so solitary — no husband, no friends, not even an animal. From New York. Doesn't know anyone in town. It's downright peculiar."

I reached out and picked up a copy of *Time*.

"She's neighbor to you," Ina went on, nodding at me now. "You or Sam been over there yet?"

Formally included, at last I could look up. "We saw the moving trucks go past last month, but didn't know who'd bought the place. You think it's a woman alone?"

Ina nodded, licking a chapped bottom lip with the point of her tongue. "Only the one of her, and she had Ted up building an addition. Fancy that. Already not enough room and she's just moved in!" She started to laugh, a sharp sound, like dry leaves skittering across the sidewalk.

I reached down to keep Jamie from decimating the magazine rack.

"He says she's some kinda artist, got a lot of big" — she

spread her arms wide — "pitchers, weird stuff, standing all around the place. Ever heard of her?"

The idea that someone other than an ordinary family might buy the old frame house on the Larson acreage had never occurred to me. "Well, what's her name?" I asked, stifling my impatience with the woman's obtuseness.

Ina paused, licking her lip again. "Can't say as I recall."

"Yesterday you said Shark, or Sharkkit, something like that," Mrs. Baskins put in, punching up my total on the register. She wiped her hands across the wide front of her apron. "That'll be fifty seventy-five, Mrs. Yates, including the magazine you're holding."

I looked down at it, startled and confused. I had never intended to buy it, and the cover story made me pull back from the idea even more. "AMERICA HUNTS ITS MISSING CHILDREN." Part of being a mother in the eighties was realizing that you couldn't leave your kids alone in the car while you ran a quick errand, you couldn't let them stand for a minute by themselves in a department store, you couldn't let them walk home from school unchaperoned. Not even in Arrowsic. Being too trusting was a luxury you couldn't afford.

My children stood in front of me, sturdy, intact, alive. I was suddenly afraid for them, and shoved the magazine back on the stand. "I don't know of any artist named Sharkkit," I answered Ina.

Mrs. Baskins stopped in the middle of bagging. "I already rung that up," she said, peering at me oddly. "You just paid for it."

"That's okay." The store seemed close, without air, full of dusty smells. I nodded thanks as she made my change and hefted the brown bags of groceries into the cart. Now she and Ina would gossip about me. I herded the children ahead of me with a sweep of my arm.

We rolled out onto the sidewalk. Anna took over pushing

the cart and Jamie grabbed my hand and began to swing it. As I looked down at his little tanned fingers, curled into mine, I thought of other women, who would never hold their children's hands again. Were those women just unlucky?

"Hey, guys, how about going to Nelson's?" I asked, feeling suddenly daring. It was nearly noon.

"Icekeem!" Jamie crowed, jumping up and down.

"Icecreem!" Meggie echoed.

"Chocolate and French vanilla!" Anna shouted. "You're my favorite mommy in the whole world!"

I shoved the groceries up into the back of the wagon, and the four of us linked hands to cross the street, skipping and singing as we went. Ice cream, I thought to myself, and so close to lunch: how my mother would disapprove, how Tobie would disapprove. Thank God, or luck, that I was the mother here.

Nelson's Sundries still made its own ice cream — old-fashioned flavors like peach and honey maple and vanilla fudge twirl — and served it in glass dishes at the kind of lunch counter they used to have in drugstores in the fifties. Sally and Herb Nelson had owned the store for the last thirty-odd years, and they were both there, every day, six days a week. Nelson's stocked everything from bubblegum baseball cards and penny candy to Doan's Pills and Pepsodent. I liked resting for a while over an occasional dish of peppermint stick, trading a little news.

Going to Nelson's brought back memories of Wednesday afternoons, summer: my mother and I walked over hot pavement to the cool blackness of the public library, where I checked out three orange Famous American Women biographies from the children's shelf, and she checked out three romances. These six books were our weekly escape. I loved reading about women's real lives and she loved reading about their imaginary ones. Then on the way home we stopped for ice cream, one-scoop cones that melted fast unless you kept up with your tongue.

My kids clambered up on the high swivel stools and had a loud discussion over which flavor was best. Herb waited behind the counter, circling his hand around his bald spot without thinking until I ordered a coffee soda. Then he made a great show of scooping and stirring, raising and lowering the glass under the soda-water siphon with a flourish. Anna finally decided on a double scoop of strawberry, her dark-brown eyes dancing in a dare, waiting for a "no" from me. I surprised her by keeping quiet. After this morning it was enough just to sit and sip and watch my three at such simple contentment.

"And how about you, sweetheart?" Mr. Nelson asked Meggie. Meggie put her finger in her mouth and ducked her head. She could never make up her mind, and her indecisiveness had irritated me from the minute I recognized it as a personality trait. Jamie leaned over to whisper in her ear and they had a private conversation, accompanied by nods and smiles.

He sat up importantly, the conference obviously at an end. "We hab chocwit!"

Herb looked at me over the top of the counter as he began to scoop from the deep barrels. "You got a fine boy there, Mrs. Yates," he said. "Looks after his sister nicely."

"She's too shy," I said, exasperated, as he set the dishes down in front of the kids. "I wish she knew her own mind."

Herb looked over at me, his thick tortoiseshell glasses shining daylight back at me as he made a dip with his head. "She's young yet." He reached over to pat Meggie's hand.

I didn't answer. I stirred my soda. I stole a quick glance at Meggie and caught her looking at me with a hurt expression on her face. She was sensitive, and she'd caught my tone. I sighed. Sometimes I forgot how much she could understand now. I leaned back on my stool, thinking that Herb was right. I saw my own insecurities in my daughter, my own faults, and I wasn't any better at tolerating them in her than I was at tolerating them in myself.

Jamie clinked his spoon against the side of the dish as if it were a cymbal, and then spun on his stool till he was just a denim blur. "Icekeem! I *yike* icekeem!"

Anna shook her straight blonde bangs out of her eyes reprovingly. "Don't do that, or Mommy won't bring us again."

He slowed to a stop and then looked over, chocolate in a ring around his mouth. He slid down off his stool and came to stand beside me, putting his sticky hand into my lap. It was as if he understood that I felt bad about Meggie. He knows what I've been thinking, I said to myself, confused, incoherent in my own mind as I looked down into his dirty face. But I shook the feeling away: after all, he was only two. I squeezed his hand and nodded at his dish. "Time to finish up now, Jamie."

Still he kept looking at me with that expression of patience, of tolerance. "I lub Mommee," he said, and then turned to climb back up on his stool.

I folded my hands in my lap and sat very still, looking down. It was the first time he'd ever said such a thing without prompting, probably the first time he'd ever named an emotion on his own.

I'd grown used to intuiting love. Anna was at an age where she was too busy flashing here and there to tell me she loved me. Meggie kept more to herself. Neither Sam nor Tobie relied on language. And then along came my small boy with his chocolate face and his three big words. I thought of losing him: in a corner of my mind I saw him on the barn floor. He had come from my body, he was part me — to lose him would be to lose myself. I pushed the thought away and wiped Meggie's face and hands.

I looked at my watch and stood reluctantly. "Well, kiddos, it's time."

"I'm not done, Mommy," Anna started to protest.

"Tobie's waiting lunch." My tone was steady and sure, and she slid down off her stool. Meggie turned from one of the counters, where she was holding a small baby doll. I walked over, and she cradled the doll in close, whispering to her. I leaned down. "We have to go, Meggie."

She looked at me silently. She didn't even have to ask. I turned over the price tag: $8.95. Reasonable, but still an $8.95 we didn't have to spare. I didn't feel like getting into another fight with Sam about the budget. On the other hand, I could always just tell him that I'd spent more at the market than I actually had. It seemed an easy solution — even though we had always made a practice of being totally honest — and was really only what my mother used to call "a white lie." I bent down to my daughter again, enlisting her in the deception. "Promise you won't tell Daddy?"

Her smile rewarded me, and I handed Herb my last twenty dollars.

"Mommy," Anna protested. "I want a new doll too!"

I shook my head.

"But that's not fair!" she sputtered angrily.

"Things aren't always fair, Anna." I crouched down to look into her eyes. "Your turn will come for something extra. Today it's Meggie's treat." I took her hand and stood up again, ignoring her lower lip, bowed into a pout.

"Say 'Thank you, Mr. Nelson,' " I instructed them.

He nodded in appreciation at their polite chorus and handed me my change from the old punch register. "Heard you got a new neighbor, Mrs. Yates."

"Ina Robards just told me," I answered, shooing the kids away from the magazine stand and toward the door. "I hear that she's an artist, but I haven't met her yet."

"Came in here Sunday," Herb went on. "For toothpaste, soap, turpentine. Opened a charge account." Like Tobie, he said it in a lump, *chahgeaccount*, as though it were one word. He shook his head. "Most people like to pay as they go. From New York, she said."

A painter, and from New York, right in my own backyard. As we waved goodbye to Herb and crowded out the door, I wondered when and where I would meet her.

Rebecca

I first met Rebecca Shardick in a dream. It was on the road to town, the night of the day I'd gone to Nelson's with the children. In my dream the sun had just set behind a wall of purple thunderheads beyond the west pasture, and dark was creeping up prematurely. An eerie green light reflected from trees broad with leaves as a woman came down the road toward me. Her face was my mother's face, but her eyes were watch-eyes, small blue circles ringed in white. In my arms I carried a baby. I peered at the baby's face and recognized it as my own, a face I'd seen hundreds of times in my baby pictures, taken thirty years before.

Around the baby's neck was a thin leather strap from which hung a star of red glass; the star winked its iridescence on and off, a beacon of orange-yellow-vermilion rays that circled through the half-light of the coming rain. Introducing herself as my new neighbor, Rebecca offered to hold the baby so that I could open my umbrella, but when I stretched my arms out to give the baby over, the infant squirmed, slipping like a fish down the length of my body to the ground. Aghast, I knelt to scoop the baby up against me, but Rebecca cried out then in warning, and I looked to see that thunderheads had piled high, in columns above us. The setting sun had reversed itself, rising back up over the western horizon, and all around us the new white light blazed.

I looked down at the child again. But the eyes swiveled, blind whites turning upward, in a convulsion. The left eye popped from its socket and rolled to the ground next to my knee, a blue marble. It flashed red-yellow-orange in the light of the star. Horrified, I pulled away. Rebecca knelt beside me, picked up the eye, and put it into the palm of my hand even as I wrestled with her grip, repulsed and desperate to get away. She folded my fingers around the eye, saying, *This is what you have left, a touchstone, and you will guard it, then use it.*

I woke, sticky with sweat and tears. A ball of tissue was wadded tight against my palm. It was morning, but the early light coming through the bedroom window did not ease my racing heart or dissipate the fear. I don't understand, I thought, starting to shiver. Sam reached out toward me and I hugged him distractedly. "Hello," he said, rubbing his scratchy face against mine.

"Mmm," I said, trying to hang on to each detail in my mind. I needed to write the dream down in my journal before I forgot it. I pulled back and rolled to the edge of the bed.

"Hey, where's my cuddle?"

"If I don't go to the john I'll explode."

"Jamie's not up yet. It's our one chance in weeks," he said softly, running his hand up under my nightie.

I caught his wrist. "He'll be in anytime now."

"Come back," he urged, "just for a minute."

But I couldn't give in this morning. "It's late." I slid out from under the covers. I didn't want to be touched, I didn't want to have to explain why I had been crying . . . or why a dream could still make me so afraid.

*   *   *

It didn't seem strange for me to have dreamt of Rebecca even though we'd never met: dreams were just another side of the waking world. I knew now that I would meet her, and soon. How she would matter to me I didn't know — but that she would matter I had already accepted.

I spent most of breakfast-time puzzling over the dream as a way of making it less frightening.

"Allie, what's with you?" Sam's irritated voice broke into my train of thought. "Joe's asked you for the milk three times."

"Sorry," I muttered, smiling at Joe distractedly and passing the pitcher. I got up and began to clear the dishes to the sink, my mind going right back to the dream. My ruminations didn't even begin to answer the import of that eye. Why had Rebecca picked it up and forced me to take it?

"Think we've got some strangles goin'," Joe said to Tobie as he poured the milk over his oatmeal. "Saw at least three mares with their noses full up."

She looked at him with distress, and the three finished quickly and tramped off to the barn. Not wanting to think about what an outbreak of disease could do to Sam's plans for the animals, I picked up the Record and turned to the horoscope page. It didn't surprise me to see my message for the day had the same mystical quality as the dream: Keep your mind open to possibilities.

Later, when I went upstairs to my studio, I managed to put the dream, the horoscope, and the farm's latest crisis out of my mind for a while and spent several hours on a pen and ink for a Hallmark anniversary card. It was to be a Maine seacoast pastoral, and I was working from a photograph of waves hurling themselves against an island with a small lighthouse. It was mindless work, and I tuned out, keeping my hands busy. I avoided looking at the oil of Jamie, which stood on an easel in the corner, or at my Red Sox cap, hanging from a peg. At last I went over and tried to assess the painting,

but I couldn't. Its presence immobilized me. I didn't like looking at its big weighty sky, its crashing colors, the small, vulnerable boy. It disturbed me. This was the first time my own
work had had that effect on me.

And the sensation continued throughout lunch, so that —
depressed by the emotional turmoil — I looked at my husband over our tunafish sandwiches and the clamor of the
twins and suddenly, desperately, wanted a little while alone
with him. "Got time for a walk after lunch?" I asked hopefully,
concealing the urgency I felt.

He shook his head. "Vet's coming up."

It must be bad if he'd called the vet, I realized. He never
called the vet unless all the magic he and Tobie could conjure
had failed.

"She's got some new shot we might try," he said, hunching
his shoulders around his plate. "Hate to think of the bill."

Tobie, too, looked grim.

"We'll manage," I said with an optimism I didn't feel. "Some
way."

"Half the time these injections don't even help," Sam went
on, sounding defeated.

"Then why do it?" I flared irritably. "Why waste the little
we've got?"

"Because I don't know what else to do!"

The children stirred under our tension. I cleared the plates;
I didn't want to argue anymore.

"Can I ride Duet today?" Anna asked Sam. "Over more
cavalletti?"

He nodded distractedly.

"Come on, honey," Joe said, pushing his chair back and
smiling up at me. Yesterday he'd led her and the pony back
and forth over the parallel bars on the ground for nearly half
an hour; Joe had a soft spot for Anna. "I'll give you a hand
tacking her up."

After the twins were in for a nap I decided to go for a walk alone, do a little mushrooming. I was still agitated, certainly not nearly ready to work or even able to sort myself out. My anxiety wouldn't be any help to Sam in the barn, either. But sometimes the woods could help me.

As I walked down the dirt path beyond our upper pasture, I started thinking about the horoscope and the dream again. I didn't take horoscopes too seriously; they were an amusement, a diversion, a junky addiction. I read them the way some people read comic strips or watched soap operas. I liked to apply a horoscope to my day like a frame around a painting: sometimes it fit, sometimes not. Still, this one teased me, in just the same way the painting and the dream nagged at me.

I took a deep breath and let the silence clear my head. Early afternoon sunlight checkered the trees, the ground, the rocks and brush, and a birdcall sounded above my head. It was a long run of notes, high-pitched, trembling, beautiful. The mate answered back. I sighed, thinking about Sam. He was the birdcall expert. He'd spent long hours with his father breaking trails in these woods, listening and watching. Love of the woods was one of the things they had shared without conflict. Sam still spent his free time here, what little of it there was, and brought the kids with him a lot. He'd been teaching Anna birdcalls, and last night she'd showed us the three he'd helped her with last week — towhee, redheaded woodpecker, cowbird — each one perfect in its alien sounds. Other people's children practiced their violin and piano; mine practiced birdcalls until they had them down pitch-perfect. I'd listened with pride, amazed at her early skill and the aplomb with which she performed. Sometimes I even got a little jealous as I watched Sam set out hand in hand with Jamie, or Meggie, or Anna. We had so little time together by ourselves these days.

The empty basket bumped my hip. It seemed Sam and I were bickering a lot — a series of tiny movements away from each other — and all about trivial, irritating details. Still, when

Sam was off working during the day, I was pleased to see that I wanted him more than ever before, to lie with him in silence, to run my hands up and down his body, to relearn him. I reassured myself that our differences were just from the pressure, the relentless work, the balance in the savings account. At night we were simply too tired for sex, and daytimes were too busy for us to talk. Our early morning lovemaking had been curtailed by Jamie's repeated appearance in our bed each day before dawn. This morning had been the exception; he'd slept late, but I'd been too upset by my dream to respond to Sam.

I squatted down at the edge of a clearing to dig up some burdock for Tobie, who loved the steamed greens alongside her chicken. It was Tobie who'd taught me how to eat them, cooked tender, with a little butter and salt, at the same time that she'd undertaken to instruct me in the art and science of mushrooming. One of the things we still shared these days was our appreciation for the wild. Tobie's disapproval of how Sam and I handled Jamie — or, more exactly, of how *I* did *not* handle Jamie — had estranged us some.

Yesterday, I'd tried to talk to Tobie, tried to reach out as I had done in the old days. Maybe she could help me through this time of squabbling with Sam. I'd faced the fact that she knew him better than I did in some ways, or maybe she could see what I couldn't. And, in truth, there was no one else to talk to, no one else to ask. For the first time in a long time I was lonely. But Tobie didn't want to hear about my problems with her son, and whenever I tried to move us around to the subject, she started in with something else, or found a new chore to do, or pulled one of the kids onto her lap.

I laid the burdock in my basket and sat for a minute, thinking about how, in the old days — before we'd had the kids and our time was so full from dawn to dusk — Sam and I would have come here and gotten the anger out, in the open, under a big tree. We liked to make up by making love, and so we'd have stripped naked, the pine needles itchy under my back, the earth cool and rocky against my spine and his knees. He would have lowered himself into me, and we'd have resolved it all with our bodies.

I reclined for a minute in the square of sunlight that had filtered through the foliage. The rays came down direct and warm over my breasts and stomach as I tilted my head back to look straight up. The woods were deep here. I was in well under the high dome of pine and maple, spruce and oak — that odd mix of evergreen and deciduous which is particular to the Northeast.

I thought of these same trees come fall, the maples violent red against the pines; the image appeared in my mind like a photograph superimposed over what I now saw. I pushed it back, glad for July against my face and the vivid green before me. I loved autumn, but today I didn't want to see it; today I only wanted summer to continue, with its long light-filled days, its hot, lush touch, its smells of ripening, the long grasses going from green to gold under a high sun.

The woods were shaded, silent. A stand of pencil-slim birch glimmered white; when I closed my eyes I saw them like a photographic negative, the reverse of the maples and elms. In a place like this I was sure of possibilities. The tree nearest me had one limb that curved upward in an odd, tension-filled arch. I wondered why it should have grown in such a strange position, and I pulled a small sketchbook from my back pocket. For a while I practiced drawing the one limb over and over, page after page, until I had that curve in space exact, until I knew just how it moved through the air. I would use that curve someday.

A shaft of sunlight came down at a slant, angled, as if it were a shower, raining infinitesimal particles of light. It re-minded me of the way sun sometimes comes through a heavy ceiling of clouds, in patches, thick cylinders of yellow rays. Once when I was a little girl I'd looked out the car window and told my mother I could see God. My father had looked alarmed, as if I were sick and needed to be taken to the doctor. When I pointed to the sky he laughed and told me I was only seeing the sun coming from behind the clouds. My mother squeezed my hand, though, and an understanding of my meaning passed between us. I did not say that day that I could see God behind those clouds, God with a big pitcher in his hands, pouring a spout of sunlight down onto the earth like melted butter onto a pancake. But I was sure my mother knew. When we got home I went straight to my room and spent the next several days drawing what I had seen, over and over, until I was satisfied I'd mastered that trick of light.

Still, despite my mother's understanding in the car that day, I was raised by two Methodists who never once took me to church. I was never christened. It appeared we were pagans. We took our holidays straight up and secular: Christmas had a tree but no crèche; Easter had a bunny but neither mourning nor celebration.

As a teenager, I sometimes went to the Episcopal church around the corner at night and crept in the unlocked door in the dark, feeling my way along until I found the matches and candles. I'd bow my head to pray — mostly for myself, selfishly — down on my knees in the hope that I would find some purpose within my life. Whenever I left there I felt better. I never told my parents. I never told my friends.

Now I hardly ever thought about God — at least, not like that. I'd relegated God to dreams or my unconscious, or to being synonymous with Nature, especially since there was so much spread out wide in the land around me. Still, maybe there was God behind every painting I did, some weird kind of God who helped pick my colors and my lines — but not a churchy God, not a God of psalms or fables.

When Sam and I first got married we'd sat in the west pasture one day, talking, and I pointed up to the cloudy sky and the breaking sun and told him what I'd pretended when

I was little. I told him how I'd painted it again and again as I grew older. And he didn't laugh. He held my hand tighter. It was one of those moments in which I loved him the most, and it remained in my memory, like the smell of fresh hay in the rain, even on the days when we argued and fought.

I stretched in the sun now, put away my sketch pad, and crossed to the foot of those birches I'd admired earlier; near the trunks, poking up their brownish heads surprisingly early, were three large king boletus. I knelt to inspect them with care. I had grown cautious after Martha Cannerby — a neighbor who had been another student under Tobie's tutelage during my first lessons in the woods — had made a bad pick, an elementary error, one day last summer on her own, mistaking an *Amanita muscaria* for an *Amanita caesaria*.

I'd grown choosy, too. I cut off one with my knife and inspected its stem carefully, then turned it upside down to look under the cap. It was reasonably clean and fresh, with little worm damage.

It had taken me a while to get used to the worms. Slicing through them as I fixed the mushrooms for cooking, I felt like a magician sawing through the trickbox with the lady inside. The tiny worms, cut lengthwise or crosswise — depending on how they were crawling when they met my knife — cooked up just fine along with everything else in my frying pan. Sam and Tobie would have nothing to do with my mushrooms. I made them for myself, mostly at night when everyone else was in bed. I'd get a craving for their dusky smell and smooth, gelatinous texture — so different from a supermarket mushroom — and go down to the kitchen to fry up a batch with butter and garlic from Tobie's herb patch. When Sam woke in the morning he would sniff the air and refuse to kiss me.

I rubbed the dirt from the cap with my thumb and reveled in the silk of its skin: its smell came from the underworld of damp earth, the breaking down of matter, fragrant mulch. The large boletus rolled on its side in my basket. The other two were too wormy to bother with. I straightened from my crouch and looked around slowly.

Mushrooming was a careful art, like following an animal's trail. If you surveyed the forest floor as you finished at one patch, you often found another close by. Nature's camouflage was powerful magic, though. Egg-yellow chanterelles sometimes nestled in the colored leaves which fell in autumn, deer mushrooms found a safe home on rotting branches, men-on-horseback poked up unnoticed among pine needles and mosses. You had to train your eye to see things which were there but hidden in surface textures and colors.

I wandered for a while then; despite my X-ray eyes, there just didn't seem to be much of anything worth taking. My basket was nearly empty, and when I looked up at the bunched branches of leaves over my head, I saw that the sun was getting into the late afternoon. If I didn't turn up anything soon, I'd have to go home and help Tobie get the kids up from their naps.

That was when I saw them, a whole tribe, glowing buff-yellow and perfect, the queen of mushrooms: morels. Sponge mushrooms. They'd fruited under an ash which had been scorched by lightning and then fallen, and their deep honeycombed caps were hidden by the tree's detritus, but not hidden enough for me to miss them. They were quite late, but, as *Morchella esculenta*, were of a variety which sometimes turned up even in early August in higher elevations such as ours. It didn't surprise me anymore to find things out of their season, especially in New Hampshire, where the weather was so erratic. Out of season, out of sync with the larger forces — it only made them more precious.

As I knelt to take them, something rustled off to my left. Not the wind, I thought, turning my head slightly, distracted for a moment. An animal maybe. I looked but there was nothing there.

I was cutting the morels carefully, my mouth remembering

their sweet, meaty taste, when I heard that same rustle again.
I'd never seen bear in these woods, nothing but squirrel and
skunk, fox and raccoon. Still, something inside me stirred in
a primitive reflex. I rose from my knees quickly and silently,
my knife still in my hand.

But there was nothing more. No sound, no movement. My
pulse returned to normal. Warily I bent to take up my basket,
reflexively brushing the dirt and needles from my knees. I
left the rest of the morels standing and turned to make my
way down the path, back toward home. I just wanted to get
out of there. But something kept me from moving in that
direction. The air around me had the strange unfocused quality of one of my dreams.

I found myself turning again, slowly, against my will really,
toward the low-lying bushes from which the noises had come.
I was pivoting as though some invisible hand were turning
my shoulders. Under that pressure I walked over to push
back the bushes, flinching even as I did it.

There was nothing there — not a rabbit, not a bird, not a
snake. Nothing but leaves and a tangle of roots from the trees
above.

That was when I knew that it was behind me. It was waiting
for me to turn around. When I did it would be real, I would
make it real by seeing it. My mouth filled with water; thick
white moths beat in front of my eyes.

Slowly I turned. Directly opposite me was an old towering
oak, its trunk nearly four feet across. In the center of it was
a woman, imprisoned by the skin of its bark. Her black hair
fell straight down her high forehead, her tall, narrow body
was trapped upright in the scaffold of the tree, like a painting
by Munch.

I closed my eyes and then opened them again. When I
looked into her face terror flooded my heart: the iris of her
right eye was an ordinary brown, but the left was blue, a
watch-eye, like the eye last night in my dream. I waited for

that eye to drop from its socket, to roll onto the ground and speak.

Then she stepped from the tree and began to walk toward me. I saw gray streaks in her black hair, fine strings of wrinkles around the corners of her mouth and eyes. The detail with which she was made was overpowering. I heard my own breath, whistling in and out. My fingers uncurled and dropped the basket.

She said nothing. I stared at her: a woman born of a tree like a child from its mother.

"I think lightning must have hit that tree," she said finally, gesturing behind her.

I kept staring and my mind returned slowly, very slowly, from the edge of total drop-off. She was real, she spoke, she was alive, and that meant she wasn't dead or a ghost or even a hallucination. Then I turned my stare from her face to the oak behind her and realized it had been cleft by lightning from the ground up: it stood like an old man with legs splayed for balance. The hollow in its trunk was an arch just large enough to walk through.

"God, you scared me," I said, half-angry now, wrapping my hand around my throat.

"Sorry about that." She smiled, a straight, direct smile, and suddenly I felt like an idiot. What had I expected to see anyway? I wondered. She wore denim jeans, a short-sleeved blue workshirt, and very muddy expensive leather loafers. She was not from Arrowsic. On each wrist was a watch: one with a leather strap, the other with a metal stretch band.

"You're the one who bought the Larson place?" I asked, trying to recover myself and not seem such a total fool.

Her face showed her surprise. "How do you know who I am?"

I shrugged. "It's a small town," I answered. "And we're neighbors. No one else'd be walking around this part of the woods." I put out my hand and she shook it. "I'm Allie Yates.

My husband, Sam, and our three kids — and my mother-in-law —," I sighed, "we live just up the road from you."
She nodded. "Rebecca Shardick," she said, and stooped to pick up my mushrooms and put them back into my basket. I let her because I still didn't want to try bending my knees; I might find myself sitting on the ground in a hurry. On top of being shaky, I was also breathless with the jolt of recognition at her name. I had indeed heard of Rebecca Shardick. I had seen her work displayed in museums, I had discussed her paintings in my theory classes. She was a *big name*, and now she was my neighbor.
"Do you really eat these things?" She handed me the basket.
"They grow on you after a while." I was trying not to stare at her: she had an arresting face, the blue eye contrasting with the brown to startle. I could see she was about to say goodbye and turn away. "Local gossip has it you're an artist," I blurted, saying the first thing that came to my mind.
"They're talking about me already?"
I laughed. "Arrowsic gossips about everyone and everything."
"Do you?"
"I wasn't born here so I don't have many people to gossip with."
She raised her thick black eyebrows. "And does that make you more trustworthy?"
"I'm not sure."
It had been a long time since I'd had a verbal fencing match. And her frankness — that's what surprised me. I realized I wasn't used to it anymore. Up here people took a while to say what they meant: there was an art to getting around to your meaning. But today I was too anxious for subtlety; today I wanted to make this woman's acquaintance. I didn't want her to hand the basket back and just walk away.
"Yes. I am an artist," she answered. "Yes, I live alone. Yes,

I am a bit bizarre." She put back her head and laughed —
a raspy sound, dry and throaty. "You can tell them or
not, whatever you like. Want to come back to my place for a
beer?"

I straightened up, thrilled and a little nervous. In Arrowsic
you usually didn't invite people over till you knew them a
bit. But I was curious, very curious. "I'd like that," I said.

I'd never been inside the Larson place, but it looked as
though she hadn't changed much, just moved her stuff right
in. It was a dusty old farmhouse not unlike ours, with wide
pegged floors of dark oak and broad wood-framed windows
that let in a reasonable amount of light. The living room had
old wallpaper in a pansy pattern. We went past, to the kitchen,
where I sat at the round oak table and sipped the Budweiser
she'd handed me, while she stood at the sink and husked a
pile of yellow corn.

"That looks like a lot for one person," I commented nosily,
wondering if she really did live here all alone and why she'd
moved to Arrowsic in the first place. "Is someone coming to
dinner?"

She shook her head. "I batch cook, then stick it in the fridge.
This way I don't have to bother about food for days and there's
no time wasted."

While nodding politely, I shuddered, thinking of week-old
precooked corn on the cob. The bowl of fruit on the table had
been there for a while, too. Fruit flies rose in a small cloud
as I ran my finger along the rim of the glass bowl, and I could
see warm brown patches on the peaches and pears. Toast
crumbs gritted under my elbows where I leaned on the edge
of the table, and there was a faint smell of mold. Open boxes
of cereal and rice, a disk of melting butter on a dish, bread
exposed to the air in an unfastened plastic bag — as Rebecca
put down an ear of corn and abandoned the pile in favor of
putting a few glasses into the sink to soak, I realized she was

the sort of distractible woman who had trouble focusing. Her kitchen was full of tasks half-done.

On the other hand, there were four clocks in the room: a Big Ben on the windowsill above the sink; a cuckoo mounted on the wall over the table; a desk clock in a walnut case on the counter; and a brass carriage clock atop the old refrigerator. None of them told exactly the same time, but they implied precision.

I didn't care about what kind of house she kept: in fact, perhaps these conflicting signs of order and chaos made me feel more at home in a strange place. What I did care about was what colors she chose, what kinds of lines she drew — how she had decided to see the world around her. I wanted to get into her studio.

My own desire took me by surprise, especially its intensity. For the first time ever, I really wanted to talk with someone else about a world I'd kept strictly private for the last twenty years. Wanting to see Rebecca's workplace, wanting to tell her that I painted too, was like an itch all over my body.

Of course, there was no reason she should let me in; after all, even Sam had barely been in my studio since I'd set up my canvases and paints five years ago. For the first time that struck me as odd. How had I managed to keep them all out for so long? I sipped my beer, wondering if other people were as secretive.

"I see you've built an addition," I said, leading around to it.

"I needed a real studio. Most of the rooms in the main house are too dark." She turned from the sink, grabbed a handful of brushes from the can of turp they were soaking in, and held them under the running water. Then she set them out to dry on a Turkish towel.

"How's your light?"

"Northern, mainly. But I've got a lot of glass."

"It looks very big from the outside."

She inspected me for a minute before answering. "It is," she acknowledged at last, returning to the corn. She bundled some of the husks and silk into a few sheets of newspaper and shoved them into a tightly packed garbage pail.

"How many hours a day do you spend working?"

"Too many, probably." She laughed. "Each day is a little different. Whatever." She shrugged.

I was quiet a minute. "You're lucky," I said after a few more sips of beer, flushing at my own deliberate ploy. "My three hours in the morning never seem long enough."

She took a sip of her beer, looking at me — weighing me and my questions — around the bottom of the green bottle. "You're certainly interested in my studio," she observed.

I looked away, rolling the bottle between my palms. "Mine's just a room in our attic."

She went back to washing brushes while I held my breath and waited, taken aback by my need to blurt myself out to this woman who was very nearly a stranger. I memorized the grain of the wood in the table — found patterns, animals, faces — put my bottle down, and pushed back my chair. The ticking of all the clocks was arrhythmic and irritating. What was the matter with me today, I wondered: had the one beer affected me so soon?

She put down her towel and sat at the table. "Are you trying to tell me we have more in common than walking in the woods?"

I colored and looked away, still on the edge of my chair, feeling foolish and embarrassed. How clumsily obvious I'd been.

"I take it you paint." It was a statement, not a question.

I nodded. "And I do some greeting card and advertising work to support myself. I started drawing when I was six." I bowed my head, angry at my own awkward description.

She sipped her beer, watching me with both eyes. It made me feel uneasy. "Have you had any shows?"

Quickly I thought back to all the times I had resisted my instructors' suggestions to be part of their exhibitions. I thought about how I had never *wanted* to have a show. I shook my head. "I was never really interested in exhibiting." My voice was casual, but my hands shifted restlessly over my knees, picking at the seams of my jeans.

She lifted the eyebrow over her blue eye, creating an illusion of unevenness in her face. She obviously didn't believe me. "It's hard for me . . . to show my work to *anybody*," I amended hesitantly. "Much less a roomful of strangers." I bit my lip, hating my own vulnerability.

She laughed and stood up. I nearly crawled under the table. It was my own fault: my confessions had opened the way for her ridicule.

"I've got news for you — it's not easy for any of us." She sighed. "Would you like to see my studio?"

I let my breath out with relief. She'd said "us," and she'd invited me in. I smiled and stood to follow her as she moved through the long hall to the back wing of the house.

As we walked through the door I stopped short, stunned by the huge space — nearly forty feet by forty feet — and the way the knotty pine of the cathedral ceiling and the floor glowed. A fine light streamed in not only through an eight-foot-high wall of glass, but through skylights as well, and the forest of white-limbed birches outside seemed a part of the room. A large sculpture dominated the center of the space.

The mess and disorganization of her kitchen extended into her studio. Across the floor huge easels were scattered helter-skelter, supporting large canvases filled with color and shape. Three long worktables overflowed with clutter: cans of turp and thinner, many jars of brushes of every sort, boxes of rags, palette knives, painting knives, marble slabs for grinding and mixing color, chisels, mallets, rollers, boxes of charcoal, trays of pastels. In one corner stood blank prestretched canvases of varying types of linen, the finest quality. A bookshelf in the other corner held stacks of paper for sketching, water-color, and pastel, and a pile of gesso panels for tempera. On one easel there was a bulletin board with a series of sketches tacked up — a study, I saw, of Rebecca's own face. She was working on a self-portrait.

The equipment, the tools, the supplies. The luxury of so much space and light all to herself. No one banging on the door demanding that she come help in the barn, no children calling and crying for her return, no meals to be cooked, no five loads of laundry a day. I was overwhelmed with jealousy.

Canvases were stacked against the walls, more than two hundred of them, I estimated quickly — and that didn't ac-count for those already sold or in museums. A few even hung on hooks around the room — finished or unfinished, it didn't seem to matter. It was as if she needed to hang them in order to see them, the way a woman needs to back off from a mirror when she's trying on a new dress.

I walked around the room slowly, absorbing, stopping here and there to look at a few. They weren't arranged in any order at all, and the different periods of her work were mixed back-to-back. Abstracts leaned against landscapes, distillations of Seurat stood side-by-side with experiments inspired by Ma-tisse. Although I'd seen a little of her work in various mu-seums over the years, it was an awesome feeling now to see so much of her at once, to feel it here, in the same room with me, and, enviously, I wanted to find fault with it. I wanted to salvage some feeling of self-respect before I left here today. She was maybe fifty years old, and she'd painted more pro-lifically than I, with my limited hours, could ever hope to. And she had no compunction about letting a total stranger into her studio, her jewel box, with its vulnerable treasure. I thought of my own studio, with its life's work locked in a small closet.

As I walked I picked on small details in her early work: little things that did not, could not, matter to the whole. I'd not been particularly taken by her style before, and I relied on that sense of distance now as a defense. I was making myself feel better by finding the mistakes she'd made.

After a while I circled back around to where Rebecca stood lighting up a thin black cigar.

"These are what I've been working on since I got up here last month," she said, gesturing to a small stack of canvases. I flipped through them, feeling nauseated: there were eleven canvases, produced in only a month. I looked casually at first, again looking for flaws, and then, despite myself, slowed to look harder.

They were almost exclusively oils, and there was something unnerving about every one of them, some interplay of light and shadow, reality and nuance, which hooked me despite my desire to remain aloof. The planes of color were flat but bold — oranges, greens, blues — and at first the subjects seemed ordinary, the objects of our daily living: tables, trees, lamps. But if you looked hard you saw more. Something nagged at you. In the still life on the top of the pile, the handle of the water jug on the bureau bothered me: I stared harder and harder, and realized finally, with a shiver, that the handle of the jug looked like the curve of a human finger. In another oil — a row of plants in terra-cotta pots on a windowsill — an embryo shape nestled on a begonia's blood-red blossom.

In these paintings everything was hidden, waiting to be discovered. They had about them the quality of an intense repression which had failed: her macabre vision surfaced regardless of conscious intent. Truth leaked out in everyday ways. I could see that the viewer would be surprised continually, never knowing what he would find if he stopped long enough to look below the surface. It was evocative, primitive, fierce.

I couldn't admit it then, but these paintings frightened me. They made me think of things I didn't want to be near. I wouldn't have wanted to hang one on my wall at home, to see it every day, but I couldn't seem to stop myself from continuing to look at them either.

"They're very . . . interesting," I said after a while.

Rebecca just looked at me and waited.

"Disturbing," I went on finally, saying then what I really meant. It was some of the most intriguing modern work I'd ever seen.

She looked at me with her one blue eye. "What sort of things do you do?"

"For my commercial jobs I use landscapes, mostly," I said, feeling miserable to admit it. "For *my* work — almost anything. Since I've been up in Arrowsic I've done a lot with what's around me." My answer sounded somehow inadequate.

But to my surprise she nodded.

"I saw a show of yours down in SoHo," I went on. "I think it was, maybe, 'seventy-eight — when I was studying in Boston."

"Oh, yes," she said, nodding. "That show." Her mouth twisted in a wry smile. "My work became unpopular after that." She flipped the stack of canvases closed and put them back against the wall. "Sometimes when I think about the solitary time you put in . . ." She shook her head. "If you want to work, really work, you're totally alone. And then, when your work is finished, you have to shove yourself out where strangers can feel and touch and see you. You do what they can't do for themselves — give shape to the ways everybody lives." She sighed and drew on her cigar. "And then you're cut apart by people who've never even lifted a brush. Maybe that's what really pisses me off! These people make their living by sucking off your effort, like ticks." The ember of the cigar glowed bright red.

I didn't say anything. What she'd said was just what I was most afraid of.

"New York is a dangerous place. It's like a cheap mirror where you're either too big or too small, very good or very bad — and it's always someone else's perception. Never your own." The ember glowed again. Her voice was controlled; the emotion lay beneath the surface. "Politics. I had to get away from all of it."

"Is that why you left Manhattan?"

"Partly." She shrugged. "I like the privacy here. This place doesn't even have a phone book!"

"I've always known I couldn't stand the criticism, or the games." Her vehemence, the pain in her voice, had brought me out of myself. And I was ashamed for the envy I'd felt before. Rebecca had suffered her paintings to be born just like anyone else. And despite the splendor, she was here all alone, all by herself. At least I could go back downstairs at night, to Sam.

"But you have to do it — if you want all this," — she gestured with her arm — "badly enough. And it makes you tougher with yourself. Forget about what other people think. You've got to be tough with yourself."

She turned away abruptly now and moved across the room to stand in front of her unfinished self-portrait. "You're married?"

I nodded. "With three kids — noisy ones."

She was silent. Outside, a woodpecker made a fresh attack on a rotting birch.

"You've got no children?" I asked after a minute.

"I'm divorced. We never had any." She crushed her cigar out in a large beanbag ashtray, and I watched a last spiral curl upward like a smoke signal. "What are they?"

"An older girl, and then twins — one girl, one boy."

"Your husband must've been glad for the boy to come along."

"In some ways, I guess," I said. "Jamie's wild streak maybe

gives him a kick, but he's got a real soft spot for the girls. Not that he doesn't dote on Jamie. It's just . . ." I stopped, thinking of all the problems lately.

She stood back from the easel, thinking and talking at the same time. "My shrinkologist used to say that men without sons have no competition."

"Competition?" I looked at her.

"Mmmm, like my father. Loved to beat my brothers at every game. I had three, older ones." She lit up another cigar. "Tag football, checkers, basketball — you name it, he couldn't bear to see them win. What a relief when I turned out to be a girl."

"Sam didn't have an easy time of it with his own dad." I circled back to the life-sized sculpture which stood in the center of the room, directly under a skylight.

"What about this?" I asked. Done in a twisted black wire, it was a woman stretching, a woman caught in the cage of her own body. Every muscle delineated, each sinew taut and tense, head tipped back toward the ceiling, both arms reaching above her head — it was a glorious, evocative piece, and I envied it, too.

"Evan Hirsch," she said, naming the creator, a renowned young sculptor who had begun working exclusively with wire in the last few years. For my twenty-sixth birthday, just before Anna was born, Sam had given me the present of a two-day trip to New York. I'd gone to every museum and gallery I could cram in, and that was when I had first admired Hirsch's work.

"You know him?"

She smiled. "He came to me ten years ago, before he was well known. I gave him an introduction at Marge Cleveland's gallery. The media snapped him up. A hotcake."

"It's a beautiful piece," I said, walking around it again.

"For inspiration I keep it here. Evan and I were, are, quite close." Her voice made me glance up, a hiss of emotion quivered out that I'd not heard from her before. She stood illuminated against the windows, and I saw strength in her profile, in the sharp, clean structure of her face — cheekbones, long straight nose, point of chin. "I miss him," she said.

"He's still in New York?"

She cleared her throat and turned slightly toward the charcoal self-portrait. "He loves the city. I don't think he could ever get enough of it. He came from a close-knit family upstate — not far from where I grew up myself."

"Where?"

"Canandaigua, New York. Where they've got the longest winters on earth. I know all about being shut up in a small provincial town." She straightened the pieces of charcoal into a line along the edge of the easel. "Evan's father and brother are both concert pianists, but his mother pushed him to find his own talent. A remarkable woman. She's an art critic — you might have heard of her?"

I shook my head ambiguously, not wanting to stop her reverie.

"Evan came to New York, we met, I sponsored him." She looked out the window at the trees. "I remembered how hard it was to get started. I thought he was very good. Very determined." She paused. "And he loved my work."

"How old is he?"

"Thirties." She sized me up. "About your age."

I was surprised. There had been an intimacy to her tone, a private sort of warmth, as she spoke of him, something implied but not stated.

"Two of, three after," she said then, checking first one wristwatch and then the other. "It's getting late."

"Why two watches?"

"Hedging my bets."

Not sure I understood, I decided to agree. "It is late." I stared at the lowered angle of the sunlight outside.

"I've got to get back to work."

"I have to get back to make supper anyway." I walked over

to where she stood. I studied the self-portrait for a minute. She hadn't caught herself yet, that haunted look.

"What do you think?" she asked.

I hesitated.

"Learn this about me," she said sharply. "If I ask, I want to know."

"The eyes are wrong," I answered then. "And you've left out the uneven quality your face has." I took up a charcoal and traced a new line on one of the studies, shading the jaw sharply, picking up the disparity of the eyes. "Here," I said. "Try a different angle here."

She looked at me, and then back at the paper. For a minute I couldn't tell what she'd thought of my comment, but then she picked up the charcoal and began to sketch the line I'd drawn. I put my hand on her arm, but she didn't turn, just sort of murmured goodbye, already lost in the possibilities.

I left, letting myself out the back door quietly. I knew what that concentration was like, how it came over you in a wave of high-shooting adrenaline. I knew how precious it was and how fast it faded. I walked slowly through the woods toward home. If I were lucky, we might be friends, I thought. If I were very lucky, she might look at my portrait of Jamie and give her opinion. And then I recoiled, again surprised with myself: the idea of showing anything at all, even a sketch, always made me queasy with anxiety — but maybe not with her. With her I felt warm and full, and it wasn't from the beer.

"I'm saying it's too late!" Tobie stood with her hands on her hips in the middle of the kitchen, arguing with Jamie. As I walked through the door he ran to me, threw his arms around my knees, and put an appealing face up toward mine.

"Pent," he said, his cap pulled down crooked over one ear. "Wanna fingapent."

I looked over at Tobie. "Dinner's already behind," she said

with exasperation. "You've been gone all afternoon, and I'll not take out a raft of those paints and have him making some big mess."

Anna and Meggie were sitting quietly and playing with the dolls in front of the fireplace. "Here," I said, slipping the basket off my arm. I handed it to my mother-in-law craftily, a peace offering. "A surprise for you. Let me worry about Jamie now."

Distracted, she peered into the basket with an exclamation of surprise. "Burdock!"

"Thought you'd be pleased," I said, shooing Jamie over to the table and quickly setting out paint, paper, and a water cup. Once settled in with his paints, he too was quiet. Tobie went to the sink and began peeling the stems carefully.

"Been out in the woods all this time?" she asked, grudgingly curious as she bent to pull a pan from the bottom cupboard with a grunt.

"For a while. Then I ran into our new neighbor." I went to the refrigerator and got out the wax beans for tonight's supper. Someone had already picked the peas, I saw. My garden was yielding a bounty this summer.

The screen door banged and Sam came in. He sat down at the table across from Jamie wearily.

I planted a kiss on the back of his sunburned neck. "I was just telling Tobie I met our new neighbor, and you'll never guess what she does for a living."

"You're right," he said, rubbing his eyes with his forefinger and thumb. "I'll never guess — better just tell me."

"Paints," I answered smugly. "She's a well-known artist, and the addition she built is the most phenomenal studio I've ever seen. She must've paid Ted Mullins a mint!"

"Seems a stretch to call making pictures earning a living," Tobie commented with acerbity, dropping the greens into the boiling water. She lit her Camel from the gas burner and inhaled while she stirred.

I ignored her sour remark, thinking of the Hallmark check in my back pocket which had come in this afternoon's mail. I crossed to the sink and began washing up my mushrooms, watching my husband. He was slumped, resting his chin on his palm, looking very discouraged. I stopped what I was doing.

"The mares?" I sat down beside him.

He nodded. "The two we lanced this morning don't seem much better."

"Duet's not sick, is she, Daddy?" Anna asked anxiously. Duet was last year's birthday present, due to foal in late August. Anna was concerned with every minute aspect of her health.

"She's fine, sweetie," Sam said reassuringly. "I even put her out in the back pasture to keep her away from the other sick horses."

"Will they get well?"

"I hope so. We gave them a new kind of shot today."

Reassured, she went back to her dolls, but I could tell from Sam's face that he wasn't nearly so certain as he'd let her think. "What about those new shots?" I asked. "You said the vet —"

"Mommee!" Jamie interrupted, demanding my attention. He had his hand palm-deep in the brand-new pots of red, yellow, and blue paint I'd special-ordered secretly from Boston last month. "See what I mek!" He held up a dripping square, once white, now totally covered with starburst swirls of red and orange. There was nothing recognizable on the page, but I noted the way he'd put the colors down, red on the bottom, yellow lying on top. Then he'd drawn a gentle finger through for a shade of orange that varied with the pressure he'd applied at different points. I was sure he had an eye for color, and then I laughed at myself a little: he was only two and already I had him competing with Gauguin. I reminded myself of Dr. Loring's cautions.

"What colors did you use, Jamie?" I asked, distracted away from Sam and the mares and leaning across the table to see better. He flipped up a clean white page and made me another picture, this time using blue and yellow. He was left-handed for sure, just like me — the only other leftie in the family.

"I mek geen," he said, holding up his stained fingertip with pleasure. "Here dak" — he pointed to the deepest part of the tone — "here light," pointing to the palest shade.

I laughed with delight. He'd figured it out so easily. Meggie didn't even like to fingerpaint yet; she hated the sensation of muddy paint against her skin. It was too messy. Maybe it even scared her a little.

Jamie's stubby fingers were stained black now from all the different tonalities of the dye, and his face was nearly as well decorated as his paper. "What's in this picture?" I asked, pointing to another on the floor. He'd lined them up, five in a row.

"That Meggee," he said, sure of himself.

I squinted at the fat round shapes, making out arms, legs, head, body, and an enormous growth under the arm, a lump nearly as big as Meggie herself. "What's this?"

"That Meggee dawl," he answered scornfully.

"Oh, of course," I nodded, smothering a laugh at my own ignorance. "And what about this picture?" I picked up the last sheet: two stick figures stood wavering inside a large square and then were duplicated on a smaller scale and looking more solid, outside the square.

"That Meggee too," he said, smiling up at me happily. "Meggee an' Jamee pay in Mommee woom."

"They were playing in your bedroom mirror earlier," Tobie explained as she sat down at the table with her plate. "He couldn't get over how there were two of Meggie and two of him." She squashed out her cigarette and scooped up the wild vegetables with a spoon.

I looked back at the fingerpainting, again amazed. "God,"

I muttered, realizing how high my hopes for him really were; if he were to regress now, it would be an enormous disappointment to me. It frightened me to think that his talent might be only my desire.

"Something wrong?" Tobie looked up.

"No," I said slowly. "How are the ferns?"

"Good thing there's one pioneer in this family," she said, butter in a shiny ring around her mouth. She'd taken her teeth out again, I saw. The burdock was soft, easy to gum. "Never could get Sam interested in anything wild."

I smiled, drawn back to her for a minute, remembering how easy things had been between us when all I'd wanted was to please her, when I'd let her be like a mother to me. Sometimes I wished it could be like that again — simple, easy, our roles well-defined. It gave me pleasure to see her enjoy what I had foraged for.

I looked over at Sam to see if he'd caught his mother's tease. But he was pushing himself back from the table and taking the bowl full of pea pods out onto the porch. I watched him through the window as he sat down in Tobie's old wooden rocker and began to shell the peas into a bowl on his lap. Anna was helping him, sort of, while Meggie played on the stoop.

I felt a pang of guilt: Sam had been talking to me and I'd let Jamie interrupt. I should have made it a point to listen, really listen, tonight, when he was so worried. I got up and went to stand in the doorway, pressing my nose against the mesh of the screen. Sam didn't look up at me. He was talking to Anna, telling her a story. Meggie was playing with her new doll on the edge of the steps.

"Where'd you get that?" Sam asked, pointing at the doll.

I shrugged, trapped into a lie. "It was one of my old ones. My mother brought it up last trip."

Sam sent me a sharp look.

"What's your problem?" I asked, irritated. Why didn't he just say what was on his mind?

"I'm short of cash to buy the mares the shots they need, and you're off buying new dolls. These kids've got enough stuff to fill a museum!"

"That's not fair, Sam! Not at all!"

"You're not going to try and tell me she *needed* a new doll?"

I was silent. I could hardly say I'd bought the doll yesterday out of guilt, that she'd needed it — yes, needed it — because her mother had been hard on her. "One doll isn't going to break the bank, Sam." I dug into my back pocket.

"And what about those fingerpaints you bought Jamie?"

"Sam, if he has talent, he's going to need special —"

"If!" he exploded. "It's a pretty big 'if' at this stage. And it doesn't change the fact we haven't got enough money for the important things, much less —"

"Nurturing his talent *is* an important thing," I interrupted angrily. "Maybe the problem is you don't have any respect for what I do. How would you feel if Jamie really turned out to be an artist?"

"Are you and Mommy going to fight again?" Anna tugged on Sam's knee.

Her remark cooled me off. I just glared at Sam and we were silent. I asked myself why we kept doing this to each other. I fished the envelope from my back pocket and handed it to him. "I was going to wait till after supper, but never mind that now," I said. "It came in this afternoon's mail. Four hundred fifty dollars should take care of the shots."

He didn't say anything, just sat on the edge of the rocker, fingering the check.

"I didn't mean that your painting isn't important," he said very quietly, after a minute. "Or that making sure Jamie gets what he needs isn't a priority. But, Allie —" His voice cracked. "Reality right now is those mares. My dream."

I went behind the rocker and put my arms around him. His dream. I should remember that more often. I stroked the back of his head.

Anna went over and began to drag Meggie's wooden horse up and down the porch on its string. She was marching back and forth, like a soldier on watch, waiting to see what would happen next. Everything was quiet except for the rolling noise the toy made over the floorboards.

The horse was built on a little stand with wheels, about six inches high, and cleverly constructed so that as the child pulled, it rocked up and down on its front legs. I let my eyes follow the horse's motion, and they grew lazy and unfocused. My brain was mesmerized. Sam had made each twin one of these horses before they were born, and they'd gotten very attached to them as soon as they could walk and pull them through the dust in the front yard: the horse left an interesting track behind it in the dirt. Jamie liked to tie his to his chair at meals, as if the table were a hitching post.

I remembered the night Sam had sat in front of the fire with Anna, showing her how he could carve the horses from a solid piece of ash. It was a night suffused with contentment: a good meal, the heat of the oak logs as it reflected off our cheeks, a deep bucket of popcorn and two mugs of hot cider, one child at Sam's feet and a pinwheel of kicks from two babies yet to be born. I'd asked him whether he hoped the twins would be boys or girls, and he'd turned from the fire, the ruddy glow turning his hair to gold, and said that a boy would be nice, but two girls would be even better. I'd been puzzled by that. "You'd be satisfied with no sons?" I'd asked in surprise. "Girls are special," he'd said, with that long, slow grin of his. "Boys . . ." He shrugged. "Maybe it makes me think too much of my own dad."

Now I watched him, out here on the porch knee-deep in his girls. And yet Jamie held a special place in his heart too.

All of a sudden I was thinking very clearly; I was seeing this scene etched against the late, low sunlight as if I were sketching it. I saw the gold light glinting off Sam's, Anna's, and Meggie's heads, falling in soft yellow patches over the cracked and comfortable wooden furniture. I heard the last heavy buzz of the cicadas before they drowsed out into evening, and from far away I heard Rebecca's voice, too, telling me about her own father, about a man who liked to beat his sons at every game. Our girls gave Sam no competition. As much as he needed Jamie, as much as he might want him to carry on what he'd done with BoxTie and with the essence of what he was, Jamie was still a male, and that made it all so much more complicated. In the generational mirror of father and son, Sam had still been arguing with Carson when he died, and so the girls were now less of an emotional threat.

Anna came to sit on the steps in front of us.

"Mommy?" She half turned, so I could see her profile silhouetted against the lowering sunlight.

"Mmm?"

"Where are my grandpas? Why don't they come to see us — like on my last birthday when Grandma Lynne came from Boston?"

All year I'd been waiting for a few pointed questions about sex, and had even prepared myself — read a book or two on what to say and how much to tell — but somehow this one had never occurred to me, and I hadn't worked up an appropriate, enough-but-not-too-much answer. I waited for a minute and looked down at Sam, wondering what he was thinking. "My father died when I was seventeen, and your daddy's when he was twenty," I said at last, going around to sit on the floor in front of the rocker. I leaned back against Sam's knees, and Anna leaned back against mine. I stroked her hair.

"Are they in cow heaven?" Anna wanted to know.

I stifled a laugh and felt Sam shift behind me, coughing suddenly to cover a snort. I elbowed him: she shouldn't think we took any of this lightly.

"What's cow heaven?" asked Sam.

"Grandma Lynne says that's where my Daisy went when she died."

I was trapped — and a little annoyed that my mother had told Anna something so preposterous. I didn't believe in heaven, but I didn't want to confuse Anna. And besides, who knew. Maybe there was some great green pasture in the sky, full of contented animals munching along in heavenly chorus.

"Well, your grandma knows a lot, and maybe Daisy is in cow heaven. But when *people* die," I underlined the word, "they're gone, that's all. We remember them in our hearts." I pointed to my chest and my head simultaneously. "We carry them with us always. I think about my daddy a lot and remember the things we did together and the good times we had." This was a pale shade of lie, but one made in a good cause.

"Why can't there be a people heaven too?" Anna asked insistently.

I opened my mouth and then shut it again. Why make her unhappy, especially when I *wasn't* sure I was right. I twisted to look up at Sam, and he shrugged. "I guess there could be," I conceded, feeling outsmarted.

"Good," she said, getting up again and banging in through the screen door. I watched her go, feeling sad for her, knowing that one day she would face my death, and Sam's. There were some things we couldn't protect her from. Still, I envied her the simplicity of her solutions: she wanted cow heaven and people heaven too, and she trusted that needing them would make them so. I hoped, for all our sakes, that this time her grandmother was right.

I moved up to sit in Sam's lap, and we hugged each other

for a minute. He kissed me, a long, slow kiss, a kiss that made me wet. Under my thigh I could feel him getting hard. We would make time to make love tonight.

I went back to the kitchen reluctantly to snap the beans. Standing at the sink, I looked over at my son finishing up his painting. An enormous surge of pride went through me, and then suddenly I felt guilty. I too played favorites, and I was certainly more patient with Jamie, even though he was the most demanding and difficult of the three. He made me feel the most needed; he made me feel the most like a mother; he made me feel everything I did feel the most intensely.

A daughter was easy familiarity, but a son was more of an adventure. Anna, Meggie, and I were all female, and I knew so much of what they would go through: the first tampon, the first hesitant kiss, the first wolf whistle, the first pair of pantyhose. These were the sorts of things I could never share with a son — but, on the other hand, a son was a chance to see the world in an entirely new way. Jamie was new territory, my lost half, the part of me never-born; on the day he emerged from me and became a separate being, a piece of my woman's body went on to become a man.

I took the colander to the stove and dumped the beans down into the kettle of boiling water. The steam came up onto my face hot and wet.

"Next Thursday we'll do the chickens," Tobie announced, going to the calendar to pencil in the date.

"Mmm," I said, thinking again of how I had been able to talk to Rebecca today. Her paintings disturbed me: she saw things which were not there. But what she'd said had helped me see something for the first time, something which had been there all along.

I shook some salt into the boiling water and went to the door to tell everyone to wash up for supper. Sam had enticed Jamie outside and, in the driveway, was teaching him how to catch a ball, his big hands engulfing those little dirty fingers. I had a hard time picturing Carson — stern, practical, single-minded — showing a young Sam how to throw a ball: maybe that's why Sam could do it now with Jamie. Their faces were intent, full of love. I smiled. Here, too, was a painting.

I liked Rebecca. Still, it never occurred to me that she might like me too — at least, not enough to come looking for me the very next day. But as I stood over my jelly kettle at the kitchen stove the next afternoon, I saw her walk through the back garden from the woods we held in common. She made an excuse, of course, about why she'd come, but I realized she must be lonely up there, all alone. Maybe even as lonely as I was down here, surrounded.

The children were shy around her: they weren't used to strangers. Meggie hid behind a chair. Anna ignored her and concentrated on her jigsaw puzzle. Only Jamie came over, after a minute, to squint at her from under his cap's duckbill visor, his mouth open, bumping against my knees for security. He tugged on my hand. "Brown," he said, pointing with one finger at Rebecca. "Boo. One brown, one boo."

I looked up at her, puzzled at first and then mortified. He was pointing right at her eyes: one brown, one blue. I pushed his hand back into my lap and tried to distract him with a book. I didn't know what to say. There was an awkward silence and then I apologized. "I'm sorry," I said. "It's an impossible age. Last week in the market he asked Mrs. Baskins how come she was so fat."

Rebecca laughed. "He's just bright, that's all." She tried to make it sound as if she didn't care, but there were two bright spots of color on her cheekbones.

"He's rude." I shook my head and laughed.

She shrugged, eased by my honesty. "At that age you probably were, too."

I offered her a cup of coffee and we sat at the kitchen table, the windows steamed over from the bubbling kettle and its deep magenta brew, the yellow nets of cheesecloth already lining the sieves for straining, the Ball jars clanking against each other in the water bath, the paraffin set over low heat to melt. The smell of strong coffee drifted and married with the fragrance of ripe berries. Jamie was fascinated by her watches, and, after a minute's hesitation, she took them off and let him play with them.

"Your kids like to fingerpaint." She gestured at the bulletin board and lit up one of her thin black cigars.

"That's Jamie," I answered proudly, untacking the stiff, wrinkled sheets and passing them over a bit anxiously. "It's very unusual for a child this young."

"You sound like a Hollywood stage mother!" She leaned back, amused.

It was my turn to blush. "Well," I said. "Well. A little, maybe."

"A young Gauguin?" she teased. "Or maybe you were fantasizing Klee?"

I looked away, then started to laugh, admitting my own hopes.

"It never hurts to dream," she said, tossing the paintings down. "If you've got the time. Better just to work, I think." She took a drag of her cigar. "Maybe when he's five you'll see whether or not *he* sees."

Tobie banged in through the screen door but stopped short when she saw I had a visitor.

As I introduced her to Rebecca I could tell from the set of her face that she wasn't inclined to like my new friend. She'd made up her mind last night. She sat down at the trestle table and pulled out her account books and began to work on balancing the ledger. With relief I saw that we could just carry on as though she weren't there: she obviously didn't want to be disturbed.

"Where do you work?" Rebecca asked, looking around her

at the clutter: bright-colored pots of fingerpaint, loose sheets
of paper, an avalanche of small wooden blocks, a red hobby-
horse, a large fire truck. I was newly aware of how much
noise the children made, as if I were seeing my own home
for the first time, through her eyes.

"I have the attic all to myself."

"That sounds a bit hot, and dark."

I wished she didn't sound so critical in front of Tobie.

Tobie straightened her back and looked up from her papers.
"We did a lot of work up there for Allie," she said. "Not
many can afford to go around just adding on to their places."

She was threatened, I realized — afraid of Rebecca, and
defensive about us and our home. I got up quickly and began
to stir the jelly to cover the ensuing silence. Tobie had never
really understood my painting or, more important, my need
to paint, so she couldn't appreciate my excitement at finding
another painter in such proximity.

"More coffee?" I asked now, hoping Rebecca would be
impervious to my mother-in-law's sarcasm.

She shook her head. "I'm fine. You spend your mornings
up there?" she went on.

"Most mornings," I said, throwing a pointed glance at Tobie.
The spoon moved through the sweet, heavy syrup in a circle;
round and round I pushed it. Rebecca wanted me to take her
up to the attic, just as she had taken me to her studio yesterday: it was to be a trade of intimacies. But I was nervous.
It was not really my studio that she wanted to see.

"How d'you find Arrowsic?" Tobie asked, looking up at
Rebecca, with one corner of her mouth tucked down in disapproval. She was inviting Rebecca to make some touristy
comment about the rustic beauty of the town.

"Quiet. A good place to work." Rebecca was playing too,
and I realized then that she could match Tobie.

Tobie grunted and looked away.

Rebecca sipped her coffee and then shook some salt into

it. Her silence pushed at me. I kept stirring. The jelly in the kettle was quite thick now. She was waiting. "Sam fixed up the attic for me so I could have a place that was *private*," I said at last, coming back to sit down.

"And that's how you like it? Private?" She raised the eyebrow over her left eye, the blue one. It was a habit. "In a closet maybe?"

I just stared at her with astonishment. I looked into her knowing face and instinctively reached to comfort myself by touching the top of Jamie's head. He sat at my feet building a tower of blocks that stretched upward, growing more and more precarious by the minute.

"Would you like to come up?" I asked, my horror at what I was doing striking down deep, like lightning to the ground.

She smiled. She'd won.

My motion to stand was nearly automatic. "Tobie?"

"Go, go — I'll finish the jelly." She motioned us away grouchily. Jamie's protest at my exit was only a small mosquito hum in my head next to the uproar of my own protest — multivoiced, a crashing of cymbal and drum at taking someone into my sanctuary.

We walked up the steep attic steps. It was silent here, the noises of the kitchen left far behind. The heat increased, probably close to 95 degrees, like nearing the source, the sun. I unlocked the door at the top of the stairs.

My space was small compared to Rebecca's airy expanse, but it had a messy, cozy feel. I cranked open the skylights Sam had installed in the roof and turned on the ceiling fan. The intense heat dropped away from us in a warmish breeze. Up here the light was soft gold, filtering through the skylights and the large windows at either end of the attic to illuminate the thousands of tiny dust motes which drifted through the dry air. There were canvases stacked along the walls, glass jars of brushes and paint lined up under the eaves, large metal cans of turpentine stacked in one corner, several heaps of stained rags mounded under the single easel. A small table was crowded with the tools of our craft. I was no better a housekeeper here than anywhere else in the house, and dust kitties were balled in the corners of the room. The old sofa on which I sometimes stretched out just to think was leaking its stuffing onto wide oak floorboards freckled with many colors.

We'd decided to leave the slope of the rafters bare, because I liked all that exposed aged wood and the sensation of being cradled beneath the slant of the eaves. Knowing I had the hands of a hundred years to back me up made everything feel solid and safe.

My canvases were stacked in neat chronological piles, probably the only area of my life in which I was orderly, logical, rooted to both concept and routine.

"Your husband did all this for you?" She lit another cigar and picked up an old coffee can lid to use as an ashtray.

I nodded. "It was just a bare space before, filled with about a hundred filthy storage boxes. He put in a lot of time."

"He's supportive of your work then." Her voice held a tinge of admiration.

"Sam never sees anything I'm working on. No one comes in here. My work is separate from my family."

"From the world," Rebecca observed, going to the corner and beginning to flip through the canvases, as if this were the most natural thing in the world to do without asking. "Still," she said over her shoulder, "he did a lot of work here. Not every man would."

I couldn't concentrate on Sam's virtues: my heart pounded and it was hard to catch my breath. I was sweating. To fight the nausea I pressed the back of my hand against my mouth.

"May I see the rest?" she asked, turning aside at last from the stacks of watercolors, oils, and charcoals.

"Rest?" I said, looking at her dumbly.

"All that you don't have out. There must be more," she

said, impatient now at having to explain. "I can tell that a lot of these are your commercial commissions. Where is your own work?"

I shrank from the request. I couldn't show her — I just couldn't. Maybe I was a coward, but I didn't care.

"To hide is safer than to show," she said shrewdly, palming her bangs off her forehead.

Still I didn't answer. I was miserable: I was failing the test I had set for myself. I thought of her canvases — those flat, bold colors, all the things hidden under everyday objects — and knew I couldn't show her. She would laugh. She was a famous artist: for as many years as I had lived, she had painted, evaluated, assessed. And my work was too different from hers. Not nearly so good as hers. She would see nothing in what I'd done, and somehow I couldn't bear the idea of that.

"Look, eventually you're going to need *someone's* reaction — if you're serious, that is. You can't paint in a vacuum forever. It all depends on what it's worth to you, what you're willing to pay to grow and get better."

I looked at her, knowing it was true. I'd been alone with all this for too many years. I would have to let someone in. I thought of the one canvas, the only one I could possibly show her. That's when my need outweighed my fear. I wanted someone else's eyes to tell me what they saw.

As if it were a dream, I went to the closet, took the key from the ledge above, and unlocked it. I shuffled through the canvases and pulled out the one of Jamie in the garden. I hadn't done anything more since the day I'd painted it. Maybe Rebecca could help me see it better. I had no objectivity about it, and I didn't know how to go on with it. I didn't even know if it was finished. Now it seemed an awkward, clumsy expression of emotion, and its faults made me stand very still, staring at it.

"Give me five more," she said.

"But —"

"Five. I want to see why you picked this one first."

I went back to the closet, numb, and selected at random. I handed them over, and then, in the light of the window, she stood studying them, silent a long time.

"You're right to pick this above the others," she said, her voice excited. "This is the best of them all — and the others aren't bad." She looked at me appraisingly. "I can't believe you're still hiding in your attic. You'll have to work very hard. But the possibilities . . ."

I turned my palms upward and bowed my head, waiting.

"I like the juxtaposition of sun and stars here. The yellow heat," she said slowly, after a minute. "The suggestion of layers of reality, something lurking behind what we see. The contradictions of the sky and land, of the seasons and colors. It's intriguing." She sighed. "Of course, it's a little bit derivative — but that's not unusual. We're all derivative from time to time. The impasto, the palette you've used — a little bit of inspiration from van Gogh." She laughed and shook her head. "But it's truly your own. And you've got to keep stretching in just that direction."

She hadn't really answered what I most wanted to know. "But what does it make you feel?"

She studied my face for a minute and then turned back to the painting. "Frightened by the pressure of this world I see leaking down through the sky. It's the opposite of the bottom falling out. Here it's the top that's falling out. And the little boy, crouching there all alone, the great weight above him."

"I don't know why I painted it."

"You didn't plan it, do a study?"

"Nothing. Just the oils onto the canvas."

"Is that how you usually work? So much here seems as if you'd done hundreds of studies . . ."

"I usually do. I map the whole thing out in my mind, and

then on paper in lots of small sketches. It's a way of keeping control."

"Too much control," she interjected. "You have to let things surprise you more. Straight from the unconscious to your brush." She put it down and backed away from it, to see it better. "Here you're looking beneath the surfaces," she mused with a smile. "And that's why I like it. Of course, I'm biased." She laughed, and I knew this was an oblique reference to her own work. "It's an unconscious vision — like an instinct. You can't sketch it first. And that's why some of the others don't . . . *complete* themselves. There's a sense of something aimed at and just missed."

I felt my face grow red and hot, and I tried to concentrate on the possibilities she saw in this canvas, not the failures she saw in the others. "But I can't seem to finish." I hesitated. "I think I'm scared to finish it."

"When a painting comes from deep inside you, it taps something, draws off something you know but don't know, something you see but don't see." She shrugged. "To me, a good painting — that is, one that *works* — helps me to see what is not, as well as what is." Again she shrugged. "I think this one's finished right now."

"But I don't want to leave it like this," I answered quickly. "I guess I don't want it to be true." I was feeling my way along, groping after something I hadn't even worked out in my own mind. "I never want Jamie to be alone like that," I said, breaking through to the truth. "I want to be there for him always. For all of them."

She looked at me with surprise. I realized how naive it sounded and stared at the floor, embarrassed again.

"Someday you'll die," she said, inhaling and then crushing the cigar out against the plastic lid. There was a faint sizzle as the synthetic scorched. "They'll be on their own then, and alone. It's a fact of life."

I nodded. Of course, she was right. It was basic. I refocused on what she was saying.

"When you unlock the closet," she went on, tapping her high forehead, "you won't always like what you find."

She turned aside, as if to let me recover, and rummaged through more of the canvases in the closet. I blocked out everything from my mind except the idea that she'd thought the painting had strength.

"You have many styles here," she said, flipping through one after the other. "Technically you've mastered a great deal. But you're relying on the technique — that sense of your own draftsmanship — far too much. Leave that to architects. Be a little less controlled and more messy. Let your heart in, as you've done in this painting of your little boy. Your own voice — it's there. Wavering maybe, young maybe, but it's there." She pulled out a small watercolor and pen of a bed of fiddleheads done in cross section, so that the root system and the rock bed beneath the earth were visible. "This one, for instance. Here I feel more of your particular sightline, although it's very different from the oil. Still, it shows an underside. I like it," she concluded. "It could really be a *New Yorker* cover."

"It could?" I was pleased that she saw such a quality.

"You might try more like this — well, not *just* like this," she amended. "But a lot of little sketches to get at the element of revealing rather than representing. That kind of exercise might help you with bigger projects."

"Do you think it's bad for me to do the other?" I asked, gesturing toward the piles of commercial work.

"You have a choice." She looked me up and down, her face stern and frank. "If you let the world into this room, eventually you might not need calendar art as a financial crutch. You might make it on the value of what *you* value. But you'll have to take a risk." She shrugged. "Concentrate here." She tapped the fiddleheads. "And remember — you never know what'll sell."

From the door came a scratching noise.

"You keep a dog up here, too?" Up went the eyebrow again.

"That's Jamie. A game we play." I laughed, suddenly exhilarated. "You can see I don't get much time to myself. That's his way of saying he wants me back downstairs."

Jamie's hand was now visible, wedged into the gap between the bottom of the door and the floor, his stubby fingers curled upward as if to touch me. Every day he called me down to lunch in just this way. I crossed over and laid my finger across his palm. A squeal of delight came from the other side of the old oak door. "Mommeecum!"

"I'd better get back to my jelly," I said, reluctant now to leave.

Rebecca nodded. "I've enjoyed this."

I blushed. "I enjoyed having you here — much to my own shock." I laughed again, amazed to realize that that was indeed true. Never before had I had someone understand what I was trying to do. Her analyses had been precise and her advice wise. Later I would try another sketch from memory. Maybe the real world was too much in my way.

"Nothing's ever as hard as you think it will be," she said, turning to go out the door. "That's one thing I've learned."

I repressed my urge to laugh, to jump up and down in delight. I felt like a little kid who just got an A. What I'd painted had power enough to make her feel something.

I couldn't wait to come back upstairs after supper, after storytime and bathtime and bedtime. I set the canvas of Jamie on the easel and did not drape it. And then, for the first time ever, I went downstairs without locking the closet door.

Slaughtering

I tied the Wyandotte's feet to the clothesline with a loop of cord and let him swing upside down, squawking and flapping against the air. Sam and Tobie and I were stained red, and our ears rang with a cacophony of protest from our victims. It was murder pure and simple, but it was murder that enabled us to eat.

Today was Thursday and — as Tobie had decided last week — we were slaughtering twenty fat cockerels of mixed breed: some Leghorn, some Barred Rock, some Rhode Island Red. We'd been at it for over an hour, ever since the children went down for naps. It was not a good day for it, far too hot for such messy work, but it was the day Tobie had set aside. I'd tried to talk her out of it and had even appealed to Sam, but my opinions had been overruled. Resentment made me angry and more aggressive than usual as we herded the fowl into a pen and separated those to be killed from the hens to be kept for laying. I could see Sam watching me as I went about the task without a trace of my usual squeamishness.

It was my job to tie them to the line and stretch their necks taut toward the ground. Then Sam slit their throats with a sharp knife. Tobie sliced open their bellies and emptied them out. Later we would pluck them, cut off their heads and feet, butcher them into cooking-sized pieces. This was the way poultry had been slaughtered at BoxTie for the last eighty years; Sam's father had learned the method from his father.

The first time we'd done it I'd begged Sam just to chop off their heads and be done with it: even a decapitated chicken running in circles seemed better than this drip-drip-drip torture. But Tobie explained it was important to let them bleed, upside down, because it made for more tender meat. I was repulsed and taken aback by my own reaction. After all, wasn't this what I'd wanted, the harsh reality of farm life? Even Frank Perdue did it this way, Sam insisted.

I'd considered becoming a vegetarian, but then I thought of chicken skin, buttery, roasted crisp with herbs, or a juicy drumstick at midnight when the rest of the house was asleep, or a bowl of chicken soup for a cold winter's lunch, and the way it made you feel nourished and coddled and cared for. No, I'd decided, it was too much to give up: I'd just have to get used to the grisly truth of how it got to the table. After all, I was getting used to a lot of things here.

The sun poured down thick and hot, like syrup from the sky, and a big botfly circled us with persistence as we worked. Tobie had crossed off the last square of July on the Purina Horse Feed wall calendar that morning, and I'd been a little sad to see the month out, despite the succession of 90-degree days, of close, unbreathable air, of acrid dust. With August the days would begin to shorten: my reading time with Sam on the porch under the last rays of sunset would end a little earlier each night, and our morning rising would be a little darker.

Until yesterday, I hadn't seen Rebecca since the week before, on the day she'd invaded my studio. She'd ended up staying for supper that night, and at first Sam had been wary around her. But then she'd teased him a little, gotten him to laugh, and that night at bedtime he told me he was glad I'd found a friend. On Tuesday, having worked a whole week on several different pieces which relied heavily on her suggestions, I'd allowed need and curiosity to take me back up to the Larson place under the pretext of delivering some of the jelly we'd made last week. Once I was inside the house, Rebecca was eager to get me into her studio: her self-portrait was finished now, and it caught not only the unevenness of her face, as I'd suggested, but a lonely, empty air as well. She had also begun a new oil painting, of Evan Hirsch, but there was something muddy and confused about it, as if she couldn't make up her mind in which direction she wanted to go, and she admitted to me that she wasn't satisfied. We spent most of my painting hours talking, and then I'd come home invigorated and ready to tackle my projects upstairs. I'd asked Tobie for the extra time away from the children and she'd given it, without comment.

This morning as I wrote last night's dream in my journal I realized that Rebecca was still buzzing around in my mind. In the dream I took the watercolor drawing of the fiddlehead ferns and went to the post office to mail it. That same afternoon Mr. Stiles's mail truck pulled up the driveway to deliver back the package I'd just sent out. Then he turned to look at Jamie, who was standing beside me, and said that he'd be expecting my son's package soon. He drove off and that was when I noticed, for the first time, that my package was wrapped up in newspaper and string — lots and lots of string, like a spiderweb. Jamie emptied his pockets then and pulled out a blue marble, a newt, a penny, a flip-top, a braided strand of mare's tail, a piece of gravel, and a star-shaped chunk of thick red glass. He waved the blue marble over the strings around my package and my painting was suddenly free of its cocoon.

I had woken this morning with a new idea in my mind, something Rebecca had suggested the week before, and after breakfast I'd gone up to my studio and pulled the watercolor from the closet. Rebecca had been right: it was a small work, but a good one. I carried it down to the kitchen table and began to wrap it, in brown paper and lots of string — enough to keep it safe, but not enough to suffocate it. Still, my hands were shaking, fumbling over the knots. I laughed at my own ridiculous growing pains and made myself tie it up, called long-distance information, got the address for the *New Yorker*, and wrote out the label. Before my subconscious could interfere, I set off for the post office, and the library in Manchester, promising Sam that I'd be back in plenty of time to help with the chickens this afternoon.

My own boldness in mailing the drawing had put me in a fine mood now. As I tied up another bird, my thumbs expert at knotting the cord, I smiled at my husband's typically impatient look. It was slippery, messy work, the sort of work his father had enjoyed, but I knew Sam only wanted to be done with it and back to his horses. He shifted the bird so that its feet stopped jerking about, and I finished securing it to the line. There were seven in a row now, beating their wings against each other, flurrying and flapping in their desperation to escape the unnatural position. They'd escape, all right.

To one side, Tobie worked methodically from her lap with a lit Camel clenched in her teeth, slitting the first load of feathered bellies with a small sharp knife and sliding the guts into the pail between her knees with a liquid *slush*. Every once in a while she exhaled the smoke through her nose like a dragon in a Chinese junk shop.

Sam and I moved to the head of the clothesline and I steadied the first, stretching its neck down toward the wet red earth so that he could make a clean cut. He did it exactly, right in between the rings of bony cartilage, slicing short the fowl's noise. Blood flowed over my hand as I held the wound open and let it collect in the pail at my feet; the cockerel gurgled as air bubbled out around the slit in its windpipe, and its thrashing slowed.

Despite the gore, I was curiously happy. Maybe I'd finally adjusted to the blood and guts of it all. Or maybe I'd just discovered some small cache of mild sadism in my personality. I'd hated those chickens for months — they'd tripped me, pecked me, shit on my sneakers — and now I was getting rid of some of them. I'd never pulled the wings off flies when I was little or put frogs in milk bottles with cherry bombs to watch them explode, and the sense of power was a new and heady pleasure.

We worked our way down the line, each incision going smoothly, one after another; I hummed a Sousa march at our precision and efficiency. There was an exhilaration in doing something few would be able to do, in confronting the cycle of life and death head-on — in a way my mother never could have — and I smiled up at my husband simply because it felt good to stand next to him.

The tension between us had eased some over the last week. The check from Hallmark had bought enough shots from the vet so that the mares looked as if they would recover, and we'd been able to inoculate the rest to prevent them from developing the infection. For some reason Jamie had been sleeping a bit later. Sam and I had been spending a little extra time in bed in the mornings, and we hadn't wasted it. Starting our day with loving had changed the way we looked at each other all day long. Even the brief skirmish over slaughtering the chickens today instead of tomorrow had remained just that: a brief skirmish. I smiled at Sam as we made our way along the clothesline, thinking that if we hurried, maybe there might be time to go upstairs before the kids woke from their naps.

But number five on the line was a big, tough bird worthy only of the soup pot: a Rhode Island Red, a hen past laying. She pecked at my hand as I reached for her, and I grabbed her hard, but she'd already sensed what was going to happen. I had to struggle to keep her wings from beating at the air and swinging her back and forth unsteadily on the line. Anna called her Mildred the Monster because of her size — a nickname I suddenly regretted as I stood bracing her throat for the cut. Her beady eye blinked at me, unforgiving and proud. She'd been one of Tobie's most regular layers for the last ten years.

I looked up at Sam in his spattered workshirt, his blond hair matted against his forehead with sweat and dirt and heat. Our gazes snagged for a minute and I knew that he, too, despite all logic, was thinking of that nickname, was maybe even a little bit saddened by it. In a rush it came back to me then, everything I'd seen in him the first time we met, everything I'd felt beating out of him, everything that was part of me now, too. I saw it clearly for the first time as I worked beside him as a willing executioner: Sam had helped me make it mine, had unknowingly shown me everything that grew up from underneath the dirt — the roots, the mold, the precious mushroom. Without Sam I might never have done my drawing of the fiddleheads.

Our hands touched as we tried to hold the chicken still, and our fingers were slippery. At last Sam made the cut, but it was a bad one. The hen struggled, beat her wings against us, rained her blood down our shirtfronts. We were immobilized there, mesmerized by the vicious struggle, feeling it, living it. My bravado caved in against her desperation. I wished she would just hurry up and die. Sam made another cut, his face grim now, and then another for good measure.

We should have gone on to the next chicken, just left behind her wretched thrashing and its inevitable result, but we couldn't move. We still held her between us, the blood spreading across our hands as her pulse and flutter gradually slowed and stopped. Sam and I looked over at one another and felt the chicken grow heavy — dead at last. We didn't take our eyes from each other's faces.

And then the hen grew lighter, as if something had escaped

out the messy gaping holes in her neck. I felt it go. I was startled and drew back, and I could tell Sam had felt it too.

"Off to cow heaven," I joked, feeling silly and a little rattled. He smiled. I thought of Anna and her never-ending questions, and then of light coming through clouds. I reached over to take his hand for a minute, glad he hadn't laughed at me, and suddenly I wanted to go into the house and lie in bed with him for the entire hot, cicada-buzzed afternoon.

But a shout from the back porch broke our concentration on each other: Anna, ready to run through the door with a wild whoop, and then Meggie and Jamie, crowding up behind her to push their pudgy little faces against the screen. The sheepdogs were there too, barking wildly and heaving themselves through the children's legs against the wire mesh. "Can we get up now?" Anna called. "We don't want to nap anymore!"

Things were pretty gory from where I stood: all the blood, and Mildred hanging upside down, a dead pile of feathers. Usually the kids napped the whole time we were slaughtering the chickens because it didn't take more than an hour or two to kill, clean, and pluck twenty or so. I looked over at Sam and shook my head vehemently.

"C'mon, Allie," he said. "I'll put the sprinkler on and they'll run around to cool off."

"I'm not sure they should see this." I gestured with a broad sweep of my arm to the mess we were making.

"This is our life here," Sam answered, his voice mild. "They've seen worse before, and they'll see worse again."

"But, Sam, look at Mildred — she's like a pet to them."

"So was Daisy," Tobie reminded us from the empty packing crate she'd been working on. "And Anna watched the vet put her down."

As Sam shouted at them to come out, I put my hands on my hips in exasperation. "The two of you . . ." I stopped midsentence, watching the kids and dogs stampede toward us, hollering and shoving. I wanted to protect them, spare them this sight, and then I thought of the trauma of my mother's overprotectiveness, of the shelter she'd tried to wrap me in and blind me with. Suddenly I remembered the importance, the urgency, of being different from that. And so when my children came barreling up to us, agape at the red earth and the dangling carcasses, I stopped myself from trying to hide anything. Explanation, logic, language — Tobie and Sam's way: that's what would keep Anna, Meggie, and Jamie safe and unafraid. Tobie whistled the dogs to her side; they panted and drooled at the sight of the blood and fresh meat, but a snap of her fingers dropped them at her feet.

"What's that, Mommee?" Jamie pointed to the pail filled with blood, which I held under the sixth chicken's neck.

"That's blood." I admired my own matter-of-factness.

"What's blood, Mommee?"

"Blood's the stuff that lives inside your skin, dodo-bird," Anna said smartly, twirling a little circle in the dust with the toe of her red Ked. "Like when you got that boo-boo on your knee and Dr. Loring gave you stitches."

Meggie nodded, obviously impressed, and Jamie bent over to look at the scar on his knee. Sam and I hid smiles.

"Where blood go?" he asked persistently, but Anna had already moved on to more important things.

"How come Mildred has three holes?" she asked, coming right up close for a better look. Meggie and Jamie gathered around in a semicircle. Blood dripped from the hen's windpipe in a steady red line, right into the dust at the tips of their sneakers.

"Daddy goofed," I said, wondering which of them would be first to cry.

"I pat Muddred," Jamie said, stretching on tiptoe to reach her head.

"I pat Mildred," Meggie said, unwilling to be outdone, but not quite tall enough to reach.

"You can't pat her," Anna said with disgust, pushing their hands away. "She's dead."

The twins looked at me, puzzled. I took a deep breath and got ready to launch into my little speech about always carrying in your heart the animals, and people, that you love. But that wouldn't, of course, explain why we would also carry Mildred to the soup pot tonight.

"Dead," Anna cut in before I could begin, her tone both important and informative, as if she were doing a "show and tell" at school, "is when you just lie around all the time. Dead is when you don't get to ride your pony or play on the tire swing or have birthday cake. Dead is when you can't see Mommy or Daddy — or even get spanked," she added, listing the one apparent asset. I caught myself hiding a grin and wanting to hug her. Sometimes she just seemed so wise, and so protective of them. Nothing I could have said would have made it nearly this concrete or understandable.

Jamie and Meggie absorbed their big sister's lecture and then turned away. My mouth flapped open. I turned to Sam, who started to grin. "They don't even care!" I felt lightened, thrilled by their resilience. "I can't believe it!" We started to laugh.

The three of them went over to the corner of the yard where the sandbox was and paid us no more attention than if we'd been hosing off the pickup. Anna got her shovel and pail and started Meggie and Jamie digging a castle for her dolls, directing them from above with her arms folded across her chest. It was clear who was boss. Sam and I watched for a minute and then went back to the clothesline.

Suddenly I couldn't wait to finish. My whole body was sticky, and it would take a long, hot bath to get rid of the red stains under my fingernails and around my cuticles. We moved quickly down the line, and after the last cut, Sam took his knife into the kitchen, out of mischief's way. I held the pail under the neck of the last chicken, and when the draining was nearly done, I set it down on the ground behind Tobie and went around to untie the first cockerel. They all had bled out nicely, and as I handed them over to my mother-in-law, I heard Anna, her voice smug with the satisfaction only a tattletale knows. "You're gonna get in *b-i-i-g* trouble, Jamie Yates. You're s'posed to paint on *paper!*"

I looked up, wiping my hands on my jeans, and saw Jamie crouched down in front of the whitewashed fence that encircled the back garden to keep out inquisitive raccoons and rabbits, his baseball cap twisted so that its visor pointed toward the ground. He glanced back over his shoulder at me, almost furtively, his hands, shirt, and pants bright red. Even the fence was streaked crimson.

He must have brought his paints from the house, I thought, and all at once was tired, irritable, sick of having to referee the adventures of a two-year-old. I gave the bird to Tobie and walked over to Jamie slowly, growing gradually more angry until I was furious, ready to put him up on the line and roast him right alongside Mildred.

He grinned up at me with mouth and teeth as red as if he'd been sucking penny-candy fireballs. He licked his stubby index finger. "I fingapent, Mommee," he said, pointing happily at the freeform design he'd smeared on the fence. "I mek wed!" And that was when I saw the half-empty pail of chicken blood at his feet.

He might as well have taken a bath in the bucket. He smelled like a charnel house, and his beautiful blond curls were matted down, his eyelashes stuck together. I gagged and turned to Sam. "Never again!" I said furiously. "I don't care what you say — next time we send the damned chickens out!"

Sam looked over from the bushel basket he was loading up with bodies. "You know we can't do that, Allie," he said, unimpressed with my disgust.

Money again, I thought: it was always money with him. Money — when our only son had been baptized with something less blessed than holy water. A blasphemy. "It's a filthy life," I cried, hugging Jamie against my chest. "And it's your fault. He's only two years old!"

"You didn't think it was so filthy a minute ago," Sam said.

"I'll clean him up." Tobie interrupted us and came over to take Jamie's hand. "No harm done. The fence'll wash."

"*I'll* take care of him," I said fiercely, pulling him back toward me and wrapping my arms around him. "They should never have been allowed out here in the first place."

"Don't get so riled," Tobie said, taking Jamie's hand again. "I've got to set the kettle on to boil so we can get started plucking. I'll just do him at the same time and you help Sam finish up here."

Like a stoked fire that suddenly combusts, my anger ignited. Resentment of my mother-in-law turned to fury. I was fed up with Tobie being rightest, oldest, wisest. I was fed up with backing up, tired of agreeing that her ways were best. I ached for something modern, something here and now, something suburban and safe — TV dinners, Herculon sofas, disposable diapers — and I held on to my son's hand, tight. "I won't let my kids grow up like this!"

Tobie just stared at me, as if I'd taken off all my clothes and were dancing around the yard naked.

Sam came over and plucked Jamie effortlessly from between us, lifted him up into the air, and tucked him beneath one arm. "Why're you so upset?" he asked, irritated at last, as he dragged the hose around the corner of the fence and squatted down to peel off Jamie's shorts and shirt. "He's just fine."

I stared at him and then looked over at Jamie, naked, tattooed red, putting his eye to the dark end of the hose and looking in to see the water on its way out.

Sam trudged back to the faucet. He turned to me, expecting a response. Tobie got up and went into the house.

I looked back again at Jamie, who was still waiting innocently for that surge of water. He wasn't hurt. He was happy.

He would wash; the fence would wash; the stains weren't permanent. My protectiveness subsided, and I saw suddenly that my fury at Tobie was not really over this incident. I'd simply gotten mad for all the other times I hadn't been able to get mad.

So I let all the angry air out of my lungs with a hiss. "He looks like a geek on the midway who bit off more than he could chew."

"That's terrible," Sam said, the corners of his mouth starting to stretch back in a grin.

"So turn the damned water on."

He smiled and twisted the spigot. The rush of cold water caught Jamie right in the face and he howled in surprise. I grabbed the hose and turned it upside down over his head. With a bar of saddle soap I scrubbed him till he faded from red to pink, despite his wriggling to get away. And as the picture of his bloodstained face faded, so did my fear.

By the time I was done washing him I was as wet as he. We were having a good time, using the hose like a giant tickle machine, and he squealed with delight as the frigid silver spray played across his back, tummy, and neck. As soon as they saw we were horsing around, the girls pulled off their clothes and sneakers and ran back and forth beneath the shining arc, trying to catch it with their hands. Anna managed to capture the hose and squirt me. I grabbed it away and squirted her back. We chased each other through the water for the better part of an hour, until I just couldn't run anymore.

Exhausted, I sat down in the grass and let the kids make a swamp of the yard. Tobie packed up the chickens and carted them off into the kitchen. Sam took down the clothesline and tied up a big garbage bag full of offal. I didn't even offer to help. I was having too much fun just sitting and watching my three urchins dance under a shower of wet stars. And I was painting in my head.

The sound of a car coming over the gravel drive out front interrupted my daydream of the painting I might do. I was still soaked from the hose, but everyone else was busy cleaning up, so I got up and went around front. A fat man with a cigarette clamped between his teeth was pushing himself out from behind the wheel of a long car with Maryland plates. I knew instantly he was a buyer. "Hang on," I said, before he could even open his mouth. "I'll get my husband for you."

I ran in the direction of the barn and found Joe on the main floor, currying Bay Lady. Looking remarkably unimpressed, he told me to calm down and then clumped off to show the buyer around. I went in search of Sam.

The day really didn't begin to cool off until around four o'clock, when the sun's light slanted down low enough to be filtered by the thick foliage of the trees. Tobie and I sat in the roomy wooden-slatted chairs in the side yard, watching Jamie and Anna fight over the tire swing. I wondered what luck Sam might be having with the fat man from Maryland.

Tobie had put her feet up and closed her eyes, her sheepdogs in a panting heap next to her chair. I watched Meggie, who was down the crest of the hill just beyond a thin stand of pine trees at the end of the driveway. I kept wondering if my mother-in-law was mad at me for what I'd said earlier, and part of me wanted to apologize, but another part wanted to leave it alone.

Meggie sat on a stool behind the table Sam set up every day in summer as a roadside stand. Both Anna and Meggie liked to play shopkeeper, selling raspberries, corn, and fresh eggs to the occasional customer, although the prices were plainly printed on a piece of cardboard and all Meggie really did was smile shyly. Generally we just left the produce out and trusted that people would put their fair share in the Ball jar, and for the most part they did — but sometimes Sam would come in swearing before supper, having discovered that some creep had emptied out the jar and walked off with the produce as well.

Now and again a car passed, slowly: I knew those people were taking a long, hard look at my pretty little girl in her checked apron. When people I didn't recognize stopped to buy a dozen eggs or a half-dozen ears of corn, I scrambled to my feet to run down the hill. I might trust them with my produce, but I didn't trust them with my kids.

The rich smell of Mildred bubbling in a kettle with fresh vegetables wafted out through the kitchen window. I'd never have thought of soup on a hot day, but Tobie insisted that hot soup on a hot night would cool you down. Anna had watched me as I'd put the plucked carcass in the pot: I had my fingers crossed that she wouldn't decide to enlighten Jamie and Meggie about the identity of our supper guest just as we sat down to eat.

Jamie came over to whine that Anna wouldn't let him on the swing. As I pushed his curls back out of his face and sent him off to argue for himself, I felt Tobie's eyes register the motion my hand had made and I stiffened, knowing what she was thinking. Haircuts were one of Tobie's specialties: she did Anna once a month and trimmed Joe and Sam at least every other week. I'd refused to let her near me — or Jamie, or even Meggie. Of course, Meggie could get away with it because she was a girl.

But I didn't say anything in defense now. She was right, of course: he looked like one of those little dogs who might or might not actually have a pair of eyes hiding under his mop of hair. Even so, the idea of cutting those golden curls made me crazy. Every morning I brushed up both his and Meggie's and wound them around my index finger like fat sausages. Without his curls Jamie would really be a little boy, not a toddler anymore, and I wasn't ready for that.

Mr. Stiles's truck pulled up the road slowly and stopped at the box nailed to a wooden post at the foot of the drive.

The telltale clank of its metal mouth dropping open galvanized Anna and Jamie, who scrambled from their argument over the swing and flew down the drive to see who could get to the box first. It was a daily contest, and Anna's long legs always made her the winner, although she could barely reach the mail by herself. I was about to yell at her to give Jamie something to carry back, when she did it without my interference, and with pride I watched her put Sam's copy of *Yankee* magazine in her little brother's hands and tell him to bring it up to me. He ran back over the gravel, holding the magazine above his head, giggling and excited with his responsibility. As he ran I saw how his legs were losing their stubby gait, how he ran faster and straighter. Soon he'd be off chasing a school bus, or a football.

"Just look at him come," I said to his grandmother, settling back with a satisfied sigh.

"He's just on loan, Allie — just on loan."

"He's my baby," I protested, beginning to feel annoyed again and unwilling to hear another old-fashioned truism.

"Children don't belong to anybody but themselves. Any mother forgets that's just asking for a lap-load of heartache."

I opened my mouth and then shut it hard.

Anna laid the mail on Tobie's knees. There was nothing but a coupon circular from the IGA and the electric and phone bills. I didn't even open them when Tobie handed them to me: I knew they'd have to wait till next month, when Duet's foal was born and, hopefully, sold. Jamie pulled up behind his sister to give me the magazine. He looked like he'd climbed Mt. Everest. "I dood tit!" he crowed.

"Good job!" I said, shaking his hand. He peered out at me through a wave of blond hair. Some demon in me finally came up with an answer to my mother-in-law's pointed glance. "Let's you and me go get a scissors," I said to my son, standing up and arching my back against tired muscles. "It's about time Mommy gave you your first haircut."

Sam came through the back door just then, letting the screen slam behind him. He held up a paper bag. "Dinner," he said. "I'm taking Allie for a supper ride!" His voice was jubilant.

"What's going on?" I asked uncertainly, delighted by his face but suspicious nevertheless. This was the last time of day I'd expect to take a ride alone with my husband. Maybe he was trying to make up for our earlier disagreement.

"I just sold Toledo's Tornado." His grin went ear to ear. "For six thousand dollars!"

I sat very still for a minute. I couldn't take it in so quickly: a flare of jealousy, thinking of the piddling check from Hallmark, but then an enormous surge of pride and pleasure at his success. I got up and put my arms around him.

Sam looked over the top of my head at his mother, who still hadn't said anything. "Well?" he demanded.

"Can't say as I'm surprised," she said, scratching a match on the arm of her chair and lighting a Camel. "After all, she's prob'ly worth closer to nine thousand." She exhaled.

Sam groaned with a smile. "Never satisfied." He shook his head. "C'mon, Allie, I've got us all tacked up."

Then I remembered the children. "But who's —"

He cut me off with a wave of his hand. "Joe's doing the feeding and Tobie'll take the kids."

I turned to her and she nodded. "He already asked," she said. "While we were cleaning up."

This was some favor: three baths, three suppers, and fifteen bedtime stories. "Thanks."

She waved gratitude away with her hand.

"Haycut, Mommee?" Jamie asked, tugging on my fingers. I looked down into his face and felt that tug against my heart instead of on my hand. "Tomorrow," I promised. "We'll do it tomorrow."

He started to protest, but I bent down to look straight into his eyes. "Mommy has to go with Daddy now," I said. "Daddy needs my help with something." His blue eyes were clouded with my desertion. His lower lip puffed out. Soon he would be crying with an anger he was still too little to put into words.

I stood quickly, wanting to divert the tantrum. "Anna, Meggie," I called, interrupting them where they were now fighting over the tire swing. "Come help your grandmother with dinner. Daddy and I are going out for a while."

I took Sam's hand and didn't look back. I just walked out on the whole complicated, tangled scene and left it with my capable mother-in-law. Manny and Lady Hill stood waiting in the paddock, a matched pair of dappled grays, bridled but not saddled because we enjoyed riding bareback the most. Sam gave me a boost and then swung himself up with no effort, and we took Harper's Trail east, a switchback that ran along one of the local mountains. The sun slanted down through thick green forest in a gold as rich as honey; the shadows were about an hour away. If you knew these woods you didn't need a watch to tell it was nearly five o'clock.

The trail led us right behind Rebecca's property, and we swung by to say hello. There was no one at home and the back door was locked up tight.

"No one around here locks their door," Sam commented. "It's paranoid."

"She's from New York. Maybe it takes a while to get used to the idea that no one wants anything you've got."

In the front yard, just off the porch, there was a large jumble of rusted metal rods. "What's all this?" Sam poked the pile with his toe and it rattled, making the horses snort and shy away, backing up against the reins as if they wanted to be gone from this place.

"TV antennas?" I guessed, doubtful. She hardly seemed the type to watch television.

"Looks like she's been dump picking," he answered. "But why would anybody want five of these? Reception in Arrowsic is terrible even *with* an antenna."

"Maybe she's working on some kind of sculpture."

Sam shook his head, mystified by the very idea, and gave me a leg up. As we rode deeper into the woods a sense of peace blanketed us: the only sounds were birdcall, animal rustle, the dry strike of hooves on occasional rocks. I watched Sam's tall, straight back as we cantered, trotted, jogged, walked, and then cantered again. We forded a brook, and then, after passing through a high meadow with tall grass, we pulled briars and ticks from our dungarees. The denim grew wet with the horses' sweat. We didn't talk. We just rode.

After a while Sam pulled up under a tree, no place in particular, a hollow where it didn't seem like there'd be too many mosquitos, and he took the paper bag off the braided rope leadline around his waist. We sat cross-legged, and he unpacked four peanut-butter-and-mayonnaise sandwiches, six pickles, and three beers.

"I'm sure glad it's not chicken," I said with my mouth full.

He smiled. "Me, too."

"Or chicken soup, either." I chewed some more. "It's too hot for soup."

"Hot soup on a hot night can cool you down."

"That's just what your mother says!"

"She's right."

I was beginning to get tired of nearly being married to my mother-in-law's implacable viewpoint. Still, I didn't want to bicker now with Sam — time alone was precious and rare — but suddenly I did want to talk. Too often we let our feelings slide away, get blocked out or covered over. Too often we just used sex to get close again. This time I wanted to get everything straight.

"Sometimes it's hard," I said, having paused a minute to gain control, "living in so close with Tobie. It makes me mad when you take her side against mine."

"About *soup*?" He was incredulous.

"About the *kids*. About the *farm*. About anything that *matters*. You could back me up a little more. Like today, I really didn't think the kids ought to have come out while we were doing the chickens."

"My mother's my mother," he said at last and with difficulty. "It's hard for me to go against her."

"Why? If you can see that she's wrong, why?"

"I owe her a lot, I guess. She always stood up to my father with me."

"Well, it's not fair to me."

"You're probably right," he acknowledged. "Still, it's hard to get around that kind of debt in your mind." He paused. "My father *never* would've allowed the kind of risks we're taking now!" Sam finished off his beer. "I went to college just to get away from his damned opinions. Ironic that when I came back here I realized he'd been right all along — I *was* happiest on my own land, with my hand up some animal's backside." He laughed shortly. "Tobie never once made me feel bad for not having made it up with him."

"Would he be proud of you today?" I asked. "Would he think it was worth the risk, if you'd told him how much you sold Tornado for?"

He shook his head. "He'd tell me I was living wild — and he didn't approve of *anything* wild. He beat the woods back out of his fields, he kept livestock that was domesticated, like chickens and cows. When I was growing up we had only three horses. He ran everything — us included — with a real tight hand." He was quiet a minute. "Maybe that's why Jamie drives me nuts."

"Jamie?" I echoed, confused by his shift in focus.

"All that high spirit, and his naughtiness. It makes me react just how *he'd* have reacted." He stopped, striking a fist softly against his bent knee, and then sighed. "Somehow it just leaks out. The girls are so much easier."

I scooted over next to him, forcing myself to listen and not respond. I wanted to hear how he felt, and my silence would make room for his emotion. He put his arm around my shoulder. "I know it can be hard for you, living with my mother," he said. His body was a comfortable warm bulk beside me and I leaned into him. "For me too, sometimes." He laughed. "She sure can wear on your nerves."

I smiled up at him. He was on my side again.

"Forget about her for a minute, though," he went on. "Because I still worry about other things."

"But we've been getting along better."

He considered, then nodded and twisted the top off his second beer. "Still, there's not enough time for just us, alone. Too much work, too much pressure, and the kids. Jamie in our bed in the mornings."

"But that's our life here," I objected. "We need the extra cash my commercial work brings in, your long hours are part of the farm, the children need what they need . . . we can't change any of those things."

"Sometimes we can," he answered firmly. "Like how we used to share things more — whole nights just making love! We've got to have more time alone."

"Like this," I said, noticing for the first time that the last bit of sun had disappeared under a wall of greenish-black clouds. "A front's coming in," I said, pointing at the sky. In the trees above us a strong, cool breeze was turning the undersides of the leaves upward. I heard thunder, soft tympani on the horizon.

"I feel like Jamie's between us," Sam went on after a minute, refusing to be distracted.

I tensed against him. He waited. I let out a deep breath.

"You're so absorbed by him. Sometimes it's like I'm interrupting. And one of these days he's going to grow up into his own life," Sam continued. "Then there'll be just the two of us again."

"Jamie's special to me," I admitted. "My only boy, for one

thing." I was quiet then, thinking. "I have big hopes, that's all." I sighed. "But I promise you, Sam — nobody and nothing's going to get between us again." I smiled into the oncoming dark and took his hand. "We'll get Tobie to do this more often."

He grinned. "There ought to be some advantage to a live-in mother-in-law."

Thunder rolled through the trees and we looked up at the sky again, startled now to see how dark it had suddenly become.

"Better head home," he said, scrambling up. "We might still beat it."

We swung onto the horses as warmed and sated from talking as we usually were from sex. We would sleep well tonight, I thought, watching my husband's strong, straight back as the horses moved out and down the trail. The animals' pace was quicker than when we had come up the mountain. They felt a storm and a dark night on the way, and they knew supper would be waiting in their grain boxes.

The double doors of the barn rolled open, and we burst onto the main floor and stood there dripping, laughing and breathless. "I thought I was going to slip right off Manny's back," I said, pulling my hair into a clump and wringing the water from it.

"At least there's no tack ruined," Sam said, picking up an empty burlap feed sack and starting to rub down Lady Hill. I started on Manny's neck and withers. "How about if you head over to the house." Sam threw a sheet over Lady's back and buckled it around her chest. "The kids might've given Tobie some trouble, what with the storm."

"You'll finish up?"

He nodded and came to take over Manny's rubdown. I gave him a long goodbye kiss, and he slid his hand under my shirt.

"I'd like more of that upstairs," he said.

I smiled and didn't reply.

It seemed August was trying to make up for everything July hadn't managed in terms of water: the rain was soft and cool on my skin, and I didn't mind getting wet now that we were home. I took my time walking back to the house, putting my face up to the sky and standing there for a minute as rivulets washed down my cheeks like a natural shower. I only wished there was time to take off all my clothes and dance around under it.

Once inside, I stripped off everything right there in the kitchen and stuffed it all into the washer. There was a lot of laundry that hadn't been put away because Sam and I had been out fooling around, so I just extracted a towel from the heap until I could get my bathrobe. Then I lugged the heavy wicker basket up the back stairs. Light dappled the floor in patches, and the door to Jamie's room was open; his crib was empty and low voices came from our bedroom.

Tobie and Jamie were sitting in the rocking chair and she was reading him *Goodnight Moon*, his favorite story. When I came in and set the laundry basket on the bed, Jamie squirmed out of his grandmother's lap and ran to throw his arms around my knees, starting to cry. I smoothed the long curls against his head with my hand.

"Has he been to sleep at all?" I asked, distressed, guilty now for having gone. I plunked him on the bed and pulled my robe from the closet.

Tobie nodded. "Storm woke him half an hour ago. He was having some kind of a bad dream. Maybe the thunder got him scared."

I picked Jamie up again and sat on the bed with him in my lap to rock him with my body. "Mommee wet!" he said, touching my hair.

"Sam out closing up for the night?"

I nodded. "We got caught by the rain, so he's giving them a good rubdown. He'll be up."

Tobie hoisted herself to her feet. "Think I'll turn in. Haven't heard peep from either of the girls."

"Small blessings." I got up and carried my son over to the rocking chair, which was still warm from my mother-in-law's body. "Thanks, Tobie. Thanks a lot."

I closed my eyes and after a minute I heard her door creak shut. I smiled to myself. She still didn't like to be thanked.

I switched off the lamp on the table beside me, and Jamie stirred in protest as the room went dark. I quieted him with a touch of my hand. The rocker was in front of the window which looked out onto the back garden: with the room in blackness the lightning was more vivid. Maybe Jamie could conquer his fear if shown there was nothing to be afraid of. But with every flash and growl, he burrowed a little more deeply against my body.

"Jamee scared," he whimpered.

I rocked him, using my body like a cradle. As we sat there in the dark he somehow rejoined me, reentered me, became once again a part of me. I felt filled up and content. He didn't squirm or wiggle; he didn't ask questions or fuss. We were silent. And gradually the storm passed on to the west, the noise and light faded. "I got bad deam," Jamie said after a while.

"What was in the bad dream?"

"Chickyfroat," he answered, turning his face up to mine, tears starting again.

"Chickyfroat?" I repeated it over in my mind, trying to decode the word.

"Chickyfroat," he confirmed. "Muddred need bannaid."

"A bad dream about the chickens and their throats — is that it?" I frowned as I translated. "You want to put a Band-Aid on Mildred's throat?"

"Yeah. Muddred need bannaid." He scrubbed at his eyes with the ball of his fist.

"Don't you worry about Mildred," I said, hugging him

tight, not knowing what else to say. How could I tell him that he'd eaten Mildred for dinner? One part of me wanted to cry, one part of me was still a little angry that Sam had let them see and that I hadn't stopped it. Then that anger dissolved: my more pragmatic side knew he'd forget all about Mildred in a couple of days.

A flash of lightning sliced to the ground outside the window as another squall line hit, illuminating the entire back garden. Tomato plants and pea vines bowed under the weight of the downpour, and the earth was one big puddle. I tensed against the enormous sizzle of thunder which followed almost immediately, and Jamie shrank into me again. Then there was another chain of light, and then another, and I could hear thunder from both east and west now, overlapping, as if two storms were facing off directly above our heads. The old house reverberated and shook under the repeating noise. It was damned loud, and suddenly I wished we had a lightning rod, or that we had on our sneakers. Another crackle of electricity cut through the air, and the light bulb in the hall fixture popped its filaments. Downstairs the bell in the phone rang out once. The night was alive around us.

I tried not to let Jamie know that I, too, was scared, and wondered if either of the girls was awake, and where my husband was. As Jamie hid his eyes against my chest, I held him tight and stopped rocking. All around us the noise went on and on, like a symphony of anger, of nature in riot, the flashing light and the crashing sound, and we banded there together against it, holding on to each other for comfort. Jamie had pushed his face inside my robe to curl up on my breast. I held him and let him be. He needed my warmth; he needed my familiar spaces.

I had been afraid of thunderstorms when I was little, too, and now I remembered going to sleep at night straining to listen to the night sounds — the crickets, the peepers, the distant highway drone — for any sign of a storm. And when thunder did interrupt my unconscious state, I told myself it was only the giants up in heaven bowling lots of strikes, like my mother had said. But I could never picture those giants, and after the peak crack of thunder I'd make a beeline for my parents' bed. For once understanding that her fantasy had not protected me from my own real fears, my mother would let me come to cuddle, and rock me until the big noise passed. Then I could go, however uneasily, back to my own cold sheets, but blanketed with her reassurance that it was all over — and about this one thing she was never wrong.

The thunder faded a bit, and the time between flash and crash lengthened little by little. I raised my head and loosened my grip, and my body began to uncoil. My son was still burrowed into me. His head was hot and damp in the crook of my shoulder and neck, his fingers were warm as they curled on my breast.

With my fear receding, I felt Jamie's touch for the first time. He was cupping my nipple with his palm, and the skin of his hand was very soft. He was stroking me the same way he stroked his blanket against his face each night as he fell asleep. Warmth began in my skin under his hand. I remembered my husband's caress earlier and my nipple rose erect. I started to take his hand away, uncomfortable, guilty; then I stopped. I didn't want to call attention to his innocent gesture and make it seem something it clearly was not. Yet I was afraid of what he had summoned up in me: a response which was taboo.

"Mommee brest." Jamie turned his small face up to me, and the delight that comes with a child's accomplishment overshadowed any other response I could have had. I hadn't realized he even knew the word. "One, two," he went on, pulling my robe aside and pointing. "One brest, two brest. Mommee got two brestzz," he said, burring his tongue over the sibilants. "I counting!" A wave of maternal love lapped at me, made me want to surrender myself to his eyes, to this

bright face full of its own newfound power. But a noise at
the door made me look up.

"He's still awake?" Sam sounded surprised.

"The thunder scared him." I shifted Jamie on my lap so
that our embrace was broken. Somehow I didn't want Sam
to see. "I'll put him in now."

"Let me kiss him first." Sam crossed over to us and gave
Jamie a big bear hug. "You okay?"

Jamie nodded, eyes enormous. "Muddred needs bannaid,"
he said.

Sam paused, translating and then said, "I'll go out to the
barn right now and patch her up." He winked at me. "You
go to sleep and don't worry." He ruffled Jamie's hair, and I
hoisted Jamie into my arms and stood. He put his arms around
my neck in a steady hug as I began to sing "Somewhere Over
the Rainbow" — his favorite bedtime song — and we moved
down the dark hall as Sam went to the bathroom to towel
off. As I laid Jamie in his crib, he immediately scrambled up
and pointed to the other side of the room. "Hossie," he cried,
demanding once again. "Hossie in kib!"

I turned and, in the faint glow of the nightlight, saw the
pull-toy Sam had carved hitched to the handle on Jamie's
bureau drawer.

"That's an outside toy," I answered. "It's dirty — you can't
take it to bed."

"Hossie," he said, his lower lip beginning to push out stubbornly. "I got bad deam."

He was only manipulating me by bringing up Mildred, I
told myself. But some doubt remained, some guilt, and if the
toy could really make him feel comforted, in control of a world
where thunder crashed and pets died, why not let him have
it? Later in life a home, children, or his wife would be the
image of safety. For now this toy was the symbol, imbued
with feelings which came from long, familiar afternoons of
playing together outside in the dust. That horse was his friend.

I handed it over. He took the string tightly in his hand and curled one arm around the horse as he lay down. "Jamee own hossie," he said protectively.

I bent to kiss him goodnight, and he turned his mouth up, puckered his soft lips against mine with a small smack; his breath smelled sweet as alfalfa as he kissed me back. Inside me a chain of tiny firecrackers exploded, ignited under my heart like the ring of flame under a gas burner, and I knew with certainty, with finality, that I would never feel this way about anyone else — not even my husband. I thought of Sam and me on the mountainside earlier, and the promise I had made about letting nothing and no one come between us. It was the right promise, but I wondered how to force my heart to keep it. Suddenly I was afraid of this love I had for my son: what sort of love was it, that saved itself only for Jamie?

If I had had a choice, I would have stayed by the crib all night long to watch my son, and then to paint the evolution of his sleep, dreaming to waking to dreaming — those interconnected phases of one reality. I stroked the damp curls back from his forehead, and his eyes closed at last. He slept.

I heard Sam click out the bedside lamp, and, reluctantly, I went back to our room. My husband was waiting for me. He used his hands to find me in the dark as I slid down into the bed the way a fish slips down into the still water of a pond. He was aroused and pressed himself against my belly. He put his mouth on my breast and pulled at the nipple with his teeth. After a while he moved his mouth up to mine, and I kissed him back with my tongue, warm and wet and strong. I let him draw me, little by little, out of my distraction into the warmth of touch; I let him use my body to capture again my mind. For that hour I did not think of anything but him and me. I kept my promise.

We rolled apart. I could still hear thunder, very distant, probably several mountains down the line. The house was silent. Lightning was only an occasional flicker against the far wall of the bedroom.

I went to the window and looked out: the moon had come from behind the clouds for a minute, blazing them with a new, and unexpected, white light. I heard Jamie call restlessly in his sleep, a half-cry, then silence. I cocked my head and started to go and check on him, but Sam beckoned from our bed. I hesitated. "Come on, Allie," he said. "He's gone back to sleep." And I went to my husband's arms and we made love again.

Later, as I fell asleep twined around Sam, I began a painting in my head, one that would symbolize my little boy's growing up and away from me: Jamie, viewed from behind, pushing open the door into the bathroom, early light falling in a glow across his naked bottom and back, the bottles of deodorants, shaving lotion, and face cream silhouetted on the sink beyond him. And in a little while my painting became my dream.

Meggie was tugging at my easel, rocking the canvas back and forth, and I was pushing her away, angry, and then I was blurred, confused. I levered myself up on one elbow and realized it was morning and I was in bed. Meggie stood by one side, pulling on the sheet. "Hungry, Mommy," she was saying insistently. "Hungry *now*."

The clock on the dresser said six-thirty and sunshine was coming through my window. I had overslept. All that late-night activity had put us behind schedule. Dimly I remembered Sam getting out of bed at five o'clock; I must have rolled over and gone back to sleep. I swore to myself irritably. The whole day was going to be off-kilter.

Tobie put her head in my door. "I'll go down and start the bacon," she said. "Joe and Sam'll be up anytime now."

I scrambled out from under the sheets and shivered, unsettled by this strange start-up. Last night's storm had crisped the air cool and dry: the first of August felt like the first of October. Anna called from the downstairs hall with impatience and Tobie turned to go.

"Have you got Jamie, too?" I tied the cord of my bathrobe and shoved my feet into my slippers.

"Asleep," she answered with a frown. "A late night for such a little one."

I paused for a minute, then shrugged and went quickly to wash up in the bathroom and pull on my jeans and shirt. The smell of the bacon grew strong, and the men's voices drifted up the back staircase. No noise came from Jamie's bedroom yet. I cocked my head, and a beat of anxiety pulsed through me then. I debated waking him. Anna yelled for me and I started down, but as I passed his door I changed my mind and went in to check on him. It nagged at me that he should still be asleep — he, who was always the first to rise.

I tiptoed across the squeaky floorboards and looked in over the side of his crib. He lay on his belly, facedown and turned away; I reached to touch him lightly on the small of his back, to feel the quick rise and fall of childish breath. My hand lay still. Puzzled, my heart beginning a strange new syncopation in my chest, I shook him gently. Something was not right: his shoulder was hard and unyielding. Fear pounded behind my eyes now. I rolled him over.

Jamie stared up at me. He didn't blink, move, or breathe. The shutter of my eye jammed — frozen forever on the sight of my son. I couldn't breathe. This had to be a dream. I shook him again, harder. Still he didn't roll away from my hand.

"Jamie," I called, bending over him, my hand searching out his. I kept thinking he must just be asleep with his eyes open. But his flesh was cold, colder than the air around me. I put my finger across his open palm: his fingers did not curl around mine. Something inside me began to scream, an endless, bone-jarring scream. I shut my mouth against it, I did not let it out. I walked around the perimeter of the room for a minute, my brain refusing to compute the facts.

I didn't know what to do. I was a wall against those screams inside me, shivering uncontrollably, my heart banging against my ribs with such force that my body shook. I went back to the crib and looked down at him again.

His mouth was open wide, and his tongue protruded a little to one side, bitten in his attempt to suck a last drop of air and call out. One hand was at his throat, a finger caught under the cord which was now imbedded deep into the swollen skin of his neck. His face was faintly blue, the color of a fresh bruise. In his yellow Dr. Denton's, his chest no longer rose and fell, and his eyes looked beyond mine. I scooped him up and hugged him against me. His head wobbled back over my arm, chin pointing at the ceiling. The toy horse swung on its string and dangled from his neck like a piece of jewelry.

I took him to the changing table, unwound the cord, and tried to erase the rope burns on his skin with my thumb: they were angry, red, indelible. With baby talc I powdered away the blue of his face. I closed his eyelids with my fingertips: *one, two, two eyes;* I could hear him counting, but his mouth did not move. I brushed his golden curls around my index finger, changed his diaper, greased his bottom with Desitin, and kissed him on the tummy, just like any morning. He was still and cold and hard as wax. I wrapped him in a blanket to try and warm him. My baby was a dead blue doll.

It seemed like ten miles to the rocking chair in my bedroom. Cradling him in my arms, I began to sing, *"Somewhere over the rainbow, way up high."* I sang out to Jamie's soul, I sang to reach him as I had once tried to reach God: my voice was a prayer, a fire, a cleansing fire, pure soprano sound rising, no lament, only faith to touch him now where he flew. *"Someday I'll wish upon a star and wake up where my dreams are far behind me."*

And then he answered me in the voice of the birds on fire outside my window, and we sang together, a duet, spiraling upward. After a while I didn't notice how still and hard he was: he was mine, I would love him any way he came. I'd just rewrite this horror, repaint the picture, alter our own history. If I waited long enough, if I loved hard enough, he would come back to me.

Still he did not move. Anna came and saw us. Anna came and touched him, recoiled, ran from the room. I hugged him tighter to my breast, opened my shirt, and put his cold cheek against my warm flesh.

But soon they came for us, found us there locked together. I would not let go of him. Dr. Loring came near. Sam and the girls came nearer and then receded; they were all like the cooling wave of the ocean, but Jamie and I were a fire which would not go out.

I bent to sing my boy's breath back into his body, but they tried to stop me. They brought to me a silvered knife, a mirrored instrument, a brush of gilt, a flashing star. My mind was unwinding like a spool of ribbon. I shook my son; I would not let him go; I explained to them that he was only sleeping. They came and laid the hypodermic against my arm, and I felt its angry, unholy fire.

They pulled my Jamie from me, they stole him from my arms and took him far, far away. I thought, I will never see him again. I lay myself down in the dark ash of love, and let my heart eat itself up with sorrow.

PART III

WHITE NIGHT

August 1986

The weeks passed half-real, not much pain, not much of anything, perhaps a little relief, mostly a *nuit blanche.* . . . Who could say his mother had lived and did not live? She had been in one place, and was in another; that was all. And his soul could not leave her, wherever she was. Now she was gone abroad into the night, and he was with her still. They were together.

— D. H. Lawrence
Sons and Lovers

In the Garden

Dr. Loring's sedation didn't help. When I woke, the loss was a white-hot searchlight inside the cave of my body. No chemical pillow could cushion this truth; no eulogy, no time passing, no language, no kiss or condolence could bring him back. My son was dead.

Only with my mind could I get around the unalterable fact: the psyche can't bear what it sees, and so it closes its eyes. I went to Jamie's funeral bandaged in love and other people's grief. My mother, my husband, my daughters, my mother-in-law, Mrs. Mack and a few other friends, to my surprise even Rebecca — they all cried. They slumped down in the wooden pews of Arrowsic's only church like small, wet birds. I held myself erect and refused. There was no pain. I would not grieve him whom I had not lost. I would simply wait for his return.

Sometimes a perfectly sane person can go through a time when reality bleeds into imagination, and imagination into reality — like a muddy portrait — and the days between my son's death and funeral were like that. I anesthetized myself with denial so that I did not have to see the colors or feel the textures as I rummaged through Jamie's drawers to choose the last pair of overalls my little boy would ever wear; I did not have to understand the look on the funeral director's face when I handed him the pink Tupperware bowl and told him it should be put on Jamie's head like a hat; I didn't have to absorb the minister's drone the next afternoon, or the shower of earth and stones that rained down on the face of the four-foot coffin which Sam, all alone, had picked.

Before the visiting hours at the funeral home, I asked to be left by myself with my little boy. The casket hadn't yet been closed. I stood on the far side of the small room, and for the first time I felt a glimmer of something down deep. Fear. Simple, primitive fear. I had never seen anyone dead before. I was afraid that he might be horrible to look at, a gruesome caricature. No one but family had ever bathed him or dressed his small body. How would anyone else know on which side to part his hair?

But this was my last chance. Although I could only let myself know that with some remote part of myself, yet it motivated me to cross the room. Random thoughts, pictures, flitted across the screen of my mind as I stood there hesitating, clutching my small best handbag: Jamie running up the drive with the mail, Jamie cuddling with rapt attention for story after story in the hayloft, Jamie's soft hands, stubby legs, dancing face. God had not rescued me this time. My son was in a box on the other side of the room, as dead as if I had tied him to the altar and lit the funeral pyre myself.

Step by step I moved closer to the casket, until at last I stood next to him. I closed my eyes before I could look, and when I finally did, a dry wind tore through me. I opened my mouth, but no sound came out. Without realizing it, I put my fist in and bit down on my knuckles to stop the room from spinning away from me. I forced myself to look again.

He lay on his back, perfectly still, a small two-year-old boy in red corduroy overalls and a plaid shirt. His sneakers were tied on his feet, but they had not put his morning hat on his head. I took his blankie from the shopping bag I carried and tucked it in alongside his cheek on the satin pillow. I tried to bend his arm to curve around and hold it, but his body was unyielding, hard. And very cold. Perhaps he would know his blankie was near. In a dream I traced the line of his nose and leaned down to kiss goodbye the small, delectable dip where one day the bridge would have appeared. I touched his hair, slicked back neatly as it had never been in life, all curl subdued. He would never have his first haircut.

They had covered the bruises — those bruises which belonged to me — fairly well. But he did not look, as they always say, just asleep. He was too stiff, lying there on his back so rigid and proper. There was no sprawl, no limb outflung, no soft *hush-hush* of breath. There was no fuzzy damp smell from a wet diaper cocooned inside warm Dr. Denton's. No, he was not asleep.

I stood there a long time. The pain devoured me, and I seized up inside, welded myself shut, iron cylinder to iron valve. Some while later Sam came and made me leave. He put his arm around me and steered me out of that room and away from my little boy for the last time. I held myself rigid: I did not look at him. I did not feel the weight of his arm. We stood side-by-side for the visiting hours, shoulders rubbing, but we did not speak.

Rebecca came early and stayed, sitting in a corner, most of the morning. She brought me a paper cup of water, a Kleenex, and she tried to distract me with sketches of the mourners. I nodded, and smiled, and throughout that rainy Saturday morning, as the women came and went, speaking words I could not hear, I smiled. But the skin of my face and palms felt dry and brittle as a fallen leaf in autumn. It itched until I thought I would go mad with the urge to scratch. But you can't scratch like that in public. Later, in the car, I pulled down the mirror to check my face. It was white, not the red I had expected.

I looked at my hair. Aloud, I idly planned to go and get it cut next week — just drive into Manchester and find someone to shear it off. It was too heavy, I said. It was a burden on my head.

"Allie," Sam said, "what nonsense are you talking?" His eyes were painfully red.

"I'm talking about getting my hair cut."

"Are you all right?"

"I'm fine. I just should have done it a long time ago." My hands pushed and shaped my hair in the mirror: I stared up into the eyes of myself and wondered who this woman was. I was on fire now, burning up.

"I love your hair," he said softly, reaching out to stroke the back of my head, down the length of the long blonde waves.

"It's too heavy," I repeated.

He turned his face to me, full of its plain misery, which I chose in that instant to ignore. I didn't want to talk. I rolled down my window and let the mist speckle my face with moisture. It felt cold and good. I wanted to freeze myself to stop the burning. Sam pulled the car up in front of Nelson's, reached out to squeeze my hand. "Allie," he said. *"Please."* I waited passively until he let go and then went in to get some hand lotion. In the afternoon we went to our son's funeral.

The sheets on our bed were smooth and cool that night. But my entire body continued to burn, and I pressed myself against the fresh cloth as if it were a new wet skin. Sam turned out the light and we lay, side-by-side, in the dark. I felt the edges of his body: elbow, shoulder, hip. I did not move nearer. In the dark the noises of the house settled around us. Down the hall I heard Anna start to cry, a small, muffled sound, and then Tobie's door opening. I heard the murmur of their voices, Tobie's gruff comfort, and two sets of footsteps going back to my mother-in-law's bedroom. In the guest room I could hear the squeak of springs as my own mother turned, and turned again, in her bed.

I could tell from the pattern of Sam's breathing that he was not asleep. Somewhere inside me I sensed that if I did not turn toward him now, if I did not reach out, take his pain and join it together with mine, it would be too late. The moon rose through the window, not unlike a few nights back when I had turned from my son's cry and gone to lie in my marriage bed. Outside the rain had stopped, but the pines were still heavy and wet in the wind. I lay without moving for a long time and finally heard my husband's breathing grow deeper, down into settled sleep. The room grew hotter and my skin started to itch again.

"He is risen; he is not here; behold the place where they laid him." I would never forget those words. They were from somewhere in the New Testament, and the minister at my father's funeral had quoted them. I remembered thinking of the irony: My father had never wanted religion in life and surely would not have wanted it in death. But my mother had wanted it because it comforted her. And me. I thought of all those sermons you hear: how the soul rises up like the smell of bread baking. And Jesus, with his big voice, how he called out at the tomb of Lazarus and then Lazarus had sauntered right out for a stroll. We needed to hear stories like these. Possibilities. The soul didn't die with the body. There was a resurrection and an ascension because there had to be. There was a cow heaven because there had to be. But the plague of my body burned and itched and I got out of bed. *Where was my little boy?*

I wandered down the hall. Jamie's room was an envelope of blackness. I drew up the shades, and moonlight searched the room. In the crib his teddy sat alone against the blanket I had knit before the twins were born. I should have put Teddy in his casket, I thought suddenly; he would be lonely without him. He had never once gone to sleep without this stuffed animal tucked beneath his arm. I had given him the blanket but forgotten the bear. I paced the room, the braided rug hard under my bare feet, and felt a strange panic grow. He was alone without his bear. I reached into the crib to scoop it up.

It nestled against my breast in a warm furry pile as I ran down the hall past my mother's room, down over the cold wood of the stairs, out over the sharp gravel of the front walk. Night moved up cool under my nightgown and against my skin: the itching eased a little as I walked toward the back garden. I didn't want anyone to know where I was, and I went deep into the tall tomato vines, hiding myself in their twining green stalks staked up on crosses against the weight of a fruit which was still hard and green in early August. I tied up a drooping branch, then sat in the dirt, cradling the bear in my arms.

The moon was high above me, the plants stretched over my head, enormous, like the girders of some green and leafy city. Their scent was of faint licorice, more pungent than usual because of the day's rain. I just sat there, for a long time, rocking Jamie's bear. Fire was consuming me, fire and pain, and there was no way to quench the thirst of that fire. The night noises were loud and distorted in my head: a background hum of night peepers, and then, staccato, a whippoorwill, the rustle of an animal — skunk, the drift of wind told me — in the underbrush.

And then a whisper came, from behind me, just the breeze perhaps, across broad leaves. I did not turn. But when it came again, I listened harder, goosebumps chilling up on my forearms. "*Mommeecum*," he said, from far, far away. "*Mommeecum.*"

He would be standing behind me in the overalls I had chosen, dirt on his face and under his fingernails from having dug his way out of that premature box.

"*Mommeecum.*" The sound caressed my soul. Pain receded for a moment in a wash of hope.

Slowly I turned my head toward him, slowly I turned to the sound of his voice. But only the tomato plants stretched their arms out on their stakes, wide, alone under the moon. There was only the voice of the night.

It came to me then that he was really gone, that I would never hold him again, never feel his sweet weight against my belly, never nuzzle the blond curls at the curve of his neck, never feel his soft inquiring fingers against my eyelids in the last dark of morning. I would never again cradle him the way I now cradled his bear. My only son was dead. I would never rage at another antic, never tie up one more shoelace. I was alone.

No, I thought then — *he* was alone. As I was without him, he was without me. I trembled for him, pictured him confused, with no one to turn to, no one to ask, no one to be comforted or held by. And I had let him go without his teddy.

I ran through the plants, searching for him, calling his name, sure he was near. But the night was stilled of noises now and the plants held only shadows. I burst out into the carrot patch and fell to my knees, holding myself and rocking. Keening. Lost in the pain, I began to dig. I dug in the mud, squatting, using my hands — an animal. I made a deep hole in the wet earth and laid his teddy bear away, praying that somehow it would reach him. I knew it made no sense and I didn't care. I only cared that he not be alone anymore. If I could have put myself into the earth alongside him, I would have.

And as I buried the bear, a hole opened in my chest. The anguish was too big. I was suffocating. I wanted to murder, to steal, to pillage, to axe it out. I pulled up the carrots, one after the other, as if I were a picking machine; I uprooted the orange shoots, still new and tender, not yet ready for harvest; I dug deep into the earth, bruising my fingers on rocks and stones, foraging for sweet red potatoes, still small and round, not come to their full weight. I cursed the bounty of my own labor: I would thwart it. Nothing should grow here. Nothing should come of nothing.

I pulled and scratched and ruined the work that had taken

months, days, of sun and rain, of cracked nails, of mosquito bites. Piles of radish, and turnip, and onion mounded toward the sky. *An eye for an eye.* Mud caked my hands, my fingernails were thick moons of black, and still the pores of my skin burned. There was a thick loamy smell all around me, a smell of earth and sowing and freshly turned dirt.

But in time my anger ran down, and without it to fuel me, I ran down too, like a child's windup toy. My own guilt was all that was left to me now. Hours had gone by. I didn't know how many or when. I only knew there were hours more to come, and I must endure this pain for all those hours; I would have to live with what we — I — had done — or had not — for the rest of my life. I lay my burned body down in the cool, dark earth of my ruined garden and, eyes still open to my own destruction, slept.

Time Passing

I dreamt I refused to give him the toy horse in his crib that
night. "No," I said to him. And so Jamie had lived.

I dreamt I heard him cry out that night. And when my
husband said, "Come back to bed, Allie," I refused him. And
so Jamie had lived.

I dreamt Jamie and I were painting in the garden, side-by-
side, and the tomatoes turned red and ripe and pulled heavy
against their vines. He had lived to inherit my gift. But he
did not.

Rebecca came to visit me every day, although I could barely
hear her and said nothing intelligent enough to encourage
her friendship. A thick buzzing filled my ears and stupefied
me. She tried to reach me anyway — bringing paintings from
her house to mine, trying to get me to talk about them. My
mother worried it was too much for me to have such a constant visitor, but Rebecca persisted. (*I'm not a visitor,* she said
flat out.) I was glad to have Rebecca there, but I hardly remembered the colors of red or blue, green or yellow. I hardly
remembered the shapes a human hand could draw.

I sat in a rocking chair on the porch in my nightgown and

moved my body back and forth silently through the hours of
the day. At Sam's insistence I wore a sweater against the chill
everyone was talking about, the dampness of this unseason-
able month. A few visitors came and went. Mrs. Mack, Mr.
Stiles in his mail truck, Herb and Sally Nelson on their way
to church. Over Tobie's protest (*Leave her be, Lynne, give her
some time*) my mother summoned Nat Loring, who gave me
no shot, no vitamin pill, no pep talk. (*She hasn't any fever,
Mrs. Sterne.*) He suggested she make us some tea. Alone, he
sat beside me and asked me how I felt. I just looked at him.
(*When a pain is very big you don't make a sound or a move against
it.*) He covered my hand where it lay like a glove on the arm
of the rocker. We sat awhile. Slowly he began to talk about
Jamie. I was jealous then, a brief flare of sensation against all
that cotton wool in my mind: his ease in remembering, the
way tears came to him so naturally. My own eyes burned and
itched, but did not so much as water. I asked Nat if he thought
I had an allergy. (*Everyone's allergic to this,* he said.)

At noon each day the girls skirted me shyly, as if I were
someone they did not know. They sensed the distance I had
gone and it upset them. At lunch I watched the family eat.
My mother stayed, week after week, unasked by me. My
mother washed, cleaned, cooked, looked after my children.
My mother tried to help me with good words (*Take Sam into
your heart,* she said). But it hurt that my mother expected me
to carry on. I felt she should have understood better than
anyone else. (*Can you imagine what you would do in my place?*
I asked with my eyes.) I was desperate and angry, yet said
nothing, nothing to her constant entreaty that I get up and
do something to make myself feel better. In the end it was
her obtuseness, her sweet single-mindedness about my duty —
to pull the family through, as if we were locked in some finite
crisis which could be surmounted, eradicated, or dimmed by
time — which made me withdraw from her, which made me

ignore her or speak irritably when she was in the room. When I was a child that same single-mindedness had made me feel safe because it had shut out a world sometimes dangerous, but now it only made me feel suffocated, alone and drowning under the great wave of the pain.

Sam and Tobie shuttled between the barn and house, splashing through pools of water lying across the paddock and driveway. Dimly, from far away, I resented the way they simply went back to work. But I knew underneath — from the way Tobie looked at me, from the way she sat next to me in the rocker on the porch at noon, when ordinarily she wouldn't have made the time — that my mother-in-law understood something of my inertia. Perhaps she remembered her own.

After a couple weeks of sitting nearly motionless, as if that might set time back, like winding a clock carefully against itself, I got out of my rocker and began to wander from room to room in the farmhouse. I had forgotten what the sitting room and parlor looked like here. I studied the faces hanging on the walls. I dusted a few tables, although my mother was being very thorough. I began to make the beds again. I even helped with the dishes. It rained. And rained. The rain of August swamped us, stunted the growth of the garden and the hay, made exercising the horses hard.

The world cried.

I could not.

At some point after the funeral someone had closed the door to Jamie's room. And it stayed that way. When I walked by it I pretended to myself that it was a linen closet: with sheets, towels, blankets, and medicines neatly arranged, it was the sort of place where order reigned, the sort of place where needs might be anticipated and then satisfied. After a few weeks I could actually see that closet in my mind as if I regularly opened it: piles of pink and blue terry, prescription jars and bottles in neat rows, enema bag, hot-water bottle, labels on the edges of the shelves — *facecloths, handtowels, queen flat and fitted.*

I pretended that there were no stairs to my attic studio, and after a while I believed that too. Rebecca kept talking about going up together, but I changed the subject to the strange weather, to the new dress my mother was sewing for Anna, to our hired hand Joe, who had had a front tooth kicked out by a mare in season.

Every night I slept curled on my side of our bed. On the edge. At first Sam asked why I was so far away and moved closer. His misery was palpable — in his touch, his skin, his breath — but I held myself back from it. I couldn't embrace it. If I took on his hurt, too, I would break apart. So I told him I was hot, that my skin still itched, that I needed some room on the mattress. And in time there was no need for my excuses, because he came to bed and went right to sleep. For all of August, Sam and I did not touch.

One night after the spaghetti was eaten but the plates were not yet cleared, Tobie crossed the last day of the month off the calendar. She lifted the page to September and lit a cigarette. My mother got up to stack the dishes and said she would be going home. Tomorrow, I heard her say. It was her way of forcing me to wake up.

"Well, try to get some rest," my mother said as she kissed me goodbye.

"I was in bed eleven hours," I answered dully, pulling my cheek away from her sticky Red Poppies mouth. It was nine in the morning and I still wasn't dressed.

"Well." She opened the car door and got in, but then just sat there and looked at me, her forehead puckered.

I waited for her to buckle her seat belt so I could close the door, shifting my feet in the gravel of the drive. Soon there would be no one to hover over me, to watch or worry. I wanted her to go. "Drive carefully," I said. "And come back soon." I sniffed at the air. Rain seemed inevitable. Again. Above us the clouds hung, gray, violet, bunched against the ridge of mountains.

"Anna didn't eat much breakfast." She put her key into the ignition. "She'll get hungry for something before noon."

"I'll fix her a snack."

"And Meggie was up asking for water three times last night, so she might poop out sooner than usual. I think —"

"An early nap," I interrupted, pushing the heavy door shut. I surprised myself by knowing all these answers.

"They need you too, you know," she said then, a little fiercely. "He was their brother."

I just stared at her. "And my son." I couldn't believe we were having this conversation in the driveway, ten seconds before she was due to leave.

"*You're* the adult," she said, stamping on the accelerator twice, "and adults are supposed to understand these things." With a roar, she started up the car.

I thought with a jolt how untrue that was, since I certainly didn't understand a bit of all that had happened to us. I shook my head slowly, from side to side.

"You've got to interpret for them, Allie. That's a mother's job," she said. With an angry sigh, she put the Buick into reverse.

"Call when you get home," I said finally.

"I'll be all right — I've got my map."

I looked over the roof of the car.

"That's not what you meant, is it?"

Once again I didn't answer.

"Look, Allie," she said with determination, keeping her foot on the brake. "If you need me to stay longer just say so. Nothing's so important at home right now."

I considered for a minute, part of me wanting to give in, craving the certainty of a parent who could take care of us, of me. But if she stayed I'd never trust myself to be on my own again. I couldn't do it with her here, making everything so nice and easy. Being taken care of could get to be an addiction. "I'm sure," I said, my voice unconvincing, "that we'll do fine."

"All right." And she put her foot on the gas and backed down the drive.

I didn't allow myself to stand and watch her go, but turned resolutely back to the house, wondering if she really thought it possible for a parent to interpret such an absurdity. She certainly hadn't interpreted it for me. I started to laugh, an ugly, harsh sound that leaked out like stained water from an old cracked tap. It was the first real sound I'd made in weeks.

Sam was over at the barn, where he'd spent all his time since Jamie died, Tobie working by his side, every minute of every day. It looked as if nothing had changed for them — they just poured themselves into their work even harder — but Sam's hurt was visible just in the way he held his body, hunched down, as if warding off a blow, and Tobie's in the vacant glaze her eyes sometimes took on. Still, a perverse part of me wanted to believe that the pain was all mine.

I had managed to begin my journal again during the last two weeks — not to record dreams as I had in the past, for where there is little sleep there is little dreaming, but only to record everyday events, a written proof that life had indeed continued. When I'd looked at the journal last night I'd seen a record of frenetic activity: three horses sold, the dryer broken and repaired, the tackroom painted, the west pasture wall rebuilt, Hallmark notified via the postman by my mother that Allie Yates would not make her deadline due to a family crisis. And Rebecca coming by every day, trying to draw me out of the gray cloud.

Letting the screen door bang, I went then into the kitchen. My mother had left everything spotless, and the second load

of laundry was already in the dryer. For a minute I felt pan-
icky. What was I meant to do at this hour and in this place?
I couldn't remember. Was I really ready to begin again?
I took two pounds of hamburger from the refrigerator to
test myself. My mother's recipe handed down orally, a story,
never written, improved upon by my own variations. Onions,
celery, green pepper loaded my hands, and I balanced them
clumsily from refrigerator to chopping block. Oatmeal from
the cupboard, eggs from the wire basket. Garlic powder, tomato soup. These were the algebraic equations of our daily
life. Had our tragedy washed my mind clean of the simple
yet complex formula for solving the riddle of the meatloaf? I
laughed at myself and trembled simultaneously.

I went to get the big crockery bowl from under the sink,
but it wasn't there, and it took me some time to find it in the
high cabinet where it didn't belong. By the time I did I was
cursing my mother, and when I banged my head reaching to
retrieve the loaf pan from the glassware cupboard, tears came
to my eyes. I blinked them back and sighed. Did I still belong
here? One short month, and neither my life nor my kitchen
felt like my own anymore. It wasn't really my mother I was
mad at, because none of this was her fault.

Straightening my back, I poured a cup of coffee shakily and
wondered where the girls were. Anna had always helped me
make the meatloaf. I called up the back stairs, but there was
no answer. Maybe they were out at the barn with Tobie.
Suddenly I hated the silence around me and I didn't want to
be alone.

With the oatmeal soaking in milk, I forced myself to start
chopping vegetables, my knife clicking unevenly against the
board, my hands herding the green stalks forward and under
the blade in a ragged bundle. After a while the shaking in
my hands settled down; the knife strokes grew more rhythmic.
Making meatloaf, riding a horse, having sex, stretching a

canvas, giving birth — no matter how much time passed, no matter what happened since you last did it, the motions of life were learned and indelible.

The simple tasks calmed me some. My hand loosened the meat, broke it apart. A pause, then memory carried me onward: I cracked the eggs over, squashed the mixture through my fingers with a turn of my hand, feeling the egg slime gradually absorb as the loaf formed, adding the chopped vegetables just then so as not to overmix it. Even with a meatloaf there was a balance to be sought: not too little, but not too much — just so, as Tobie would say.

I turned the loaf into the pan and washed my hands, wiping the water on the backside of my bathrobe, and went to sit at the kitchen table for a minute. I took a deep breath as the girls clattered up the back porch. "Snack, please," Anna announced.

With relief, I got out the orange juice and began to pour it into two glasses.

"Mommy, that's not right," Anna said, surprised. "Juice goes in our red cups." I stared at her, puzzled for a minute, then I moved toward the cupboard, not knowing what I would do when I got there. When I opened the glass door, I saw three red plastic cups.

"Sorry," I muttered, rattled now. I took out the three cups and poured the juice into them. But as I set them on the table, I saw my own mistake. Quickly I sat down in front of Jamie's cup and took a cookie I didn't want. I used action to calm myself, believing that if the girls perceived my distress they would become upset. After crayoning a few pictures, we went upstairs to change Meggie's soggy overalls. I went into my room to get dressed, deciding that I'd been in my robe long enough. The girls tagged along, sitting to watch me, perched on the edge of our big bed like swallows on the barn fence.

"Tell me again about the marks on your tummy," Anna asked, as I pulled up my underwear.

"Baby lines," I answered slowly. She used to come over at least once a week to trace the silvery streaks of stretch across my abdomen with her finger. "The first ones came from you, and the rest . . ." The sentence trailed off into silence. We didn't look at each other. She burrowed into my open closet and I was relieved to have the subject changed. I pulled my shirt over my head, and when I emerged she had my city pocketbook over her arm and my blue pumps over her red Keds. They seemed like articles which ought to be up in some attic trunk. I couldn't imagine being brave enough now to go, all alone, into the city.

I was surprised, and gladdened, to see how quickly the girls were picking up the old routines, so I refrained from commenting on Anna's costume and turned instead to make the bed. Meggie slid off and went to stand beside her sister, who was swiveling and posing in front of the long mirror next to the window.

"When can I have my first high heels?" Anna asked, catching her toe in the braided rug and nearly toppling over.

"When you're big enough to walk without killing yourself." I thought back to my own mother, taking me to Grover Cronin's basement to look for my first pair of black pumps. Sixth grade. She'd elbowed other women aside to scoop up the only pair of black patent leather with a moderate heel; they were mated together by a piece of plastic punched right through their insteps. "Probably twelve or thirteen."

"*Thirteen!*" she wailed in dismay. "That's —" She tried to count on her fingers. "That's probably twenty years away!"

I smiled and pulled the quilt up. My anxiety lessened a little as I talked with Anna. I didn't feel quite so sick to my stomach now.

"I'd rather have a pair of real riding boots anyway," she said with disgust, taking off the heels.

I didn't comment, thinking of the Miller's catalogue with its prices close to two hundred dollars for a good pair of black show boots. And Anna would want that, I knew, for she was getting to be a fine rider. By the time she was six she'd be ready to enter the children's classes in the summer circuit.

She got up on the bed now and started to jump, everything forgotten for a moment in the sheer exhilaration of motion. She clapped her hands at the height of each bounce, and the sight of her stabbed at me: Jamie had been the one who always tested me by making my bed a trampoline. With his blond curls flying up and down, it had been his favorite naughty game. I turned away, wordless, and watched Meggie pull a pair of tights off the closet doorknob and put them over her head. She stood in front of the mirror, arranging one leg over each shoulder. She caught me looking.

"Bunny?" she asked hopefully.

I knelt behind her to hug her, anything to distract myself. "Yes," I answered, my voice still thick and choked. "Let's make long ears like a bunny." I pulled them up so she could imagine it better, but in the glass I could still see Anna flying up and down behind me. The springs of the bed creaked, threatening, but my chest and throat constricted: irritated by the noise, afraid for the bed, I still couldn't tell her to stop.

"Mommy, why did Jamie go away?" Anna flew into the air one last time and then just bounced down to sit without moving, her legs straight in front of her, waiting for my answer.

My breath caught in my throat, but still I didn't turn from the mirror or from Meggie. I glimpsed my older daughter's face in the glass. "I don't know," I said, trying to think up answers quickly. I wasn't ready for this. Then I stopped my own panic. Perhaps I should simply be honest, just give her the kind of answer I'd always wanted from my own mother. "Jamie took a toy to bed that was dangerous," I went on, swallowing hard. "I made a terrible mistake. That toy got tangled up around his neck."

"And then he just died? From that old toy?" She wanted

specifics, I saw, the mechanics of her brother's death: examining how it had worked would make it less magical and, therefore, safer.

Still crouched behind Meggie, I tied my sneaker laces very slowly. "When it got tight around his neck he couldn't breathe anymore."

She sat and thought about that for a minute. "When will he breathe again?"

"Do you think people who are dead can breathe, Anna?" I felt a little annoyed suddenly, and worried about Meggie. Anna knew Jamie wouldn't breathe, ever again, but Meggie was so young. How much could she, and how much did I want her to, understand? There was an enormous weight pushing behind my eyes, and my knees quivered from the strain of simply getting through this day. Anxiety revved in my chest, and I dropped my gaze from the mirror to lay my cheek against the nape of my youngest's neck.

"I guess not." Anna hung her head. It occurred to me then that maybe she was trying to ask something else.

"But I want him to! Won't we ever see him again, not ever?" Her voice had a quality of desperation to it now, and it was her desperation that reached me at last.

"We'll always keep Jamie in our hearts." I looked at her, feeling tears behind my eyes for the first time, but sensing that to become too emotional now might upset her and stop these questions she needed so badly to ask. "We'll remember him and love him always. But I don't think we will ever see him again." I closed my eyes and buried my face in Meggie's overall straps.

"Well, how long will he be dead?"

"When people die they're dead forever." My voice was so choked now it was a miracle I could form an answer at all. I wondered how much longer I could go on.

She wrinkled up her nose. "You mean, like Mildred?"

I nodded.

"But what about heaven? Are you sure he's not just in heaven?" Her face was troubled, and there were tears shining now over the surface of her eyes.

"No," I said at last, my voice quavering. "I'm not sure."

"Grandma Lynne said he might be in his heaven place, and that we could see him when we got there. Maybe I should go and look for him. I bet he's scared to be there all alone."

"Only people who die can go to heaven."

"You mean I'd have to die first?" she asked earnestly.

I nodded, and swallowed against the lump in my throat. "After you die — *if* you've been a very, very good person when you were on earth — you get to go to heaven and stay with God. That's what some people believe."

"But not you."

I shook my head, wishing with all my heart that I could believe my little boy was in a warm, beautiful place eating cake from a silver plate, being loved and cared for. In that instant I wished my mother — the instigator of all these heavenly questions — were here by my side right now to answer for me. If she had told me about heaven at this moment maybe I would have believed her. "Not me."

"Can you come back here afterwards?" she asked, with hope.

I shook my head again.

"I wouldn't get to be with Daddy or Meggie or Grandma Tobie?"

"Not if you died."

"Oh," she said, pausing a minute to consider all her options. "Well, will Jamie ever have ice cream again? Or how about a bath?"

"I don't think so." I shut my eyes against the picture of his small body locked away, deep, under the weight of all that dirt.

"I think you're wrong, Mom," Anna said, sliding down off the bed and taking my sun hat out of the closet. She came over to pose once again in front of the mirror. "I mean, they've got to have ice cream in heaven," she explained, settling the hat more firmly on her head with a little frown. "And I'm *sure* that God must make you take a bath."

I got up and went to sit on the bed, a smile turning up the corners of my mouth, relieved that the questions were over. Meggie clambered up beside me and snuggled in close. I put my arm around her, and with that motion I realized at last how long it had been since I'd cuddled either girl.

"Can I brush your hair?" Anna asked, breaking away from her reflection.

I shook my head. "Not now, honey." I still didn't want to be touched — not by anyone.

"Puh-lease, puh-lease, puh-lease!" She danced a circle in front of me, and when I hesitated, trying to think of how I could explain, she grabbed the brush and jumped up on the bed behind me.

Her small fingers burrowed down deep into the weight of my hair to lift it, bunched in her hand, off the nape of my neck. She brushed. Meggie leaned in closer. I felt the surround of my daughters — their love and need for the old ways, the familiar rituals. The side where Jamie used to lean was unguarded. My left arm hung empty. Anna's brushing was rhythmic, soothing, and warm. Once I had brushed my own mother's hair, fascinated by the long, shining wave of auburn — by that beauty — incongruous with the seams of her face. It was April, the sun mild against our winter skin, the grass still not green. She pulled the loose hairs from the brush and matted them into a soft ball with her fingers. "For the birds' nests," she said, letting it skitter out onto the wind.

Now it seemed there was no beauty anywhere, but only the cold wash of the waves, a gray rhythm of self-reproach inside my head, submerging me: my guilt, my guilt, my greatest guilt. Yet I could feel my daughters' touch gently pulling me back, and I was not sure I wanted to come. Depression was numb and safe. My girls' trusting, open faces made me ashamed. They asked me to show them how to continue, when continuing was the one thing I couldn't seem to manage.

Brush-brush, brush-brush: sensation spread, warmed my body, and little by little I leaned into it. I let my head hang, the weight bowing my neck, eyelids sleepy, and allowed pleasure in.

The tears came then too; those tears that I had been denying welled up strong and hot and soft. I had been alone so long: I had not wanted my girls to touch me, I realized, afraid I might harm them through some magical and deadly osmosis. I had not wanted Sam to touch me, afraid I would know at last my own aloneness. I had not wanted to cry, for to cry meant Jamie was truly gone.

Now the tears fell in a steady stream, silently, dropping over my lap, onto my hands, onto Meggie's small fist. Neither of them said anything. Anna stopped brushing and put her arms around my neck, tight, in a hug. Meggie's small hand stroked my arm, as if to say, as my own mother once had, "there, there." My daughters were comforting me. I could feel Anna's wet cheek against my own, and for the first time I felt someone else's suffering.

After a while Anna went back to my hair. She made a long, fat plait that hung slightly askew down the center of my back. "It's nearly time for lunch," I managed, wiping my face with my palms.

"Grilled cheese, grilled cheese, let's have grilled cheese!" Anna shouted, starting to bounce again. I slid from the bed and picked up my tights and hat from the floor. Jamie had never liked grilled cheese. Now I could make it for lunch without argument.

"French toasted cheese or plain?" I asked then, resolving to make it a special treat.

"French toasted!" she cried, running out of the room and down the hall.

Meggie and I followed more slowly, and when we got to the top of the stairs I saw Anna had made a detour. She'd opened the door into my imaginary linen closet. Jamie's room. She was sitting on his toy chest, cradling a stuffed giraffe in her arms. The feelings crossing her face were ones familiar to me, but I had not been able to do what she now did. Slowly, as if awaking from deep sleep, I looked around me.

A parade of animals lined the twin bed my son would never be big enough to sleep in. Trucks were parked in a row against the walls — my mother's handiwork. The books were stacked neatly, the puzzles laid out with all their pieces carefully interlocked. The clown-shaped bop bag, listing to the left, stood in the corner losing its air.

Meggie stepped across the threshold, tentatively. Even she could see that everything was still in place. "Where did Jamie's bear go?" she asked after a minute.

I stared at her, my mouth going dry. "Jamie took Teddy with him," I got out at last.

"To heaven?" Anna persisted.

"If Jamie's in heaven, his teddy's with him for sure." She was still hugging the giraffe. Now I remembered that it was the one she'd picked out at Nelson's to give Jamie for his second birthday. I went and sat down beside her to stroke its head. "Jamie would want you to take care of Stretch for him," I said. "He wouldn't like Stretch being lonely."

Anna studied the animal's face for a moment. "I think that's a good idea," she said gravely after a minute. "He could sleep on my bed with my stuffies."

I turned to ask Meggie if there was an animal she'd like to take to her room, but she was standing in front of the mirror, studying her reflection. On her head was Jamie's red baseball cap. I bit my lip. I didn't know if I had the strength to watch her wear it day after day. I walked over to stand behind her, and she looked up at me over her shoulder. She pointed at her reflection, touching the glass with the tip of her index finger. "I go 'way too, Mommy?"

For a moment I didn't speak, dumbfounded. Then I realized she was remembering that day more than a month ago, when Jamie and she had played before the mirror, studying their reflections and trying to puzzle out their own sheer numbers. Now she was a twin without a twin. I put my arms around her and pulled her against me. "You'll stay right here with me, Megg-o." I felt her tiny body tremble against mine and then straighten up. "And," I added, trying desperately to sound nonchalant, "maybe you'd better take Jamie's cap for now — you remember he didn't like it ever to be off his head? This way you could keep it warm for him." She nodded, taken with the importance of her task.

I knew if we didn't get downstairs right away I was going to submerge again into my safe gray cloud. The pain was back, turned up full, and I struggled to control it with my mind. I herded the girls toward sandwiches, wondering if there would come a time when every detail of our living would cease to be colored by his going.

Tobie's sharp eye took in the changes immediately: lunch on the table, a daughter-in-law who was at least dressed and trying to look somewhat in charge. She sat down, polished her fork with her napkin, and then poked suspiciously at her hamburger to make sure it was well done. Nothing turned her stomach faster, she claimed, than blood in her meat. I didn't say anything as her familiar examination continued, but just poured the girls' milk. She insisted that eating his meat rare was what had killed Carson so early in life, although Sam and I kept telling her that was an old fish tale.

Once reassured, Tobie began straightaway to eat, cutting

Meggie's grilled cheese into bite-sized pieces with one hand while she put her hamburger away with the other.

"Where's Sam?" I asked, getting up to slide another burger onto the griddle for her.

"Got someone interested in buying an animal out to the pasture," she said, jerking her thumb in the direction Sam must have gone. "Fellow who bought Tornado told this guy 'bout us, so he came down from Sunapee. Been on vacation in one of those condos on the lake."

"What's he looking for?" I asked, trying to sound interested. A potential buyer was good news, but I couldn't muster much excitement.

"Something young. For their eight-year-old girl." She lifted her eyebrows and tipped her head slightly in Anna's direction, telling me without words that the buyer was interested in Duet's first foal, due any day now. Anna was not going to like the sale of this foal, the first she'd have witnessed out of her pony.

"It seems too hard," I murmured.

She looked at me without smiling or nodding in agreement, sizing me up, and not really listening to what I'd said. I waited, but she put her head back down and went on eating.

"When Carson died," she said after a while, "it took me a long time to make myself a decent meal. Then all of a sudden I got hungry again. Panfried up a big hamburger with onions." She ran her tongue over her lips: she was remembering the taste of living again.

I didn't answer: sometimes with Tobie you had to wait a bit before she got around to her point.

"Good to see you dressed."

I laughed sadly. "Took me long enough."

Sam stomped the mud from his boots on the back porch and came through the door. He slid into his chair and scooped up his burger in one motion, taking a huge bite. "Flip another in for me, Allie?" he asked, looking at me with the spatula in my hand and smiling.

I busied myself at the stove to hide the anxiety on my face.

"Why is that man looking at Duet?" Anna's voice quivered but did not break.

Sam looked at me, then Tobie, then cleared his throat. He reached across to pat Anna's hand. "You did such a good job taking care of her that he wants to buy the foal." His voice was gentle but firm.

Anna chewed her grilled cheese slower and slower. "But the foal isn't born yet, Daddy." She put the sandwich down and poked at it.

"It will be any day now. When it's big enough, Mr. Shapiro will come down to pick it up. He's got a little girl just a bit older than you." He reached over to ruffle her hair, but she drew back.

The room fell silent except for the spatter of grease in the frying pan. I stabbed at the meat, thinking again how unfair it was. For a minute I hated him. Sam poured more ketchup on his plate. Tobie drank her tea and watched Anna over the rim of her cup. Anna sat very still, very straight, in her chair.

"You knew we'd have to sell that foal," Sam said at last, keeping his voice low and matter-of-fact. He didn't look at Anna now. "That's how we earn the bread and butter here."

"It's not even born yet," Anna repeated plaintively. "How can you talk about sending it away when it's not even born?"

"You knew all about it." His face changed then, moving from worry to fatigue to a set stubbornness — an expression which looked, I imagined, quite a bit like one his father might have used. "When it's weaned at four months it'll be time. These animals aren't pets."

As I put the hamburger on his plate, I put my hand on Anna's shoulder. "Sam," I began tentatively.

He shook his head sharply. "That's how it is, Allie," he

said. "The two of us went over all this before the pony was even bred."

Anna's face puckered up and she slid from behind the table to shoot out of the room, knocking her chair over in her haste to escape.

"She can't remember all that now!" Color and heat rose to my face. "Why should she have to lose everything at once?"

"Life's life," he insisted mechanically. "It's got to be faced."

"It stinks!" I strode to the sink and turned the cold water into the hot pan. A hiss of steam rose around me.

"Seeing and knowing are two different things, Sam," Tobie observed, getting up to follow Anna.

"Damn you." I turned back to him. "I'll finish my commission and earn the money so she can keep the foal."

"You!" He laughed bitterly. "This is the first time in a month you've been dressed! The first time you've cooked a meal! How can you even talk of taking on some new drawing?"

Stung, I stared at him.

"If you're thinking of finally doing something, why don't you get Jamie's room cleaned out? It gives me the willies, everything just sitting there like it was waiting for him to come back through the door."

I lurched as if he had hit me. To pack up Jamie's clothes, his toys — his living . . . it was too soon, too cruel. I could only shake my head: there were no words in my mouth. Over the intercom next to the sink came the distant sounds of Anna sobbing and Tobie comforting.

"It's got to be done," Sam went on insistently. His voice grew choked and thick. "Anna with his giraffe, the cap on Meggie's head — it's not right, Allie."

"What do you want me to do, rub out the fact that he even existed?" Rage filled me. "It helps them to have his things, to remember and know it's all right to remember. You just go about your business, spend all your time in that damned barn pretending he's not gone!"

"Don't kid yourself. I know he's gone every minute of every day." He looked at me with pure hate in his face, and anguish too. I felt like I was really seeing him for the first time in weeks. "*You're* the one won't talk about what's happened, Allie."

I didn't answer, because I knew he was right. I was the one unwilling to share.

"Remembering is fine," he went on, his voice still tight with anger. "But keeping him alive is something else. Wearing his clothes, using his toys . . . I took care of all the —" He broke off; his voice sounded like it had a bubble in it. " — arrangements. All by myself. Now it's your turn!"

A whimper from Meggie made us realize she was still sitting at the table, strapped into her highchair, watching. She clutched the cap in both her hands, as if we might take it from her. I went over and started scrubbing ketchup off her face.

"Allie," Sam whispered then, putting his forehead against the edge of the table. "It's been so hard without you . . ."

I was silent. The enormous cost of the grief he had carried alone was painted for me vividly as he slumped against the table. But I couldn't let go of my anger. I used it as a shield.

"Allie, please — can't we talk? We could go upstairs —"

"Don't worry, Meggie," I comforted my daughter, "no one's going to take it away from you." I set the cap on her head defiantly and lifted her from the chair. Cradling her against me, I left the room without answering my husband and went to put Meggie in for her nap. When I came back downstairs his chair was empty.

My anger with Sam drove me to my studio then, in the hope that I might finish the abandoned watercolor for Hallmark, earn some extra money, and so spare my daughter the pain of another loss. I didn't put on my Red Sox cap though, but only took out a fresh canvas and set up my acrylics. The brushes felt strange in my hands. It seemed better to paint something imaginary, a scene conjured from my mind: Jamie and Meggie, hiding in the high grasses behind the barn. It might end up as an illustration for the month of July on a calendar, but it could still be a testament to my son.

I squeezed my eyes shut and tried to imagine what they might have looked like on such a day. Against the screen of my eyelids I waited for a scene to bloom. But everything remained dark. Silent. My fingers trembled slightly, and I opened my eyes to dip into the color: perhaps this painting would simply emerge from my hand.

I drew a long brown line down the center of the canvas. My hand rose and fell again and again, and the white space became crowded with long, shaky brown stripes. These were the lines of my own impotence. I couldn't get beyond my mind, to Jamie. It was too much to draw even his face.

I leaned my head against the edge of the easel in fatigue and despair. Nothing was the same anymore. How could I possibly pretend it was? How could I pretend that I continued?

A knock on the door startled me, and I ignored it at first, hoping Sam would go away. Then it came again, and with it, Rebecca's voice calling my name. Hurriedly I pulled a drape down over the canvas.

I swung it open without looking into her face, because I wanted to hide the fact that I had been crying.

"You finally made it up here," she said, unzipping her yellow rain slicker.

"Is it raining again?"

"Mostly just drizzling. I'm glad you're back at work," she said, pulling her coat off and a pack of thin cigars from the back pocket of her jeans.

"I'm not," I answered then. "Not really."

"But at least you're up where you can make a start."

"I tried, Rebecca," I said around the lump in my throat, "I really did. But I can't do it." I lifted my hands in a gesture of despair and started to cry. It struck me that now that I'd started crying it was impossible to stop. "It's like being blind."

She patted my shoulder awkwardly, and we stood there for a while as I cried weakly. "I know it's overwhelming," she said in a low voice after some time had passed. "But now you've got it out where you can see it — and you've got to use it." She went over to stand moodily in front of the window, backlit, as I blew my nose. "It's time now to make it work *for* you."

I stared at her, my chest tight and queer. I hated her for making it sound as if all I needed to do was set my mind to it and suddenly I would heal, paint great pictures, and go back to living an ordinary life. I hated her for being able to walk away from my pain so casually and light up her thin cigar.

"It hurts too much," I answered angrily. "You can't possibly understand."

"I've never had a child," she admitted slowly, "so I don't understand *exactly.*" Her voice was a little tight and defensive now. "Still, I *have* lost some people I loved. And it did hurt. For a long time. But then I made something of the pain, and that helped the hurt."

I brooded over her words and stood at the table rearranging brushes in a jar, refusing to acknowledge that she could know what I felt. My pain was as precious and special as Jamie himself had been.

"I had to let go of Evan," she said after I'd been silent a few more minutes. Her voice was a low, gravelly whisper.

"Evan?" I looked up, disconcerted. I went and sat on the couch. "Evan Hirsch?"

She nodded. "After my divorce I shied away from letting people get close." She shrugged awkwardly, and I could see it was hard for her to talk about it. "But Evan — he just sneaks

up on you. You're so distracted by his brash and noisy out-
sides that you don't even realize . . ." She drifted off, turning
slowly from the window, and came to sit beside me on the
couch, picking at paint-stained cuticles with her long fingers.
I remembered the first time she'd spoken of him, back in July,
on the day I'd met her, and the way I'd intuited there was
more between them than friendship.

"I broke it off when I moved up here," Rebecca went on.
"More to the point — I moved up here as one way of getting
away from him. He was too much a part of everything. I
couldn't go anyplace without thinking of him, the gallery,
moviehouses, museums, vegetable stands, restaurants — even
the Chinese laundry." She lit up another cigar. "I didn't want
to mope around like some romantic fool." She laughed, a
smoky rasp from deep in her throat. "Which is all I really
was of course. So I came to Arrowsic. I went back to work."

"Why did you break it off?" I asked hesitantly.

"It was only a matter of time before he found something,
or someone, that excited him more than me. I'd been left once
before, don't forget." She sighed and got up again, went back
to the window, puffing on her cigar.

"Your husband left you?" Somehow I had envisioned it the
other way around.

Again she shrugged. "As I suspected, it wasn't hard to
convince Evan we should just be friends." Her voice tightened. "You'll see what I mean when you meet him. I'm picking him up on the five o'clock Greyhound." She pushed up
her sleeve and looked at the watch on her right arm and then
at the one on her left.

"Today?"

She nodded. "That's why I came over. I was down at the
IGA stocking up: sardines, pumpernickel, cheddar, and beer."
She made a face and picked up a small canvas which lay on
the worktable, examining it under a light. "He's a picky eater."

"I can't meet anyone new now, Rebecca," I said irritably,

annoyed at her persistence and insensitivity. Surely she could understand that I wasn't ready to start socializing.

"It'd be good for you," she said. "And you'd make things easier for me, too."

"You want a favor? At a time like this?" I asked incredulously.

"You could be saying that the rest of your life." She came over to me, pinning me with the direct gaze of her different eyes. "It's really for both of us anyway, because in the long run you're going to have to let the real world in up here. Sometime or other."

"I'm not ready."

"Evan's a bald talker," she went on, as if I hadn't refused her. "Never lies, never hedges about what he thinks of someone else's work. He isn't threatened when you do something good, keeps his own ego out of his opinions so you can trust him. He'll get a lift out of knowing he's the first New Yorker to see your stuff."

I walked over and took the painting from her hands. "I'm not meeting Evan Hirsch, I'm not showing anyone anything."

"Why not?"

"I don't feel up to it."

"Why not?"

"Jamie was the one who was going to show things," I answered dreamily, turning away and moving toward the window, still holding the painting. I stood looking out into the branches as they moved against the sky, and then stared down into my own work. "Jamie would have been brave enough."

"That's some fantasy. Just one big way of avoiding what *you* have to do. Even if he hadn't died he couldn't have painted for you, exhibited for you, or lived for you."

A slow fuse of anger began to glow inside my brain. "You still don't understand," I said tightly, putting my back to her as I went to the closet and put the canvas back, locking the door.

She sighed. "There are degrees of pain in life, Allie, but basically all pain is the same. The question is solely one of intensity. Paint about Jamie," she said, putting her hand on my shoulder and forcing me to turn back to her. She looked into my eyes, her voice an entreaty. "Remember him here" — she tapped her heart — "and bring it out for us to see. To share."

I got up and crossed to the easel. I lifted the drape on the acrylic. "There," I said, my voice bitter again. "That's what I can share right now. That's all I can share."

She came closer and stared for a while. "Some people in New York would think that was art," she said at last.

"I don't."

"Neither do I. At least, not from you."

I was in no mood to be flattered. "Oh, stop it. The point is I can't do anything at all!"

"Maybe you don't want to badly enough."

"But I do!" I said heatedly. "Sam and I just had a fight about selling Anna's new foal when it comes. If I could finish this damned commission, then she could keep the foal."

"That's the stupidest thing I ever heard."

My cheeks were hot, as if she'd slapped me. "What is?"

"Start painting again — but not for some romantic notion of saving Anna from reality. Worry about yourself! Worry about Sam!"

"Stop being so melodramatic!"

"Stop using self-pity to block everything out and start to *paint* again."

"It's too soon," I answered defensively.

"Don't you see how lucky you are?" Her voice was suddenly loud, and I backed away from her. "You have two other children and a husband who loves you." She put up her hand

and ticked off statements on her fingers. "But your children need you and you haven't been there. You've let your husband live through this terrible time alone — you froze him out, and he's a damned sensitive man. His mother's been the one holding him when he cries."

I stared at her, stunned she should know something as intimate as that — something even I did not know. "How —"

"Even worse," she went on, "you haven't *used* the pain. Do it now, before it's too late."

"I got enough pushing and shoving when my mother was here," I said through gritted teeth. Suddenly I wanted to be alone again, to retreat into my gray wooly world. "Why don't you go now?"

"Fine," she said, still angry, biting the end of her cigar in frustration and squashing it out on my watercolor palette. Picking up her rainslicker, she strode through the door and down the stairs.

I flew around the studio in a rage, kicking the couch, the cans of turpentine, striking the edge of my easel with my foot till it hurt and tears came to my eyes. And, little by little, it occurred to me that I was not angry with Rebecca for being her pushy, direct self, or with my mother for misunderstanding me so completely and rearranging my pots, or with Tobie and Sam for going back to work. I sat down at my worktable and doodled with a pencil, as a way of releasing my thoughts. I watched my hand sketch a woman: she stood at a window, a man on one side of her, a child on the other.

I stared at the drawing and knew then that I was angry with Sam for having called me back to bed that night, and with myself — for having gone. With resignation and finality I let my mind touch the thought that I had handed my son the toy that killed him. And then I hadn't gone to check when he called out for me. I couldn't blame Sam anymore.

I started to cry, really cry, like a child, with sobs that squeezed my entire body. I cried until my nose dripped and the sleeve of my blouse grew soggy from being used as a tissue. I cried until my eyelids were red and swollen into fat sausages. I cried until the bitter taste left my mouth and there was only a deep, hollowed-out emptiness inside me. And I knew that this was only the beginning.

I pushed myself up. I walked across the room to draw the cover off the painting of Jamie in the garden, under that chrome-yellow sun. He was in another world now, somewhere I could not go. Perhaps Rebecca, with her hard, blunt words, was right. Perhaps painting was the answer. I went over to the window again, wiping my cheeks with the backs of my hands, blowing my nose on an old rag. The clouds were still low, belly-flat against the mountains. The pastures were washed-out green, mauve, lavender. In the distance Sam and Meggie and Anna hovered over an animal which was prone. It looked as if Duet's time had come. I wondered where Tobie was, and if the foal had been born.

Slowly I took the painting of brown stripes and, using my mat knife, sliced it into pieces small enough to fit in the trash. Maybe I would paint a picture of Jamie. I still couldn't see it with my mind, but suddenly I believed that I might see it someday. Meggie would be in it, and perhaps Anna. Or maybe just Meggie, with Jamie's baseball cap, as the central focus, and soft, aching colors — colors drawn out of the pain I felt. I went to the door, but I looked back over my shoulder. This room was where I would begin to work it all out.

Downstairs I headed for the kitchen, but stopped short outside the door, hearing Rebecca's sharp exclamations over Tobie's low growl. It didn't even occur to me not to listen. "I like her too much to worry if she gets pissed at me!" Rebecca said to my mother-in-law. "I've always said what I thought, and I'm not about to stop now!"

I heard Tobie scratch a match over the hearth. "She did do lunch today, and took care of the girls this morning. I think she's comin' around." She cleared her throat with a phlegmy cough. "Sometimes you need someone to slap you hard and wake you up." In her voice was a grudging sort of admiration. Rebecca sighed and said she'd be back tomorrow. With a start I realized then how Rebecca knew so much about Sam. She and Tobie had shared their worry about me, and about him. Worry had united them and made them almost neighborly.

"Mom, I've decided I want to name him Jamie." Anna's head was high, but her chin quivered. "Can I?"

The foal was coal black, with a star on his forehead and two white socks. He was wet and trembly and hugged his mother's flank. Slowly Sam reached out to take my hand, and for the first time in weeks, we touched. I squeezed his fingers in an apology. In our daughter's eyes was the courage for which I was still groping, the courage to face Jamie's death — not to run, not to blank it out and be numb. The courage to acknowledge that life would continue without him.

"Yes, Anna," I said, taking her small bony frame in my arms and hugging her with all my strength. "I think that would be just fine."

"That way when he leaves here, part of our family will go with him. He'll always be a part of us."

Sam and I got a little teary then, and we all stood in a clump, watching the mare and her nursing foal. From behind the clouds, the sun began to shine forth in patches, and I saw that Rebecca was right. We had to rely on one another to help heal the wound. But what I could not see that clearing afternoon in the west pasture was the shadow and the cunning of my own inner division: to lay my son to rest at last, and to keep him yet alive.

Inner Divisions

The next day I resolved to pack away Jamie's belongings, and Tobie caught me staring moodily out the window after breakfast. It was warming up, promising to be hot for the first time in several weeks. "You planning to work today?" She lit a Camel as she finished the dishes and hung the drying cloth over the handle of the oven.

"I was thinking about getting to Jamie's room." My eyes filled again and I blinked furiously. "I'd like to take care of it. It's hard on Sam."

Tobie nodded. "Your mother wanted to do it before she left, but —" She looked away and took a deep drag, exhaling as she went on. "I told her I thought it was yours to do."

"You're probably right." I sighed. "Still, part of me wishes . . ." My voice drifted off. "I just dread the thought of going through all those drawers alone."

"We're going to be busy this morning with getting the mares ready to trailer down to Maryland," Tobie said, worry creasing her voice. "But this afternoon, late, I could —"

"No." I shook my head. "Now I've made my mind up, I want to get it over with."

"Rebecca will probably come by sometime this morning. Expect she'd be happy to give you a hand."

I nodded and decided I didn't want to wait for Rebecca to turn up. I called her instead, pretty sure she wouldn't still be angry over our argument yesterday. And, although she simply agreed to help, saying she'd be by at eleven, her voice sounded as if she were pleased I had phoned. Later that morning we climbed the stairs to his room without speaking; I cast a sideways glance at her strong profile, grateful she had come.

At the door to Jamie's room I didn't allow myself to hesitate, but twisted the knob and stepped over the threshold in one fluid motion. I put the box of trash bags on the dresser and set my two cartons down near the toy shelf. Rebecca did the same.

"So."

"So," I echoed.

"Do you want to save anything? For Anna or Meggie?"

I shook my head.

"How about yourself?"

"I thought about it, but . . ."

She waited for me to finish.

"It hurts to see someone else using his things. I gave each of the girls one toy, and it really upset Sam."

"If you wait awhile" — she shrugged — "he might find it easier as time goes on."

"That's good," I agreed, trying to sound positive. "Maybe I'll start with the dresser."

"What do you want me to do? The toys?"

"Well." I looked up at the toys. I couldn't imagine parting with a single one. Slowly I walked over to the shelves. Nearly everything was worn, a few were broken, some had pieces missing. I picked up his top. "I remember the day he learned how to make this go," I said, putting it down on the floor and pumping it to see the train inside trundle down its circular track with a whistle. "It was Christmas, and he got so excited." I gave it another push as I thought back to that wonderful day, overflowing with happy squeals from the kids, the smell of Tobie's roasting goose, the litter of wrapping paper, and the dry hiss — a blizzard — against the window glass. How safe we'd felt, how rich, how untouchable. My nose prickled. "He was very coordinated. Even Anna had trouble working it at first."

"What about these?" Rebecca held up a set of nesting boxes. "They're beautiful. Look at the craft."

"Sam made them, and then I did the painting." Jamie's first birthday: he'd just learned how to say Mama, Dadda, Toe-bee, and damm; I was learning how to watch my mouth. I took the boxes from Rebecca, turning them slowly in my hands, saddened. I studied the grain of the maple, the carefully joined edges — made like a piece of fine cabinetry — and my own precise brush strokes decorating each box with scenes of our family life: Sam milking a cow, Jamie and me collecting eggs, Anna currying Duet, Meggie patting a foal, Tobie raking out the paddock. I swallowed around the lump in my throat, and my voice was low. "He loved these."

"Allie." She dug her pack of cigars out of her back pocket. "Don't make a mistake here. Some of these things are your family heritage. You can't just unload everything into a Salvation Army dumpster."

"Maybe I could put them in a box in the attic."

"Maybe you could put them on the shelves in Meggie's room."

I nodded then, reluctantly, not trusting my voice, and she touched my shoulder lightly. Tears made a fine sheen in front of my vision. I pulled down *Goodnight Moon* and flipped through, blinking. How many nights had we made a game of tracking the mouse, who popped up in a different spot on each page? There was so much to remember — too much. The pain was a tight surcingle around my chest: it was keeping me together; it was cracking me in two.

I understood suddenly that remembering must be the purpose of this activity, all this packing and sorting. I couldn't let someone else fold away his life; I couldn't give up this moment of knowing how much Jamie had given me. And so I was glad suddenly for the remembering, for the special, bittersweet pain — a pain which meant he had lived, was loved, had made a dent in this life he'd found so intriguing, so full of areas to explore and conquer. I saw him once again, climbing into the tire swing, clambering up the ladder, "mekking" his eggs as I fried the bacon. Once again the softness of the kiss, the touch, all that was Jamie.

"Thank you."

She ducked her head in a nod, seeming preoccupied. "When I got divorced I had to pack up my husband's stuff," she said after a minute. "And everything I touched either made me angry or sad. I couldn't stand the sight of those boxes stacked in the foyer, so I ended up shoving it all out into the hall. The garbage people nearly took off with it." She started to laugh. "My husband didn't think it was too funny. He was really pissed. My shrink told me to use all that emotion for my work, which really pissed *me* off. At the time." She inhaled hard on her thin cigar and looked over at me. "See — you get the same good advice, but it doesn't cost."

I smiled weakly. "You *were* right. Or rather, your psychiatrist was. Sorry I was so mad."

She laughed and gave me a gentle poke. "Your turn on the condolence bandwagon will come. Just wait till I get my next crappy review — then I'll be taking it out on you."

I smiled, distracted again by the weight of all the objects in front of us and the choices we had to make.

Rebecca took down the Fisher Price stacking rings, a Raggedy Andy, and a soccer ball and began putting them into the carton.

"How did you get through losing someone you'd lived with for so long?" I asked, fiddling with the box of trash bags.

"Once he was gone it wasn't so bad. It was the waiting for him to leave that was the worst."

"You never told me about your husband before."

"Probably never will." She rasped out another laugh. "And with Evan," she went on, bending to put another armload into the carton, "packing up was just the same. Maybe even harder. Seeing him again this soon has been tough."

"Then why did you let him come?"

"We're friends, remember?" She grinned, but I could see the pain behind the lopsided smile. "He doesn't know how I feel, and I don't want him to. I want him to think it was all clean and easy."

"But —"

"What does it matter how I *feel?* I know what's right to *do.*" She shrugged. "The end would've been the same no matter how I handled it. Some things you can't change."

I was quiet, then got up and went over to the dresser. For me this was the hardest part: so much in those drawers was acutely Jamie, the last things to touch his body. Even though everything had been laundered, his sweet smell still clung in the folds of denim and cotton. Bravely I pulled open the top drawer, pants and shorts, and took out a stack. Holding it pinched between my chest and chin, I shook out a trash bag and dumped it in. It was September second. In another few weeks I would have been packing away his summer clothes and laying in those for winter. Instead, the drawers would remain empty.

Behind me Rebecca kept laying things in the carton. A brand-new baseball glove that he would never use, a bat that he liked to drag around in the dirt but had never hefted over his shoulder. All the pieces of life he would never live.

We were quiet, stacking, sorting, folding. I decided to keep all the books. The girls would want them. But I couldn't bring myself to save any of his clothes: it was as Sam had said — just too painful to see someone else in his things. From the changing table I threw out the Desitin, the cotton swabs, the jar of ointment Dr. Loring had prescribed for his rash. Jamie's brush held a web of fine blond hair. I rolled it into a soft ball between my fingers and slipped it into my shirt pocket. This I would keep.

I transferred three bags of diapers from his closet into Meggie's. When I came back, Rebecca was folding up the quilt from his crib, the quilt I had made before he was born, appliquéd with barnyard animals. There was finality to the stripping of the bedding. The bars guarded nothing now, an empty box with a mattress of stained white plastic. A lump rose in my throat, a lump that was difficult to swallow around. "Hard, isn't it?" Rebecca touched my shoulder lightly.

"It isn't goodbye," I answered automatically, in defense.

"No?"

"I won't say goodbye. Not like that."

She looked at me sadly, and I shut my mouth before I could tell her about the hope which had soared in me for one brief moment this morning as I was working upstairs. Instead I tied the trash bags closed. "I went up to my studio again this morning," I said. "I will get back to work."

"What first?"

I shook my head in amazement at her. "All I did was open the windows and air the place out, stack my old work in the closet, and put my new stuff where I could see it. To remember where I left off before . . ."

She nodded. "Have you changed your mind about coming over?"

I hesitated. "I thought maybe I'd stop in and meet him this afternoon — but that's all! No showing anybody anything!"

"Why don't you do what you feel like when you feel like it? I know you and he are going to hit it off anyway."

"I just want to get back to work, start feeling normal."

"That may take a long time. You may never be done with this." She gestured with a sweep of her arm to the empty room. Our voices echoed now.

As we closed the door, I thought of my morning in the studio. It had helped to clean it out, to let in light and air where only dark gloom had been before. It had helped to look at the work I'd done earlier in the summer and see progress. Time away from working had given me some perspective. But then I'd been startled out of my self-analysis by a disconcerting sound from behind me — a noise I'd never expected to hear again: Jamie's fingers, scratching under the door in our old game.

I nearly turned and called out to him. I forgot, in that instant, that he was gone. But then I froze. It couldn't be. The sound came again and even his voice was calling, high above the strong wind that sailed suddenly through the room.

I stayed motionless while the wind and his voice licked at my body. *Mommeecum.* I stayed motionless until I was calm and clear, until I was like a weather-smoothed stone. I managed to shut hope off then: I could not bear to turn and see the empty space. I could not stand the pain. So after a minute I picked up a can of turp and set it down with a loud thump. I went and cranked the windows down. I did not once turn toward that door, and after a while the room was silent and once more my own. The episode had shaken me: my mind knew how to provide me with the things I wanted to see.

As I said goodbye to Rebecca now I knew I didn't really want to see, meet, or talk with Evan Hirsch. Shyness overwhelmed me. Some things you do because you want to, some things because you have to, some because you're sure you're supposed to. Meeting Evan fell in the latter category. So, later that afternoon, I dressed myself carefully: a clean chintz skirt, a soft cotton shirt, my hair washed and loosed in waves down my back. I even shaved my legs for the first time since the funeral. I slipped on my sandals and walked over through the woods.

He wasn't at all what I'd expected. Wiry, five foot ten, with frizzy brown hair that haloed his head and dark blue eyes that continually challenged, he was the most intense man I'd ever met. It was a shock after all the weeks in such a cloistered atmosphere, after my mother's tentative conversation, Sam's and Tobie's silences, my own interior echo. Rebecca's "bald talker" turned out to be an electric current of words: harsh, brash, to the point, uncensored. And he had no difficulty in talking about himself either. Within one short hour and two Heinekens, he'd managed to cram in his entire history, tossing it off as if it were mere factual data. Only a few years older than I, he came from a big Jewish family and had spent most of his life competing with his father and his older brother. His mother had encouraged him to try something different from the others when she saw early talent budding in the shapes he punched into his Play-Doh, and I envied him that early support. I thought about how my own life might have differed if I'd had even one parent who understood what was happening to me. Evan dropped out of Ithaca College in his sophomore year, took a job in a grade school teaching papier-mâché, and late at night sculpted, sculpted, sculpted, developing a distinctive style with wire. That style was soon caught up by the New York elite, and, as easy as that — he claimed with a wide gesture — he was made.

As we talked I could feel Rebecca watching him, could see the fondness on her face. She was still in love with him, I realized then. But I wasn't sure if I liked him. He was like a very large mouthful of some strange and foreign food: either great or ghastly, but I wasn't sure which. I felt a smart of jealousy at their history together and was glad to be a painter, not a sculptor. At least Rebecca and I shared a means of expression which Evan did not.

Being a prolific talker about himself didn't mean that he monopolized the conversation, though. It seemed as if telling his history was a kind of preliminary, his way of laying himself out before his listeners and saying, Now let's get on with it: who are you? As the two of us left Rebecca to her work and walked down the path back toward our farm, he kept at it: he wasn't going to let me hide, and he was determined to know me — which I found puzzling as well as threatening.

"Why are you so interested in all this?" I asked at last in exasperation, having already told him more than I wanted to. He'd worn me down with his continual questions.

"You don't see it, do you?"

"What?"

"How *unusual* you are! That you could've been painting for twenty-odd years and never even tried to go public. It's really hard to believe." He grinned, those blue eyes widening and deepening. He pulled a pair of dark glasses from his pocket and put them on. "Most people are out there hawking their fish long before they're ready, and here you are, shut up in an attic. A real Emily Dickinson routine." He sounded delighted with me, as if I were a steal and he were a sleazy car salesman. "You have to admire someone who puts the actual work, the painting itself, first, and doesn't worry at all about the recognition."

He'd done it again: complimented me just as I was thinking something derogatory about him. It kept me off balance, and I looked down at the ground, feeling resentful. One minute he was aggressive and obnoxious, and the next, perceptive and sensitive. What was it that Rebecca found attractive in him?

We turned the corner and came from the path into the west

pasture. I motioned toward the house and back garden and we kept walking. "How did you meet Rebecca?" I asked, steering the subject off me again.

"Wrote her a fan letter and asked to come see her."

"And she wrote back?" I could hear my own incredulity.

He nodded. "Invited me down to her place in SoHo. I went. There was chemistry. She sponsored me at the gallery. The rest you know."

I knew a lot more than he thought, but I didn't say anything, thinking that I never would have had the self-confidence or the gall to write to a famous artist and suggest a meeting. For the first time, then, I understood what Rebecca could do for me, if I was willing to let her.

"Rebecca has a habit," he said, speeding up a bit so that he passed me and then walked backward in front of me, half running on the tips of his toes, but still talking, "of picking up stray dogs — know what I mean? Likes pulling people into her orbit, especially talented *young* people. Jazzes her up. Like fuel. When she told me she was moving up here I was really bummed. Where? I said. No one leaves the city. But you can see it in her work — she's tripled her output, gotten more experimental."

I realized suddenly, instinctively, that he didn't know about Rebecca's real reasons for leaving New York. He'd known her longer, but already I knew her more intimately. He was too bouncily self-involved to see the pain on her face. I felt sorry for her and understood suddenly why she'd moved away from him. He was too much of a child to resist anything, or anyone, tempting — and he wasn't the sort to be discreet, either.

"Now that there's nothing to distract her she's like a machine," Evan went on. Again he grinned, taking off his sunglasses, and his eyes caught the late-afternoon light and turned an even darker, more mesmeric blue. "Nothing except you, that is. And you're quite a distraction, I can tell."

I flushed, picking up the innuendo, and looked away. Inside me a small voice was repeating a string of words over and over, like a cycle, a wheel of thought that had no beginning or end, just the cadence of its question: *Whywhywhy are you taking him back with you?*

Because he'd insisted, because he'd dared me, because he'd irritated and upset and teased me. Because I didn't want him to know how vulnerable I really felt. If I showed him my paintings I wouldn't have to show myself. Which was irrational, considering the two were interchangeable.

"The sun's turning your hair red." He stopped running and I nearly bumped into him as he blocked my way. We were nose to nose: his hand lifted a wave of my hair, lying loose across my shoulder. "Incredible." A smell of fresh sweat came off him as he raised his arm to touch me, his blue jeans outlined the hard muscles of his thighs and caught him in the crotch. Sam would never have worn pants that tight.

I moved around him, not at all prepared to handle what might follow. "There're my little girls," I said, pointing over to the paddock in the distance where they were helping Tobie tie Duet and her foal to the fence. Evan turned to squint at them and said nothing. We walked through the back garden and into the house. The screen door slammed behind us. He looked around, but I didn't pause, just went through the kitchen to the stairs, and then up, up, up, passing Jamie's empty room on the way. I wondered if Rebecca had told him that my son had died recently.

The heat was fading from the day, but the studio was still stuffy, so I occupied myself with cranking open the windows while Evan made himself a tour of everything standing anywhere in the room. Fresh air whipped through as the wind found its way in. He flipped without comment through stacks of my commercial artwork and my most serious pieces alike. After a while I sat down on the couch and just waited. He didn't stop until he'd come to the end, and to my surprise I was not sweating or shaking. It all felt distant somehow, not really important enough to get anxious over.

He selected five canvases and took them to the easel. "Like a lot of it," he commented swiftly in his telegraphic style. "But these are outstanding."

I flushed with pleasure. I'd never had anyone use such a superlative in connection with my work.

"I like this barn a lot," he said, putting a different one up on the stand. I had done it right before Jamie died, after I'd met Rebecca, in tempera. "Reminds me of home. And the way you've got the shadows — like it's night, but the color of the sky tells you it's day . . . well, I just like it." Suddenly he seemed shy, more in slow motion, more relaxed, talking about what he liked, as if he were speaking of desire instead of a painting.

He put the one of Jamie up and stood silent in front of it, thinking. "This makes me sad, and afraid," he said after a while. "The angular lines and the hard colors. Was this your little boy?"

I nodded silently, my question about what Rebecca might have told him answered.

"How did you have the guts to do this so soon after he died?"

I found my voice and went to stand beside him. "I did it before."

A chill passed over us. He reached out and put his hand on my shoulder. He was silent, nonplussed for a minute.

I spoke slowly, a new idea forming with my words. "It was a warning, I think — but I didn't want to see it."

"Do you really believe in things like that?"

I looked at the floor. "Maybe." I felt surprise as I said the word, and laughed awkwardly. "But if I had the power to stop it . . ." My voice fell to a whisper in the silence. I didn't finish my thought.

"I don't know what to say."

"I don't know what to do, so that makes two of us." I raised my head, cleared my throat, and pushed the idea away from me.

"Have you done any new work since?"

Evan had left his hand on my shoulder, and it rested lightly, but the warmth of his palm came right through the thin cotton of my shirt and was distracting. After a minute I said that I couldn't seem to paint at all right now.

"You will," he said, moving his hand from my shoulder onto my back. "There's a little gray here," he said, hooking a few locks of hair off my neck with his long fingers. Warmth crept up, and I tried to ignore it. Sam and I hadn't touched in so long. It felt good, and for a second I hung in the moment, waiting to see what we both would do. He was attractive; I imagined him naked, and for an instant I thought of losing all my pain in the sensation of someone new, someone who held no reminders of the child we had made. And then I was horrified with myself: this was the man Rebecca loved.

I moved and broke his touch, severed the current connecting us. I would not cross that line: even apart from my concern for my friend, I was far too confused about Sam and the girls, and Jamie. I was too confused about myself.

He cleared his throat and went on as though he had only been talking about the colors in the painting. For a minute I wondered if that had been all there was to it. "This I could take to New York for you," he said, gesturing to the portrait of Jamie. "I'm going back the beginning of next week."

"I don't know," I said in a voice thick with the debris of all my emotions.

"What's to know?" His eyebrows went up under his curly hair in extreme surprise. "I'm offering you an introduction."

"Well," I answered lamely, not wanting to admit that I didn't want to give the portrait up — not for fear, but because it was of Jamie, a link to my son, perhaps the only link left. "There's Rebecca to think of."

"Rebecca suggested it. In fact, she already called the gallery."

I turned away to catch my breath, feeling angry at first — at Rebecca for being so presumptuous, and then at him for making it sound as though he was doing the favor when Rebecca had already called — but suddenly I saw my own childishness. They were giving me an opportunity. I had no reason to turn it down. I took the canvas from the easel and put it in his hands. "Take good care of him," I said, feeling the tears on their way.

His face changed then, an acknowledgment of how hard it was for me to give it up, and of how readily I had done it. He had been prepared for more argument. "Promise," he said, holding up three fingers in the Boy Scout sign.

I laughed a little and turned away to wipe my eyes on the back of my hand.

"Have to get back to Rebecca's in time to rescue dinner," he said, carefully wrapping the canvas in a sheet of blank newsprint. "Did you know what a terrible cook she is?"

I laughed again, harder this time. "That's funny — she said you were a terrible eater. You make a good pair."

We walked downstairs. At the back door he put out his hand and again the current ran between us. He was carrying away part of me, and that opened me to him, made me want to hang on or travel with him. "Goodbye," I said reluctantly.

"I'll see you again before I go."

I went back to the kitchen to begin supper and opened the refrigerator door. I hadn't planned anything, hadn't thought past cleaning out Jamie's room and meeting Evan Hirsch. Nothing inspired me now, as I stood there, ground down by the hot, stressful day. The bottles of relish and soda were beaded with sweat, the celery looked limp. I wasn't hungry. Evan had my painting of Jamie under his arm, all the way through those woods. What if it rained?

Anxiously I checked the sky through the window over the sink. A cloudless sky vibrated with the deep red orange of the lowering sun. More heat tomorrow.

An omelette, I decided — that's light. And even the girls would eat it if I made it look like scrambled eggs. Cold sliced ham, fresh tomatoes with salt and pepper. A loaf of Tobie's oatmeal bread. I took the serrated knife and began to slice it, piling the square pieces on the plate.

Over the intercom I could hear the girls suddenly. They must have gone up the front stairs to their room. They were playing house.

"I'm the daddy," said Anna.

"I the mommy," agreed Meggie peaceably.

"Get Stretch," Anna urged, "he's a good baby."

"Feed Stretch baby?"

"No, it's my turn. You do the dishes." Anna's tone had turned imperious. I wondered if that's how Sam and I seemed to them, ordering each other about.

"Kiss?" enquired Meggie.

"Smack, smack."

Meggie made slurping noises to imitate the hungry baby.

I smiled, cracked the brown eggs against the rim of the white crockery mixing bowl, and started to beat them with a fork.

"*Mommeecum.*"

I froze.

"*Mommeecum.*" His voice was a distant whisper over the noise of the girls. I shook my head against it.

"*Mommeecum pease.*"

I turned slowly.

His voice came from the second intercom. I'd never shut it off, not since that night. I hadn't been able to. Now I knew why: I'd been waiting.

I picked it up in my hand. Nothing. I shook it, gently at

first, then harder. After a minute there was a sharp crackle of static, and then, once again, his voice from the speaker, calling for me in a faint, disturbed whisper.

I dropped it on the counter as if it were hot and ran to the back stairs, breasting the risers two at a time: my heart struggled like a live fish inside my chest, and waves of nausea beat up my throat. Clearing the last step, I raced around the corner, flung open the door to his room, and stopped. It was empty.

Gooseflesh prickled up all over my body. I crossed to the transmitter box of the intercom. Someone had switched it to the off position. Even if he had been here, I could not possibly have heard him. Dizziness swept up in a black wave, and orange haloed spots rose like a million miniature suns in front of my eyes. A chorus of buzzing, an army of cicadas, sang in my ears. I tottered to the bed and sat down, put my head between my legs. Slowly my vision cleared, my hearing returned.

There was water running in the bathroom. The girls were giving Stretch a bath. The sound of water slopping onto the floor. I didn't move. From the barn the shouts of the men's voices floated up on the late summer day, Tobie's growl, horses stomping impatiently for their feed.

After a time I got up and stumbled back downstairs, leaning on the banister for support. In the kitchen Evan stood, looking around. "I forgot my sunglasses," he said, gesturing to the kitchen table. "I knocked but there wasn't any answer."

I nodded dumbly and tried to speak, but only a low noise, not a word at all, came out of my mouth. I gulped, tried again, but started to cry softly instead.

Evan blinked and looked uncharacteristically startled. "What is it?"

"He's gone," I said, my hands hanging by my side like huge white weights. "I'll never see him again." And I bowed my head and surrendered to the pain — all of it. Evan came to me, looking overwhelmed, but put his arms around me and patted my back while I gasped for air. There was none of the electric touch from this afternoon: just solid, human comfort.

After a while the sobs stopped. I stood there without moving, still sagging against him. It was good to be held. "I thought I heard him," I whispered at last. "Over the intercom — I swear I heard him calling me."

"You're serious?" Evan's body tightened up against me.

I nodded into his shoulder. "But he wasn't there when I went. His room was empty."

"I've heard stranger things," he said with an uneasy laugh, and I knew he hadn't, not really.

"I'll be okay," I said quickly then, to cover myself. He loosened his hold but didn't let go. "Sometimes the intercom picks up the truckers' C.B.'s on the interstate. Maybe this was just a crossed circuit with some other house nearby." I wiped my cheek on the rough serge of his shirt.

"Are you all right, Allie?" Sam's concerned voice came from the screen door.

Immediately I stepped back from Evan, flustered. "Sam."

There was a long moment of silence. I cleared my throat. "I'm fine." I smiled, pretending I hadn't been crying. I didn't want him to ask me any questions.

He stepped into the room warily, staring at Evan. "And you are . . .?"

"Evan Hirsch." Evan held out his hand, but Sam didn't take it. After a minute Evan let it drop to his side with a shrug. The snub didn't bother him, but I was mortified.

"When's supper, Allie?" Sam poked into the pots on the stove, trying to cover the awkwardness of finding his wife in a stranger's arms. I could tell from the square of his shoulders that he was very angry. "Doesn't look like you've got much of anything here."

"I've been busy this afternoon," I said defensively, hating his tone even more than what he'd said. "And it's hot." A perverse urge took over then and I turned to Evan. "Would you like to stay — cold ham and an omelette?"

Sam shot me a look.

Evan laughed. "Good as it sounds to escape Rebecca's cooking, I think I'd better get back." He hefted the canvas under his arm and put his sunglasses in his pocket. "Don't worry about this. If I find my way back over there it'll get to the city."

I nodded my thanks and let him out the door with a wave.

"Who's he?" asked Sam belligerently as I came back to the kitchen and began slicing the ham.

"I told you this morning. He's a sculptor from New York. And he liked my work a lot."

"What the hell was he doing with his arm around you — sculpting?"

"I was a little upset, and he was just being nice."

A heavy silence pervaded the room then, broken only by squeals of joy and the sound of splashing water over the intercom. Sam stood up. "When am I going to be the one you turn to?"

It was a simple question, almost a statement of fact — and one I had no answer for. I just stood there, moving the knife through the greasy pink meat, with my back to him. How could I possibly explain why I had allowed a near-stranger to hold me while I cried? Whatever Sam was thinking was better than knowing that I'd just heard Jamie's voice.

"I'll check on the girls," Sam said after a minute, his voice sad. His step was heavy and forlorn as he turned and left me to the cooking. And I kept slicing, the knife grating against the bone. I'd lied to Evan. There were no other families with young children living near BoxTie farm.

I heard nothing more come over the intercom connected to Jamie's room, even though for nearly a week I made excuses, unconscious ones, which enabled me to hang around the kitchen. During the rest of that first week in September, I baked five loaves of bread, put up twenty more jars of jam, stitched assiduously to finish my older daughter's new dress for her first day of preschool next week, and canned twenty pounds of tomatoes. But after five days passed with no further sign, I forced myself to recognize that soon we'd float down the river on all the food I was putting up. I reassured myself about the incident by listing all the stress I'd been under, counting it as if it were money in the bank: I had cleaned out Jamie's room, showed Evan Hirsch my paintings, and then felt the pain of separation as I let go, for the first time, physically and emotionally, of a piece of my art. Or perhaps, I argued with myself, they were all separations, and, as such, linked by some invisible thread in my mind.

By Sunday morning I had begun once again to focus on my work, using it as a lever to thrust away all other thoughts and distractions. Evan had dropped in the Monday before, at the end of his stay with Rebecca, to say goodbye. Again there had been that electric look in his eye when we were alone, and again I'd ignored it and concentrated on business: he promised to call me as soon as he got back to the city and had a reaction from the gallery. It didn't surprise me that I hadn't heard from him since.

Sunday noon came down hot, near ninety. As August had been atypically chilly and wet, September had begun unseasonably, and breathlessly, hot. This was the tail end of summer, when I was longing for fall. The trees had faded to a dusty, parched green but not yet turned color, the grasses had yellowed but the hay had not quite ripened, and the cicadas still buzzed, louder and louder until it seemed they should drop from the trees with their vibration. The air lay across the mountains in a thick haze which didn't burn off even on the sunniest days. The animals stood in the fields with their heads hanging low, too heat-tired to graze or even switch flies. Sam and Joe went on with their work — even heavy labor — the same as always, but flopped into the kitchen at the end of the day flushed dull red and breathless. Sam needed a long, cold bath before he could really function again. A few nights we took supper sandwiches over to the edge of the river and just sat on the boulders to dangle our feet in the water. The river was cold and clear as rubbing alcohol, making the bottom look close enough to touch, the beige speckled stones camouflaging minnows you could catch by the handful if you were quick enough. Sam and I sat there with the girls, but we didn't talk. We were wary of each other now, unsure of how to reach out and bridge the silence which had fallen between us since Evan Hirsch's visit.

Tobie had decided it was too hot to bake today and had come out to the garden with me and Meggie. She'd fallen asleep in the old wooden wingback next to my easel where I was working on a watercolor of the garden for my overdue Hallmark commission. Anna and Sam were out in the barn, currying Duet's foal; his new owner, a little girl just a few years older than Anna, was coming by to meet him this afternoon, and Anna had been subdued all day long. She was already preparing her heart for the foal's departure after weaning. Maybe Sam had been right after all, maybe she was learning to roll with life. It was Meggie who had me worried.

Meggie kept seeing Jamie around every corner, up in the hayloft, in the chicken coop. And she continued to talk to him as if he were right there. Each night over the last week she'd blown him a kiss and then told him to "seep tight an' don't let the bebbugs bite" as I listened to her settling in over her intercom. It was as if Jamie had become her imaginary playmate. I hadn't mentioned to Sam Meggie's continuing contact with her twin: in fact, the thought of bringing it up filled me with dread. I was loath to upset the fragile balance of the family any more than it already had been.

I'd brought Meggie out to work with me today, hoping that with a little extra attention she might open up some. She'd always been a private little girl, sharing herself mostly with Anna and Jamie, shy around grown-ups. Now the distance between us made me sad.

Meggie had carried her doll along with her and was playing house at the foot of the old oak which stood at the back of the garden. I tried putting the tree into my watercolor, its arms snaking out in black lines over the fluid contours of the bright blue, green, and pink flowerbed. I sighed. The contrast between the black tree limbs and the bright soft wash of the garden was a little ominous, and I knew Hallmark wouldn't like it. It reminded me some of Homer's "Bermuda." The bright sun hurt my eyes. I pulled my baseball cap down tight over my forehead for shade, then closed my eyes and rotated my head on my neck to relax. Even with my eyes shut I still saw those black lines against the backdrop of my lids. It came to me then, a new painting, the one which had been percolating inside me since that day in the attic when I'd made up my mind to start working again. Quickly I leaned forward to take my watercolor paper down and put up a canvas, which I had — presciently, it seemed — brought with me. I took out my oils. My hands were shaking as the idea buzzed and grew larger and stronger.

I prepared a palette of opposing forces: blacks, whites, browns, yellows, bright blue. Thinning the black to a transparent hue, I drew a bold black box at the back of the canvas to represent a mirror. With strong edges, angles, and lines, the shape was substantial, yet still flat and hollow. I hesitated and then left it. In front of the mirror my brush flickered away for a while and the face of a little girl began to emerge. Again the lines were angular, the impasto thicker, the paint more reflective and white-toned. Her face was nearly a wedge, sharply pointed toward the chin, and the skin tone was bright yellow-beige. The eyes were enormous, milky-blue — the color of a malamute's — and disproportionate to the rest of the face. I wanted those eyes to talk, to rivet, to be a focal point.

The hair was a halo of orange-yellow, almost interchangeable with the skin tone, throwing the attention and emphasis back onto the eyes. This was Meggie on fire that day in Jamie's room, burning up with her question, "Will I go 'way too?"

I kept painting without pause, absorbed now, my brush dipping again and again into the harsh, bright colors. The body appeared: small, shoulders slight and bowed, turned away from the mirror with her eye level rising as if she spoke to someone — an adult, high up, outside the painting. I went back to her eyes again and thickened the impasto. Daubing in a darker tone of blue with tiny strokes, I gave her a look of appeal, of sorrow, the sadness I myself felt at the inexplicable nature of our lives. Behind her the mirror shimmered transparent silver, almost a watery reflection, a pool which beckoned with its icelike purity, promising rest and anesthesia from pain. I redid the outline of the mirror, made it even darker black, and narrowed the lines from front to back, like a tunnel entrance, giving it a three-dimensional quality. The mirror had an interior now, as if it were a room. Across its surface wavered an image, blurred white, hard to distinguish: another face, rising from the depths of the tunnel like the moon. At first it appeared to be the reflection of the child in the foreground, but soon it became clear it was not, for her face was turned outward and only the back of her head would have been reflected. This face belonged to someone else: this was the face of Jamie.

After a while, with her face, the mirror, and the reflection blocked in, I sat back to rest for a minute. The remainder could wait. I closed my eyes, wondering where the painting should be set, what the background or foreground should be. It would come to me eventually. I sighed. It was still hard for me to let control of a painting pass to my inner resources, and go without a map or a sketch.

Some time had passed; I didn't know how much. Tobie was snoring now to my right. The rest of the garden was quiet. The sun beat down on my face and made me nearly sleepy. I felt contented, drained after my burst of energy. Another vision had come after all. I was not a void. I would go on to paint more and better paintings. Already instinct told me this was one of the best I'd done. Nothing about it was a hedge, nothing pretty or pastel, just strong, bold colors for a strong, bold idea. A portrait of a girl before a mirror — traditional in composition, but all mine in interpretation.

I looked up to check on Meggie. The oak tree was empty, the garden quiet. My heart thudded unevenly for a moment. I stood and craned my neck to see if she could have wandered down to the roadside stand. She hadn't. I ran forward a few steps, but she was nowhere. In my mind a confused jumble of ideas streamed together: lightning won't strike twice, she's just hiding, she's been stolen, please, God, don't let anything have happened to her. I offered up everything I had for the safety of my little girl, offered it up and remembered how God had not deigned to save Jamie.

From the high grasses beyond the back of the garden came a squeal of childish laughter. I swung toward the sound.

Jamie was standing at the very edge of the grass, bathed in sunlight, radiating sunlight as if he himself were the source. Again the sound of laughter floated across the yard to me. All the objects around us subsided in my vision, shrouded by a heavy light-struck mist, as if we stood under a waterfall. I could see only Jamie, shining in the sunlight before me, emanating light. In a daze, I felt a peculiar combination of fear and longing: I wanted to go to him, scoop him up in my arms, hug him — but I was also frightened of him. Drawn to his brightness, I took a step toward him. The laughter stopped. The cicadas buzzed louder, loudest, in my ears. I took another step, and then another, and soon I was running, eager as for a lover, a butterfly to the sun, a fox to the fire.

He stepped back quickly into the long grasses, which were already over his head, and they closed around him like a sea.

I skidded up to the edge of the field and called out to him. His name floated, reedlike, on the stillness of the day. Again, the laughter drifted up, maddening me, taunting, teasing, enticing. I could see the grasses move in a snakelike path, giving away his position as he pushed in toward the middle of the field. I ran, the waist-high grasses twining around and clinging to my legs, and began to wade toward him, still calling, still eager to touch his soft face. He pushed on. But I was gaining on him and at last he was not ten feet from me. I called one last time and then leapt the remaining distance, thinking I flew perhaps, to part the feathered grasses above his shining yellow head. He looked up into my face.

I looked down into the face of Meggie.

My mouth went dry, and I sagged toward the ground. Dusty earth gritted against my knees and thighs. The grasses closed over my head and I thought I would faint. The heat beat on my back, but a wash of cold, freezing cold, as if I stood in a current of the river, ran up and down my body.

Standing beside me as I knelt, Meggie patted my bowed head tentatively. I fought for control of my stomach, and the rasping in my ears faded a bit.

"Mommy play hide-see?" she asked hopefully.

"That's what you were doing?"

"I play hide-see with Jamie," she went on, explaining the situation to me. "But he hided a long time."

I recoiled. For a moment I thought I couldn't stand to ask any further. "With Jamie?"

She nodded. "We played hide-see but then" — she paused and frowned, struggling to make me understand — "then I think he wented away."

I nodded. "Jamie is gone now. We won't see him anymore." I looked up into her face, so hopeful, and started to cry.

"But I wanna see him!" Her big blue eyes filled with tears, too. "Jamie's a bad boy. He hided and won't come out. *You* call him."

I shook my head and put my arms around her as she started to sob. I rocked her and she put her arms around me, patting my back. I couldn't stop crying. I thought of Rebecca's saying, "You may never be done with this." Meggie curled up on my lap like a cat, and we sat there, holding each other for a while till the tears petered out. An ant crawled over the instep of my foot, and we both watched it as it tried to drag a small piece of a flower stem across my big toe. A bee buzzed by our hiding spot, and I wished we could stay there like that, forever. I pulled out a long blade of grass and tickled Meggie's nose with its furry end, and she laughed then, a clear musical scale of pleasure. She pointed toward the high blue sky. "Sheep, Mommy." I looked up. The clouds did indeed look like a field of furry white fleece. I smiled and kissed her upturned, wondering face, then stood, pulling her by her hand. We began to trudge back through the long grass, swinging our linked hands, all quiet around us except for the crickets. I realized then that Anna and I had had two private years to know each other before the twins came. Jamie I had loved, despite my earnest efforts, the best of all three. But this was the first time Meggie and I had ever shared a sense of companionship. It had taken our mutual loss for me to give her the chance. It was a depressing realization, and I distracted myself from it by turning to practical matters — like what to make for supper and how we'd probably both be covered with grass ticks by the time we got back to the house.

Meggie did have a lot of ticks: sixteen, in fact, all tenaciously attached to her scalp and bloating by the minute. It took Tobie and me over an hour, working together, to burn them out. Throughout it all Meggie sat quietly, hands folded in her lap, without flinching. My heart went out to her for her bravery, and I saw then how much her mien resembled her grandmother's.

Sam came in as we were finishing up, trailing a sad Anna

by the hand. I could see from the looks on their faces that the afternoon had worn on both of them. Sam poured himself and Anna a glass of lemonade. I set Anna to coloring with her crayons, while Tobie checked Meggie's head one last time.

"Mr. Lovell came by," Sam said, draining his glass. "The headstone's in place. He'd like for us to stop in there and check it over."

Bud Lovell was the minister who'd done Jamie's funeral service. Thompson's Monuments must have finally gotten around to installing the stone Sam had picked the week of the burial. I didn't say anything, just busied myself showing Anna how to draw a tail-wagging dog.

"You want to go by before supper?"

I hesitated, caught between two strong emotions. I wanted to do as Sam asked and make an effort to pull us closer together. At the same time, the very idea of visiting my son's grave made me nauseated. I hadn't been there since that blurry day we buried him. I swallowed hard against the sick feeling rising up my throat and knew I wasn't ready to go back yet, especially not after this afternoon's vision in the garden.

Tobie studied me as Sam's question lay over us in the air. "I'll go, Sam. Maybe Allie should stay here with the girls." Tobie gestured toward Anna with a significant raise of her eyebrow.

Sam stood abruptly and pushed back his chair. "Fine. I'll bring the wagon around."

I gave Tobie a grateful look and pulled Meggie onto my lap with a hug. The sense of escape made me nearly giddy. "I'll have supper started by the time you're back."

Sam honked out front. Tobie started out, then turned to me and gave my shoulder a pat.

The girls and I spent the rest of the afternoon in the garden. I blocked out all thought of what Sam and Tobie were doing and packed up my paints and easel. The strength of the painting was apparent to me. It was clear and direct, not muddy like some of my early work. It made a statement with the clean, sure sweep of its lines. It spoke of bewilderment, pain, loss, fear: bereavement. The lines and colors belonged to me — they were an extension of my mind, my fingerprint. I took the canvas up to my studio, put it out on the easel where I could work on it tomorrow, and then covered it with a drape.

By five, when Sam and Tobie returned, I had the Sunday roast in the oven, the potatoes boiling, the salad made. While the girls set the table, I picked fresh dahlias from my garden. I didn't ask Sam or Tobie about the headstone: to know it was there was enough. We sat down at the table to eat.

"A little grace tonight," Tobie said, bowing her head and motioning that we all should follow. I stared at her, shocked at this departure from the usual. Anna twitched with a grumble in her chair, eyeing the roast, which streamed its red juices onto the platter, and the mound of steaming mashed potatoes wafting the scent of butter and cream into the air.

"Watch over our Jamie," Tobie began, enunciating around her dentures and addressing her entreaty to no one in particular, "in his new resting spot. Take care now that we're not able, and keep all of us here safe. Thanks for this bounty, our fine home, a loving family."

We sat silently for a second, thinking of the empty place at this table which would never again be filled. Then we picked up our forks and the clamor of the meal began.

It wasn't until we were in bed that Sam spoke of the monument. "Looks pretty good," he said, settling himself under the covers and turning out the light. "They did a neat job on carving the angels."

"Angels?" Incredulity strained my tone.

"I told you I had them do a border of little angels and flowers up around the edge of the granite. Children's stones usually have some decoration like that." He was silent for a minute and so was I. The description made it so real.

"I wanted it to be special." His voice dropped to a whisper and it sounded as if he might cry. I reached over and took his hand, then rolled across to him all in a rush. I put my face up to his and kissed him, greedy at last for the warmth of his body — anything to fight the cold inside me. He kissed me back; he took me up in his arms and caressed my breast. I reached down to hold him, but he broke our embrace and rolled away as soon as my hand touched him.

"Not tonight, Allie. It doesn't feel right tonight."

"It's been over a month now. I know I haven't wanted to before, but . . ."

He didn't answer, and the darkness and the silence lay between us. "We've got to get back to each other," I said. "End this separateness."

When he still did not speak I rolled back to my own side, miserable and rejected. "Will it ever be the same?" I asked angrily after a minute. "Will you ever forgive me?"

"Forgive you for what?" He sounded tired, bewildered, beaten.

"I know you're blaming me. I know you think it's all my fault. That I gave him the horse that night."

"How could I possibly? Jamie was your favorite — you'd never have done anything to hurt him." He rolled from his back to his side and raised himself up on one elbow so he could see my face in the moonlight.

"I put the toy in the crib with him!" My voice was filled with bitter recrimination. I didn't look at him. "And *you* wouldn't let me go to him when he called!"

"I know," he said, his voice choking again. "I've gone over and over it in my head, what would've happened. If only . . ."

"If I —" I couldn't go on, but started to sob instead. He slid across to me.

"If," he said sadly. "I guess we'll be swallowing against that one little word the rest of our lives."

I lay on my side and he put his arms around me from behind. "We didn't mean it to be like this," he said, his voice tortured. I could feel his body shaking now too. "Why is it like this?"

There was no answer. We held on to each other and cried together. Sam curled his large body around mine, knee to knee, stomach to buttocks, like a shield against the flame that licked up and around us, and after a long time we stopped crying. Sam blew his nose and passed me the box of tissues.

"It's just a crapshoot with kids this young," he said then. "Think of that day he was up on the ladder, or the time he nearly got hit by the mail truck." He reached out and touched my hand where it lay on top of the sheet. "Sometimes you get caught. You do your best at protecting, but you can't put them in a padded cell or they'd grow up afraid. Your parents were like that and look how you hated it."

"If only I'd checked."

"If only I'd let you."

"Do you think he forgives us?"

"I don't know, Allie."

I was silent then, wondering if, even together, we could stand to live with the pain. Even though the feel of my hand in his was good, even though his body was warm and big against mine. "He was so upset, with all the thunder and his dream about Mildred. I wanted him to be comforted, that's all."

Sam pulled me tight against his chest. "Why wouldn't you let *me* comfort you? And why wouldn't you come today? It was something we should have shared."

"Because it's too hard," I said softly. "If I let you comfort me, if I go to see his grave, I have to know, really know, that he's gone. Forever." I started to choke on my words, and the tears started down my cheeks again.

"But he really *is* gone, and if you won't let me comfort you, then we're even more alone. You can't protect yourself by pretending."

"But if I let you comfort me then I'll feel better — and I'm too guilty to let you do that."

"You let Evan Hirsch comfort you." He lay still against me, remembering. "That really hurt."

"He was safe," I got out at last, turning on my back so I could see his face. "He was a stranger! He didn't matter to me, or to us. I didn't have to admit to him that I was the one put the toy in Jamie's crib. I didn't have to justify anything — not to him, not even to myself."

"You can't walk around shutting us out. We need you."

I put my arms around his neck and he pulled me close. I could feel the wetness of his tears on my shoulders and on my face as he kissed me. "Let's go check the girls."

"I do every night now," I confessed, swinging my legs out of bed. "I've been waiting till you were asleep."

We went hand in hand down the hall. At Anna's room he drew the sheet up over her. "She was so brave today," he whispered, smoothing her hair back off her forehead. "It killed me to sell that damned foal. She was a real soldier, showing that other girl how to brush him, pick out his hooves. If only she'd carried on a little, then I wouldn't have felt so mean." He sighed. "Or at least cried." I kissed Anna's head: she was a deep sleeper, she never stirred.

In Meggie's room moonlight silvered her hair as she lay in the crib beneath the window. "I'm worried about her," I confided in Sam's ear.

He raised an eyebrow.

"She keeps telling me she sees Jamie all the time. I heard her over the intercom talking to him again tonight." My voice had a tremor to it. I was talking about Meggie; I was talking about myself.

"She's just trying to live with it, that's all. She was probably closer to him than any of us."

I was silent. "Should we take her to the doctor?" I asked after a minute.

"Give her a little time, Allie." Sam reached into the crib and stroked her head. She shifted at his touch and we held our breath, waiting to see if she would wake. She turned over, settled into some deeper layer of dreaming. "That's what each of us needs."

He took my hand then and we went back to bed and cuddled up together. We didn't want sex, we just wanted comfort, company, solace. We curled into one another's arms for the first time since that terrible night, and at last I did indeed sleep, and at last I did indeed dream, and in my dream, Jamie was once again alive.

The Face of Jamie

The high-bush blueberries on Salter's Island were ripe, and every green branch was loaded with the tiny indigo berries. The summer day was warm, and sun beat down on our backs, reflected off the ocean rolling up on the rocky shore. The skin of my nose was beginning to sting with sunburn. Salter's was a tiny island with nothing on it but blueberries: no houses, no people, no telegraph poles, no roads. Jamie and I had filled our pails to the brim and then eaten our sweet way to the shiny tin bottom twice. My father called to us that the tide was turning, and we must come back to the boat. I reached for Jamie's hand, but he ran from me in a wild circle and disappeared into the high grass. As I ran after him I heard my father yelling, more distant now, "Come on, Allie, time's running out." I stopped and he gestured toward the motorboat. The wind had chopped the surf into whitecaps, and even the stunted pines bowed a little under its force. "Come on," my father called, cupping his hands so his words wouldn't be sucked out to sea. "We're leaving." I turned back to Jamie, but he stood far from me, high on a patch of exposed rock at the very edge of the surf. The sun gilded his hair. I ran toward him as the outboard coughed, then started up with a whine.

I turned to see my parents moving out to sea, their backs straight and their heads dipping in and out of my sight as the boat cut through the swells. I ran to my son, and he put his small face up against mine: it was warm from the sun. He laughed as we touched, and suddenly I didn't care that my parents had gone on without us. Jamie and I would live here alone; we would live on wild blueberries and seawater and love.

With a start I woke up. I looked over the foot of our double bed and saw the lavender light creeping into the room. "It was just a dream," I murmured, pulling the blanket around my shoulders and comforting myself as if I were one of my own children. And then I remembered that Jamie had been dead for a month and a half now. With my waking I had killed him again. Tears rolled down my cheeks into my ears. Beside me Sam began to stir, wakened by the faint rocking of the bed as I cried.

He reached out and pulled me to him.

"I dreamt he was alive," I said, breaking the rhythm of my sorrow. "I dreamt Jamie and I were picking blueberries."

He lay back and put his hands under his head in a cradle. His arms made a bony triangle. "I dream about him too," he said softly. "When I wake up it takes me a minute to realize he's gone."

I nodded, surprised to hear him describe my own reaction so exactly.

He put his arms around me in a strong circle, and in that moment I really did want to be protected, and to protect him. I put my face up to his and we started to kiss. My body wanted some physical solace where there could be no emotional solace. I was tired of being alone.

His hands moved up under my nightgown and caressed my breasts. I stayed quiet, almost passive, afraid that if I moved, my own fragile sensations would stop. He didn't seem to mind being in charge. I let his hands rove all across and into me. "I've missed it, Allie," he whispered in my ear. And then, certain of myself once again, I put my hands in his hair, pulled his head up so that I could kiss his mouth. From the hall came the sounds of the girls beginning to stir. "Hurry," I urged him, craving him now, sliding underneath and opening my legs, body, heart.

But he didn't hurry. His eyes flickered over to the half-open door, and he pulled the sheet up above our heads. The room was still dim. Then he slid into me slowly, inch by inch, and I was ready — liquid and dark and very hot. He moved in and out, quickening as we both grew closer. From our mouths came the small muffled noises of our pleasure. But that pleasure was almost painful to us: it was painful to feel, to know, that out of these two bodies had come one body which was now lost to us, a small body we could never hold or cuddle or touch again. We had forfeited a part of ourselves, part of the very same unity we now found so precious. As the pleasure increased we began to cry silently, each of us seeing with clarity the other's tears, each of us knowing just where we were, and when we came, me first and then Sam a minute later, we rubbed our wet faces against each other like cats.

Afterward we lay together, unmoving, Sam still inside me, even though the girls were up now in their rooms. Nothing seemed to matter right then except what we had shared. And the moment held on, and continued.

Finally, with one lingering kiss, we rolled apart. We swung our legs over the edge of the bed and began our day. But the sex we'd shared was like a warm golden light inside us; it was with us all through breakfast, through the noise and the bustle of two small children, a panful of eggs, three toastersful of toast, six glasses of juice. It was there between us as we moved, just like that, into the old routine, and for the first time since our son had died, it did feel more like the old routine. I finished up the dishes, started the laundry, packed the girls off with Tobie. Then I climbed the stairs to my studio, ready to begin working again on the painting of Meggie I'd started yesterday in the garden.

I bustled around, opening the windows a crack for air, letting the light in. But it was a gray day, a sharp break from the heat of the last two weeks, and the lavender hue of the early dawn remained. As I looked out the window I saw Sam walk from barn to paddock. The hayfields were nearly ready for cutting. This morning over breakfast he had worried that a stretch of wet weather now might delay things more than the rain of August already had.

I turned on the lamp over my drafting table. It was a good day to work indoors, a day where I would find the right setting for the painting of Meggie. Most of the painting had come as a gift. Now I would have to sweat a little to see the rest. In what room did that mirror hang? What should be the background and foreground on which Meggie stood?

I took out my box of oils and began unscrewing the tops of the tubes. Jamie's room probably should be the background, perhaps the empty crib and a few stuffed animals. I frowned then. It mustn't seem melodramatic, or dilute with sentiment. Suddenly I couldn't wait to see what I'd done yesterday. I longed for that familiar feeling of rediscovery, of looking back at the previous day's work. There was always a sense of satisfaction for having begun, and then dissatisfaction for all that was left to do. I crossed to the easel and took hold of the bottom edge of the drape.

Someone knocked at the door. Startled, I stopped still and didn't move, not even when another knock sounded. Once again fantasy overwhelmed me as I remembered the sounds I'd heard the other day under the door, and Jamie's old games. Who was on the other side today? Sam and Tobie and the girls were all out at the barn.

"Open up, Allie!" The voice was male, excited, demanding.

"Let us in!" I recognized with relief Rebecca's voice and realized that it was Evan and she who were pounding my door down.

They barreled past me as soon as I swung the latch free.

"What are you —"

"Just be quiet," Evan interrupted, "and we'll tell you. It's a surprise."

I looked to Rebecca. She smiled, her crooked grin more crooked than usual with a bigger smile than usual.

Evan took a deep breath. "I took the painting over to my gallery in Manhattan last Monday. Marge Cleveland — she's the owner — asked me to leave it with her —"

"You left it with a stranger?"

"Stop interrupting." He shot Rebecca a look. She shrugged and pulled her package of cigars from her back pocket.

"Anyway," Evan continued, "she asked me to leave it, and then she called me back a few days later. She had some people she trusts in to see it." He paused and smiled at me. "Rebecca and I are cosponsoring a show of emerging artists at the gallery in February. We've picked six of the best new talents we could find, unheard of, some painters, some sculptors, and we'll be showcasing them alongside our own work." He paused and let the moment spin out.

I stood there blankly, waiting.

Rebecca scratched a match and inhaled. "We'd like you to be one of them."

I looked back and forth at their faces. "Part of your show?" I echoed.

"A group show," Rebecca went on. "But it's a start. There'll probably be ten of my canvases, and ten of Evan's sculptures. I'd guess we'll use about five or six pieces from each of the new artists."

I stared at them, gradually comprehending what they were talking about. They had brought me news better than anything I could ever have dreamed. A quick rush of excitement flushed my face, and I smiled tentatively. "Six pieces," I repeated. And then I pictured the faces, the expressions, the remarks, the criticism — all directed at my work. I panicked. "I don't have anything for a show like that."

Evan put his arm around my shoulder and smiled nonchalantly. "Of course you do. You just don't know which ones they are. That's why Rebecca and I are here."

"We're going to pick them for you," Rebecca said, going to the closet and opening it. "The gallery's sending the van for them Wednesday, so we've got to decide fast."

"So soon?"

"Photos, press releases, advertising, catalogues, mounting — there's a lot of work that goes into this kind of show. I would have asked you a month ago, but . . ." Her voice trailed off and I flashed back in my mind to the blank grayness of August.

"But who's going to pay for all that?" I worried after a moment.

"They front all the expenses and take sixty percent of whatever you might sell."

"More than half?" I'd known it before, in the abstract, but it suddenly seemed so much. And it meant losing a painting, sketch, or charcoal for good — giving away small chunks of myself permanently.

He nodded. "Sixty percent. And it's worth it. A good gallery show with good reviews can make you."

"Or break you," I said sourly.

"It's better than hiding in an attic."

I was silent.

"At least you'll know you tried," Rebecca added. "Now, let's get going," she said directively to Evan. "We haven't got all day. Before you know it'll be lunchtime and she'll make some excuse about getting the girls sandwiches."

I smiled. She knew me too well. "Could you just give me a minute to digest all this?" I sank slowly onto the couch, trying to realize what it meant. "You spend your life waiting for a break, and then when it comes you don't know what to do with it."

Rebecca sat down beside me. "I knew you'd get overwhelmed, and that's why we came up. Don't be so self-effacing. You can handle this, and a lot more too."

Evan was making a slow study of several different canvases. "Of course, they want the one of Jamie in the garden. And this barn here might be my favorite," he said, musing.

Rebecca crossed to Evan. "Where's the one of Sam?" She began to flip through.

I didn't like having people digging around in my work. Going to the closet, I gently shoved them both aside and took charge. "Let me show you some," I suggested, making them sit on the couch while I put up one canvas after another on the easel. "Here's the one of the men stowing bales in the loft, which I think is one of the better ones I did in July. And there's a good oil of Tobie, and one also of Joe."

Rebecca got up again and stood in front of the easel, staring and assessing. She took her time. She turned the overhead light up full so they were illuminated in a harsh and searching glare. Under her silent scrutiny I despaired over what immature, poor attempts they seemed at that moment.

"Yes," Rebecca said, "they're very fine." Her words made me suddenly objective again. The raw strength of Tobie's and Joe's plain faces was captured in the paint. The oil of the three men piling bales in the hayloft held its own, too, with each line and angle of their weary and overwhelmed bodies: three small men against an insurmountable task.

Evan and Rebecca and I worked together for several hours, picking, choosing, debating, changing our minds. All around us my work stood stacked, and I stopped feeling self-conscious. Rebecca and Evan were looking for a balance in what they chose, a variety in both subject and medium. Rebecca finally put her foot down and insisted on having her own way, reminding us that she had seniority, and, in the end, we acquiesced to her judgment. We sat down on the couch, relieved to be finished, and I looked at my watch. "My God, it's nearly three o'clock," I said. "No wonder my stomach's growling. I can't believe someone didn't come up looking for me."

"We warned Sam when we ran into him earlier," Evan said with a sly smile. "He promised he'd leave us alone. He seemed really pleased with the news."

"You told him already?" I was disappointed. I had looked forward to doing it myself.

"We figured if we were going to crash in on you without permission we'd better have a damned good reason," Rebecca said, shrugging. "And he's like a watchdog. He wouldn't let us come up till he knew why we were here."

I was surprised. Sam had never struck me as being so protective of my working hours before.

"What's this over here?" Evan said then, going to stand before the draped easel where the canvas of Meggie still stood, untouched.

"It's not done," I answered, leaping to my feet, feeling shy again.

"Nonsense," Rebecca said. "I've heard that from you before. And it's always an excuse." She crossed and tugged the drape off even as I began to protest again, this time angrily. But she and Evan just stood in front of the canvas, blocking my view. They didn't say a word.

"I told you it's not ready," I said with exasperation, trying to squeeze between them. "Once in a while you should listen to me."

"I'll never listen to you again," Evan said, his voice low. "This is phenomenal. Why on earth would you have held it back?"

"I can't believe you don't see why," I said, shoving him aside to cover it up again. I stopped short.

The painting was finished. The background behind and in front of the mirror, the setting of the portrait, was complete. In swirls of glossy Cadmium red and Ultramarine — made even more bright by the addition of a lot of Zinc white — and blended with a fingertip, not a brush, my garden was depicted in full bloom. What had been a blank white space yesterday was full of color today.

"This one canvas must be the center — the focus — of your part in the show," Rebecca said, thinking aloud. "I hope Marge hangs it by itself. Why did you say it wasn't done?"

I opened my mouth and then shut it. I had left this canvas unfinished yesterday, and today it appeared to me like a miracle, a burning bush, complete. "Nothing ever seems finished to me," I muttered, trying to collect myself with an excuse I knew they'd buy.

Rebecca snorted. I kept staring at it in disbelief.

"The contrast between the transparent black and the white of these reds and blues, and the difference in impasto . . ." Rebecca sighed. "It's a wonderful painting, Allie."

As I stared I knew that it was indeed a remarkable painting — far more remarkable than I had ever envisioned. The mirror rose right up out of the garden bed, was surrounded by that garden bed. The garden itself was alive, twining up in a jungle around Meggie's legs. Had I walked in my sleep, painted in my sleep, to do this? Had I left my bed and come here as dark purpled into dawn? Had I just blocked out my own final vision?

"I love the way the mirror turns into a tunnel and has a force of its own, like a suction," Rebecca went on, admiring and drawing on her cigar. "It's a portal, inviting but threatening at the same time — and out of it comes this specter. What will you call it?"

I stared at her, struck by the accuracy of her analysis. "Death of Her Twin," I answered automatically, but really shocking myself again because I had not given a single thought to a title. Suddenly I wanted them to go, to leave me alone so I could think. I reached deep into memory. I reached out to touch reality, but nothing met my hands, as if I were searching in a darkened room for the light switch on the wall. The longer I stumbled in the blackness, the more frightened I became.

"If you varnish it tonight it will be dry in time to go," Rebecca said.

"I'm not sure I want to send it."

"You're sending it," she said with finality. "Now we need to do a written inventory." She turned aside from the painting and rummaged in the pockets of her rainslicker. "Where's that paper?"

"I'll do it myself tomorrow," I answered, wishing they would go. "I think I'd like to rest for a while," I said then, going over to the door and opening it. "I'm bushed."

"Is she kicking us out?" Rebecca said, lifting an eyebrow at Evan.

"It's a definite hint," he agreed, sending me another one of his electric looks.

"Am I at least allowed to use the bathroom before I leave?" Rebecca growled, stubbing out her cigar in the coffee can lid.

I nodded and she disappeared downstairs. I began to follow, but Evan caught me by the arm. "Are you pleased?"

"Of course," I answered, distracted, feeling the urgent need to be totally alone, wishing he would just walk through the door quietly and take Rebecca home.

"You're not acting like it," he said. "You'd think it was nothing to you." He pulled me tight against him then, up against the heat and the shape of his body.

Though I was caught by surprise, I still pulled away, hard, and stepped on his foot by mistake. All my distraction fled now that I had something concrete to focus on. As he hopped up and down, massaging his foot, I didn't even bother to apologize. "I'm not acting *grateful* enough — is that what you're trying to say?"

"Stop, stop!" He raised his arms in the air in self-defense. "I thought there was an attraction between us, that's all."

"Attraction or no attraction, I'm married."

"So, okay." He nodded and bounced on his toes. "I'm not looking for anything you're not willing to give freely. Maybe some other time, or place." He looked a little amused, as if I were just playing with him, fighting him for fighting's sake, but possibly ready to give in later. He put his weight on his foot gingerly and smiled at me. "Like I said the other day, you're a real Emily Dickinson."

"I'm not interested," I said flatly, thinking of the splendor this morning with my husband. "Not at all, not now, not here, not anywhere." I looked straight at him, knowing I had better be very clear. "And if you don't want me to be part of the show anymore, you're off the hook. I won't even tell Rebecca why."

He smiled with a new gleam in his eye. "I think I'll enjoy watching everything that happens to you with this show. And how you handle it." There was a taunt in his voice and I knew we weren't finished with this.

"Evan," Rebecca's gravelly voice floated up the staircase, interrupting before I could say anything more. "I'm leaving now."

"He's coming," I said, taking his arm and pushing him out the door.

I escorted them out through the kitchen and then sat down at the trestle table to think, my mind turning immediately from Evan back to the portrait. Outside, a cold, gray rain had begun to fall. I got up to turn on the lamp at the end of the table and sat in Tobie's rocker before the fireplace. I was so chilled I was shivering. I thought of going upstairs to get a sweater but was just too tired. I pulled the afghan which

always lay on the rocker around me tightly and picked at the
little pills of fuzz which had accumulated on its surface over
the years.

Shock was wearing off and giving way to fear. I was scared,
truly scared. I couldn't even think about the gallery showing.
Anxiety made my heart pound, and to calm myself I closed
my eyes, put my head back, and tried to slow my breathing.
After a minute I opened my eyes again. The first thing I saw
was the bulletin board of the children's artwork above the
fireplace. There was Jamie's early talent, all gone to waste
now, but still enriching my room and my life. I got up, went
over, and unpinned my favorite fingerpainting, the last one
he had done in July, when he'd discovered how to blend the
colors with his fingertips and make new tones by varying the
pressure. I held it in my lap, ran my fingers across the thick
paint, and felt tears begin once again.

Everything stopped then, quivered, held. The moment extended as, in a flash, my mind saw and encompassed the
significance of it all. The garden which twined around Meggie's legs in the portrait on my easel upstairs was twin to this
fingerpainting in its childlike technique.

As I sat there, riveted, the world moved forward again:
crickets creaked, water dripped from the tap, a bucket clanged
in the barn, wind rustled the leaves of the maple by the back
door. But all up and down my back, the tiny hairs lifted in
fear. My skin prickled up into goosebumps. My mind injected
itself with a dose of novocaine, and reality rolled back under
the numbing influence of simple fear. I turned like a robot
and went to climb upstairs to the attic. I had to see the portrait
again. I had to know for sure.

At the top of the stairs I stopped for a moment, hands
hanging by my side. The fear was enormous inside my chest.
I was pregnant with it; it pushed against my lungs and made
it nearly impossible to breathe. I was afraid to know and afraid

not to know. I had come here to learn more about all I did not want to know. I pushed the flat of my hand against the door and it swung open.

The overhead lamps were turned off, and the studio reflected only the dark lavender light of this day. I stepped across the threshold into the tunneled mirror of my own painting. In the far corner of the room, on the middle of the sagging sofa, with Teddy tucked under his arm, sat my son.

PART IV

POSSIBILITIES

September 1986

And Jesus rebuked the devil; and he was departed out of him: and the child was cured from that very hour.

Then came the disciples to Jesus apart, and said, Why could not we cast him out?

And Jesus said unto them, Because of your unbelief: for verily I say unto you, If ye have faith as a grain of mustard seed, ye shall say unto this mountain, Remove hence to yonder place; and it shall remove; and nothing shall be impossible unto you.

— Matthew 17:18–20

Home Again

He sat cross-legged, his pose relaxed and natural, his thumb in his mouth. Despite the shadows of the room he seemed to glow with a buttery yellow light. Motionless, trembling, I watched my beautiful boy. His hair still curled soft and blond, his skin was ruddy and fine. There was no mark of tragedy anywhere on him. But he had yet to move, and I waited to see whether he would turn from a mere vision, a glossy portrait, into a living, breathing being.

I opened my mouth to say his name but no words came out. Fear stood shoulder to shoulder with love as I struggled with my own disbelief. Much as I wanted to go to him, a simple truth remained: I was afraid.

"Mommee," he said, stretching his arms out to me. I heard the sharp hiss of my breath as it left my body, and realized then I had been holding it. In that instant I accepted what I saw, believed in my own vision, took into my heart the impossible. But I didn't let myself move: at the back of my mind was the memory of yesterday afternoon, and how he had run when I tried to come near.

"Mommeecum," he said again persistently, persuasively, but this time it grated on my ear a little. In the month he'd been gone Meggie had dropped so much of her babytalk. Jamie had not been able to grow, I realized, the conclusion floating lazily through my mind as down a summer river, seemingly detached from the excitement vibrating through the rest of my body. My mind was nearly calm, computing, adding up all available information. Wherever my son had been all this time must have been a stationary place, a place of waiting.

The teddy bear slipped to the floor as he shifted on the couch, and without thinking I took a step closer, ready to pick it up and hand it to him. But with my movement Jamie dimmed, like the sun going behind a cloud. He was fading, receding, just as the tide pulls itself farther and farther from the shore. He held out his arms again and once more entreated me to come. I knew I was losing him, and now my fear of that loss was greater than my fear of the unknown, and so I ran forward a few steps, stretching out my own arms hungrily, craving the feel of him with my entire body.

But he was going, just as mysteriously as he had come, sucked out of my world into some other, invisible, layer of reality. A black wake swept up over me, pulling me under with sorrow, and the air around me seemed crowded with a million glowing particles, all fibrillating in front of my eyes. I sank to my knees, dizzy, nearly passing out from the intense sensation of suction and backwash in the air.

And then the wind lifted my hair back from my head — a strong wind that emanated from nowhere — and there was a touch, a soft and tender caress down the length of my cheek, as Jamie passed through me on that powerful breeze. For a moment I felt him inside me as though he were once again yet to be born.

"Jamie." My voice was a banner of hope across the disturbed air. My body tingled with his touch, his passage, and was electrified by the static of the air. Then the room quieted again and he was gone. It was as if he had never been here.

But I knew better. He was alive somewhere, somehow. And I knew I would give my life to reach him.

I sat there, alone, for a long time, exhausted and exhilarated simultaneously. He might be gone for now, but he would return. I was sure of it. The touch of him inside me stayed in a warm yellow incandescence and did not dim as the minutes passed. I needed something with which to calm myself, so I began to prepare some new canvases. There was reassurance in the cool, solid metal of my stretching pliers and tack hammer. As I fit the wooden frames together, stretched and tacked the strong white linen from side to side on the chassis, then end to end, and finally tapped the keys home into their corners, I went through it all in my mind step-by-step. I had heard Jamie, but not wanted to believe my own ears, that first night in the garden and then later over the intercom; I had seen him, but not wanted to believe my own eyes, yesterday in the field of grass. But now I believed. I believed because he had touched me, and touched me in a way no one else ever would or could. By the time I had five canvases ready, I had made up my mind. My son truly had come back to me.

The studio slowly faded from lavender to deep purple, the grayness of the day bringing dusk early. It was nearly dinnertime and I didn't even have a start on supper. I'd have to force myself to be practical from now on; I had to remember the needs of my family even as I plotted about the needs of my son, taken from me too soon, caught now in some limbo of time and space. And I would have to be very careful or Sam might suspect. Yet, even as it occurred to me to conceal Jamie's return, I saw how much I wanted to share the news with Sam. To have found Jamie once again was miraculous joy, a joy his father had a right to as well.

I went slowly downstairs, preparing face, mind, and soul, unsure of what I would do. I stood at the threshold of the kitchen, feeling caught in a time warp. Here everything moved as usual, unchanged: the stove steamed with pots and pans; the TV blared with Oscar grouching, Telly trembling, and Maria mediating; Meggie and Anna chased each other in circles while the dogs dozed in the middle of the floor, providing obstacles to be leapt over; crayons and paper were strewn helter-skelter across the kitchen table. I started gathering up the children's art materials, silently appraising their efforts. "What do you need help with, Tobie?"

Startled, she looked up over her shoulder from her mixing bowl. "I thought you were working late tonight."

"I lost track of time," I admitted.

She shifted her body away from me and the set of her shoulders was tense. I wondered if she was angry.

"Salad greens need picking," she growled.

Feeling guilty that I hadn't been down to start the meal, I was glad to volunteer. Sliding into my yellow slicker, I escaped to the garden with the basket over my arm, looking forward to being outside. But tonight was not a good night for sunsets. The light rain had stopped, and a gray dusk obscured the sky. The air was heavy with moisture, chill against my face, and my sneakers immediately soaked through at the toes as I walked across the yard. Everything seemed dull and dreary except my own exhilaration.

The garden had come back somewhat after my massacre midseason, and as I squatted I was able to pick a few carrots and sweet onions along with the last of the soft Boston lettuce. We had eaten everything I had dug up that night — none of it had gone to waste — but my own hysteria had hurt me anyway because every time I walked by the garden I was reminded of my own, more important, denudation. Now I burrowed my fingers into the dirt and it felt good: damp, pungent, fruitful. I no longer cared about past destructions. I could only think that I had seen Jamie, and that I would see him again.

With a whoop Sam hoisted me up by my armpits and swung his arms around me for a big bear hug. "Allie, I'm so proud!" he said softly in my ear. "You've worked such a long time for this."

He was talking about the exhibition, I realized. I'd forgotten it in the last few hours. I smiled up at him. "It's good news, isn't it?" My comment was casual, distracted, made as I was thinking about other things. We began walking back toward the house. Under the clammy rubber of the slicker my bare arms were cold, and I wished for my sweater. It might well drop into the fifties tonight. Could Jamie feel the cold?

"Just think what it could mean to us if you really sold a few paintings — all the things we could fix that we've been putting off, a new fridge, maybe some real riding lessons for Anna —" He interrupted himself and put his arm around me. "Not that it wouldn't be great news even without the money. It's enough just to get some credit for all you've done on your own the last few years."

"I'm nervous about it, Sam. Showing my work to strangers?" I shuddered. "I won't want to see their faces when they're looking."

"I know it's private to you," Sam said drily, "because I never get to see any of it." He snorted, a sound that reminded me of Rebecca this afternoon when I'd said the oil of Meggie wasn't finished. It looked as if everyone could see through my defenses these days. "Still," Sam went on, "it seems to me that paintings were meant to be hung up and looked at, not hidden away."

I sighed. "You've been talking to Rebecca."

"She really believes in you." His voice was thoughtful. "And she's been a good friend to us this summer. Someone we could really count on." He smiled. "So, when you're rich and famous, will you still want to live in this burg?" His voice held a tease.

I laughed and didn't say anything.

"You probably won't be happy just hanging around some old farm anymore," he joked as we went up the steps into the house. "You'll want to move to New York and hobnob with all those educated types." Suddenly a tingle of insecurity was audible in his tone. He was questioning me about how the sudden opportunity might change our lives. But it was hard for me to focus on any of it: it seemed almost unimportant. I crossed my arms over my chest and hugged myself hard, remembering the way I'd felt my son move through me this afternoon. "Don't be silly," I answered mildly.

Dinner was difficult. All I could do was stare helplessly at the fingerpaintings behind Sam's head; the children were noisy, excited, and all my husband wanted to hear about was my news. Even Tobie seemed interested. She wanted to know how many pictures I was sending and what they were of.

"There's one of you." I scooped up a forkful of chicken stew, trying to concentrate on the conversation. "Out at the barn, tending to Cloverleaf's calf."

She paused in her chewing to stare at me. "You're sending a picture of me down there?"

I nodded.

"Could somebody buy it?"

"That's the idea," I answered, around a mouthful. "And if they do, things'll go a lot easier around here. No more dribs and drabs from Hallmark."

"How much could you get for a painting of an old woman?" She snorted.

"It's an oil, a big one. And one of my best. Rebecca mentioned two thousand."

Her eyebrows shot up and she squawked with laughter. "Two thousand dollars!" She settled back into her chair, still shaking her head. "It's plain peculiar, the idea of me hanging on someone else's wall —" She broke off and clicked her dentures against the roof of her mouth. "I'm not sure I like that one bit."

Now it was my turn to be curious. "Why not?"

"Gives me the shivers to think of some stranger staring at my bald face day after day." She paused, and then chuckled. "But I guess for two thousand I might be willing to part with a fair-sized chunk of myself."

I was reminded of an article I'd read in *National Geographic* by a photographer on safari in Kenya. The natives always hid their faces behind their hands, he reported, afraid the camera would steal their souls.

Tobie cleared the table and I got up to begin washing the dishes. "Sit down, now, we're not finished yet," she said gruffly, disappearing into the pantry.

I went back to the table, puzzled, and looked to Sam; he shrugged, professing ignorance, but smiled as he wiped off Meggie's hands and face.

Tobie reappeared, carrying a high, round cake. "*Congratulations*" sloped across the top, squirted out in a shaky hand. "Your favorite lemon-on-lemon," she said, setting it down in front of me, "with raspberry filling. A little way of saying we're proud."

I was stunned and just looked up at her, speechless.

"Don't sit there flapping your jaw," she said, sitting down again. "Start cutting." The children began banging their forks on the table in a clamor for me to hurry.

"When did you get the chance?" I asked after my first mouthful of pure heaven. Tobie's lemon-on-lemon was the most luxurious cake I'd ever tasted, but it was exacting to make and took time, so usually we only had it for grand occasions, like birthdays and anniversaries.

"Caught me with my knife in the frosting bowl and nearly ruined the surprise." She slipped her dentures from her mouth and put them beside her plate and began to eat the cake eagerly. Tobie believed she could taste things better with her dentures out, as long as she didn't need to chew.

"That's what you were up to! I thought you were mad because I hadn't started supper."

She snorted again and I concentrated on enjoying my cake. Her incomprehension of the long hours I spent on my work had always come between us in the past, but my mother-in-law was a woman who needed proof, who lived by what she could see, feel, and touch. Rebecca's news must have provided her with just that.

"McKinnon's will drop it off tomorrow afternoon," Tobie said to Sam, cake leaking out of the corner of her mouth.

I raised an eyebrow enquiringly.

"A new haybaler," Sam answered grimly. "You'd better sell some of those paintings, Allie."

"He spent the afternoon tinkering with the old machine," Tobie confirmed. "But she'd just been patched together once too many."

They wouldn't let me help clean up and kicked me out of the kitchen into the sitting room, where Sam lit the first fire of the season to fight off the raw chill of the rainy evening. He went up to bathe and bed the kids while I sat and enjoyed my moment of peace and quiet. In the summer we spent our evenings on the porch, but one of the nicest things about fall and winter was using this parlor, with its roomy rockers, big, broken-in couches covered in faded chintz, and pottery lamps. When she'd come as a bride to the farmhouse, Tobie had decorated the walls with black-and-white photographs of generations of Yateses and Ronins: baby photos and annual picnics, Christmases, Easters, even funerals. And, of course, there was a story to go with each. Aunt Maude had run off with the dog catcher from New Canaan, Uncle Lucius turned out to be touched in the head, Cecile had ten children and managed the place alone after her husband died, Walter moved to New York City and went into banking, while his brother

Farley had lived on the Ronin farm in Nova Scotia till they planted him. There was a little of everything here. Now the photos had faded to sepia and gave the room warmth. Family gathered in this room, surrounded by family. I parked myself in my rocker, pulled a woolen shawl around my shoulders, and put my feet up on the three-legged stool in front of the fire.

"You know, I'm surprised," Sam said, talking to me as he squatted, poking the logs he'd laid.

"What at?" I picked up my sewing. I was still working on Anna's clothes for school, even though she started in a few days. There was never enough time to finish everything no matter how early I began.

"You." He came over and sat beside me in his rocker. "Here I thought you'd be wild over all this, and you're cool as a cat." He squinted at me.

I looked away, fighting my own urge to tell him what had me so distracted. What could career news mean next to the idea that Jamie had come home again?

"Why aren't you more excited?"

I worked the red thread in and out of the plaid material of the dress, trying to mesmerize myself. A secret would only come between us, and last night we'd promised that nothing would set us apart again. Still, I wasn't sure I wanted to tell him because I wasn't sure how he would react. "I'm probably a little stunned, that's all," I said after a minute, making a great show of trying to keep my hemming even and so not look up at him, resisting the temptation to blurt everything out.

"Or scared."

"I guess."

"You're not really focusing on this at all, are you?"

He might try and talk you out of it, a small voice inside me said. He might even laugh at you. He might lock you away.

"It just doesn't seem that important," I murmured, trying to put a new piece of thread through my needle. My hands were shaking and I couldn't manage it, so I crossed nearer to the lamp and tried again, this time with my back to Sam.

"What could be more important?" He was startled, irritated suddenly. "Right now there's nothing more important."

"There's Jamie." The words leaked out before I could stop them. I threaded the needle, and to cover my agitation, I went back to the rocker and rummaged in my sewing box, making noise to disguise the fact that the room was now totally silent.

He looked nonplussed. After a minute he cleared his throat. "You can't feel guilty because your life is starting up again. It's absurd."

I shook my head. "You don't understand!"

"Then make me."

I was silent. How could I even begin to explain?

"We promised each other," Sam said softly, slipping from his chair to kneel before me and take my hands. "Just last night we promised to talk and be open and share everything. Come on, Allie. Trust me."

His face beseeched me. "It's Jamie," I said then, the ecstasy of my news filling me, overflowing onto my face and into my eyes. "He's home again." And as I said the words I realized how deeply I believed them. I was sure of it, and in that sureness, eager suddenly to share my joy.

But Sam's eyes still searched my face, troubled, trying to understand what I meant.

"This afternoon." I smiled, remembering the feel of him inside me. "I *saw* him. He *touched* me."

His eyes widened, but still he said nothing.

"In my studio," I went on, the news spilling out of my mouth. "He came to me after Rebecca and Evan left."

"You saw him." Sam repeated my words carefully, as if trying to get hold of them.

"Actually it was yesterday I saw him first, back in the garden while I was painting." I rushed on, still gripping his hands tightly. "And I heard him once before over the intercom — that was the day you walked in and found Evan comforting me. I didn't want to tell you I'd heard him — I thought I was having a nervous breakdown then."

"And now?" he asked, dropping my hands and standing up abruptly. He went to the fireplace and fiddled with the poker, turning his face away from me.

"Now I'm *sure* it's him." I went to put my arms around him from behind and pressed my cheek against his strong back. "Sam, I know it sounds crazy, but I'm positive."

"What sounds crazy?" Tobie asked from the doorway.

I looked over at her, startled, the privacy of our moment broken. Horrified, I realized she might have overheard the entire conversation, and I hadn't even considered telling her yet. This was something private between Sam and me.

"Allie's been telling me —"

"Sam," I interrupted in a warning tone, catching at his arm, imploring him with my expression not to reveal our secret. But he had turned now toward his mother, and his distress was plain. I cast about in my mind for some way to explain without really explaining.

He looked down at me, distraught. "We're a family, Allie, and we don't keep secrets — especially not this kind."

He didn't want to be alone with it, I realized. And so my anger began. He was still including her in everything. I had trusted him, and now he would betray that trust.

Tobie came in, switched the table lamp off, pulled her cigarettes out of her pocket, settled into her rocker. The red light of the fire made wild patterns against the white walls. I looked at Sam, and he looked from me to his mother and then back again. He raised his hands in the air, helplessly. She was clearly here to stay and determined to hear it all.

"Allie thinks she's seen Jamie," he said at last, in a low voice.

Tobie's eyebrows shot up. For a moment she said nothing,

just looked from one of us to the other as Sam had done the minute before.

"I don't think it — I know it," I asserted then. My tone was quietly stubborn. "Jamie's come home to us."

"Meggie's been saying much the same thing," Tobie observed, beginning to rock back and forth.

"Then you believe me?" Quickly I sat down in my rocker, next to her, catching her gaze so that she would look at me directly. "If you could've been with me today in the studio, you'd know. It was like magic! I walked in and he was sitting there as if he belonged. He even spoke to me, but when I tried to get near him . . . then he faded out." I stood up again and paced. "But he touched me as he went." I stopped still, in the middle of the braided rug, and put my hand on my chest, remembering the warmth of that touch. "It was as if he passed right through my body."

"A child's mind can get overexcited," Tobie said, returning, it seemed, to the subject of Meggie. I wondered if she'd heard me at all. "Like having an imaginary playmate. Sam's first was called Georgie." She threw him a look. "But, Allie — what a child sees is not always reliable."

"So you *don't* believe me," I said flatly.

"It's not a question of believing. I believe you *want* to see Jamie, to know he's well wherever he may be. I know you need the comfort of that. Any mother would."

"Comfort has nothing to do with it," I answered stonily. "Look, I can prove it to you. I started a painting of Meggie on Sunday and I didn't finish it. When I went up to my studio today it was completed!" I looked back and forth from one to the other. "*Jamie* finished it for me!" My voice grew loud and excited. "The foreground uses exactly the same style as his fingerpaintings from July. Nothing could make me more certain." Their faces were still serious and unrelenting. "Come upstairs and I'll show you."

"How d'you know you didn't do it yourself?" Sam demanded.

"Don't you think I'd remember finishing a painting? Could you breed one of the mares and then just plain forget it?"

"If I was upset enough."

I bit my lip with frustration.

Tobie got up and scratched a match on the hearth, lit her Camel. "When Carson died I thought I heard all sorts of things." She inhaled and let the smoke stream out through her nose as she went back to her chair. "I was crazed with grieving. And you always know your husband'll die — just a question of who'll go first. Carson took his own time about it, and I was ready. But your *boy* . . . that's a different stew altogether. Can't explain it to yourself no matter which way you turn it. No religious folderol can whitewash it, either."

Her words fell into silence. I knew she meant to comfort me, but I didn't want that sort of comfort. Sam cleared his throat and faced me again. "Are you really serious about this?"

I just looked at him: I knew I'd lost the chance to win them over and there was no way to fight it. "I should've known the two of you would be too damned sensible to listen to me!" The anger vibrated in my voice. "I should've known you'd call it crazy."

Tobie's rocker creaked back and forth. "I didn't mean to say I thought you were crazy, Allie."

I looked over at her, only slightly mollified. "Then what did you mean?"

"Just that grieving as hard as you do when you lose someone real important — and someone you don't expect to lose right then — can make you hear and see what you wish were the day-to-day truth. I wanted Carson back, so I kept his room ready a whole year. I woke from dreaming and could've sworn he was sleeping right there beside me. I could even smell the smell of him. The mind's a strange animal, and it conjures up what it wants." Her gruff face was tense now with the memory. "Sam here kept me pulled together in the end." She looked over at him. I could tell that everything his mother was saying was new to him: he'd heard none of this before. "It was Sam needing me, and his need greater than my own. I just put my ideas aside and went back to living in the here and now. Stopped dreaming about Carson and what might have been. Got good and grateful for what was. My son."

"You've got two little girls who need you, Allie." Sam leaned across to put his hand on my arm. "I think we better go talk to the doctor. Tomorrow —"

"Weren't you the one who said there was no kind of medicine for this kind of pain?"

"I only meant —"

"I know very well what you meant." I got up and went to stand at the fire with my back toward them, trying to control my despair and my fury.

"We just want to help." Sam came and put his arms around me.

I turned to stare at him and then Tobie. Their faces were striving for calm, trying to conceal their worry. The firelight flickered over us, gave us a healthy, ruddy glow, made everything look normal and ordinary. We might have been discussing the *Farmer's Almanac*.

They thought I was having a breakdown even though they wouldn't admit it. I realized that I'd never convince either one of them that Jamie had returned to me. And in that split second I saw there was only one way to handle the situation.

"Yes," I agreed, turning back and pretending to warm my hands before the fire. "I know you want to help." The lie slid out easily as I stepped back from my husband, and from my marriage. "And maybe Nat Loring could make me feel better — but I'd rather go alone. Tomorrow I'll call." I sighed, and stared into the flames pensively, using the drama of my pose. They must believe me. Everything depended on it. I put my hand to my forehead and rubbed it. "Maybe I'm tired."

Sam put his arm across my shoulder. "Just talking to him might help."

"I'm sure you're right." I was furious inside. The words felt like sugared pills inside my mouth, and I wanted to spit them out. But I would not let Sam and Tobie stop me.

"A good night's sleep won't hurt you any either," Tobie observed, standing up and checking her watch. She knelt to bank the fire. "Past nine already, and it's been a big day."

I turned without a word and we left the room, Sam's arm across my shoulders. Loneliness pooled in my chest, and I had to fight the urge to cry as we trudged together up the worn risers. I had lost no matter how you looked at it: if Sam was right, then my son was truly gone, and lost to me forever. And if I was right and Jamie had returned home to us, I could never be close to my husband again.

"It's a hard thing to live with." My voice trembled and I stroked my fingertips across the grain of the chair's wooden arms. I was sitting in Nat Loring's office, trying to explain myself. He'd done a physical exam, taken my weight, pulse, and blood pressure, and then pronounced me sound. "I just can't sleep anymore," I went on. "The harder I try the worse it gets." I let a few tears slip down through my lashes.

"The insomnia began after Jamie's funeral?" He reached across his battered desk and pulled the prescription pad toward him. As he frowned, his large face grew more deeply creased. He began to scribble. "I'm making this a very small prescription, Allie. Ordinarily I don't even give out sleeping medications, but this seems a bit different from what I usually see."

"And what's that?" I asked curiously.

"Abused women, overworked farmers, accidents, women inundated with too many kids too soon." He shrugged. "Mostly a lot of people with troubles that can't be solved by pills. Which brings us to you." He looked at me directly, his brown eyes kind but firm.

"Me?" I looked away. I didn't want him asking any more questions.

"You say it's just that you can't sleep, but that's not all of it, is it?"

"All?" I echoed. I studied the diploma hanging on the wall behind his desk.

"Sam called me after you did. He said you'd been seeing Jamie again." His gaze held steady, never wavered. I looked away, embarrassed that he'd caught me in a lie of omission, enraged that Sam didn't trust me enough to talk to Nat alone. "He was pretty upset when I spoke to him this morning. Want to talk about it?"

"Not really." I looked at the floor and let my voice reflect my discomfort. "I mean — I realize now that it was all just a fantasy. Sam didn't need to call like that. It's embarrassing." I concentrated fiercely as I said the lie, knowing how important it was to convince him that this was what I truly believed.

He was still looking at me, then he pushed his chair back from his desk and came around to sit beside me. "A colleague of mine practices down in Manchester, treating people who've had someone die suddenly, especially parents who've lost children." He sighed and rubbed his palm across his thick, bushy hair. "I think it might help you to see him. He's set up a program where you can go and live in a wing of the hospital temporarily. Sometimes it helps to get away from all the pressures of home and family when you're trying to work through this sort of loss." He reached toward his desk and note pad. "I'll give you his name and then I'll call him —"

I put up my hand. "I won't need it. I'm fine now, really."

"You're a lot less than fine if you need a pill to sleep."

"Only temporarily." I stood up. "I won't be back for a refill. Part of it might be from the strain of work right now."

He looked up from the prescription blank. "I didn't know you'd gone back to work."

I nodded and smiled convincingly. "I'm having my first New York show in a few months," I said proudly. "It's been a rush to get it organized and ready to ship. In fact," I added, checking my watch, "I've got to get back and finish my inventory."

"Any of it show off our native habitat?"

A teasing smile came to my face. "There's even one of you."

"Me?" He was taken aback at first, but, an instant later, pleased.

I nodded. "That time Meggie cut her leg and you had to come out to the farm to bandage her up. I did a charcoal of that."

"It never occurred to me that an artist could paint a picture without the subject's knowledge," he said thoughtfully. Then he smiled, tickled at the idea of being included. "It's a little sneaky, isn't it?"

I smiled and put my hand out.

"Good luck with New York," he said, opening the door for me. "And let me know if you change your mind about Manchester. Or if you'd just like to talk with a friendly ear." He grinned and I nodded, hurrying through his waiting room onto the sidewalk.

Escaping out to the pavement, I took a deep breath. He'd believed me, and now I even had physical evidence — the prescription — with which to allay Sam's and Tobie's fears. I looked up and down the street. Nothing had changed in Arrowsic since I'd last been to town a month ago. It was only me who was different, my mind and my eyes. Probably nothing would ever look the same to me again.

As I crossed the street to Nelson's, the late-morning sun heated my back through my shirt. It was a hot day, welcome after yesterday's cool rain. Sam would be pleased with the dry heat — today's sun should guarantee the second cutting of our fields tomorrow. He'd get a chance to try out the new baler.

The shop bell jangled as I pushed the door open, but I came in slowly, making a show of getting the prescription from my bag. I hadn't been in since before Jamie died, since the day we'd all been here for ice creams. I walked up to the counter casually, but my eyes stung and I blinked against tears. This store was a part of my life before. It was painful to walk back.

"Why, hello, Mrs. Yates," Herb Nelson greeted me, his tortoiseshell glasses thick mirrors in which I could see my own reflection, small and wavery, very far away, nearly a miniature of myself. "Good to see you again."

"And you, Herb." I held out my prescription blank. "Think you could take care of this while I wait?"

"Only if you'll sit for a coffee soda while Sally fills it."

I laughed. "You don't have to twist my arm." I climbed up on the high swivel stool and fought my own memories. In the long glass behind the counter, I saw us all as if we were really here: Meggie, then Anna, then Jamie, on the far end, covered in chocolate ice cream. Jamie, spinning on his stool. Jamie, enjoying every rich minute of our outing. Jamie, his dancing face. I closed my eyes.

"Haven't seen you in a bit," Herb said, setting the soda in front of me.

I busied myself with the straw, and with sucking up sweet. "Been working hard," I answered after a minute.

He nodded. "Sally and me, well, we wanted you to know how much — how sorry —"

I cut him off by looking at him directly. "Herb, I know you were very fond of Jamie."

He nodded. "Such tragedy — and you and Sam so young. The other little ones must be a real comfort to you now."

I was spared having to answer or continue by the jangle of

the shop bell as a new customer entered. In the mirror I saw that it was Rebecca, hiding behind dark glasses. On her head she wore a large straw hat with a red bandanna tied from brim to chin. When she saw me, she stopped.

"You're finished?" she asked, coming over to me quickly.

"I just started," I answered, startled, gesturing to my soda glass.

"Not that." She was impatient. "I mean the inventory."

"I can't see your eyes behind those things," I observed, peering at her.

She took them off and slipped them into her pocket, then sat on the stool beside me.

"Anything I can get you?" Herb asked politely. I could see he was trying hard not to stare. It came to me then that Rebecca was embarrassed about her eyes and had probably been hiding behind her dark glasses since the day she moved to Arrowsic.

"Not unless you've got a cold beer."

He shook his head. She shrugged and turned back to me. "So?" she asked again.

I returned to my soda. "I haven't started yet," I answered vaguely. "I'll get to it sometime later."

"They're coming tomorrow, you know." She looked at me speculatively. "Maybe you're really not ready for this step."

I felt unsteady suddenly. "I didn't think it would take very long."

"It probably won't. But leaving it till the last — well . . ." Her irritation was plain. "Look, if you don't want this, then skip it. No one can tell you when you'll be prepared for the public. Maybe you never will be."

I was silent. Herb came back over to us and handed me my prescription bottle. "Dalmane, twenty-five milligrams." He read the instructions out loud, as was customary. "Doctor says to take one capsule each night before bed."

"Dalmane," Rebecca repeated, staring. "You can't sleep?"

I pocketed the bottle. "Haven't been able to since Jamie died."

"I got hooked on those things once. You'd be better off painting your way through the night."

"He only gave me twenty." I was starting to feel a little testy. Rebecca aggravated me sometimes: once in a while she got too pushy and too nosy for her own good. Or mine.

"If you start with those you'll be groggy for hours after you wake up."

"Will you cut it out? When I want the advice of such an expert, I'll ask." My chin quivered and I realized with horror that I was about to cry. I bit my lip to try and stop, but confusion, grief, and anxiety were washing through me in a powerful wave. I stood up quickly, put a twenty on the counter, tapped my foot and kept blinking against the tears while Herb made change. I rushed from the store with Rebecca trailing me, scenting distress, pelting me with questions.

"What's going on here?" She backed me up against my car as I fumbled in my purse for the car keys.

"Could you just leave me alone please?"

"No, I can't. A friend doesn't leave you alone when you're in a state." She put her arm out toward me, hesitantly at first. We had never really touched much before. And then she swept me in against her tall, thin body and held me, rocked me awkwardly while I sobbed. After a few minutes she took my purse, upended it on the roof, and rooted through the mess till she got my keys. Sweeping the contents back in helter-skelter, she unlocked the doors, buckled me into the passenger seat, started the old wagon up, and drove off down the street. She was taking care of me.

We drove for a while in silence. I was still crying, but not sobbing anymore. When I finally looked up, I saw we'd turned into my driveway.

"Feel better?"

I nodded, oddly relieved. "I'm still a mess these days. Sorry for the scene."

"*I'm* sorry for jumping on you. Being around Evan makes me bitchy." She grinned her lopsided grin. "Besides, I always liked scenes. It used to drive my husband crazy."

"Do you want me to take you back to your car?" I was thinking practically again.

She shook her head. "I'll come in and help you start the inventorying. That is . . . if you want me to."

I paused for a moment, wondering what it was I really did want. Then I nodded. "Thanks," I said. "I could use some help."

Rebecca drew the steel measuring tape along the sides of the canvas. "Thirty-two," she said aloud. "Write it up this way: open quote, Haybaling, period, close quote. Oil on canvas, comma, thirty-two inches by twenty inches, period. Nineteen eighty-six, period."

Faithfully I transcribed the formula onto the long yellow pad with my pen. I smiled. I had to admit it: I was getting a little excited about the show.

Rebecca set the next canvas up on the worktable and began to measure. "Thirty-two by forty." She looked at it as I wrote it up: "*Death of Her Twin.*" Oil on canvas, 32" x 40". 1986.

"You know," she said thoughtfully after a minute, "this reminds me of something."

I didn't answer, just fiddled with my pencil and paper.

"I can't place it," she went on. "But it's nagging at me. How did you manage this part of the garden here?" she asked, gesturing to the masses of color twining up around Meggie's legs. "The intensity of color, the impasto pretty thick, but not too thick. And the layering of different colors really works. The blending is remarkable." She peered at it closely. "You didn't use a brush, did you? It's done with a fingertip?" She looked over enquiringly.

I shook my head. "I didn't use anything at all."

"What do you mean?" She was puzzled.

I sighed. "I mean that I didn't do that part of the painting."

"Someone else did it?" Her voice was incredulous. "Who?"

I was silent, then crossed the room to the closet and took out the fingerpaintings Jamie had done earlier in the summer. I handed them to her. She stared at me, at them, then flipped through the stack quickly, holding paper up against canvas, comparing fingerpaint to oil.

"That's what I was remembering," she whispered. "Jamie's fingerpaintings. But it's deceptive — it looks so different done with oil. Still, the layering and blending are just the same."

I stood silent, waiting.

"You're saying his paintings inspired you?"

I shook my head.

Her tanned face paled. Now she said nothing.

"I'm saying that this painting was unfinished on Sunday when I brought it up here, and finished when you and Evan uncovered it Monday morning. I was just getting ready to work on it when you two stormed in on me." My voice grew loud, excited. "I nearly passed out when you took the drape off because I wasn't kidding around when I said it wasn't done." I crossed the room to stand beside her, and pointed. "Here. Here — all this was white space. I hadn't even *decided* how to finish it. I was thinking of using Jamie's room as the background. Of course, this is much better." I looked at her. She was eyeing me warily.

"You don't believe me," I said, going to sit on the couch wearily.

"Don't believe what? You still haven't told me who finished the painting for you."

"Jamie finished it."

She stared at me, then fumbled in her pocket and lit up

one of her thin black cigars. "Jamie's dead," she said after her first drag.

"I've seen him, Rebecca. He's come home again."

She exhaled a plume of gray smoke. "A ghost?"

I shrugged. "You can call it whatever you like. He sat right here" — I patted the couch beside me — "and spoke to me yesterday. He finished my painting, I'm sure of it. And he'll be back — I'm sure about that too."

"Is this why you went to see Loring today?"

"Sam and Tobie made me. They think I'm nuts."

She tapped her ash onto the floor. "Well, the thought did cross my mind."

I shook my head vehemently. "I'm not. And I don't need those sleeping pills either. It was just a ruse to satisfy Sam, because I'm telling you, Rebecca, if he's here I won't let anyone stand in the way of my being with him."

"Maybe you painted it yourself and just don't remember," she said, turning back to the painting.

I glared at her. "Do you really think that's even a possibility?"

She didn't answer, but kept staring at me. "What about Meggie and Anna? What about your husband?"

"What about them?" Passion and grief for my lost son rose up hot inside me. "Don't you see? He's come back to me, Rebecca, I can't turn away from him."

"They need you too."

"Not as much as he does. He's out there alone." I went and stood before the window, staring into the tree outside the glass. The leaves swayed with the wind, their tips barely tinged with color. Fall was here. Soon the cold would come. I had to find shelter for Jamie before then, find a way to bring him back into my world, or forward into his own. "Out there where I put him."

"You still can't be blaming —"

"If I'd only *checked* —"

"Stop it! Just stop." Her voice was loud and angry again. She scratched around on the table for the coffee can lid in which to tap the long ash. I handed it to her silently. "You can't indulge in this kind of fantasy without having it cost something somewhere. What about Sam? What does he say?"

My voice was bitter and hard. "He told Tobie."

"He's probably scared, Allie."

"I don't care! I wanted it to stay between us."

Rebecca sighed. "Well, what did Nat Loring say?" she asked impatiently.

I shrugged. "He gave me the pills."

"You told him you were seeing Jamie and he gave you a *prescription?*" Her growly voice was incredulous.

"I told him I couldn't sleep. I lied to him."

"Allie." Rebecca's voice was low now, despairing. She came over to stand beside me at the window. "I could call my old shrink in Manhattan and see if he knows anyone up here."

I shook my head. "Nat already tried that routine with me. I said no to him and I'll say it again to you."

"Your little boy is dead. You've got to go on with what's still here."

"We had this conversation already, a week ago," I answered, angry now. "And I accepted my loss and I started trying to live again, and then *he came back*. If I were going to make all this up, why would I have waited so long to do it?"

"I don't know. But I'll tell you this — you're going to destroy yourself if you keep on." She put her hands on my shoulders and forcibly turned me so that I had to look into her face. "Allie, listen to me. Your life is too full now for this kind of nonsense." She gestured to all the canvases standing around us. "Don't turn away from this. Stop the torture."

I looked straight into her eyes without flinching, my anger helping me be sure of myself. I was tired of doubters. I needed some support. I wanted a little belief from the people I loved.

"I won't turn away from my son." My voice was fierce. I felt I had nearly bared my teeth at her.

"Your son is gone."

"Are you so sure?"

She hesitated, dropped her hands from my shoulders.

"Are you so sure?" I repeated, homing in as I sensed the chink in her defense.

She stared at me and still did not answer.

"Are you so sure you understand *everything* about life? Who's to say what comes after?"

She took a step away from me and my vehemence. She had no answer.

"You're my friend — believe in me now." My tone entreated, and then faltered a little. "I need someone to believe instead of arguing."

"All right, Allie," she answered slowly, still troubled. "I'll try. But I'm frightened for you."

"Now you sound like my mother." I laughed, relieved. At least I could count on her not to go to Sam.

She laughed too, a little unsteadily. "Well, sometimes I feel like your mother as well as your friend."

I picked up a charcoal sketch and laid it on the worktable. "Come tell me what you think of this," I said. "I did it last night when everyone was asleep. I've still got to spray the fixative." I moved away so she could see it better. "It's a detail from the oil of Meggie in the garden. I'm calling it 'The Face of Jamie.' "

At bedtime Sam brought me a glass of milk to wash down my Dalmane. He seemed relieved that someone knew what to do for me; he was as fooled as I had hoped he would be. Even as I swallowed the capsule my mind was busy again with thoughts of Jamie, busy planning what to do when he appeared next, how I would entice him nearer — perhaps even onto my lap. I fell asleep dreaming of our reunion, but despite the drug I was restless. I tossed under the technicolor quality of my dreams, which came in an unending stream that night. At two o'clock I sat up, dazed, rubbed my eyes, looked at the clock.

I lay back on the pillow. Sam snored beside me, reaching out to rub his arm against my side. I fell back to dreaming. It was an old dream this time, a nightmare I had had early in the summer. In it, the sun had just set behind a wall of purple thunderheads beyond the west pasture, and dark was creeping up prematurely. An eerie green light reflected from trees broad with leaves as a woman came down the road toward me. Her face was my mother's face, but her eyes were watch-eyes, small blue circles ringed in white. In my arms I carried a baby. I peered at the baby's face and recognized it as my own, a face I'd seen hundreds of times in my baby pictures, taken thirty years before.

Around the baby's neck was a thin leather strap from which hung a star of red glass; the star winked its iridescence on and off, a beacon of orange-yellow-vermilion rays that circled through the half-light of the coming rain. Introducing herself as my new neighbor, Rebecca offered to hold the baby so that I could open my umbrella, but when I stretched my arms out to give the baby over, the infant squirmed, slipping like a fish down the length of my body to the ground. Aghast, I knelt to scoop the baby up against me, but Rebecca cried out then, in warning, and I looked to see that thunderheads had piled high, in columns above us. The setting sun had reversed itself, rising back up over the western horizon, and all around the new white light blazed.

I looked down at the child again. But the eyes swiveled, blind whites turning upward, in a convulsion. The left eye popped from its socket and rolled to the ground next to my knee, a blue marble. It flashed red-yellow-orange in the light of the star. Horrified, I pulled away. Rebecca knelt beside

me, picked up the eye, and put it into the palm of my hand
even as I wrestled with her grip, repulsed and desperate
to get away. She folded my fingers around the eye saying,
*This is what you have left, a touchstone, and you will guard it,
then use it.*

I woke, sticky with sweat and tears. It was still night. Now
I understood that the dream had been a harbinger, a map. It
would tell me what to do. I got out of bed and went up the
stairs to my studio. I swung open the door to a room empty
with moonlight. Stacked edge-to-edge along the worktables
and walls were the canvases to be crated tomorrow. I walked
through them, looking carefully at each, saying goodbye to
the lines, the planes, the colors of my life. They would be
sold, they would be hung in other people's houses. They
would no longer be mine.

Then I turned to see Jamie, sitting once again on the couch.
This time I was not afraid. Across the shadowed room I went
to him and, without speaking, sat down. He turned his face
up to mine, smiled, then crawled into my lap. I put my nose
down into the curl of his hair, took in his scent. Amazement
flooded through me in a warm golden light. I stroked his
cheek, looked deeply into his eyes, which were dark with the
blackness of this room. He wore his Dr. Denton's. The weight
of his wet diaper pressed against my knee. He cuddled in
close and I leaned back and began to sing. And a strange
thing happened then, for although he did not ask, I knew
which songs he wanted to hear; I knew as clearly as if he had
spoken, as if his thoughts had simply appeared in my mind.
And as my voice lifted itself up out of the hush of the dark
room, Jamie and I were yet again as one.

Reunion

Nothing about him was different, nothing had changed. He felt the same, he smelled the same, and as he spoke into my mind he even sounded the same. After a while I stopped singing and leaned back against the hard lumpiness of the couch. I relaxed, just like I used to every night as I cradled him in the rocker in our bedroom. His body went warm and soft and limp with sleep; the weight across my chest and stomach and thighs made me drowsy too, and at peace. With the Dalmane clouding my consciousness at last, I slowly drifted off to sleep, my arms still locked around him. I did not dream. For the first time in over a month I did not need to dream.

Sometime later I woke. My lap was empty. I sat up, swallowing quickly against the sticky bad taste the pill had left in my mouth. "Jamie?" My voice was a tense whisper in the darkened room.

"Mommee." I looked over to the easel, where the oil of Meggie still stood. Jamie was staring at the painting. He turned back toward me, a half-turn. He looked almost like a painting himself, silhouetted by moonlight, the shadows creating deep chiaroscuro on the planes of his face. I held my breath. He was beautiful.

"Mommee bye-bye."

The words shimmered, gossamer, fragile, across the screen of my mind. I shook my head against them, put my arms out to him. This time he did not come to me.

He began to fade, the color bleaching away first in his clothing, then in his hair, and last of all in his face, tender, scared, knowing. Stock-still for only a second, I rushed to the spot. I was losing him again, and there was a great, rending tear inside my body. Again I felt the backwash of air; my arms clasped only themselves and the thin black night. Desperately I called out his name, begged him, *Wait! Wait for me!* The silence of the room echoed back in my face. I panicked: how, having held him once more, could I now bear to live without him? A wail broke from me and I shoved my fist against my mouth.

What if he didn't come back? Then there would be only one way out of this trap, only one escape. My palette knife glinted in the moonlight. I closed my eyes as I picked it up. I waited for courage to strengthen me as love had strengthened me, but there was nothing — no miraculous pulse of energy. My hand hung limp by my side.

Slowly I opened my eyes. Meggie haunted the air in front of me, her eyes an entreaty, and I reached out slowly to touch her, feeling the thick impasto of oil paints, the energy and toil of each brushstroke, knowing that if I went, this too would be lost. Never to hold Meggie or Anna, or to kiss Sam again; never to fill a palette again, lift a brush, face a blank canvas. Or never to hold my son, rub my cheek against the soft curl of his hair. To leave Jamie alone, adrift in the night. I cried out against the painful weight of such a choice and backed away to the window in despair.

Through the branches of the tree the stars burned coldly

in their heaven. I fell on my knees and began to sob, slumped down on the floor of my studio. Only my paintings watched. Dust and dirt from the unswept planking gritted against my cheek and lips, and tears rolled down into my ears, my mouth. I thought I would crack in two from pain, a pain worse than any I had ever known; the pain of letting Jamie leave this world made the pain of bringing him in look meek.

Craving human warmth, I went numbly down the stairs. I sat on the edge of Anna's bed and stroked her hair. She was nestled into her sheets, and when I listened carefully I could just hear her soft breathing. Unconsciously, my own breath synchronized itself with hers. We too were linked. She was my firstborn, my experiment into motherhood. I remembered a late, unexpectedly snowy night one November, with Sam stuck down in Manchester getting an old truck part replaced. Anna had been restless — only four months old — and I, too inexperienced to know any better, had rocked her, walked her, sung to her to make her sleepy again. I'd put her up on my shoulder as I paced, the floorboards creaking, and when I thought she'd finally drifted off to sleep, I brought her down gently into my arms. As soon as I moved to lay her back in the bassinet her eyes flew open like a china doll's, deep, firstborn blue. Angrily I stared into that stubborn face, so exhausted now I was ready to kill her. And in that moment of my desperation she let fly her first real smile: not a shy, average, half-moon smile — but an openmouthed, toothless, silly wide gas of delight. She chortled at me, and despite my stupor, I laughed back. She'd taken me by surprise, and exhaustion dropped away, flooded out on waves of pure maternal bliss. Later, when she was finally asleep again, I'd tried to sketch our exchange. Her smile had matured and her teeth had come in, but the spirit — that wild sense of humor — had been Anna and stayed Anna from that minute on.

Now I put my finger into her palm and she curled her fingers around mine, opened her eyes, saw me watching. I had wanted her to wake up, I realized, to see her smile again. One grin, sleepily, then she turned her face back into the pillow.

At Meggie's crib I remembered how I used to watch Jamie every night, and for the first time allowed myself really to see the physical similarities between the twins. I had fought those similarities all along, even when friends and neighbors had commented on how much they'd turned out to look alike, despite their different sizes. I had wanted them to be separate because I'd wanted Jamie to be closest to me. As I stood looking down on Meggie, I knew why I might have mistaken her for Jamie the other day in the field — if indeed I had: the same curly blonde hair, the same snubbed nose. He had been bigger; she was a miniature, yet all her own. And now too I recognized my own face mirrored in hers for the first time. But she wasn't Jamie. Or me. Jamie was gone, lost to me unless I chose to follow.

I went back to our room, half hoping Sam would wake. Head under the pillow, blanket over his shoulders, he was only a hump, sprawled halfway across the bed. A wide and restless sleeper, he had overtaken my space as soon as I left it earlier. Something was bothering me, working itself into a persistent voice at the back of my mind, but I couldn't pinpoint what it was saying.

I climbed back to my studio. In the dark room the moon sifted through the skylight onto the bare floor. I crossed to the easel and took down the painting of Meggie. I remembered how Jamie had stood on this very spot: I remembered the contours of his face. A white canvas beckoned, the largest I had ever attempted. I would paint it as I wanted us to be. And, as van Gogh himself had once proposed, I would paint it only by moonlight. I balanced the big canvas on the easel carefully and shifted it so that it was directly beneath the skylight. There was a sharp inward pull of air then, as if the night were holding its breath.

I set up a simplified palette of soft but bright oils: Zinc white, Cadmium and Naples yellows, Viridian, Burnt green earth, Mars violet, Manganese blue. My eyes ached in the darkness, and instinctively I pulled my cap on my head, a tight band around my skull. Then I took out my bristle brushes and a few red sable flats for blending. I waited for a moment, poised in front of the white linen, waited for the vibration inside of me to increase until I felt it extend out to my hand, to my fingers, until it became clear as a song inside my head. Then I began to paint.

A field. Trees and mountains of the background done in a flat wash of Burnt green earth, Mars violet, and Viridian, diluted with a lot of turp so as to be transparent, floating, nearly ethereal. The hayfield stretched to the bottom edge of the canvas, Cadmium yellow, also diluted soft and transparent. The boy squatted in the foreground, picking a sunflower. His crouch was strong and sturdy, the ground around him littered with the heads of flowers. I did his hair in a bright tone of Naples yellow, mixed with a small amount of white, to contrast with his face: his face was done with deep chiaroscuro, with depth and intensity, the only three-dimensional object on the flat surface. In the sky above him the sun shone, but so gently that the moon and stars were still visible, dim shapes in a bleached-down sky of dilute Manganese blue.

As I worked, the moonlight shifted above my head. I kept moving the easel to new spots. I didn't want the harshness of electricity; there was magic in this painting, done by a half-light which allowed my vision to bloom undisturbed and my eyes to see in a new way.

Behind the boy I painted four other figures working the field: on the left two young girls planted seedlings; on the right a man hefted square blocks of hay onto the back of a pickup truck; in the center the woman stood, a baling hook in her right hand. I painted her shirt the same lemony shade as the boy's hair, using lots of Zinc white mixed into the

Naples yellow, forging an inextricable visual link between them. I painted her stretching toward the sky, her left arm curved out sinewy and disproportionately long — longer than the right — and tense with the agony of her reach, but finding what it sought as she caught a descending shooting star. The star burned as it touched her fingertips: the Naples yellow reached fire brilliance as I mixed it with more and more white. The curve of her arm was the curve I had practiced over and over, the curve I'd found in a tree limb one July day, so long ago, in our woods.

The star rained light downward, over the face of the field, down onto the head of the boy. Using the very tip of my brush in tiny strokes, I created points of light showering down to catch in his curls. And so he shimmered, bright as a meteor against the dark face of the earth, with a fine net, almost a halo of fire, surrounding him.

The family stood, united, under a sky of night and day, on a field where spring and fall, sunrise and dusk, met. This was my answer, but still I was not sure of what I meant. I had painted it as I wished we could be: a family reunited. The vibration inside me remained, unabated.

Gray dawn came through the skylight and began to change the tones of the paints I'd used. I looked at my watch: five-thirty. I began to see what I had really painted in the half-dark and it frightened me with its strength and statement. It was telling me what had to be done, but I was not sure I could do it. I staggered to the couch and slept.

Sam woke me, alarm on his face. "What are you doing here?"

I sat up, groggy. "I couldn't sleep. I painted most of the night." I looked at my watch to orient myself. Six-fifteen.

"I've been looking for you all over." Upset, he paced past my painting and paid it no notice. "Didn't you take the sleeping pill?"

"It gave me weird dreams," I answered, rubbing my eyes. The vibration was still there, humming through my body. I stretched out my arm and saw the tremor, and for the first time I was frightened. The air seemed close, hard to breathe. What was my own terrible answer?

"Maybe tonight will be better," he said comfortingly. He stopped pacing and looked around. "This is the stuff you're sending?" It was one of the only times he had been in my studio, and to my surprise I didn't mind his eyes on what I had done. He walked from one canvas to the next. I could tell from his face that he was awed by the number of canvases stacked around the room, by the intricacy, detail, color, and line of each, by these scenes of our everyday life captured and reinterpreted.

"I don't know anything about art," he said at last.

"You don't need to."

"You've kept all this out of our marriage — and it's a big part of you, Allie."

I looked at him slowly. "I've kept it in a closet, Sam. Don't take it personally."

"I wish we could share it some — a little — just the way you share my work here." He looked at me with a question in his dark brown eyes.

"Maybe." My voice was noncommittal.

"You're ready to let the world see it now?"

"I'm not sure," I said. I got up and stretched, trying to breathe around the motor humming at high speed in my chest. My body felt sore and out of sorts from my short sleep on the lumpy couch. "I need a shower, that's what I'm sure of."

"I'll get the girls' breakfast," he said, stopping to stare at the oil I had done last night. I went to stand beside him. As I looked at it the vibration increased: my entire body quivered as my eyes met my work. The colors were maybe too strong. They might have to be muted. I would get Rebecca's reaction later when they came to crate the others. And there was still work to be done on the faces of the two girls, and in the shape of the man's back, which needed to be more angular and strained, more in harmony with the square geometry of the bales he hefted.

"I don't understand this one at all," Sam said.

I smiled, amused and distracted from my anxiety. "I don't mind."

"The little boy here —" He pointed with his index finger. "Is this Jamie?"

I dropped my head, and he nodded.

"I don't understand the meaning," Sam repeated. "But it makes me see."

"See?"

"How hard you work — how difficult this all is. How much of yourself you have to open up." He sighed and put his arm around me. "How do you feel today? Any better?"

"Fine." I nodded, breathing through an open mouth. "Just fine."

"You haven't" — he broke off, cleared his throat — "seen him again?"

I hesitated, then plunged into the lie. "Nope." The anxiety swelled up, a response that made my heart pound. I swallowed against it, shook my head for reinforcement, and turned to pick up my brushes, which lay thick and stiff with color. Filling a jar with turp, I suspended them on a rack to soak. I'd broken them in carefully, and I didn't want to lose them now.

Sam came up behind me as if he sensed my tension. "We need you, Allie." He put his arms around me and rocked me from behind. I relaxed against him. It felt so good to be held. When he held me the vibration idled more slowly. "The movers from the gallery are coming when?"

"Ten."

"Will you need any help?"

I shook my head. "Rebecca will be here. We've only got to supervise anyway. But I can't come baling with you this morning."

"That's all right. Tobie and the girls will. I won't be alone."

"I'll be down this afternoon."

He nodded and kissed the back of my head. "Tonight maybe we'll go over to the drive-in — it's the last kids' night before it closes for the season. Take the girls for a treat?"

I nodded. "Lobster rolls."

"And Anna asked if we could watch for shooting stars after."

I stiffened. "It'll make an awfully long night."

"Her school starts Monday. They can sleep late tomorrow if they need to."

"All right." We went downstairs then, his arm supporting me, but my mind was already elsewhere, living in the world of my painting, thinking about Jamie, wondering how and when we would get there.

They came to crate my paintings at ten o'clock. I was working on the large canvas when the van rumbled over the gravel outside, and then there was the slamming of metal doors, footsteps trudging toward the house, toward me and my inner life. I put down my brush and palette slowly and went to meet them with reluctance, the vibration trapped inside my chest and desperate to get out now. Greeting them, I heard my own breathless, gasping tone and hoped they wouldn't think me very strange. At least, not so strange as I felt.

They climbed upstairs behind me, puffing a bit, and I looked at my watch. Rebecca was late. I was almost angry that she was late today.

The two men were a Mutt and Jeff team: one with bulging forearms and a tight, grubby teeshirt; the other thin, gawky, with his hair parted meticulously, his fingernails scrubbed clean. They were both young, in their twenties; they sounded like Brooklyn; their names were Jake and Bob. I was glad to see how strong Jake looked. The canvases weren't heavy, but they were precious. From the truck Jake brought Bob the packing materials and spread them through the already crowded studio.

"Don't worry, Miz Yates," Jake said, grinning at me. "We done this a lot. We're used to you temper-mental types." He unrolled a stack of blank newsprint and Bob got ready to begin the wrapping. Jake wiped sweat from his forehead onto his sleeve. "Radio says it's gonna be a scorcher," he went on conversationally.

I knew he was trying to be friendly, to make me less crazy, but I could hardly breathe and it had nothing to do with the heat that was beginning to build up in the room. For a brief moment I considered telling them to stop and go back to New York, to forget they ever heard my name or address. And in that instant, Rebecca sauntered in, one of her thin cigars clamped between her teeth.

"You're late." My welcome was not exactly hospitable but Rebecca met my gaze, assessing me.

"Jake, Bob." She greeted the men with a nod of her head. "How's Marge?"

Jake smiled and I noticed how uneven, but white, his teeth were. "She told us you'd probably be here today."

Rebecca smiled. "Well, I did oversleep," she admitted, taking a long drag, and turning to me. "You nervous?"

"Who could sleep? I painted all night long." I was furious with her: she knew I was depending on her.

"Are you calmer now?" She peered at me. "You don't look very calm."

"She don't know us yet, Miz Shardick," Jake said, absorbing a little of my glare and irritation. There was something about his burly body that just soaked up the tension. He looked trustworthy, I decided. So far it seemed he did all the talking while Bob moved swiftly, in silence, pushing his glasses high up on the bridge of his nose. I watched the care with which his hands worked, each piece treated reverently. Jake muscled things about, nailing together frames in which the canvases would sit and opening the crates, while Bob began to wrap a painting with delicacy.

Rebecca saw me watching. "Marge stole Bob from a museum," she said in a low voice, "and hired him full-time. I've done a lot of shows with her, and Bob packs the work like eggs into a carton." She was trying to comfort me, and my anger evaporated: I couldn't ask for more loyalty and support than Rebecca had given in the last two months. I was ashamed at my own unfairness.

"Does he ever talk?"

She shook her head. "He just *concentrates*. Let's leave them alone to do their work. We'll come back to sign the inventory lists when they've finished. It won't take long."

"Coffee?"

She nodded and we went down to the kitchen, our voices surfacing to normal levels again. "Did you really work all night?" she asked, as we settled into our chairs.

"I couldn't sleep. Even with the Dalmane."

"What did you work on?"

"Something new. I'd like you to look at it."

"Try and keep me away." She grinned her lopsided smile and lit up a cigar.

"When they've gone then." We sat for a while, listening to nothing in particular, just sipping companionably.

"How are you feeling?"

I forced a smile. "Better."

"Don't lie to me, Allie," she said softly. "I can see through it all. Every last bit."

I looked into her different eyes and let my anxiety show for the first time all morning by standing up to pace. "It's eating away at me. I can't take much more." The vibration increased as I spoke of it. "Look." I held my hand up for her to see: it shook like a spring branch in an April blizzard.

"You can't have done much painting with a tremor like that," she observed.

"It stopped when I started to paint. Funny, isn't it?" I sighed. "But the feeling won't go away."

"What feeling?"

"Dread." I had finally named it. I sat down again and put my head in my hands. "I'm so scared."

"What of?" She came around the table to sit beside me and took my hand awkwardly in her worn one. There was still green paint beneath her fingernails.

"Myself," I answered slowly. "Of what I'm doing. I can't stop it. These paintings are a waterfall that just keeps coming out of me. I've got no control over any of it."

She frowned. "I was the one who told you to let go."

"But should it feel like this? Should I be so frightened?"

"I'm not sure," she said after a minute. "If it was just your work . . ." She paused, looked straight at me. "Have you seen Jamie again?"

I was silent and dropped my gaze. "Last night, late. I think for the last time — I'm afraid he won't come back." Tears filled my eyes.

She sighed, relieved. "Good."

"No!" I twisted in my chair and pulled my hand free from hers. "I won't let him die a second time! I won't let him go again."

She inhaled slowly. "Did you tell Sam?"

I shook my head vehemently.

"Maybe *I* should." Her face was set. "Can't you see how you're hurting yourself with all this craziness?"

"I was already hurt! Irreparably. Damaged, undone — that happened the day he died!"

"Sam should know —"

"If you tell him anything, I'll deny it all." My voice was sharp and firm; inside me the anxiety fibrillated away. "It's none of your business anyway. And you promised!"

"Ladies?" Jake called to us from the doorway. "Sorry to interrupt, but we need your eyeballs on this list."

I stood up abruptly. Rebecca stared at me and then, after a minute, nodded. "All right," she said. "But I can't be quiet forever, you know."

I went to the stairs and she followed. When I reached the door of the studio I stopped short. Some of the color had been taken from the room, and the packing crates were nailed shut, ready to go. My eyes filled with tears again and I turned aside to the window.

Rebecca took over, went through the inventory with Bob quickly, and then signed the release papers. Jake hefted the first crate and went down the stairs. In a few minutes he had everything outside.

"Show me the painting," she said as they shook our hands goodbye and then left for the last time.

"Not now." I went and sat on the couch, despondent, stripped.

She took my arm. "Stop being melodramatic. You know, when Evan had his first show he was just as scared as you are."

I looked at her, startled. "Evan? Scared?"

She nodded. "Under all that bravado Evan has his insecurities, too. He called me last night to ask for the third time which sculpture should be the focus of his part of the show. He's tense — and don't kid yourself about why he's willing to participate."

"What do you mean?"

Her face took on a patient expression and she shook another cigar from the pack. "I mean that if some of you new people are judged to be worthy, it will reflect well on our taste and instincts, and if any of you are judged to be mediocre, it will distract the public from the mistakes we make in our own pieces." She shrugged. "That's how it works."

"You're both established! What could you possibly have to worry about?"

"Collectors are fickle, and fashions change. Sometimes artists do not mature, or make a great leap. The public expects a great leap every time." She smiled, an ironic twist to her mouth acknowledging the absurdity of what she'd said.

"Still," I said grudgingly, "it hardly seems Evan should be nervous."

"Don't be so naive. *Every time* you will be nervous. You reveal yourself — you're tense about being judged." She sighed. "Who can be indifferent to their own work?"

"I wish I were."

She distracted me by standing up and going toward the easel on which stood the not-yet-dry oil. "Is this it, over here?"

We crossed the room to where I'd shoved the painting into the corner, out of the way. There was no drape on it because it was still wet, so Rebecca had space and opportunity to see it as we approached. She stood in front of it quietly. "You really have taken off," she said musingly after a while. "Does it feel good? Different? So much yourself at last?"

"I'm not sure. This just felt like the answer."

"What do you mean?"

I glanced over and saw from her face that she was taken aback by what I'd said. I tugged on my earlobe in frustration. "I don't know . . . I don't know anything anymore."

"Allie, please —"

I waved her off. I didn't want to argue anymore. Fatigue blanketed me.

"I wish you could send it to Marge," she went on, after a time.

"It's barely dry yet."

"I know, I know. Still, it should hang with the painting of Meggie and the mirror. She'll be furious not to have it."

I shrugged, not caring about that. I wanted to hear what Rebecca thought. I wanted Rebecca to interpret the painting for me. I wanted to know what she saw. I waited. "This painting scares me," I admitted finally, hoping to elicit more response than I was getting.

"That's what you were talking about when we were downstairs?"

I nodded. "I'm not sure I know what I meant with this one yet."

"Funny how you can paint something and not even know what you really intend. Sometimes I start out with one thing and end up someplace totally different. Sometimes I can't see it at all until it's hung. Or until a critic says something intelligent about it — and that doesn't happen often."

"What do you see in this?"

She was silent a long time. "A reunion," she admitted, reluctantly. "You may not see what you meant, but anyone who knows you could."

"Yes," I said, turning to her slowly, the anxiety inside me crystallizing with her words into something like resolve. "And 'Reunion' would make a good title, too."

I drifted away from her toward the window. She had somehow released me from my pain. Bob and Jake had finished putting the crates into the truck and were tying them down amidst other boxes. I watched them while Rebecca studied the canvas.

"This show will be a good start for you, Allie."

I didn't answer. She came and stood beside me, and we looked out at them as they started the truck up with a roar and backed down the drive. "It's hard to lose all this," I said at last. "I may never see those paintings again."

"When you see them hung, at the gallery, you'll know why

you painted them, and they'll seem different to you then. Much as you may believe it, Allie, you did not do all this work to have it go unappreciated here in your hermitage. Those paintings are your personal expressions, your experiences, and you recorded them with a purpose — to make other people feel what you feel."

I shook my head. I heard her words, but I felt something quite different now, an intense, euphoric determination that was not to be spoken of. "I hope I can make it," I whispered, leaning my head against the cool, clear plane of glass.

She put her arm around my shoulders. "You will," she said, misunderstanding my meaning. "You have to."

The sun burned relentlessly in the deep blue sky. There was not even a cloud for cover. I squinted up and down the length of the field and noted the neat job of mowing that Sam and Tobie had managed this morning. The even rows would make our job of scooping up the fallen hay and baling it into neat, tight bundles a lot easier. And I was glad to have something physical to do with myself this afternoon, something which would blot out thought, idea, and emotion. I wanted to be a moving, bending, working machine.

Today's heat — over a hundred in the direct sun — had been too much for Tobie and the girls this morning. Anna and Meggie were exhausted, while Tobie was sick to her stomach, shaky and pale. Sam had insisted all three stay in the house this afternoon and rest. I would help him to finish up, and from our hard labor would come all the hay needed for our livestock's winter fodder. Without it we would have to spend a lot of money we didn't have to feed the animals. Every year we sowed, mowed, and baled our three fields twice, and so far we'd managed to squeak by, although Sam was already counting on clearing and planting more land to the west next year to fill the ever-increasing demand at BoxTie.

"No worry of rain today." I pulled my hair up tight on my

head in a knot, out of the way, and jammed my baseball cap over it.

Sam nodded. His fine blond hair was already slicked down dark with sweat. "Only yesterday's heat and this kind of burning sun would've dried it out so quick." There were two more fields down the road still to be mowed and then baled, but they would wait until later in the week because Sam preferred to do our fields one by one, taking no chance that the mowed grasses would be rained on in the meantime. This was one of the first years we weren't fighting rain. It had been such a wet August that the field was late in ripening, and it was always chancier to bale in September rather than late August, because September usually brought cooler weather and more rain. But this year we'd had no choice. We'd had to wait.

"Might as well get started," Sam said with a sigh, swinging up onto the new baler. He patted the steering wheel as I clambered up beside him. "And we'll just have to see if she's any better than the old one."

I nodded absentmindedly as the engine started up with a snort and a puff of diesel exhaust. Skillfully Sam began to manipulate the controls so that the machine moved slowly and efficiently along the row, sweeping up as much of the loose hay as possible into its mouth. I turned in the seat beside him. My job was to watch the bales as they came out the other end of the machine. One jammed bale could take hours to unsnag. The first bale came through, a tight-packed oblong, easy to handle and move about. We rode in silence, concentrating, the machinery noisy enough to discourage talking, but I could tell from Sam's face that he liked the feel of her and the way she handled.

I watched the bales fall from the inner workings of the machine, mesmerized by the rhythm of the whirring blades, the squeak, pack, and thump as the bale was spit back onto the land. I felt sleepy, lethargic, and distracted. In my head

I tried to plan our outing to the movies tonight, to remember everything I would need to take. Already it seemed I'd forgotten something, and it nagged at me. There were ritual items not to be left behind when we were going to the drive-in, items of comfort and convenience and purpose. A sweater for each girl because it almost always cooled off when the sun set. I'd pop a batch of popcorn when we got home and put it in a paper bag. Beer for Sam. Meggie's blanket. Anna's small pillow. Although the list seemed long, there was still something missing. It scrolled through my mind over and over. I made myself concentrate on it so as not to think of other bigger, harder issues: everything I would do but did not want to face. The humming and buzzing of the machinery was in my head now, and I shook it from side to side to clear it, but the buzzing continued.

The sun beat down on my head, right through my cap. I could feel heat radiate from my scalp, and a rivulet of sweat ran under my breasts and trickled down my side. I didn't want to think about how hot we would be in a little while when we stopped sitting and driving, and moved on to the hard physical labor of going through the field in the truck to pick up the bales. It wouldn't be long now, because the baler was moving quickly down the rows without a snag.

Waves of heat shimmered through the field in a curtain. It almost looked like water rising from the earth — a mirage. The bales fell regularly. I kept close watch, facing the back of the machine, away from Sam. I looked over to the edge of the field behind us. Jamie was there, his small body undulating on layers of moving, rising air. I watched him quietly, nearly lazily; I wasn't sure this time of what I really saw. I wasn't sure this time if my own desire had called him forth. But he didn't fade. He danced on the waves and I felt as if I were on some drugged-up high, lighter than a cloud. He put his hand toward me and beckoned and I knew I would come.

"Allie!" Sam shouted as a grinding noise came from inside

the baler and a big vibration shook us. "You're not paying attention!"

I couldn't turn to look at him: I was watching Jamie, who was rising now on the hot waves of air, elevating upward, carried in the heat and the sun, up into the blue, blue sky. Stuporous, unable to answer, I put my hand on Sam's arm and leaned my head against him sickly.

He stopped the machine with a quick jolt and turned the engine off. "What are you staring at?" he asked angrily. Around us the field lay bathed in the heat; the crickets sang, raspy and loud. I was drugged with the heat, and yet freed by it.

"Are you all right?" He took my chin in his hands and forced me to look into his face.

I nodded. "Jamie," I choked out at last. I turned my head back to the left and was not surprised to see the field of mowed hay stretching flat and empty now.

"You saw him again?" Sam asked with alarm.

"No." I shook my head. "Look!" I pointed. "A rainbow."

"Allie, it hasn't rained." He looked at me strangely. "You can't see a rainbow if it hasn't rained."

"I see a rainbow," I said, more insistently now, because indeed I did. Even though it had not rained and rainbows came only after showers in the sun, I saw the giant arc of its color spectrum bending over the field. "Maybe he painted it."

"Who?" Sam's face was drawn, and I reached out to stroke the length of his cheek.

"Don't be so worried," I said. "I'll help you get the machine unclogged." I unstuck my body from the seat and climbed down. Sam followed: he didn't know what else to do, so he moved under the machine, freed the mechanism as I pulled matted hay from the choked tube. It only took five minutes.

"Wasn't so bad," Sam said as he slid out from under the baler. We stood there, facing each other, and he smiled at me uncertainly, almost tremulously, and we climbed back up. He reached across and put a gentle kiss on my cheek. I smiled at him, filled with soporific warm light. He reached to turn the ignition key, using the motion to hide his confusion and fear.

In a short while we had finished baling the field. The sun was a little lower, but not low enough to dissipate the intense heat too much. I didn't mind now. We began the long, hard process of gathering the bales onto the bed of the truck. Sam stripped off his shirt. I pulled my cap from my head and wiped my face. Sam hefted the first bales onto the pickup, bouncing them off his thighs. The muscles in his forearms and back stood out like a relief map.

Using my baling hook, I stacked the bales on top of each other. My palms stung as the blisters rose, but the labor felt good. My own terrible thought, the knowledge that I carried deep inside, receded as I worked. I swung the hook in a short arc, bedded it deep into the tightly packed bale, and hefted it up. Swing, hook, heft — there was rhythm to this: I found it, used it. I swung again, and it came to me, the item I'd forgotten for my list, the item I couldn't do without: *I'll have to pack Jamie's sweater too*, I thought, *I'll need that even though it's not finished yet.* And my swing went wild.

"Watch it!" Sam's voice came to me as if we were underwater, garbled and strange. His face was frightened, pale beneath his sunburn. My swing had grazed his hand and a thin streak of red blood attested to the sharpness of my hook. I couldn't speak, couldn't say I was sorry. I just climbed into the pickup and got out the first-aid kit. I put the soft white bandage over the cut, then lifted his thin wrist to my mouth and kissed it.

He was staring at me now. "You're not all right, are you?" His eyes burned in on me; I closed my eyes against him like the sun.

"I am." This was all I could manage, and my voice didn't sound real. Inside my head another voice was reciting the litany: popcorn, beer, glasses, pillow, blanket, sweaters. A chant — low, rhythmic, soothing. Soon it would all be taken care of. Soon I could rest.

"Should we go back to the house?" He was shaken. I could feel his fear in the silence.

I shook my head, hefted my hook, and smiled slowly. "I'll stay out of your way."

"I can't believe it's not going to rain." He was trying to draw me into a normal conversation to reassure himself.

I smiled at him, gently, beatifically. I couldn't talk but I could still smile. We were fighting for time, but for a different sort than he supposed.

We went back to work, moving up and down the fields like ants carrying away crumbs. I could feel the presence of the wide and empty sky, pressing down on us, pushing me upward. It was only a matter of time before I could rest. I didn't feel my body anymore, didn't feel my exhaustion. I was just sleepy. The rainbow shimmered in front of me, red, violet, turquoise, green, yellow. Jamie was near, I could feel his breath in the way the wind lifted the shirt off my sticky body. I put my head back and looked up over me, opened my mouth to swallow the sky. I was elevating, the sky was lifting me up, it was inside me now, big and intense and blue, and empty, with the hot sun burning its way out of my chest. It was only a matter of time.

The sky was inside me the rest of the day in the field, later as I packed up the car for the movies, as I got the girls dressed, as I brought Tobie tea in her bed, as I popped the popcorn, put the beer into the cooler, stood in my studio and looked around. It was with me when Sam asked why I had brought the old sweater I'd been knitting for Jamie, when I lied about finishing it and giving it to Meggie. It was with me through two cartoon shorts and the Disney feature, through messy lobster rolls and Sam's third beer, through the girls' predictable crankiness as the evening grew late. It was with me as I drove us to the bottom pasture and parked, turning out the headlights and killing the engine. We all settled back, waiting for someone to see the first shooting star.

I passed Sam his fourth and final beer. That was always his limit. He yawned. Alcohol and today's hot, hard work made him sleepy. The air had grown chill around us, as it always does at night toward autumn in New Hampshire. The girls pressed their faces to the glass of the windows in the backseats.

"Why can't we get out?" Anna complained. "We'd see much better."

"Your mother and I don't want to be up all night putting calamine on mosquito bites," Sam said, talking around another yawn. "Not like last time. You can see just fine from here."

Last time Jamie had been with us. Last time Jamie had seen the first one, dropping through the velvet night sky and out of sight with elusive speed. It was always hard to believe you'd really seen one, because it was gone nearly as soon as you spotted it.

Sam inched his window down and sniffed. "Rain. I smell rain." He rolled it up again.

I leaned my head back against the cracked plastic of the seat.

"Won't be able to do the next field if it rains," he said, worried.

"Take a day off," I managed. The words were thick and sticky in my mouth. It was very hard to talk. As if I had forgotten how.

"Mmm." He had put his head back too, I saw, and closed his eyes. In a minute his breathing drowsed over into sleep. His mouth dropped open and he began to snore.

The girls began to squeal in the backseat. "There's one!" Anna clamored. "I saw it first!"

"Me too," Meggie chimed in.

"No — me," Anna insisted.

"Shh," I said. "Daddy's sleeping." But Sam showed no signs of stirring despite the noise.

"Another and another!"

"There!" said Meggie, pointing her stubby finger.

I rolled the wool stitches of Jamie's sweater between my fingers. It was a tight weave. It would do the job. I pulled it off the knitting needles and waited.

I put my forehead against the glass of my window. The moon was out full and fat, the stars were bright pricks of light. But on the western horizon a thick bank of clouds was moving toward us — a front rolling across to obscure the stars. Every once in a while those clouds lit up from within. Lightning. Sam might be right about the rain.

I turned and looked into the backseat. The girls were still pressed up against the glass, looking into the aquarium of the night sky, but their eyelids were getting droopy. Meggie rubbed her face with the back of her hand and leaned against Anna. I ran my hand down the length of Sam's arm, and still he slept.

"Be back in a sec," I said, slipping from the seat as I opened the door. They were too tired to ask what I was doing.

The tall, stiff grass prickled my bare legs as I went around to the back of the station wagon and bent to stuff the thick roll of knitting up the tailpipe. I stood, looked at the stars above me, and felt the heat of their light inside me. A breeze grew restless in the leaves of the trees — the storm signaling. I got back in the car and turned on the ignition.

"Wait, Mommy! Just one more," Anna begged sleepily, as I had known she would.

"Okay, sweetie," I said agreeably, settling back. And then we all waited together, waited for one more. I could hear thunder now, coming toward us fast, but still distant. The motor idled and a sweet perfume seeped up through the old floorboards, in around the rusty muffler, up, and into our air. I looked through my window and saw the banks of clouds cover the moon now, slowly blotting out the stars. I closed my eyes.

"Sleepy, Mom," Anna mumbled.

"On our way home now," I answered, turning slowly to look at them one last time. They were slumped together in the back, their heads leaning against each other, the baseball cap knocked askew on Meggie's head. I took Sam's hand, curled my fingers through his, closed my eyes again. And then I felt it: a quiet, sleepy dizziness, suction coming from blackness, and a shower of stars blooming down over me, taking me with it. In a spiraling upward rush I went out, into the white night.

EPILOGUE

Fall 1 9 8 6

. . . Every year
everything
I have ever learned

in my lifetime
leads back to this: the fires
and the black river of loss
whose other side

is salvation,
whose meaning
none of us will ever know.
To live in this world

you must be able
to do three things:
to love what is mortal;
to hold it

against your bones knowing
your own life depends on it;
and, when the time comes to let it go,
to let it go.

— Mary Oliver
"In Blackwater Woods"

. . . his tears burned my cheeks and his heart moved in mine.

— Dylan Thomas
"Poem in October"

A Mother's Song

"*I* dreamt we were swinging on the stars." I did not meet Sam's eyes, but rubbed my toes back and forth under the cool sheets. "From point to point across the night sky." I turned my hand over, and there were star-shaped blisters on my palms. I looked up at him at last, then closed my eyes quickly to lean back into the pillow.

He had a mug of coffee for me and set it down on the side table. Still, we didn't look at each other directly, but when he made as if to sit down on the bed beside me, I slid toward the center. "It's late," I said. "You should have woken me."

"You needed the sleep." His voice was quiet.

"I remember," I went on slowly, speaking to myself in a near-whisper of horror and despair and self-loathing, "how slippery the door handle was. And Meggie coughing in the back." I looked up at him and then away again, picking at the fuzzy pills on the blanket. "It woke me up. Her calling me."

He reached over and took my hand.

I wondered if he could still love me after everything I'd done. "You were the one who rolled the windows down and turned off the key, weren't you?" My voice was low.

"Only after *you* woke me."

Looking into his dark brown eyes at last, I saw they were steady. I pushed the blankets back and sat up, trembling. "I'm scared, Sam. Part of me would do it again." My lower lip quivered. "I don't know how to live without him. With that part of me . . . extinguished."

He put his arms around me and leaned his forehead against mine. "You'll find a way. From somewhere inside."

I sat up straight. "My child." I rubbed my lips with the back of my hand. They felt swollen, as though I had eaten too much salt. "My children." I lay my cheek back down against him, against the soft flannel of his shirt. "Maybe I'll never heal from this, Sam."

"Maybe not." He stopped for a minute. "Maybe we'll just learn to bear the pain."

"How? How can such pain be borne?"

"Maybe, somehow, we'll live past it."

We sat there, arms around each other in a fierce embrace.

"Nat Loring can see us, this morning." Sam pulled back to look into my eyes and stroked the side of my face. His hand shook a little and I knew in that instant how scared he must be. I caught his fingers and held them against my cheek, hard. The bones of his hand told me who and where I was.

"We aren't going to hide anymore." He cleared his throat and I knew that meant he was afraid he was going to cry. "I lost my son already. I'm not willing to lose you, too." His voice was thick and choked.

I bowed my head. "Will you come with me?"

"I made the appointment for us both — not just you."

"What does Tobie say?"

"I wasn't planning to ask her."

We were quiet for a while, and I found peace in the motion of his hand against my cheek. It made me sleepy, relaxed almost. "Isn't there some way . . ." My voice trailed off.

His face flickered from sad to angry and back again. "Allie,

I don't know of any way. What you did last night — I can't handle this on my own."

I was silent. Some things could never be retreated from: apology could not change, or absolve, the hurt I had done; love could not erase the pain I had caused. "I'd better get up now," I said after a minute. "Breakfast is going to be awfully late."

"Tobie's down starting it," he said, sliding off the bed. "She said you could stay in bed, if I'd give her a hand. But, if you want —"

"I do."

"Then the girls," he said, standing at the doorway, "they're still asleep. Can you manage?"

I nodded slowly, thinking of another morning not so long ago when the household had overslept, another morning when I had gone to wake my son. Another crisp, sunny morning which was, and was not, just like this one. I swung my legs over the edge.

In the girls' room I snapped up the shades to let in the sunshine. I sat on the side of Anna's bed and nuzzled her cheek until her eyelids raised droopily. I touched her face and knew she was here. Leaning into Meggie's crib, I watched her stretch both fists above her head, yawn, and smile up into my eyes. I touched her face and knew she was here. Twice I was rewarded with kisses and hugs, and I hated myself for what I had almost done to them. The shame was bitter and deep, but I pulled myself from it to dry my eyes, knowing that I couldn't help my daughters with guilt or self-pity. Love required that I be strong. With a resolute smile I promised them a treat, blueberry pancakes and maple syrup. I laid out their overalls, shirts, sneakers, and socks and headed out the door for the back stairs to the kitchen.

I was halfway down when there came a noise from behind me, half heard. I turned, sure it was Anna or Meggie unable to manage some button or maybe a sneaker lace.

But it was Jamie who stood on the top step of the landing, a yellow swath of sunshine lighting his golden curls in a fiery halo against the dark outline of the window frame behind him. His small fist clutched the string of his toy horse, and for a minute we stood there, without moving or speaking. Then he smiled at me, his grin sly, his eyes cobalt against his black lashes.

Squeals of laughter from the girls' rooms diverted me, and I took my eyes away from him for just a second, turned my mind for a moment to them. When I looked back he seemed to shimmer even harder, growing more beautiful as I watched. I knew then that I would paint him just like this, forever a part of me, standing on the top riser in all his allure and with such determination. I would paint him — for this was what I had left. I would set up easel and canvas in the back garden, draw down deep into memory's riches, deep into what had passed and what had yet to come. I would fold him into my heart and so offer up the moment when mother and son exchange something immutable, something untranslatable. It would be a beautiful painting, in oils — idyllic, lyric, soaring. A mother's song. A goodbye song.

I turned my body from him and took another step away. A sob escaped me, tears slid from my cheek onto my chin, the banister pressed hard against my palm as I leaned into it, step by step. For an instant I felt the flicker of him inside me, his incandescent presence, and then he was gone. I had made my choice: I had let him go.

The crisp smell of September blew in through the open window at the head of the stairs, laid over with sausage, eggs frying, coffee. From their bedrooms above, Anna and Meggie swooped down, chattering, tugging on me, pulling me back into the river of family life. I took my daughters' warm hands in mine, and they crowded me through the kitchen door to breakfast.